THE WARNING

The big ranger settled his gaze on the fire, his voice gentle but still carrying a mountain of weight.

"Do like I tell you, son," Sazes said. "This is bad country, and it turns things wild in a hurry. Get some sleep, and tomorrow you will leave."

Samuel thought of his friend, butchered and murdered for no other reason than the greed and viciousness of other men.

"But I've got to do *something*."

Sazes nodded. "And you will do something, come morning. Just don't look back tonight. Tomorrow, you go to Wakely, sell your buffalo hides, buy yourself a train ticket back to Memphis, and get the hell away from here. Go home and try to forget this nightmare ever happened. You've got no business out here, boy. Can't you see that? This place was made just to rip the heart right out of you."

His eyes moved from the fire and found Samuel.

"Get out while you still can."

BLOOD ROCK

Ralph Cotton

A SIGNET BOOK

SIGNET
Published by New American Library, a division of
Penguin Putnam Inc., 375 Hudson Street,
New York, New York 10014, U.S.A.
Penguin Books Ltd, 27 Wrights Lane,
London W8 5TZ, England
Penguin Books Australia Ltd,
Ringwood, Victoria, Australia
Penguin Books Canada Ltd, 10 Alcorn Avenue,
Toronto, Ontario, Canada M4V 3B2
Penguin Books (N.Z.) Ltd, 182–190 Wairau Road,
Auckland 10, New Zealand

Penguin Books Ltd, Registered Offices:
Harmondsworth, Middlesex, England

First published by Signet, an imprint of New American Library,
a division of Penguin Putnam Inc.

First Printing, March 2001
10 9 8 7 6 5 4 3 2 1

For Mary Lynn . . . *of course.*

And for my good friend, Jacky Otto,
whose faith inspires me.

PART 1

Chapter 1

When he'd finished, he patted the rocky dirt down into place with his gloved hands and stood beside the fresh mound of earth for a moment until he caught his breath. The big blue cur stepped forward and touched its nose down to the fresh grave. He nudged the dog back with the side of his boot, saying, "Get back, Blue." Then he took his battered hat from his head and held it to his chest with his head bowed, although he knew there was no reason for such formality.

He could have left his hat on, or held it down at his side. He could have sailed it through the air; he could have slapped it to the ground and stomped on it and cursed heaven and earth alike, for that matter. Nobody would have seen him. Nobody would have heard him.

His name was Samuel Burrack, and whatever he might have done at this point made no difference—leastwise not to Davey Riley. Davey Riley was dead and buried. Nothing would change that now. So Samuel stood for a moment longer, and at length he let out a sigh. He knew no prayers and had no Bible for reference. Finally, when the roar of the hot wind slackened enough for him to hear his own voice, he whispered under his breath, "Davey, I'm sorry."

His chest tightened and, knowing nothing more to say, his eyes swept away from the small sad grave and toward the overpowering magnitude of this brutal endless land. The big short-haired cur sat back a few feet, watching him. Sam put his hat back atop his head and drew it down against the howling wind.

Thirty yards from Davey Riley's earthbound remains, out on the edge of the sand flats, lay the dead paint horse. The horse's legs had stiffened beneath the boiling sun, and stuck out from its trunk like brittle limbs on deadfall timber. Hot wind licked at the paint horse's mane and tail. Dust had already begun to bank up along the animal's windward side, as if the earth could not wait to swallow it up. "I'll send your part of the money home, all right, Davey?" He lingered for a second longer as if waiting for an answer he knew would never come. Then he lifted his eyes upward. "He was a good friend."

Amen . . .

"Let's go, Blue." He stooped down, picked up the small spade shovel and wiped it clean, then carried it to the oxcart and pitched it up atop the load of curing hides. A glistening sheet of blowflies rose up and spun in an angry cloud above the stench of salt and rancid viscera. He and the big cur walked past the front of the heavy, two-wheeled cart and stopped beside the team of oxen.

"That's all we can do for him," he spoke to the dog, then turned to the oxen. The big beasts stood beneath the double yoke, spills of white froth swinging from their lips, their broad chests rising slowly in and out, their breathing labored by the scorching heat. "Let's take up, Oscar, Jim. We're a long ways out." He picked up the long whip from the ground, and as he cracked it out above the beasts' sweaty backs, he leaned his shoulder into the lead ox's side until its big hooves came loose from the sand, trudging forward.

Hidden in the harsh glare of sunlight and the distance of a thousand wavering yards of sand, Ranger Clyde "Outrider" Sazes held the scene in the circle of his field lens and watched the big oxcart lumber across the sand. "Now the fool's forgot his rifle," Sazes murmured to the big Appaloosa stallion beneath him. He shook his head and started to lower the lens from his eye. But then he lifted it back into place as he saw the young man and the blue-spotted cur run back a few yards to the unmarked grave.

"Good, you remembered it." Sazes watched the young man pick up the long buffalo rifle from the ground. "There you go, pick it up. That's it, look it over. Uh-huh, wipe a hand down it. Check it out."

Poor dumb pilgrim . . . As the young man and the dog trotted back to the slow moving cart, Ranger Sazes smiled grimly to himself and lowered the field lens from his right eye, closing it between the palms of his hands. "Now he'll go get himself killed I reckon." He backed the Appaloosa a step and turned it on the narrow rocky path that led down to the sand flats. "Come on, Black-Pot. Let's see what he's up to . . ."

When the burning sand grew too hot for his boot soles, Samuel Burrack climbed atop the lead ox and carried the buffalo rifle across his lap. An hour had passed before he noticed the first dark splotch of blood amid the trail of horses' hooves he followed. He looked down at the dried blood in passing, and did not stop until he saw another, larger spot, a hundred yards further.

"Get back, Blue," he said, seeing the dog sniff curiously at the dried blood. He stepped down from the moving oxen and slowly drew the team to a halt. Tipping his hat sidelong against the sun's glare, he searched ahead along the snaking trail of fresh-turned sand. In the near distance, the hoofprints sank down over a low rise and rose up again beyond it, leading on toward jagged crests of upward-sloping rocky land.

Beside him, the cur whined and panted and circled near his boot heel; but he paid no attention to the dog as he took a .50-caliber cartridge from his shirt pocket. Slipping it into the breech, he drove it shut with his gloved hand. He stared out into the distance for a long while, hearing nothing but the roar of hot wind lapping at his hat brim.

"You'd do better flanking them," said a voice behind him. The sound came so suddenly and took him by such surprise that Samuel jerked around toward it before having either the time or the presence of mind to cock the big rifle.

Ranger Clyde Sazes's hand caught the rifle barrel and held it to one side, away from his chest. "That is what you're planning, ain't it, boy? To go after them? Get your staples back? Avenge your friend's death?"

Samuel tugged back on the rifle stock, his thumb trying to pull the hammer back. But Sazes tightened his grip on the barrel.

"Boy, if I'd wantcd you dead, you would be already." Beside Sazes, Samuel saw the big cur sitting at rest, Sazes' free hand hanging down, absently scratching the big cur's ears. "See? You should have listened to your dog. He tried to tell you I was coming."

"Mister, who are you?" Samuel tugged once more on the rifle.

"I ain't one of them. That's the main thing." Sazes shook his head, still holding the barrel tight in his hand. "Settle down now. You've had bad reckonings all day. Don't end it on a worse note." Lifting his free hand from the blue cur's head and slowly pulling aside the lapel of his faded riding duster, he allowed a crooked questioning smile. "What do you say, boy? Why don't you turn it loose? It's hard to talk to a rifle bore." A battered tin badge glinted in the sunlight.

"You a lawman?" Samuel stared at him, skeptical.

"I've been tracking that bunch for nigh three weeks—I'm Clyde Sazes, Arizona Ranger." He turned the lapel loose and let the wind blow it closed. "If you won't give me the rifle, at least let it down. Take your thumb off the hammer."

Samuel eased his grip. Sazes opened his hand, making a show of turning the rifle barrel loose. "See, we're getting along real well." He nodded down toward the big cur. "He ain't much of a watchdog, is he?"

"I thought he was," Samuel said, letting out a breath. "Maybe I was wrong."

"Well, don't be hard on him. He's young, still got some pup in him. And he ain't been out here long, I can tell. I have my ways with dogs and horses. Dogs catch on to things about as quick as their masters do." He flashed his crooked smile, looked at the team of oxen, then back to Samuel. "So, you're going to overtake those four knotheads, ride them down? Set things right for what they did back there?"

When Samuel neither answered nor returned the smile Sazes nodded back toward the big Appaloosa. "Don't suppose you could use some water, could ya? I saw they took your whole water keg."

Sazes turned toward the canteens hanging from his saddle horn. But before he could lift one, Samuel said, "Wait a minute. You saw them take it? Where were you, mister?"

Sazes raised the canteen and pitched it to him. "Don't get cross. I was too far above to get down to yas. But yessir, I saw it . . . saw it all from way up there."

"Who are they?"

Sazes cocked a bushy eyebrow. "You going after them?"

"I'd like to know who they are."

"Why?"

"I just think I oughta know, that's all."

Sazes looked him up and down. "Junior Lake is the leader. He just watched. Daggett and Braydon held your friend, and the one with the beard cut his throat, if you must hear it. I don't know the bearded one. He's a new one. I figured they'd even take your friend's boots, but then you showed up out of the draw." He cocked his head to one side. "Out here it ain't wise going astray to take yourself a jake. I reckon you learned that much today if nothing else."

Samuel uncapped the canteen and raised it to his parched lips. When he lowered it, he poured a trickle into his cupped hand and held it down to the big cur's muzzle. The dog leaned forward and lapped it up. "We've spent the whole season out here . . . never had any trouble, before now."

"Then you was lucky as hell, is all I can tell ya. From here to the badlands border, all you've got is your renegade *comadrejas,* your *banditos,* and your throat-cutting outlaws. What were you doing out on the sand flats anyway? There's no herd comes through this way."

"We were cutting over to Wakely. This was our last haul."

Samuel looked down at the dried blood at his feet, then off along the hoofprints in the sand. "I shot one of them in the shoulder."

"I know . . . I saw it. That was Daggett. He always was an unfortunate rascal. They say his pa once nailed his foot to a wall to keep him from walking in his sleep."

Samuel just looked at him, unsure if he was serious or not. Sazes squinted in the harsh glare of sunlight. "Never kilt a man have ya, boy?"

"No, I haven't. I never even shot at one till now."

"I knew it . . . saw how you drew your shot off at the last second." He turned back to Samuel. "It's a whole different thing than shooting buffalo, ain't it?"

Samuel let the question pass. "That's my best friend buried back there. We go all the way back to Tennessee together. He's got family back in Memphis."

"Family . . ." Sazes said it in a flat tone, then fell silent for a second. "Well, can you eat something before you take after them? You are planning on tracking them down, I suspect."

Samuel still didn't answer. "I can eat something, sure enough. They took it all. Our only horse, food, water, tarps . . . everything we had. I suppose they would have taken the hides—"

"Hides? Ha!" Sazes cut him off. "Hides is work, boy. If them knotheads had a day's work in them, they wouldn't be in the life they're in. Come on, the day's nigh over. Let's pitch a tarp. I've got dried shank and some airtights. You'll need your strength if you're going after them in the morning."

"There's two or more hours of daylight," Samuel said. "They're getting away."

"No they're not." Sazes turned, took up the reins to the Appaloosa, and asked over his shoulder, "What's your name, boy?"

"Samuel Burrack. Why do you keep asking me if I'm going after them?"

Sazes turned a glance to him as he slung the canteen strap back around the saddle horn. "Because so far you ain't answered me yet," Sazes replied. "It's my job to know who's doing what out here." He tied the Appaloosa's reins to the rear of the oxcart. "I've had my sights on those four for quite a while, biding my time, waiting till they got in rifle range. Junior's horse was lame. I would have taken them by nightfall if they hadn't found a horse, some food, and water."

As he spoke, Sazes untied a rolled tarpaulin from behind his saddle. He let it fall open and shook it out, spilling four wooden stakes to the ground. "Now I'll be lucky to catch them in a week." He stooped and picked up the stakes. "But they *ain't* getting away. You can bet on that."

Sam took the end of the tarpaulin and walked it alongside the oxcart. As he tied it to the side of the cart and the two of them stretched it out, he said in a sullen tone, "If you had made a move on them sooner they wouldn't have killed my friend."

Sazes had bent over to stake the end of the tarpaulin to the ground. Now he stopped and looked up at Samuel. "Well, that's true in one sense. In another sense, you could say if he hadn't left Memphis he'd still be alive." He jammed a short stake into the ground and stomped down on it with his boot heel as he continued. "Or, in a much *greater* sense, you could say if he'd never been born, he could have avoided this ugly mess altogether." He grunted, straightening up, and stretched the other end of the tarpaulin. "But that's 'twixt him and God."

"You know what I mean," Samuel said.

"Yeah, I know." Sazes drove another stake tight into the ground with his boot heel as wind whipped at the tarpaulin. "It's not sitting well with you . . . me up there watching, while your friend got his throat cut."

"Can you blame me?" Sam asked above the wind. As soon as the tarpaulin was staked into place, the big cur slipped beneath it into the shade and lay down against the wheel of the oxcart.

Sazes finished staking the tarp and dusted his hands, looking Sam up and down once more. "Sammy-boy, do you have a pistol? A side arm of any sort?"

"My name is Samuel. And no I don't. I had an old Hoard .44, but it was in the supplies. Now they've got it."

"Figures," Sazes grunted. He took the canteens and saddlebags from atop the Appaloosa and bent down to move into the shade of the tarpaulin. Samuel followed. Beneath the slanting tarpaulin, Sazes threw back the flap on the saddlebags, took out the remnant of a dried elk quarter shank, and pitched it to Samuel. "Have you at least got a knife, to feed yourself?"

"I've got one." Samuel took a long knife from his boot well and wiped the blade back and forth across his grease-stained trouser leg. Sazes shook his head and looked away as Samuel carved off a modest helping of dried meat.

"The fact is," Sazes offered, "I could have gotten there a little bit sooner, but still not in time to save your friend's life. I would've pushed my horse too hard coming down through the rock spurs, maybe killed him and broke my neck in the bargain. Then those boys would've had nobody to stop them on their way to the border. See how that works, Sammy?"

"Yeah, I suppose so. I'm just regretting it, is all." Samuel took a small bite of the dried, grainy elk meat, chewing as he spoke. "They'll head for Mexico, huh?"

"That depends." Sazes uncapped a canteen, wiped his hand across the top of it, and took a drink. Hot gales of wind continued to slap at the tarpaulin. "If they don't know I'm on them, they might hole up in Wakely long enough to get Daggett's wound looked at."

"They don't know they're being tracked?" Samuel took the canteen when Sazes handed it to him.

"Of course they know they're being followed. They've known it for a while. They just might not know it's *me* on their trail yet. That would make all the difference in the world to them."

"Why's that?" Samuel swallowed the dried elk meat and washed it down with warm water.

Sazes gave him a narrowed stare. "How long have you been out here, Sammy-boy?"

"My name's not Sammy-boy. Like I said, we've been out here all season."

"Ain't been to town much, I don't suppose?" Sazes said, taking the canteen back from Samuel's outstretched arm.

"No. Just long enough to drop hides and resupply. Why?"

"Oh, nothing . . ." Sazes shoved the blue cur to one side and leaned back against the cart wheel. "Can't expect a newcomer to know everybody out here all at once, I reckon."

Samuel took another bite of the dried meat and chewed it as he stared down at the dirt. A sliver of wind passed beneath the bottom edge of the tarpaulin and swept bits of sand against the toe of his boot. Dark contemplation shrouded his brow, and Clyde Sazes watched him quit chewing as his shoulders shivered slightly. Then Samuel spit the chewed meat into the palm of his hand and pitched it over near the big cur. The dog snatched it up, gulping it down before looking at him for more. A silence passed. "I—I should have moved quicker."

"Oh . . . ?" Sazes's voice trailed off. He listened quietly.

"I saw them when I topped out of the draw. They . . . were down off their horses. Davey looked worried, so worried. And they circled him like wolves. "He shook his head slowly. "But I thought that whatever I did, I might cause them to—" He stopped and swallowed a tight knot in his throat. "Lord have mercy."

"I know, boy. It's a terrible thing, seeing a man die—especially a friend," Sazes said in a soft tone, keeping a steady searching gaze on Samuel Burrack as the wind lessened against the side of the tarpaulin.

"If I had known they were really going to . . . to do what they did!" Samuel felt his eyes well up. He turned his face away and looked out in tight silence across the glistening sand.

Sazes's words came soft into the quietness, as if careful not to disturb something. "I was up there, boy. I could see it coming but couldn't help. You were down here. You could've helped but you didn't see it coming. Neither of us failed your friend. We just didn't save him. He knows you ain't to blame."

"I *was* going after them . . . I think." Samuel held his voice steady in spite of the heaviness in his chest. "I meant to. He would if it was the other way around. I know I should go after them . . . but I don't know if I can." He slumped forward as if having turned something loose inside himself, and shook his bowed head back and forth slowly. "I'm sorry, Davey, but I don't know if I can now."

Sazes spoke once more as the hot wind stopped altogether, seeming to catch its breath. "That's it, boy, let it out." He started to reach out and place his hand on Samuel's shoulder. But then he thought better of it, and dropped his hand to the pistol butt on his hip and let it rest there. "You've had your water . . . a bite to eat." His voice stayed soft. "Now sort this out and put it away. I'm on these boys, and I'll get them. I always do. We'll get you to Wakely, and I'll take it from there."

"I need to do *something,* though." Samuel rubbed the heels of his hands in his eyes and took a deep breath. He looked at Ranger Clyde Sazes. "Don't I?"

"No, you don't." Sazes shrugged a shoulder and turned the cap back down on the canteen. His free hand went out to the big cur's head, patting it as he spoke. "You don't want to go into the world those boys live in. Once you get in there, it's hard to get out."

"You're there."

"Yes, I am. That's how I know . . ."

Later, as the wind howled flat and mournful, and pressed the flames of their campfire sideways across the sand in racing sparks, bouncing and fleeing off only to be swallowed by the darkness, the big cur's howl cut long and haunting into the desert silence. Samuel stood up quickly and dusted the seat of his trousers and looked out across the black pools of shadow among the lower pitches of land.

"Is it them? Is it?"

"No, boy," Sazes answered from above the glow and the spinning curl of smoke from his briar pipe. "Don't you know what that is?"

"Oh, yes, it's only coyotes." Samuel looked out forty yards at darting red eyes in the night. In the pale moonlight he saw the shadowy figures moving past them like ghosts, back along their trail. He eased a bit. "But I've seldom seen this many of them at once. Usually you hear them calling out to one another across the flats."

"Not tonight, though." Sazes stood up and cupped the pipe to his chest and pointed out with his free hand toward a darting pair of red eyes moving past them about forty yards out. "Tonight they already know where they're headed."

"What?" Samuel looked at him.

Behind them, the big cur began another long blast of baying. When his howling ended, Sazes sat back down with a stoic expression. "Don't you understand, Sammy? Do I have to say it to you?" Racing firelight streaked across his shadowed features.

"You don't mean—? Oh, Lord, no."

"There were no available rocks around, Sammy-boy. You did all you could." Sazes drew on the briar pipe and let go a wisp of smoke onto the wind. "Best go on to sleep now."

"Sleep? How in God's name can I sleep?"

"Then cut some more meat for your dog," Sazes offered, "and tie him to the oxcart." His voice fell soft once more. "You don't want him going back there tonight."

Samuel's face looked ghastly and drawn in the flickering firelight. "He wouldn't . . . I mean, I know my dog, Ranger Sazes. Blue would never—"

"Do like I tell you, son," Sazes cut him off gently. "This

place turns things wild in a hurry. Get him tied, then get yourself some sleep."

"I can't just sit here, knowing what's going on back there—"

Sazes cut him off again. "You don't want to go back there either, boy. Are you going to tie the dog, or am I?"

"I've got to do something."

Sazes nodded. "And you will do something, come morning. Just don't look back tonight." His eyes went to the cart in the darkness. "Tomorrow, you go to Wakely, sell your hides, get yourself a train ticket back to Memphis, boy. Go home and try to forget this nightmare ever happened." His eyes moved across the blue cur, then back to Samuel, his face taking on a firm expression. He added, "You've got no business out here, boy. Can't you see? This place will rip your heart right out of you."

Chapter 2

"I don't know who the blue hell it is out there," Morris Braydon said, slipping back down beside the jagged rock that sheltered their firelight from both wind and vision. He'd squinted out into the dark basin below, seeing the tiny glow in the distance. He rubbed his strained eyes and looked at the other three men. "I can't figure it being that buff hunter, though. If it is, I ain't too worried." He grinned, cruel and tight. "We didn't leave him much to work with, did we?"

"Should have shot the oxen, just in case," Junior Lake said, stirring the end of a brittle stick into the flames. "You saw what that big rifle did to Daggett's shoulder."

"What shoulder?" Braydon's grin widened, nodding at the bloody blanket wrapped around Andrew Daggett.

"That's what I mean," Junior Lake said. "If this poor bastard ain't dead tonight, he's good for the next hundred years." He looked at Braydon, then slid his eyes across to the other two men huddled around the low flames. Daggett sat a few inches from the new man, Sherman Ellsworth, and hadn't moved for the past hour. Earlier, Daggett had slumped forward with the dirty blood-soaked blanket wrapped tight around his shoulders, letting out a long groan. Now he appeared to be lifeless, an empty canteen lying open in his lap.

Sherman Ellsworth ran his fingers into his long beard, picking something from it and flicking it into the fire. "I say it's the same one who's been dogging us all along. We'd do

well to sit tight and wait for him. Kill him and get it over
with. We're starting to leave too many signs behind us."

"Ordinarily I'd agree," Junior Lake said, sucking a sliver
of dried buffalo meat from between his teeth. "But if that's
Outrider Sazes down there, I'll be honest with yas. I don't
want no part of him . . . unless I can catch him asleep and
round his head out with a shotgun. You're new to these parts.
You don't know him like I do. He carries a big Russian-
model six-shooter. Calls it the *Mad Russian*—crazy bastard
talks to it like it's alive."

"Still . . . kill him in his sleep? That ain't how we do
things in Texas," Sherman Ellsworth said, jutting out his
chest as he spoke.

"Well, of course it ain't." Junior Lake cocked his head
with an air of sarcasm, the newly stolen Hoard pistol hanging from his neck on a long strip of rawhide. "We all know
how you big bold strapping *Tejas* boys are," he said, raising
a long dirty finger for emphasis, "and I know how pale all
us poor Kansas trash must look by comparison. But if that *is*
Ranger Sazes out there fanning us . . . you feel free to march
your proud pan-handle arse down there and square him off
face-to-face. See if he don't blow you to hell quicker than
your sister can whisper my name."

"Hey—!" Ellsworth bristled. "You don't *know* my sister.
So don't be running your mouth."

"You're right, I don't know your sister." Junior Lake's
expression stayed the same; flat and sarcastic. "Your *mother,*
then." His hand closed around the handle of the big Hoard
pistol, cocking it as he rose slightly, pitching the brittle stick
into the fire with his free hand. Sparks spun upward.

"Whoa, boys! Damn it now!" Braydon raised his hands
chest-high toward them, seeing Sherman Ellsworth tighten
his grip on the Henry rifle across his lap. "Let's not draw
blood here! We're having a reasonable discussion . . . like
smart men do. Look at ole Daggett there, for God sakes. We
don't want no more of that, do we? Huh? Hell no, we
don't!"

Ellsworth relented first, easing back down, running a hand across his face. "I don't if you don't," he said to Junior Lake.

"Forget it, then." Junior Lake shrugged and dropped his hand from the pistol. "We're all a bit what you call *tense* here. But you've got to admit, you could cut all that Texas talk in half and it'd still be a lot for us Kansas boys to swallow."

"All right." Ellsworth nodded. "I'll note that, and will try my best to correct it. Let's leave mothers and sisters alone from here on, though. I come from good folks."

"Right." Junior Lake tossed a disbelieving glance skyward, then leveled his gaze on Braydon, who sat eyeing Daggett's sturdy-looking boots, one of them thickly coated with dark dried blood. "Any ideas, Braydon?"

"Huh? Me?" Braydon had to snap his eyes up from Daggett's gear. Daggett sat still as stone, firelight shimmering on the metal-trimmed canteen in his lap. "I ran out of ideas the minute we ran out of whiskey. I agree . . . we might should have shot the oxen before we left."

Junior looked disgusted. "Come on, Braydon. We're no longer talking about what we *should* have done. Take your mind off Daggett's footwear and try to get with us. It ain't natural, a man staying on your trail this long. We've killed good horses, run out of grub—"

"Yeah, and that's Cherokee Cousins' paint horse you run to death," Braydon cut in. "You better think about *that*, too. He won't forget what you did to him."

Junior Lake let out an exasperated breath toward Braydon. "To hell with Cherokee Cousins. I'll stop his clock anytime he wants it. That's got nothing to do with nothing. I'm worn plumb to my nubs here." He cast a glance to Sherman Ellsworth. "What about it, Sherm? Think we need to split up? Get together later on across the border?"

"Maybe. But what about Reed and Dannard, and the rest of them? We was suppose to meet them last week."

Junior Lake closed his eyes for a second. Then he said,

trying to sound patient, "Boys, listen to me. Reed knows by now that we've hit a snag. Him and the others are gone on. If they ain't, then God love them, they're too damn stupid to deal with in the first place. We'll meet up with them later on somewhere."

"I hate splitting up," Braydon said, thinking about it as his eyes fixed once more on Daggett's boots.

"I know it's hard on all of us." Junior nodded. "But I truly believe we better do it. I've just got a feeling that's Outrider Sazes tracking us."

Sherman Ellsworth said, "I still believe we oughta—"

"Don't start again with your *Tejas* bullshit, Sherman," Junior said, cutting him off with a raised hand. "Because I'm really tired, and starting not to like you. We're splitting up for a while and that's that."

"I just don't understand why you're afraid of a ranger."

"Did I say I was afraid of him?" Junior Lake's eyes on Ellsworth turned hard as iron. "Don't push it, Sherm."

Sherman Ellsworth sat back, sullen and quiet.

"What about him?" Braydon nodded toward Daggett, his voice lowering.

"What about him?" Junior just stared at Braydon with a flat expression.

"Well, I mean, you know . . ." Braydon gestured a coveting glance at Daggett's boots. "If he's dead, he ain't gonna be needing them."

"Shit . . ." Junior Lake whispered. He sighed and turned toward Daggett, kicking his boot toe. "Daggett? Wake up! Braydon's ready to strip you naked as a jaybird. Are you dead or are you hearing any of this?"

"I'm a little bit of both." Daggett's rasping voice whispered from under his lowered hat brim. "I'm done for, I think. Just leave me be here. He can have these boots. I won't need them."

"See? He don't care." Braydon moved in quick, his hands already reaching for Daggett's feet.

But Junior straight-armed him back. "Jesus, Braydon,

calm yourself down." Braydon landed on his back with a grunt.

"Just leave you here?" Junior asked Daggett.

A short silence passed. Then, without raising his head, Daggett's labored voice spoke once more. "That's right. I've been doing some hard praying sitting here. . . . I believe I'm prepared to face the music."

"Daggett, I don't want to appear as a stumbling stone on your road to salvation. But do you understand that we can't leave you here alive? You know too much, all our hiding places—"

"I won't be alive that long," Daggett cut in.

"Well, who can really say?" Junior looked at Braydon and Ellsworth as he spoke to Daggett. "Again . . . not to question whatever deal you *think* you've cut with the Almighty—but let's be honest, a lousy dirty bastard like you? No matter what God told you, you better look out for a double-cross. I can safely promise that the minute you're dead, you're going straight to hell and burn there forever. No offense intended."

"You don't know that," Daggett rasped. "You can't say what God's gonna do."

"Okay, then. But I can tell you what *I'm* gonna do. We can't leave you here alive."

"I don't know why not."

"We just can't, Daggett. Maybe God'll explain it to you better than I can now that you're getting to know one another. But we can't risk a gunshot out here." He raised a knife from his boot well, making sure Daggett heard the sound of the blade across the leather. "Best we can do is stab you to death. I'm sorry, of course—"

"Wait just a minute," Daggett said, summoning strength in his voice. "I . . . can ride, I believe. If you'll help me up on a horse."

Junior Lake spread a faint smile, looking back and forth between the other two men. "Are you sure, Daggett? It'll only take me a second to put a little sharp steel to ya." He slapped the knife blade against the palm of his hand.

"Son of a bitch. Get me up! Get my foot in a stirrup. I can ride, damn you, Junior!" Daggett struggled in place trying to stand up in his rage.

"See? God ain't going to waste His time on something like you." Junior stood up, dusted his seat, and chuckled under his breath. "Get this fool on a horse, and get him out of here, Sherm." He shot Sherman Ellsworth a glance. "You and Daggett head to Wakely, get him to a doctor. Me and Braydon will go the other way."

"Huh-uh. You ain't going to jackpot me this way," Ellsworth said. "*You* take this bleeding sumbitch to town. I'll ride with Braydon."

"You wouldn't make it two days with Braydon before he'd have you picked blind and walking barefoot." Junior grinned. "Right, Braydon?"

Braydon had stepped out of the firelight, pulling the four horses in by their reins. He looked ashamed, and just shrugged. "Well, I *will* steal things. It's something I can't stop myself from doing. A warden back in Kentucky said it's because when I was a little boy, something happened that—"

"Hush, Braydon." Junior shut him up and turned to Sherman Ellsworth. "See? He's probably already got your daddy's watch with your mama's picture in it."

"No I don't," Braydon protested.

Ellsworth's hand went idly to his vest pocket, checking it, feeling the watch there as he spoke. "All the same, why am I being given this shot-up bastard to look after?" He nodded toward Daggett as the wounded outlaw struggled hand-over-hand up the side of his horse.

"Because I trust you, Sherm," Junior said. He reached out and boosted Daggett up into his saddle, then spread his hands toward Sherman Ellsworth in a show of submission. "There, I admit it. I believe you'll do the right thing. Besides, you're new around here. Cut off five pounds of beard and hair, and nobody'd know you if you stood up in their soup."

"Still . . ." Ellsworth considered it, running a hand down his long dusty beard. Atop his horse, Daggett wobbled back and forth until he firmed his hands around the saddle horn and managed to right himself.

"Listen to me," Junior said to Ellsworth, his voice now low and friendly. "I wouldn't jackpot a pal—never have before. Daggett knows the trail down from here. Me and Braydon will give you a head start. Once you've got clear away, we'll backtrack down and give whoever that is out there something to follow. All you got to do is get out across these badland hills and ease down into town. How hard is that for a big ole Texan?"

"Ali right. But be sure you give us plenty of time," Sherman Ellsworth said after thinking about it for another second.

"Don't worry. I'm talking an hour or two at the very least." Junior took the reins to two of the horses from Braydon's hands and shoved them to one side.

"Here," Braydon said to Ellsworth, brushing past him as he handed him the reins to a big roan gelding. "Take my horse. He's the best of the bunch. I'll get him back from you next time we meet up."

"When and where will that be?" Sherman Ellsworth turned back to face Junior Lake with the question.

Junior pushed up his hat brim. "Go to Blood Rock, just over the border. We'll meet you there."

"What if you ain't there when I get there?" Ellsworth looked concerned.

"Shit . . ." Junior whispered, shaking his head, getting disgusted again. "Then take along some marbles and reading material, I reckon. We'll get there when we can."

Sherman Ellsworth grumbled and stepped up into his saddle and jerked his horse around beside Daggett. Junior Lake slapped both horses on their dusty rumps, and as the two men goaded the horses away along the rocky trail into the darkness, Junior chuckled to Braydon. "I hate a Texan worse than I hate a snake."

"But you've got folks there," Braydon remarked.

"Yes I do. I even married a girl from down in the panhandle once, remember? She did things that no sane white man could abide."

"What'd she do?"

"I won't say . . . but it was things that would curl your hair if you heard them. Wasn't married six weeks. Had to shoot her to get rid of her. I still wake up nights in a cold sweat."

"Then I don't want to hear it." Braydon sat down beside the fire and leaned back. "We just as well get comfortable for the next hour or so."

"Get up, Braydon." Junior took the pistol from the rawhide string around his neck, checked it, and spun it on his finger.

"Huh? Why?" Braydon looked at Junior's pistol spinning in the glow of firelight.

"I said get up." Junior's pistol stopped spinning and was now pointed at Braydon. The skinny little outlaw sprang to his feet. Junior grinned. "Now how much money have you got?"

"Lord, Junior! You ain't gonna shoot me, are ya?"

"Yeah, I might, if you don't answer me. How much?"

"Six dollars . . . you can have it, though."

"No, Braydon, I mean how much counting what you snuck out of ole Sherm's saddlebags whilst he wasn't looking."

"Oh . . ." Braydon squirmed in place. "Maybe, forty, fifty dollars. But you can have that, too."

"How much of that do you want to bet that Daggett don't end up dumped alongside the road before daylight?"

"Ellsworth said he'd take him to Wakely, Junior. Don't you believe him?"

"If I did I wouldn't be wanting to bet, would I? I lay you

twenty dollars against this ole Hoard pistol the Texan leaves him dying in the dirt. What do you say?"

"Naw, that's a sucker bet. Besides, that stolen pistol didn't cost you a thing."

"So? Your money's stolen, too." Junior slipped the rawhide string back through the trigger guard and let the pistol drop down his chest. Braydon sat back down. But Junior said, "Huh-uh, get up. We're leaving, damn it! Can't you understand anything?" He kicked Braydon's leg.

"Hell, I don't know what you want." Braydon sprang back up to his feet. "Want me to put the fire out?"

"No, let it burn." Junior stepped over, got the reins to the horses and pulled them into the firelight. "Anybody comes in, they'll see Ellsworth and Daggett's tracks and follow them out of here. We're gonna lead these horses over the rocks, then head down the flats and haul arse. You ready?"

"I always am." Braydon flashed his crooked weasel grin, dusted the loose seat of his dirty trousers and took the reins to his horse.

On the trail, a quarter of a mile ahead, Sherman Ellsworth stopped beside Daggett before nudging their horses around a sharp turn in a steep switchback. He asked Daggett in a concerned voice, "Are you sure you're up to this, ole buddy? You're bleeding pretty bad."

"I'll make out." Daggett's voice sounded weak but determined. "Just help me up if I fall off this saddle."

"I'm worried about you." Ellsworth shook his head in the darkness. "Maybe it ain't a good idea, you trying to ride. You might oughta point the way down for me, then sit back in these rocks till morning, see if you feel better by then."

"Don't shit me, Ellsworth. If you want to cut out, go ahead. But it'll be dangerous going in the dark, with no direction."

Sherman Ellsworth considered it. "Naw, I gave my word. I'll stick with you."

"I thought you would." Daggett spread a weak smile.

Sherman Ellsworth turned in his saddle and looked back toward the thin glow of light behind them. "I hope two hours' head start is enough time."

Daggett tried to laugh under his breath, but it turned into a painful wheeze. "You don't know nothing, do ya?"

"I know more than you think." Ellsworth straightened in his saddle and looked out across the black land beneath them.

"Yeah? Well, do you know Braydon got your watch?"

"No, he didn't. I checked it, remember?"

"Then you check again. He got it when he gave you his horse and brushed past you . . . you dumb peckerwood." Daggett coughed and wheezed.

"What the—?" Ellsworth patted his empty vest pocket. "That little rat-bastard! I'm going back. I'll kill him!" He started to spin his horse around on the narrow trail, but Daggett turned his horse and blocked his way.

"Save yourself the trouble, Ellsworth. They left no sooner than we got out of sight."

In the gray hour before dawn, Samuel Burrack had already untied the big cur and let him bound out, running in a wide circle with his nose to the ground. Samuel unhobbled the oxen, yoked them, and had them hitched to the big cart while Ranger Sazes still sat crosslegged near the smoldering campfire with his rifle across his lap, his briar pipe hanging from his mouth. Beside Sazes, the Appaloosa stallion stood scraping a restless hoof in the sand. "It'll soon be daylight," Samuel ventured, getting restless himself.

"I know it." Sazes lowered the pipe from his lips, looked down into the dark bowl, then tapped it empty against the sole of his boot. He put the pipe away inside his riding duster and gazed straight ahead toward the badlands hills.

"Shouldn't we be moving on?" Samuel leveled his battered hat on his forehead.

"When it's time." Sazes didn't look at him. His eyes seemed to search every thin ledge and crevice in the purple light. In the east a silver wreath of sunlight glowed beneath the dome of the horizon. "I want to see what kind of message they send us from up there."

Samuel looked up along the black outline of hills, then back down to Sazes. "They've seen our campfire plain as day from up there."

"I meant for them to." Sazes still searched the hill line as he spoke. "Now we'll see what they think of us. They were expecting me sometime in the night, but I never do what they expect. Sit down. Have some tea, boy. It'll take the edge off ya."

But Samuel didn't sit down. "Maybe they're waiting to ambush you once you start up there."

"That's not Junior Lake's style. He's not the smartest man in the world, but in this kind of situation he's as good as they come. He won't take a stand until he's got the odds on his side. I figure he's still on the move. I just need to see which direction he's headed. No sense in chasing my own tail, is there?"

Samuel didn't answer. He walked over to the oxcart and sat down, leaning back against the wheel.

When a few more minutes had passed and the silver wreath spread upward in the sky, Clyde Sazes stood up and stretched without taking his eyes from the distant hills. "There it is. We can go now. We'll get you headed for Wakely. I'll get on Junior's trail."

Samuel stood up and stared off with him. From within a faraway dark crevice a sliver of smoke twisted skyward on a breath of wind, drifting slantwise. "That's it? That's the message you've been waiting for?"

"Yep, there it is." Sazes took up the reins to the Appaloosa. "Junior has split his men up during the night." He gazed off southward across the flatlands leading toward the border, then northeast across the hills toward the road to Wakely. "He's headed down for old Mex. Wants me to find their campsite up there and go off after whoever rode north."

Samuel looked at him in silence for a second. "How can you be sure?"

"Can't be. But that's the way I call it. He's feeding me somebody while he makes his getaway. That's the way this ole boy works. Nobody knows this desert better than Junior Lake—except me, of course. By now he's probably figured out it's me on his back. So he'll be at his best. This'll turn into a dance between just him and me."

"You're going after him and letting the others get away?"

"They won't get away for long. But Junior's the head of the snake. Once I cut him off the rest is easy. Junior has a knack for leading thugs and killers. More than likely Daggett will be getting medical treatment. But he'll get it and go. He won't stick around town."

"As soon as I get there, I'll go to the sheriff," Samuel said.

"Yeah, you do that. His name is Kemp, and he's a good man. Tell him what happened, then you keep your nose out of it," Sazes advised. "You don't want the kind of trouble these boys carry with them."

"If I run into them on the trail, I'll defend myself."

"Of course. But don't go out of your way looking for a fight. The sooner you can shake this mess from your boots, the better off you'll be. These are the worst sort of men on earth. They have a way of drawing you into their world."

"I'll be careful. I want no part of it." Samuel spoke, but Sazes didn't seem to hear him as he went on.

"They live without the benefit or hindrance of any moral restraint whatsoever. They'll kill you for a plate of beans or a barrel hoop. Give them wide berth. Let the law deal with them."

"That's what I fully intend to do," Samuel said. He walked to the oxcart, picked up the whip from against its side, and goaded the oxen into a slow plodding walk. Sazes stood looking at him as the cart struggled forward on the loose sand. Then he stepped up onto the Appaloosa's back and heeled it forward, the big cur falling in behind the horse, following with its nose still to the ground.

As cart and horseman and dog grew small in the flatlands, silence spread across the sand with the first rays of morning. A spotted lizard slipped up as if from out of the belly of the earth. It froze in place with its clawed feet planted firmly beneath it, searching instinctively for any sign of life supplicant to itself on this barren lower plane. There was none.

Chapter 3

At daylight, on the flat trail toward Wakely, Sherman Ellsworth stopped and took Daggett's horse by its bridle. Daggett sat slumped in his saddle, knowing what was about to come. But he was too weak now to do anything about it. All through the night, he'd kept a hand on the cocked pistol in his lap, expecting Ellsworth to make a move on him as soon as the big Texan felt he could make it the rest of the way down alone. The blood from his shoulder wound had crusted deep down Daggett's arm and his heavily coated hand was now stuck to the pistol butt. "Guess what, Daggett?" Ellsworth spread a sly, knowing grin, and gave a nod toward the stretch of flatland ahead.

"You son . . . of a . . . bitch," Daggett said in a strained, halting voice, looking up at Ellsworth from under his hat brim.

"Give me that pistol." Ellsworth grabbed Daggett's weak gunhand and raised it from his lap. "Turn it loose."

"I . . . can't." Daggett's arm flopped back and forth loosely.

"Then I'll help you, you bloody wretch." Ellsworth twisted his hand until the pistol came free. Then he raised a boot and kicked Daggett from his saddle. "I'll take the horse, too. You won't be needing him where you're going."

Daggett landed with a groan in a spray of dust, and rolled over on his back and looked up at Ellsworth. "I wish . . . I had lived long enough . . . to kill you."

"Can't have everything, can we?" Ellsworth said, staring grimly down at Daggett. Ellsworth steadied the blood-crusted pistol in his hand and aimed it at Daggett's head. He pulled the trigger. But the hammer wouldn't fall. "Damn it!" He slapped the pistol in the palm of his other hand, then tried again. Nothing happened.

"You must have been living on roof tar and straight hog grease, Daggett." He tried the pistol again, but as he tried to get the hammer unstuck, Daggett crawled forward, took a weak hold on Ellsworth's stirrup and managed to drag himself up a few inches.

"Get off of there!" Sherman Ellsworth kicked him away. "Hell, you're dead anyway." He slung the cocked pistol off into a stand of creosote bush. "*Adios,* Daggett, you unlucky horse's arse. Go see if God's offer is still open for ya." He spat and grinned, then kicked his horse out onto the trail, leading Daggett's blood-soaked mount behind him.

"I'm done for . . . " Daggett murmured to himself. He rolled over onto his stomach and crawled off to the creosote bush, sand clumping and turning dark on his bloody chest.

Sherman Ellsworth pushed the big roan hard, pulling the other horse by its reins, not stopping until he found a turnoff toward a stand of cottonwood trees a hundred yards off the trail. He grinned and spoke to himself. "Ain't been a Texan born yet that can't find water when he wants to bad enough." He gigged the horse toward the trees. "Junior Lake ain't *seen* the jackpot he can put me in."

At the dark, thin pool of murky water in the bottom of a wash beneath bare cottonwood roots, he slipped down from the roan and let the horses drink. He dipped a hand into the water, rubbed it into his long beard, and took out a big Bowie knife from its sheath behind his back. "What say, boys?" He laughed, looking at the tired horses with dirty water dribbling from their muzzles. "Time to clean up a little, huh?" He held out a length of wet beard and cut it off, letting it fall from his fingers onto the passing wind.

While he didn't yet know how far it was to Wakely, Ellsworth knew it was getting closer all the time. Once there, with a shave, a new shirt, maybe a change into some spanking new pin-stripped trousers . . . hell. He chuckled as he continued cutting his coarse long beard and letting it flutter and fall. His own mother wouldn't recognize him.

At midmorning, Samuel and Ranger Sazes had split up near the base of the hills. Sazes had cut left across the desert basin. Samuel, with his oxcart and the big cur beside him, had pushed on to the right along the low trail and into the sparse grassland and brush country toward town. Before Sazes had left him, the old ranger had given him a canteen of water and a small-caliber single-shot Uhrlinger pistol, and advised him to keep his eyes open toward the badlands hills. "There's two water holes 'twixt here and Wakely, but use caution around them. I wish I could ride farther on with you," Sazes had told him. But Samuel had assured him he'd be all right.

"I'll keep the dog out front and circling," Samuel had said to him. "He'll let me know if anybody's nearby. I'll listen to him better from now on."

"You do that." Sazes scratched the big cur's head and stepped up into the saddle. "You both could use a heap of learning." Then he'd turned the Appaloosa stallion and rode off onto the desert floor.

It was past noon when Samuel saw the horses, hoofprints leading down from the hills, and only a few minutes later he came to the scrapings in the dirt where Ellsworth had kicked Daggett from his horse and left him to die. Samuel brought the cart to a halt, seeing the wide mark of blood-streaked sand where Daggett had crawled away. The big cur had moved out twenty yards into the brush while Samuel waited beside the cart, with the small pistol in one hand and his buffalo rifle in the other.

"Blue, get back here!" He called out, fearing for the dog's life. But the dog would have none of it. He'd found something in the creosote bushes and wasn't about to give it up. He reared back from the bush a few feet and stood low on his front paws, bellowing and snarling with his hackles raised high.

"Blue! Get back here!" Samuel swung the rifle over the edge of the cart and aimed a few feet ahead of the dog. "You in there. Come out where I can see you!" The cur moved back, but only a couple of feet, grudgingly, and lowered its voice into a quieter growl.

"Call . . . him off," Daggett's weak voice cried out. "I can't move . . . let alone come out. I'm done for."

"Then show your hands." Samuel heard the unsteadiness in his own voice. "I'm on you with a .50-caliber."

"A buff rifle—?" Daggett's words halted for a second. "Then you're . . . the one who killed me."

"I haven't killed anybody. Not yet." Samuel searched the land around him as he spoke, leery that the man was not alone. "Now show me your hands and keep them raised."

"Hell . . . young man." Daggett's voice seemed to grow a bit stronger as he spoke. "I can't do nothing. Either . . . come get me, or let me die in peace."

Samuel hesitated, needing to think, but feeling too pressed for time. "Blue! Get out here! Right now!" The big cur whined, bowing, circling, keeping its eyes on the creosote bush. Then it pulled back slowly, turned, and bounded out to the cart, jerking back and forth toward the brush as if pleading for Samuel to follow.

"Good boy." Samuel ran a gloved hand across the dog's head, keeping his eyes on the spot where the voice came from. "I'm coming in, mister. Don't try anything funny."

"Funny?" Daggett coughed and choked. "Ain't . . . *nothing* funny about it. I'm going fast."

Samuel and the big cur moved forward into the sand and brush in a wide cautious half circle until the body of the wounded outlaw appeared through the spindly branches. Samuel saw the dark blood pooling beneath the man's body, and saw the man peering out toward the cart, a small pocket pistol hanging limp in his hand, expecting Samuel to come from that direction. Samuel moved in from the side; and at a distance of fifteen feet called out in a quiet tone, "Drop the gun, Mister. Drop it now."

"Oh . . . there you are." Daggett turned his face sideways toward Samuel as the dog moved in closer. Daggett let the pistol fall from his bloody fingertips and let out a sigh. "I wasn't going to shoot. It's just . . . force of habit."

"Keep your hands out front," Samuel said, his breath rushing a bit. "I don't want to hurt you, but I will if you make me."

"You already have." Daggett nodded at his wound where the big bullet had come out, taking flesh and bone with it.

"You brought it on yourself. You killed my friend."

"Not me." Daggett wheezed and fell back as Samuel moved in beside him. "That was the others, Lake, Braydon, and Ellsworth. I'm Andrew Johnson, I only held him. The others did . . . the killing. That's the truth." He eyed Samuel to see how that sounded to him.

Samuel picked up the bloody revolver, forced the hammer down on it, and shoved the gun down inside his belt, keeping his eyes on the wounded outlaw. "Your name's not Johnson—it's Daggett." He reached down with his free hand and helped Daggett lift himself to his feet.

"That's right . . . but us Daggetts all come from Johnson stock. So I often mistake—"

"Save your breath." Samuel looped Daggett's arm around his shoulder and together they struggled toward the oxcart, the blue cur close at Daggett's heel, sniffing with his hackles still raised. "I'm taking you to Wakely. You can tell it all to the sheriff."

"I'll never make it . . . that far. Can't you see I'm done in? Leave me here . . . let me go on to my maker."

At the cart, Samuel leaned him back against the wheel

and searched him for any other weapons, taking Daggett's boot knife and tossing it out into the brush. "How'd you know my name?" Daggett asked, his strength coming back more, his mind already at work, looking for a way out.

"A ranger named Sazes told me. Lucky for me he came along when he did. He stopped me from riding into your laps last night."

"Sazes? *Outrider* Sazes? He was behind us . . . when we—I mean *they* killed your friend? So that really was him?"

"Yep." Samuel looked around and alongside the cart. "Stay right here. I've got to find a way to tie your hands."

"Tie my hands? Lord, boy, nobody . . . ties a man's hands. I'm too far gone . . . to be any danger. Look at me." Daggett slumped a little more than he had to and touched a hand to his bloody shoulder. "You did this to me. You killed me." He watched Samuel's eyes for a reaction.

Samuel winced. "Sorry. You gave me no choice."

Sorry . . . ? That was a good sign, the boy apologizing, Daggett thought. "No choice? You shoot a man in the back, kill him . . . then say he gave you no choice? You're as cold-blooded as a snake. You just as well finish me off . . . here and now."

Samuel looked him up and down, seeing the heavy coat of blood-crusted sand on his chest. "We need to get you cleaned up."

"No. The sand has stopped the bleeding," Daggett said. "Don't meddle with it. I'll be dead . . . soon enough as it is."

Samuel considered it, then said, "All right, we'll leave it alone. And I won't tie up your hands, so long as you do as I say." He gestured upward onto the pile of sweltering buffalo hides in the oxcart. "You'll have to ride up there."

"In that nasty, stinking—?"

"It's either that or walk." Samuel cut him off. "It's over thirty miles to Wakely. I'm not about to carry you." He moved away a couple of steps, leaned the rifle against the cart and came back. Daggett watched, feeling stronger now, but knowing he wasn't able to make a leap for the rifle. "Here," Samuel added, taking him by his shoulders, "I'll help you up."

Daggett groaned, stepping up the side of the cart and falling over onto the hides. Flies swirled. He fanned them away with a bloody hand. "Never thought I'd end up this way; dying on a stinking gut wagon."

Samuel picked up his rifle and the whip, and goaded the oxen forward with the whip handle. He walked a few feet out from the cart, keeping an eye on the wounded outlaw while the big cur kept an even wider distance, still glaring at the blood-soaked stranger. On the ground, Samuel took note of the two sets of hoofprints left by the other outlaw as the oxen plodded along the trail.

Over an hour had passed when they came to the turnoff toward the stand of cottonwood trees. Smelling water, the team of oxen tried to turn instinctively toward it. But seeing the hoofprints turn off in that direction, and being leery of an ambush, Samuel took a firm hold on the team and straightened them forward. The blue cur stopped and looked back, already headed for the wash; and when he saw the cart still moving along the trail, he whined and came back to Samuel's side. "I see it, Blue," Samuel said down to him. "We'll find more water on the way to town."

"You'll kill these ox if you don't get 'em watered," Daggett called down to him.

Samuel didn't answer.

"You hear me?" Daggett leaned out over the side. "You'll kill them, and us, too. This sun is scorching our bones."

"There's another hole on ahead," Samuel said, walking on.

"Like hell there is. I know this trek. There's nothing from here on, until we get to town."

"Yes there is. Ranger Sazes told me about it." He gazed ahead into the wavering heat.

"Sazes . . . ha! If you listen to that lunatic, you're as crazy as he is."

"We're not stopping," Samuel said in a firm voice. He goaded the oxen with the whip handle and kept moving, the big cur whining and panting at his side.

Chapter 4

In the heat of midafternoon, they turned off the trail and stopped long enough to rest the oxen, taking to the slim shade beneath two tall saguaro that stood atop a swell of rocky ground. With his knife, Samuel cut chunks of cactus for the oxen to chew. As the big animals' jaws crushed water from the tough fibrous plants, Samuel passed the canteen to the wounded outlaw, then took it back, drank from it himself, and poured water in his cupped hand for the dog.

"I'd like to eat something . . . before I die," Daggett said, lying back against the edge of the low rock shelf.

"You appear to be feeling better." Samuel looked him up and down. "I've got some dried buffalo, and some tea Ranger Sazes gave me. We'll eat when we get to the next water hole."

"Won't matter to me. I'll be dead by then. What I need is something to eat right now." Daggett stared at his dusty boots and muffled a cough with the back of his dirty hand. "I might appear better . . . but I ain't." He lifted his eyes to Samuel. "Even if I make it to Wakely, like as not they'll hang me."

"That's up to the judge." Samuel looked off across the dry hot land for a moment, then got up, went to the cart, and came back with a handful of dried meat. "Here, this will have to do for now. The more you eat, the more you'll want to drink."

"Ever seen a man hang?" Daggett took the meat and tore off a piece between his teeth, chewing loudly.

"Nope. But I saw my friend cut from ear to ear." His eyes fixed hard on the outlaw. "I can't imagine hanging being any worse than that."

"I told you, I never done the cutting. It was that bearded bastard, Ellsworth."

"Ellsworth, huh? I'll remember that. What's his first name?"

"Hell, what's the difference? He'll head back for Texas. You'll never find him. But he's the killer, for sure. Not me."

"You only held him." Samuel's eyes stayed fixed upon him.

"Yeah, I only held him . . . and that wasn't nothing." Daggett winced at the pain in his shoulder and adjusted his back against the rock. "Anyway, I had to . . . can't you understand? Junior Lake would've killed me if I didn't help. That's how he is. You can't cross a man like Junior." As he spoke, Daggett scraped a spur rowel back and forth in the dirt.

"Your friend, Junior Lake, will have to answer to Ranger Sazes. And you'll have to answer to the judge. All I want is to see justice done for Davey Riley. He didn't deserve to die."

"Was that his name, Davey Riley?" Daggett gave him a look of remorse and shook his head. "Well, all I can say is, I'm sorry for what Junior and the others did to the poor young man. But my hands are clean. That's a fact."

Samuel studied his eyes for a second, seeing that this man actually believed what he was saying, that somehow in his own mind Daggett held himself blameless for Davey Riley's murder. There was no point in discussing it. He stood up with the rifle in his hand and dusted off his trousers. "Let's go. I've got nothing more to say to you. " With his free hand, he reached down and pulled Daggett to his feet and nudged him forward toward the cart.

"Hey, easy there," Daggett cried, looking back over his shoulder. "I'm in bad shape . . . and I'm still eating!"

"You're alive, mister. That's more than I can say for my friend." At the cart, he boosted the reluctant outlaw upward until a snarl of flies rose and swarmed in a glistening dark cloud. "If I were you, I'd be careful what I say from here on."

"Hell, what have I got to lose?" Daggett swatted flies from his face and tore off anther bite of dried buffalo. "I either die out here . . . or hang when I get where we're going. Either way, I'm dead." He shrugged his good shoulder and slapped a grimy hand through the air. "Damn flies. I'll be lucky if this wound don't fester up on me. Well, what the hell's the difference . . . ?"

Samuel just looked at him, knowing that to this man's way of thinking, what he said was true. Samuel was sure that whatever other terrible things Daggett had done in his life had meant no more or less to him than holding Davey Riley while another man cut his throat. Looking at Daggett, Samuel remembered what Ranger Sazes had told him— about how these kind of men had a way of drawing a person into their world. But for the life of him, Samuel couldn't see how. He picked up the whip from against the side of the wagon and goaded the oxen forward.

They moved on, with the heat of the afternoon sun pressing hard, draining substance from man and beast alike on this scorching blanket of coarse earth. Across sloping sand flats, broad-terraced layers of rock and patches of sparse brittle foliage and cacti, the oxen trudged with their big heads bowed and their thick shoulders struck forward against the weight of their heavy load. Twenty yards ahead of the cart, the cur held a slow steady pace, his shoulders low and his tongue lolling back and forth beneath his chin.

As streaks of evening shadows stretched long beneath the dog, the oxen, and the cart, Samuel saw the team bearing left off the trail toward a long downward slope, where at the bottom a thin stream ran serpentine out of a rise of rock. This time when the oxen drew toward water, he let them have their way and followed them, his hot boot soles dragging a bit underneath his unsteady gait.

In the lower belly of the falling terrain, sunlight cut short, and shade from the rising land behind them spread across Samuel's shoulders. Soothed, he sank to the ground and watched the oxen trudge forward the last few yards and stop at the water's edge. The big cur plopped down beside him, his tongue rising and falling with his panting breath. "Go on and get some water, Blue. You don't have to wait for me." But the dog only whined under his breath and didn't move. After a second, Samuel stood up and added, "All right, come on then. We'll drink together."

At the edge of the water, Daggett had climbed down from the cart, stretched out on his belly and sank his face into the meager stream. He raised his wet face sideways and wiped a hand across his eyes as Samuel stooped down beside him and lowered the canteen to fill it. "Looks like Ranger Sazes told you right," he said, water dripping from his chin. He grinned. "I must've forgotten it was here."

"Yep, you must have." Samuel answered in a flat tone, dipping his cupped hand into the water and pitching it up onto his face. The buffalo rifle rested across his lap. Beside him, the big cur lapped water eagerly, laid down in it, and rolled back and forth. "We'll make a camp here tonight." Samuel looked back and forth along the long streaked shadows among the low pitch of land. "With an early start, we should make town by tomorrow evening."

Daggett rose up onto his haunches and touched a hand to the caked blood and sand on his shoulder. "I hate to see what this'll look like once I get it cleaned up."

"We can clean it here," Samuel offered.

But Daggett drew back at the suggestion. "No . . . it'll start bleeding again."

"Suit yourself." Samuel stood up with the canteen in one

hand, the rifle in the other. "You're stronger now. I can tell by looking at you."

"I'm still . . . in bad shape, though." Daggett's voice sounded weaker all of a sudden. He sank back on the ground and scraped the rowels of his spurs idly back and forth in the rocky dirt.

Samuel slept lightly throughout the night, leaning back against the wheel of the oxcart with the rifle cradled in his arms. Along the side of his leg, Blue lay with his head resting on Samuel's knee. Twice, Samuel stirred and blinked his weary eyes when the dog lifted its chin and growled low in its chest. But looking over at Daggett, seeing him asleep, wrapped in a ragged blanket closer to the low glowing fire, Samuel patted the dog's head, murmuring, "Good boy, Blue," and drifted back into his cautious slumber.

Before dawn, Samuel and the dog were up, the big cur sniffing back and forth along the water's edge where during the night small creatures had come and gone, taking water and leaving footprints behind them. "Time to go, mister." Samuel reached out with a boot toe and tapped it against the ragged blanket.

"Lord . . ." Daggett rose slightly on his good elbow and shook his head. "What's the big rush? A man oughta get some sleep before trekking out like this."

"You slept good all night. Let's get moving." Samuel turned and walked away a few feet to the oxen. He untied their traces from around a short stand of rock and led them back to the cart. Daggett sat up and moaned, running his fingers through his hair.

After Samuel yoked the oxen, he saw that Daggett had laid back down and thrown the ragged blanket over himself. He walked back over and nudged his boot against his leg, harder this time. "Come on. We want to beat as much of the heat as we can."

"All right, damn it." Daggett slung the blanket off and sat

up once more. Samuel turned and stepped over to the water, stooping down, and raising a cupped handful to his mouth. He drank, hearing Daggett grumble under his breath as he moved down across the loose rock behind him. "I reckon now is as good a time as any."

Samuel slung water from his hand, then adjusted the rifle in his other hand and started to stand up. "The earlier we get started—"

But halfway to his feet his words cut short. Something suddenly struck him low and hard on the side of his neck; and it struck him again, this time on his collarbone, even as he pulled away instinctively. Pain shot through his body. He tried to swing the rifle back like a club, but Daggett quickly swept atop his back, stabbing vicious blow upon blow with the sharp rowel of his spur.

Across the trickle of water, the big cur sprang back and forth in place with his hackles raised, growling, barking, but staying back out of the melee. Daggett grunted aloud with each hard blow of the rowel, his wounded shoulder opening with a fresh flow of blood. Samuel struggled beneath him, the rifle kicked away from his hands now, his right forearm raised over his head for protection. Blood flew.

With his left hand groping back over his shoulder, Samuel found purchase around the outlaw's throat and squeezed with all his strength. Bowing forward on his knees, Samuel felt Daggett fall across his shoulder onto the ground, the sharp rowel embedded deep in Samuel's ribs. Daggett rolled forward a few feet. "You son of a bitch!" he gasped, then scrambled to the rifle in the dirt a few feet away.

"Drop it!" Samuel cried out, his voice more of a plea than a threat. But Daggett stood up, weaving unsteadily, cocking the rifle.

"I'll blow your stupid arse to hell!" Daggett swung the cocked rifle around toward him as Samuel ducked to one side, blood running down his gashed forehead into his eyes, blinding him.

Blue darted in at Daggett's boots, but then jerked back as a hard boot toe caught him a solid blow to his jaw. He yelped and circled. Daggett pointed the rifle into Samuel's bleeding face, and at a distance of four feet pulled the trigger. "Damn it!" He cursed, snarling, when the hammer fell on an empty chamber.

"Drop it!" Samuel yelled, swabbing thick blood from his stinging eyes. "*Please . . . !*"

"Like hell!" Daggett slung the rifle back sidelong by its long barrel, and moved forward for a final crushing blow.

The small, crisp pop of the Uhrlinger pistol caused Daggett to let out a hard grunt and jackknife forward at the waist. The rifle barrel slumped, Daggett's hand going to the small hole in his upper thigh. "You sneaking little coward—!" He caught himself and righted the rifle barrel once more.

"*Please!*" Samuel cried out, his slick trembling fingers hurrying with a reload.

But Daggett stepped forward, a look of killing lust in his red-rimmed eyes. "There . . . ain't nothing going to keep me from—"

The Uhrlinger popped again, this time the bullet hitting Daggett higher up in his side, sending him into a bowed, staggering gait sideways. The rifle fell from Daggett's grasp to the ground. Samuel hurried, scrambling forward on his hands and knees. He snatched up the rifle. Fumbling with a bullet from his shirt pocket, he drove it into the breech, slammed it shut and cocked the loaded bore in Daggett's face.

"Stop!" Samuel's voice turned solid as steel. Seeing the look in the young man's bloody eyes, Daggett froze two feet from the tip of the big rifle barrel. The big cur darted in, nipped at Daggett's boot, then ducked back, circling and darting in again. "Back, Blue. Good boy!" The dog settled and growled low, staying back with ears perked, its hackles standing high. Daggett's breath pounded in and out. "All right. I'm . . . quitting here." His hands raised chest high. "Don't . . . shoot me no more."

"On the ground." Samuel struggled to his feet as he spoke, his breath tight, his head pounding.

"Now, boy . . . there's no need—"

"On the ground!" This time he bellowed the words, the blue cur even slinking back at the sound of his voice. Before Daggett could do as he demanded, Samuel swung the rifle barrel sideways, cracking it into the outlaw's knee. Daggett crumbled; and as he hit the ground face first, Samuel planted his boot sole on the back of his neck and pressed down. Daggett's face was rasped by sand and sharp stones.

Samuel uncocked the big rifle and leaned it against his thigh. Loosening the wide leather belt from around his waist, he stooped down, jerked Daggett's arms back behind him and bound his wrists together. Daggett sliced out a low painful groan, feeling the wound in his shoulder stretch and break open further. "Boy, you can't . . . truss a man up like an animal." Even in his defeat, Daggett still tested, seeing how far he could push.

"Don't say one more word about it, or I'll crack your head and *drag* you back to the cart!" Samuel pressed his boot down harder. The sound of his own voice seemed foreign and distant to him. His heart raced in his chest. "I tried being decent . . . *decent,* but it didn't work." He jerked upward on Daggett's bound wrists, forcing the outlaw onto his feet. Then he shoved him forward, Daggett limping toward the cart where the oxen stood watching, detached and uninterested in the workings of men now that the sound of the pistol fire had been swallowed up by the gray silence of morning.

"But . . . what about this bleeding?" Daggett spoke back to Samuel over his shoulder. Samuel stalked close behind him, nudging the outlaw on with the rifle barrel. "We can't go on, both of us in this shape," Daggett said. "You're going to die . . . right along with me!"

"Better hope I don't die first, *murderer.*" Samuel felt a tight bitterness in his words and in his being. Something hot and dark boiled in his chest. "If I feel myself go, the last thing I'll do is open your gullet with a spur rowel and watch you spill in the dirt." As Daggett tried to slow, Samuel turned the big rifle butt forward in his hands and launched a firm blow in the small of his back. "You're going to Wakely, either face up, or face down. From here on in, I don't care which . . ."

Chapter 5

Sherman Ellsworth had held out as long as he could without a drink. But on the morning of the third day in Wakely, he'd started tossing back shots of rye no sooner than the doors to the Little Egypt Saloon swung open. Alone at one end of the bar, he stood slumped forward on his forearms, the brim of his new bowler hat riding low on his forehead. A loose bow tie lay dangling from his open white collar band. On his waist hung a .45-caliber Colt. His freshly shaved cheeks were pale where the beard had long shielded his face from the harsh sun.

"Do it again," he called out to the bartender, pushing his empty whiskey glass forward with a fingertip. There'd been no sign of whoever had been following him and the others. He felt good and rested now, the whiskey making him ready for some action.

"Why don't I just leave the bottle, Mr. Potts?" The bartender poured the shot glass full and stood the bottle of rye beside it.

"Yeah, why don't you do that?" Sherman Ellsworth spoke with a whiskey-laden sneer. He hadn't pulled the name Potts out of thin air. Potts was the name of a dry goods drummer he'd shot in a poker game two years earlier in Santa Fe. *Warren Potts* . . . He grinned to himself. Make that *Mister Potts*, he thought, glancing down at his new pin-striped trousers.

In his pocket he had three hundred dollars that had laid damp and sweaty for the past three weeks on the trail. Now that the money was dry and crisp, he wanted to throw it around a little. Yet he cautioned himself to play it quiet for a while longer—not make himself too visible all at once.

He'd ridden one of the horses to death on his way to Wakely. He'd dropped the saddle from the other horse and set it free a quarter of a mile out of town, the animal exhausted and staggering blindly out onto the sand flats. When he'd first come into town he'd slipped in on foot from behind the livery barn, carrying only his saddle and tack. He pitched the gear onto a public rail, and washed himself off in a bucket of water.

Ellsworth hadn't gone straight to the saloon as he would have liked to. Rather, he'd made his transformation a little at a time, going first to the barbershop, then to the mercantile store where he'd suited himself up in a white shirt, a swallow-tailed dress jacket, and pinstriped trousers. Then, with a new bowler hat riding high on his head, he'd bought a coat-pocketful of cigars and a leather travel valise and hung around the stage depot for a couple of hours until a stagecoach arrived from the north.

He'd strolled the boardwalk with the valise in his hand after the wide Studebaker stagecoach unloaded its passengers, just letting himself be seen coming from that direction, looking here and there inspecting the town—getting everybody used to seeing him. Sure, he could play it straight a little longer if he wanted to, but . . .

Hell with it, he thought, throwing back the fresh shot of rye. He was safe enough here. Why go on forever, acting like some polite, dandy-mac just blown in from a New Jersey boarding school. It wasn't his nature. Money was made to be blown; whisky was made to be swilled; and trouble? Well, trouble was just made to be *made* . . . period. *Amen.*

"You there, rock-busters," he called down along the bar to a small gathering of miners who'd stood laughing among themselves drinking foamy beer from their own tin cups. "Any of you fit for a few hands?" As he spoke he nodded toward an empty poker table near the back wall.

"We're all tapped out," one of the miners answered for the entire group. "Just winding down from a week's worth of faro and drinking."

"Then don't waste my time." Ellsworth swung his head from them as they looked at one another bemused. They shrugged and went back to their beer and conversation. Ellsworth eyed a young man at the far end of the bar who stood with his wide Stetson brim bowed above a glass of whiskey. "Hey, big hat," Ellsworth called out in a half-drunken slur. When the man's eyes raised slowly and faced him from underneath the Stetson brim, Ellsworth grinned. "Yeah, you with the headful of hat. You looking for some poker action? Win a few . . . lose a few? What do you say?"

"What *about* my hat?" The words came low and strong like the low warning hiss of a snake.

But before Sherman Ellsworth could reply, the bartender cut in with a strained nervous laugh. "Now, Larry, hold on. Mr. Potts meant it in a friendly way, I'm sure. He's new in town. Sounds like he's trying to make acquaintances here and—"

"Shut up, Thurman," the man's low hiss cut him off. A pair of cold green eyes cut to the bartender's sweating face, then fixed back onto Sherman Ellsworth. "What *about* my hat?" he asked again. A tight black glove raised a shiny bone-handled pistol as he spoke. He lay the pistol slowly down onto the bartop, flicked a fingertip across the tip of the barrel as if to clear it of any dust, then rested the gloved hand down six inches away from it. Miners moved back from the bar in dead silence, then slipped farther back inches at a time until nothing stood between the two men but the wet bartop and a circling fly. Sherman Ellsworth felt his pale cheeks grow flushed and hot behind his tight whiskey smile. He noted that the front sight was missing from the shiny pistol lying pointed at him twenty feet away—a gunfighter's gun. Ellsworth held the young man's gaze without wavering.

"Well now, *Larry*," he said in a mimicking tone, using the

name he'd heard the bartender call the young man. "Had I but known how touchy you are about your headgear, I might have asked differently—no insult intended. All I wanted was to ask if you'd like to play a little poker." A tense, silent second passed. "So do you?"

"Let's get settled on my hat first," the young man said, his voice the same flat near-whisper. He raised the Stetson from atop his head, laying it down on the bar and running his hand back across his oiled, well groomed hair. He pushed the Stetson forward with his gloved fingers. "Tell me what you *really* think of it. Be honest now," he added in a dark playful tone. His cold green eyes looked calm, yet in them something seemed coiled, ready to strike. He flicked an imaginary speck of dust from the tip of the black hat's crown, the same way he'd done with his pistol barrel.

Damn it . . . Why hadn't he just kept his drunken mouth shut, Sherman Ellsworth chastised himself. He tried to hold the man's stare, but felt ready to slip at any second, his eyes nervous and dry, needing to blink. His whiskey glow faded. He'd tickled the belly of a rattler. Now he had to face it down somehow. Well . . . it's only a gunslinger. *Here goes* . . . Still holding his tight smile, judging how far his hand was from his pistol butt without looking down at it, Sherman shrugged. "It's one fine-looking hat. I wish I owned one like it. To tell the truth, if there's another one like it, I'd—"

"You're a damn *liar*." The low hiss interrupted him mid spiel, then fell silent as stone.

From behind the bar, the bartender whined, "Larry, for God sakes! Think about this mirror!" He faded back against the counterful of bottles along the wall, his arms spread out as if to protect it.

Ellsworth's spine stiffened. *Liar?* That cooked it. Near the door, the miners huddled, watching, hearing every word. Drunk or sober, he couldn't be shamed like this. "Mister, we don't stand for that kind of talk in Texas." He straightened up but kept his hand on the bar. How fast was this young man, this Larry whomever-the-hell-he-was.

"Texas, huh?" The young man hadn't moved an inch. But Sherman thought he'd seen something flicker in those cold green eyes, so he had to play toward it.

"That's right, Texas," Ellsworth said, taking on a little bolder tone, for the sake of the onlooking miners and himself as well. "That's where I'm from." He tilted his chin a bit, defiant.

"So am I," the young man hissed. "I never saw you there." As he spoke he reached out to a bottle a few inches away, filled his glass and tossed it back and swallowed, his eyes never leaving Ellsworth's face. "I believe you're lying again." He saw Sherman Ellsworth start to say something but before he could, the young man went on. "I believe you're a liar . . . a cowardly piece of punk . . . and a no-good son of a wet-bitch dog." After a pause, the young man turned his eyes from him in disregard as if Sherman Ellsworth had left the room. "There's not a true Texan alive would listen to that kind of insult without bringing up a handful of iron, now is there?"

Sherman Ellsworth stood stunned and whipped, his face burning, his rage boiling but his mind not letting him make a move for the pistol. The young man had routed him down; and now he'd waited too long to make a move. All he could do was stand and take it. "You don't know me, mister."

"No, Potts, you drunken fool," the bartender cut in. "And you don't know Fast Larry. This man ain't to be messed with. If you're from Texas, you oughta know that!"

Sherman Ellsworth swallowed a tight knot in his throat, feeling the whiskey leave him flat. He said in shaky voice, "Lawrence Shaw? From El Paso? *Fast* Larry Shaw? Nobody mentioned Fast Larry . . . he only called you Larry."

The young gunslinger lifted his chin and gazed back at him without a word.

"Nobody should have to tell you, you stupid bastard." The bartender yanked the bottle from in front of Ellsworth and ran a damp rag beneath it. "You came in here, got drunk, couldn't keep your mouth shut about the man's hat. Now he's ready to kill ya for it, unless you crawfish out of here like an ass-bit dog!" The bartender grew bolder as he spoke, and reached out and snatched up the money lying on the bar near Ellsworth's whiskey glass. "Get out, and don't come back! I'm sick of replacing mirrors over trash like you!"

"Trash? Hey, there was forty dollars laying there." Ellsworth turned to the bartender now. "Is this how you treat customers? Get them drunk, take their money? Call them trash?"

Fast Larry Shaw had only watched for a second. Now he spun the pistol on the bar top, his gloved finger down through the trigger guard. "Get moving, pinstripe, before I change my mind and decide you're worth wasting a bullet on." The pistol stopped spinning, pointing right back at Ellsworth.

Sherman Ellsworth struggled to keep from blurting out some drunken insult. He turned woodenly and stomped to the door where miners parted and stared at his red face. But once at the swinging batwings, he stopped and turned, feeling he had to get in some last drunken babble in parting. "Where the hell am I suppose to drink, then? This is the only saloon in town!"

"That's not my problem," Fast Larry said. "But if I ever hear you mention being from Texas again, I'll just figure it's your way of telling me you're tired of living. Understand?"

"Yeah, I understand," Ellsworth grumbled.

"There's a place called Mama Roby's, outside of town near the dump," the bartender called out. "It's for bummers and punks like you. Now get out before I kick your ass myself!" The stubby little bartender had grown full of himself, knowing Fast Larry had him covered. He gestured as if ready to come around the bar toward Sherman Ellsworth.

"All right, then, I'm gone, damn it!" Sherman Ellsworth spun around in his drunken rage and stomped out onto the boardwalk. *Rotten, dirty, no good . . .* He seethed and paced back and forth in the dirt. For two cents he'd get a shotgun and clean the whole place out—Fast Larry and all. The sonsabitches! He staggered a bit and caught himself on the hitch rail. Two women and a little girl rode slowly past him in a buggy, looking down at him as he righted himself and kicked at the dirt.

"What are ya'll looking at?" Ellsworth raged at them. One of the women placed her hand across the little girl's eyes and turned her face away as the buggy moved on. "You want to see something, do ya?" He staggered along beside the buggy a few feet, his fists clenched at his sides, his loose bow tie string working free and fluttering to the ground. "I'll show you something!" He grabbed his crotch and shook it at them, but they'd already looked away.

From the dusty window of his office across the street, Sheriff Earl Kemp looked out at the drunk shouting in the street like a lunatic. "What's this all about?" He spoke to himself in the empty office. Outside, Sherman Ellsworth sneered and cursed at the townsfolk passing by. Sheriff Kemp shook his head, walked over to his desk, picked up a long billy bat, tested it against the palm of his hand, and headed for the door.

Inside the Little Egypt, the bartender had set up fresh beer for the miners and walked down to where Fast Larry stood with his gloved hands spread along the edge of the bar. *"Mister Potts,* my Aunt Lucy's bloomers." He chuckled and filled Larry's glass to the brim. "Think our pale-jawed friend is an outlaw? I say if he ain't, there's not a dog in Georgia. What do you say?"

"Yep. There's not a doubt in my mind." Larry Shaw raised the glass in salute, took a sip, and sat it down. "He's part of somebody's bad dream. Put a clean shirt on one and he'll fool you for a while. But sooner or later it has to come busting out." He gave the bartender a curious look. "Why'd you try to stop it a while ago?"

"Just hoped for a second that I could keep it from getting

out of hand in here. I meant what I said about the mirror. You wouldn't believe what they cost. " He ran a hand back along the side of his sweating bald head. "Think he'll come back?" He cocked his head slightly, waiting for Larry's opinion.

"Yep, he'll be back most any minute. I'd bet on it."

"You gonna kill him?"

"Naw, he's a nobody. I'll shoot him when he comes through the doors. " He shrugged. "But I'm not going to kill him. Then I'd have to explain it all, wait for the judge to come to town and rule on it. Nope, too much aggravation for me. That's one more reason I want out of the gunman business. It's getting too complicated."

"He might catch you from behind some night while you're not looking."

"Watch your language." Fast Larry smiled. "I'm always looking, and you know it." He picked up the pistol, spun it, checked it, and spun it again, this time letting it hang across his forearm on the bar. "That's why you pay me to drink here. I sort them out for you—keep the good eggs, and send the bad ones out to Mama Roby's."

They both chuckled. "I don't know what I'll do when you head back to Texas," Thurman said. "You don't really want out, do you?"

"Oh, yes I do." Fast Larry just looked at him. "The sooner the better."

"You've been saying that for the past three weeks. I'll believe it when I see it."

"Then watch close, Thurman. I'm leaving here tomorrow."

"You mean it this time? You're headed back tomorrow?" Thurman looked skeptical.

"Yep, tomorrow. I've got a fine Mexican wife waiting for me. I don't mind telling you I miss her something awful. Besides, there's always plenty of other work to be had in good ole *Tejas*. A man who can't build himself a new life there ain't really trying."

"Yeah, that's true, but—" Thurman started to say something else when the doors flew open wide and Sherman Ellsworth stood with his feet planted firmly beneath him and his Colt pistol out and cocked. *To hell with a shotgun . . .* He'd kill this gunslinger with his pistol. Miners dove to the floor in a spray of spilled beer. "Look out, Larry!" Thurman yelled, then ducked straight down.

Sheriff Kemp had been coming across the street with his billy bat when he saw the drunk in the pinstriped trousers raise the pistol and step through the doors. *Aw, hell!* He quickened his pace, weaving around a buckboard in the street, dropping the billy bat and going for the pistol at his hip. "Hold it, mister!" He yelled, but it was too late. A pistol exploded inside the Little Egypt. As Sheriff Kemp ducked to one side, he saw the man in the pinstriped trousers fly backward through the swinging doors, and bounce off the boardwalk; Sherman Ellsworth landed flat on his back in the middle of the packed dirt street. Dust swirled.

Amid rearing horses and the sound of a woman's scream, Sheriff Kemp hurried forward. Ellsworth rolled over onto his stomach, raised up onto the palms of his hands, and shook his bleeding head. "Oh, Lord, God . . ." Ellsworth groaned. He struggled forward to where his pistol had fallen a few feet from him. But Kemp got there in time to clamp a boot down on his wrist.

"It's over! Lay still!" Sheriff Kemp kept a hand on his holstered pistol, and reached out and picked up Sherman Ellsworth's gun from the ground. As if from out of heaven, Ellsworth's new bowler hat fell to the ground with a soft plop and sat there upright, smoke curling from the burning felt around the hole in the center of its crown.

"Let me go," Ellsworth pleaded in a slurred voice. "I'll kill him. I swear I will!"

"You better keep still, before he blows your fool head off!" Kemp glanced up and saw Fast Larry Shaw standing in the open doors of the Little Egypt with his pistol hanging down his side. Gray smoke circled Shaw's hand, drifting up his forearm. "Afternoon, Sheriff." Fast Larry smiled and touched two fingers to his wide Stetson brim. "Just doing a little *cleaning up* here, before the evening drinking crowd arrives."

"I can't have this kind of stuff, Shaw," Kemp called out to him, raising Sherman Ellsworth to his wobbly feet. A dark streak of burnt felt ran back across the top of his forehead. Blood trickled from the middle of it where the bullet had creased his scalp.

Shaw chuckled. "It goes without saying, Sheriff. Pin-stripe there started it. I just finished it for him."

"I'm not questioning who started it, Shaw. I saw him head in there primed and cocked. But there's innocent people passing back and forth out here. I won't have their lives in danger."

"I understand, Sheriff." Lawrence Shaw nodded. "I'm leaving here tomorrow. It won't happen again, unless somebody else throws down on me. You can't blame me for defending myself." He spread his gloved hands, the shiny pistol lying in one palm, looking bold and brash between the open doors.

"Tomorrow? I'm glad to hear it." Sheriff Kemp gave him a stern look. "Who is this peckerwood anyway?" He held Sherman Ellsworth by the back of his shirt collar, shaking him back and forth.

Before answering the sheriff, Shaw turned to the bartender behind him. "What do you say, Thurman? Should I feed this idiot to the law or not?"

"I don't care what you do with him," the bartender replied.

Fast Larry Shaw turned back to the street and called out to Sheriff Kemp. "He's just some traveling peddler named Potts. He got a little drunk and let his mouth get the better of him. I won't be pressing charges."

"It doesn't matter whether you do or not." The sheriff shook Ellsworth again. "You didn't see what he did to poor Ella and Clara Wheeler out here. I'm gonna let him sleep it off for a while. Then he's got some charges of public drunkenness and indecent exposure to account for."

"Do as you must, Sheriff." Shaw tipped his fingers to his hat brim, turned, and walked back over to the bar.

"Come on, Mr. Potts," Sheriff Kemp said. He reached down with his free hand, picked up the bowler hat, dusted it against his leg and jammed it down on Sherman Ellsworth's wounded head.

"Easy, Sheriff." Ellsworth winced and sliced a breath in pain.

"I'll show you *easy*. You better hope you've got enough money to pay a stiff fine, or you'll be mopping out the jail for the next month." Kemp turned him by his collar and shoved him along across the street.

"I've got some money, Sheriff. There's still close to a hundred dollars in my boot."

"Oh? Well, then." Kemp cut a quick glance back and forth to see who might have heard them. "Let's get you behind bars while I add up the bill for your little drunken spree."

Inside the Little Egypt, Thurman, Larry Shaw, and the miners watched across the top of the saloon's swinging doors. When Sheriff Kemp had led his prisoner up onto the boardwalk and into his office, one miner turned to Fast Larry with a raised tin cup full of foamy beer. "With you here, sir, who needs a piano!" He laughed and the others chuckled with him.

"Nice of you to say so." Shaw smiled, spun his bone-handled pistol and let it fall loosely into his holster.

"This round is on the house, gentlemen," Thurman announced. He started to pour Shaw a glass full of rye, but Shaw put his hand over the glass, stopping him.

"Not now," Shaw said. "I think I'll ride out a ways. My horse needs a good working before I head home." He adjusted the Stetson on his forehead and turned to the miners. "Boys, keep an eye on Thurman for me. You wouldn't believe what he does to that beer when you're not looking."

The miners laughed and cheered until he'd walked out the doors. Outside on the boardwalk, Shaw felt the old lonesome hollowness well up inside him. But he put it away, squared his shoulders back, and took his time walking the boardwalk. One more day, he reminded himself, although he had to admit, there were parts of all this he would miss. A part of him still liked knowing that heads turned when he walked the streets, that his name was whispered in awe. He'd made his mark, and he liked the image—Fast Larry Shaw, cool, calm, confident. There wasn't doubt in his mind, or anybody else's. He was the fastest gun alive.

Chapter 6

Three hours later as evening shadows slanted from across the rooftops of Wakely, Sherman Ellsworth was back on the dirt street, with a hangover, his forehead crusted with dried blood. Something pounded inside his head like a hammer striking a steel anvil. His bow tie was gone, so was his stiff clip-on collar. The crisp white shirt had turned wrinkled with sweat stains, and was now the color of street dust, spotted with blood.

Somewhere in the mix of things Ellsworth's swallow-tailed coat had vanished. One pocket of his new pinstriped trousers had gotten ripped down the seam somehow, and now the pocket lining lapped back and forth like a dog's tongue as he walked along on unsteady legs. He'd gone to hell here in a hurry, he thought. The sheriff had cleaned him out. He was down to three dollars now, most of his money going to pay the fine for being drunk and exposing himself—Wait a minute! *Exposing myself . . . ?* What the hell kind of charge was that? All he'd done was jiggled his crotch. He hadn't *exposed* anything! Not to the best of his memory, anyway.

He stopped for a moment in the gathering shades of night and looked over at the Little Egypt Saloon where beyond the swinging doors laughter and voices spilled amid the sound of racy banjo music. For two cents he'd go there right now and . . . His hand searched instinctively at his waist before he remembered that the sheriff had kept his pistol. *Damn it!*

Well, he'd get another pistol soon enough. The main thing was, he'd gotten out of jail.

The sheriff had spent over an hour going through wanted posters and asking him questions, grilling him. But when the sheriff found no charges on him anywhere, he'd fined him and sent him on his way. Ellsworth knew the money was going into the sheriff's own pocket. But so what? That was the price a man like him paid now and then. It had been a close call, but it was over. Forget it.

Now all he had to do, Sherman thought, was to get back on track. He'd get a few drinks to clear his head, then he'd get busy. He needed another pistol, and he needed transportation. He took off the bowler and ran a finger through the hole in the crown. He'd get out of these dress clothes and into his *real* clothes. With a gun in his hand and a horse between his knees, he would snatch up a handful of money from somewhere and blow out of this jerkwater town. Yes, sir! Sherman Ellsworth was not going to be treated this way.

He looked back and forth along the darkening street as he moved along. There was a bank here, a mercantile store, and a telegraph office. He'd rob something, he didn't care what. This town had taken his money and made a fool of him. He wasn't leaving here broke, with his scalp creased. He placed the dusty bowler down carefully on his sore, pounding head. As soon as he got his mind clear, he'd get to work and settle things here. First things first, he needed a drink. Ellsworth wiped his palms up and down his dusty trouser legs. He needed one bad.

Mama Roby's Cafe, part shack, part crumbing adobe hovel, leaned up out of the sand and rock a mile out of Wakely, as if the town gave itself wide berth to this spot where broken bottles and refuse lay strewn from generations past. The bleached calcium remains of an ancient buffalo lay sunk in the earth near the broken door, its rib cage half covered with sand, a timeless receptacle now for cigar stubs and bottle corks. Three scrubby range horses stood bowed at the hitch rail.

Sherman Ellsworth arrived in the darkness, looking the horses over and shaking his head at their sorry condition. One of the horses raised its scraggly mane when Ellsworth ran a hand across its damp withers. "Go back to sleep, fool," he whispered, "before you fall down and die." Then he moved past the horses, shoved the battered door open, and stepped into the lantern light, saying in a boisterous voice, "What's a man have to do to get a drink around this dump?"

On the flatland, three miles past Mama Roby's Cafe, Lawrence Shaw pulled his horse up at the sight of the lumbering team of oxen as they topped a low rise and struggled along the rutted trail toward town. In the grainy darkness, at a distance of twenty yards, Shaw saw something atop one of the oxen's broad back. But he did not realize it was a man until he heeled his horse up along the slow moving cart. Samuel stirred, half conscious, and offered resistance when Lawrence Shaw's gloved hand reached out and pulled him from the ox's back.

"Take it easy," Shaw said, stepping his horse away from the cart, dropping Samuel to the ground. "You're in no condition to turn down a helping hand." He dropped from his saddle, swinging his canteen strap from around the saddle horn. The blue cur staggered in, its panting breath close to Lawrence Shaw's face, Shaw stooping down and cradling Samuel up on his knee. Shaw shoved the dog away. "What the blazes happened to you?" he asked the bloody young man, uncapping the canteen, pouring a thin trickle down Samuel's forehead. Shaw saw the rowel of the spur sticking out between Samuel's ribs. He started to pull it free, but seeing how deep it was imbedded he thought better of it. "We're going to have to get you to the doctor."

Samuel struggled with his words, saying, "Don't let them get away." He tried raising a pointing finger toward the cart, but his hand fell limp. "I have . . . a prisoner in there."

"They won't get away." Shaw stared after the cart, then gave Samuel a drink from the canteen. "A prisoner? You don't look like any lawman I've ever seen." Shaw poured a small puddle of water into his free hand and held it out for the blue cur. The dog seemed to absorb it.

"I'm not . . . a lawman." Samuel managed to sit up on his own. Lawrence Shaw helped him stagger to his feet. "I've got to stay with the cart."

"Don't worry, you will." Lawrence Shaw shoved him up atop his horse. "Come on, dog, you can ride, too. He picked up the exhausted cur and pitched him up across Samuel's lap. Then he swung up on the horse's back and heeled it forward.

On the way to town, Samuel told him what had happened. Lawrence Shaw only shook his head, leading the oxen on a length of rope he'd looped around one of their necks. "I always say, if a man weighs two hundred pounds in the badlands, at least a hundred of it should be gun and bullets." Passing Mama Roby's Cafe, Shaw thought about stopping. But as blown as the big animals were, if they came to a complete halt now, he might never get them started again. "How're you holding up?" he asked Samuel.

"I'm . . . doing all right, mister. The bleeding has stopped."

"Good. We've got another mile or so. I don't want to let these animals stop if I can keep from it." The cart lumbered on as he spoke.

"I wonder how's he doing?" Samuel turned his head toward the cart where Daggett lay atop the mound of rancid-smelling hides.

Shaw chuckled, saying in a wry tone, "To hell with him. Let him rot."

"Then keep them moving," Samuel replied, sounding weak but determined.

Lawrence Shaw looked down at the big cur, its head bobbing on the young man's leg with each step of the big buckskin. "Buffalo hunters," Shaw whispered to himself, smiling in contempt. He drew the slack out of the rope until he felt the weight of the oxen on the other end. Then he wrapped two turns of rope around his saddle horn and moved on, feeling Samuel sway against his chest, the dim light of Mama Roby's Cafe fading behind them.

Inside Mama Roby's, Sherman Ellsworth leaned back in his chair, a short cigar stub glowing between his teeth. "I say a man is a pure damned fool to be treated this way and not do something about it." Sherman Ellsworth raised the greasy bottle of shag-rye and sucked back a mouthful. To hell with sobering up. He swallowed, let out a whiskey hiss, and continued. "I don't plan on letting them get by with it. You won't, either, if there's a lick of fur on your backsides." He leveled a drunken gaze on the three pairs of blurred and hollow eyes gathered around the grimy tabletop.

Sherman had told them what happened at the Little Egypt Saloon, changing it a little to where he'd been unarmed at the time and passed out at the bar when Fast Larry Shaw had attacked him for no reason—otherwise he would have killed that gunslinger dead on the spot. As he stared at the three faces, the one in the middle, a lean, sharp-featured Missourian named Dillard Moore, looked back and forth at the other two, then turned his eyes back to Ellsworth.

"I can't speak for Cockeyed Clayton Mumpe here, but it wouldn't be the first time me and Brother Kirby put a gun to some yahoo's chin and took his money—would it, Kirb?" Beside Dillard Moore, Clayton Mumpe gazed at him with contempt through crossed eyes, then looked away and shook his head.

"Tell it, brother." Kirby Moore blotted whiskey from the edge of his drooping mustache onto the back of his gloved hand and grinned. "Although I can't say anybody at the Little Egypt ever mistreated me personally. I just don't go there because it's not my kind of crowd." He shrugged with an arrogant tilt of his chin. "As far as Fast Larry goes—there ain't a gunslinger alive that can't be had, given the right circumstances."

"I'll drink to that," Ellsworth said in salute.

"Humph." Clayton Mumpe sat listening in silence. Over

the next hour the conversation swung from killing gun-slingers to robbing banks, to burning the Little Egypt to the ground and shooting everybody as they tried to leave. Fi-nally, as the Moore brothers and this new drinker, Ellsworth, had fallen deeper and deeper into a rye stupor, Mumpe checked his battered pocket watch, put it away, slid his chair back and stood up.

"No offense, boys," Mumpe said, "but this is where I get off. I'm no outlaw. Count me out. I came this far to build a reputation, not end one on a rope." He turned and walked, staggering slightly, to the barrel-topped bar where a fourth man stood in the shadows drinking alone.

Behind the bar, a squat little woman stood on a short wooden crate in order to reach the bartop. "The bull got too deep for you, huh?" She ran a dirty wet rag back and forth and slapped at a large roach.

Clayton Mumpe only looked at her for a second with his crossed eyes, then turned without answering to the drinker beside him. "I didn't see your horse out front when we got here. Are you afoot?"

The lone drinker turned his dark eyes to him, looking him up and down. His hand rested on the pistol butt at his hip. "I've learned to be careful where I leave my horse of late. Why do you ask?"

Clayton Mumpe tapped a coin on the bar and gestured to-ward a row of bottles. "Give me another one, mama." He turned his crossed eyes back to the tall half-breed. "Just making conversation, is all."

"There's been a lot of that going around." The man nod-ded toward the table where Sherman Ellsworth and the Moore brothers had drawn into a huddle. "Who's the pin-striped peckerwood?"

"Beats me. We were here when he came in, same as you." Clayton Mumpe turned a faint wry smile toward him. "We were just lucky enough to draw his attention first, I reckon."

"Yeah, just lucky." The man returned his grin. Clayton Mumpe tossed back his drink. The tall half-breed picked up the bottle at his elbow and refilled it for him. "I'm Cherokee Cousins. Think he's just blowing air, or does he really know the people he claims to know?"

"Thanks, Mr. Cousins." Clayton Mumpe sipped the warm rye. "I'm Clayton Mumpe." He gestured toward the table. "Hell, who knows if he's lying or not? Once the talk gets down to doing some serious thieving and burning, I move away. It's easy enough to get tangled up with the wrong bunch but hard as hell to get out. I'm a shootist, myself—trying to be, anyway." He raised the glass and drained it. "I threw in with the Moores crossing the badlands. Don't know a thing about them, though. Can't say I want to, either."

Cherokee Cousins kept his eyes on Sherman Ellsworth as he spoke to Clayton Mumpe. "Didn't I hear him mention Junior Lake a while ago?"

"Probably. He's mentioned every other desperado between here and hell. He'd have to be a hundred years old to meet everybody he knows and do half of what he says he's done. You'd think he'd have enough sense to keep his mouth shut. You or I could be the law for all he knows." Clayton Mumpe hesitated for a second, then asked in a guarded tone, "You're not, are you? The law, that is?"

"Naw," Cherokee Cousins chuckled. "If I was, I'd already put a bullet about an inch lower than the crease on that idiot's forehead." He pointed a gloved finger toward Sherman Ellsworth, taking aim, then clicked his thumb as if it were a pistol hammer. "I ride police off and on for Judge Parker, down in Indian Nations," he added. "But I get tired of beating the hell out of all my kinfolks. Mostly I shoot a little pool—nothing serious."

"I understand," said Clayton Mumpe.

Cherokee Cousins saw Sherman Ellsworth look over at him with bloodshot eyes just as Cherokee lowered his gloved finger. "Hold on a minute," Ellsworth said to the Moore brothers, raising a hand to cut them off. Then he stared closer at Cherokee Cousins and asked, "Something I can do for you, redskin?"

Cherokee let the insult pass. "Maybe. Did I hear you say you just saw Junior Lake a few days back?"

"What's it to ya?" Sherman Ellsworth pushed his chair back a few inches and out of force of habit hooked his thumbs in his waist, forgetting for a second that he had no pistol there.

"Just asking." Cherokee shrugged. "Was he riding a big paint horse by any chance?"

Sherman Ellsworth turned surly. "Do I look like the kind of man who passes loose information about his friends?"

Mama Roby cut in. "That's all you *have* done, ever since your stinking arse walked through the door!"

"You don't *want* to hear what you look like to me," Cherokee replied, his voice growing a bit stronger. "I asked you a simple question. Unless you're packing something besides a big mouth, just answer me, and we'll be done with it."

As Cherokee spoke, the Moore brothers scooted their chairs back out of the way. Sherman Ellsworth suddenly remembered that his pistol was gone, and he sat silent for a second. Then he answered in a grudging voice, "Yes, he *was* riding a big paint. But he rode it down lame and left it dead on the desert floor."

Cherokee Cousins clenched his teeth at the news. "Damn Junior Lake," he whispered under his breath. He collected himself, and looked back at Ellsworth. "Where's Junior now? Where can I find him?"

"That's for him to know, and for you to find out, mister." Ellsworth stood up slowly and nodded the Moore brothers toward the door. "Come on, boys . . . let's talk business somewhere a little less crowded." He snatched the bottle of rye off the table and turned, keeping his eyes on Cherokee Cousins as the Moore brothers stood up to follow him out the door.

"Are you going with us, Cockeyed Clayton?" Kirby asked Mumpe.

"I'll just hang around here," Clayton Mumpe replied, a bitter twist to his voice. "Maybe I'll run into you both again down the trail somewhere."

"Leave that cross-eyed fool here." Sherman Ellsworth staggered sideways and caught himself in the open doorway. "Are you two coming or not?" The Moore brothers filed past him, and he slammed the door behind them. Dust bellowed in their wake.

"That dirty punk," Mama Roby said to the closed door. "I'd love to sink a hatchet in his back. Those boys would have drank here all night, hadn't been for him."

The sound of hooves resounded outside; and as they moved away, Clayton Mumpe took on a bemused look and said, "Didn't he say he walked out here from Wakely?"

"Yes he did." Mama Roby nodded, rubbing the dirty rag back and forth on the bartop. "He said he almost walked right past us in the dark."

"Aw, hell!" Clayton Mumpe raced to the door and slung it open.

"Bet he's not walking now," Cherokee Cousins murmured under his breath. He raised a glass of rye toward Mama Roby as if offering a toast, then tossing the fiery liquor back in one gulp, he blew out a hot breath and sat the glass down on the bar.

On the flat stretch of sand and rock leading back toward town, Sherman Ellsworth and the Moore brothers batted their heels to the tired horses' sides, Ellsworth giving it a little extra effort, wanting to see what the shaggy little dun beneath him could still do. He rode the dun out away from the other two onto the desert floor and spun it back toward them letting out a loud drunken war cry. The game little dun puffed and blew and kicked up sand, until Sherman Ellsworth slid it around to a halt beside the Moores.

"Damn it, boys!" Ellsworth slapped the dun's damp neck

and ruffled its scraggly mane with his hand. "This little horse says he can't see no reason to wait till morning. Says he thinks he could rob a thing or two tonight. Right, hoss?" He took a handful of mane and shook it roughly back and forth. The dun raised its head and blew out a breath.

Kirby and Dillard Moore looked at one another with flat expressions. Dillard asked, "What the hell can we rob tonight? Everybody's in bed by now, except the bunch at the Little Egypt. You want to rob *it?*"

But Sherman Ellsworth pictured Fast Larry Shaw at the end of the bar and thought better of the idea. "Naw, not tonight anyway. But there's nothing to keep us from doing a little backdoor stealing—just enough to see how we work together."

"Me and Kirby ain't burglars . . . we wouldn't know where to start."

"Shit, boys. That's why I'm here, to show you! I cut my teeth on stolen biscuits. All we do is kick in a door, grab what suits us, then cut out. Whatever we get we can sell somewhere in the morning."

"Sell to who?" Dillard looked confused.

"Mama Roby . . . anybody who wants it. Hell, I don't know who. But that ain't the point. The point is, I can pick me out a pistol, a decent hat. We can pick up some cash if there's any under the counter—"

"So, you're talking about the mercantile store?" Kirby cut in.

"Well, come to think of it, yes, I reckon I am. They've got it all. Shelf after shelf of anything we want. What do you say?"

"I've never been one to shun away from something different," Dillard said, spreading a wide whiskey-lit grin. "What about you, Kirb?"

"Well, it's a brand-new thing for us . . . but you know me. I'm game as a warthog."

"Then come on," Sherman Ellsworth said. "Let's go toss that place and see what shakes out of it." He maneuvered the little dun in between Dillard and Kirby Moore and jumped it forward a couple of feet, taking the lead, swiping the bottle of rye from Dillard's hand as he brushed past him. Dillard and Kirby laughed and heeled their horses forward, the three of them riding abreast, pushing the tired animals along the dark trail to Wakely.

The streets of Wakely lay empty and dark when they stopped for a moment at the edge of town. The only lights burning were the overhead lantern fixtures inside the Little Egypt Saloon, a single flickering oil lantern inside the doctor's office halfway down the street, and another shining through the board cracks of the livery barn. As they sat their tired horses, the door of the livery barn squeaked shut, and inside, the livery hostler pulled back with all his weight until the team of oxen stopped, blowing and milling about on exhausted hooves.

"Let's quiet down from here on," Ellsworth whispered, nudging the dun forward, cutting across the empty street toward the alley alongside the mercantile store. Outside the doctor's office, the big cur rose up on his tired feet and stepped forward to the edge of the boardwalk, growling low in his throat until the three horses moved past him and disappeared into the alley.

Behind the dog, the door to the doctor's office opened a crack and Sheriff Kemp looked out, sweeping his gaze back and forth along the empty street. "Hush up out there," he called out to the dog, cutting another quick glance in both directions, then down at the half-empty water bucket on the boardwalk where the cur had drank his fill. "Lay down there, boy, your friend is going to be all right."

"Like I said, Sheriff," Lawrence Shaw continued as the door closed and Kemp turned to face him, "he was laying across one of the oxen when I found him." Shaw winced. "I saw the spur stuck in his side and didn't think I ought to pull it out." As Lawrence Shaw spoke, he brushed a tight black glove up and down his shirt, searching for any signs of bloodstains. "You know how these buff hunters are—you can't hardly kill one."

Shaw chuckled and stood up from where he'd leaned back against the doctor's cluttered desk. Beyond an open door, the white-haired doctor stood between two gurneys, bowed over the one on his right where the toes of Samuel's worn boot soles lay pointed upward. "How's . . . Blue?" Samuel asked in a strained, cracked voice.

"Blue?" The doctor stopped for a second and raised the scalpel in his bloody hand. "Oh, the dog? He's fine." He pressed a hand on Samuel's chest. "You're the one you should be worrying about. You just about bled dry, young man. Now lie still. I've got to cut this rowel out of your ribs."

Lawrence Shaw and the sheriff listened and watched through the open door. Samuel rolled his head to one side toward the other gurney. "What about him?"

"He'll make it. He's in better shape than you are. Now be still."

"If . . . I don't make it. Tell the law . . . that he killed a man named Davey Riley. That's why I brought him here."

The old doctor stopped and looked over at the unconscious face of Andrew Daggett on the other gurney. He spoke over his shoulder to Kemp. "Sheriff, maybe you best step in here."

"I heard him." Sheriff Kemp moved in beside the doctor. "Now what's this? Who'd he kill?"

"My partner, Davey Riley. You can ask . . . Ranger Clyde Sazes about it. He saw it happen."

"Sazes? All I need is Outrider Sazes sending his trouble into Wakely. Where'd you run into that ole ranger? He usually won't even let himself be seen out there. He's nearly a hermit."

The doctor stepped back for a second and stood beside Lawrence Shaw while Samuel told Kemp what had happened. When he finished, the sheriff shook his head and moved to one side to let the doctor go back to work. "I've heard enough for now," Kemp said. "Let this boy get some rest and heal up." He gestured a nod at the outlaw. "I'll have to deputize somebody to keep an eye on this bird until we get things sorted out here. What about you, Shaw? Care to sit guard tonight?"

"Whoa, Sheriff." Lawrence Shaw raised a hand. "If I wanted to do law work, I would've started a long time ago. This is my last night in town. I need to get some rest before heading out tomorrow."

"All I'm asking is for you to sit here and—" Kemp stopped at the sound of two shots exploding from the direction of the mercantile store. "Gunfire?" He looked at Shaw.

"I'd say so, Sheriff." Lawrence Shaw had already started for the door. Outside, the sound of horses' hooves pounded away toward the desert. The sound of a woman's scream echoed along the street, and upon hearing it, even as Sheriff Kemp raced outside and raised his pistol at the two vanishing riders, Shaw ran toward the mercantile store, his pistol out, cocked and searching back and forth in the darkness.

Chapter 7

Sherman Ellsworth ran limping down the alley and turned left in the direction of the backyard of Vera's Boarding House. He didn't understand why things went wrong, but at least he'd gotten a pistol and a hat out of the deal. The pistol lay warm against his belly; the hat swung back and forth in his hand as he ran. *Damn that horse!* When he'd stepped up into the stirrup, the whole saddle slid down the horse's side, then the horse bolted forward without him! The Moores didn't stop for him, so there he'd laid with a twisted ankle, an armload of socks, a cured ham, and sugar cookies lying all around him in the dirt.

The whiskey seemed to wear off quickly now that he was on the run. He heard the woman scream again as he batted through refuse at the town dump, threw himself over a picket fence, and eased across the yard to the back door of the boarding house. This was the best he could do for now. He'd just have to sit tight and see what happened. Pain shot up from his twisted ankle. Back along the street, the sound of a barking dog split the silence. Well, the dog couldn't identify him . . . and neither could anybody else if it came down to it.

The store owner was dead; the woman hadn't seen him. All she could have seen was the two slices of pistolfire in the darkness of the stock room. It wasn't his fault, having to kill the man. Hell, he hadn't expected anybody to be there. What were they doing sleeping in the stockroom, anyway? Guarding the place? Christ, didn't they trust anybody? To hell with it. At least he was safe.

He caught his breath, slipped around the side of the house, and ambled up onto the dark porch. He pulled the key from his pocket, fumbling with it before letting himself into the hallway. For a second, he stood in the dark silence, making sure no one was up and around. Then he climbed the stairs and went into his rented room. *Jesus! What a night . . .*

On the dark street, Lawrence Shaw had grabbed the dangling reins to the little dun horse, its saddle now hanging down its side. "Easy, boy." On the boardwalk, the blue cur roared and growled, bouncing back and forth, but like a soldier standing guard, it did not move from its position outside the doctor's office. Lanterns sprang alive in windows. Doors opened and slammed shut as townsmen came forward, shoving their shirts down in their trousers. Shotgun barrels glinted in the pale moonlight. Customers ran forward from the Little Egypt, some with beer mugs in hand.

"Somebody shut that blasted dog up!" Sheriff Kemp yelled as he bounded out of the mercantile store and over to Lawrence Shaw in the middle of the street. "Lord, it's a mess in there! Lou Baines is shot dead—twice in the chest!" He looked back and forth along the dark street as more faces came forward.

"Everybody stay back, now! We've got a robber on foot somewhere! Spread out!" He fanned the sleepy faces away. "Start looking!"

Lawrence Shaw handed him the reins to the little dun. "What about Martha Baines?" he asked.

"What? Oh, she's hysterical! Can't tell me nothing. The blacksmith's with her now."

"Maybe one of them was riding double."

"Naw. I didn't get a good look at them, but there was only one on each horse, that much I could tell." His breath rushed. The blue cur bellowed. "Somebody shut that damned hound up!" The sheriff spun in the street. "I've got to get up a posse!" He added looking back and forth along the street again, "Lord! I can't just leave with one of them running loose here!"

"Settle down, Sheriff," Shaw advised. "The one running loose has found a horse by now, I'd imagine. If not, he's looking for one." Before Kemp could say another word, Shaw turned to three townsmen who held shotguns. His voice sounded calm, detached. "You men, get over to the livery barn. Keep it covered." As Shaw spoke, he moved over to the boardwalk outside the doctor's office where the hound flew into a higher pitch of barking.

"Damn that stupid dog!" Kemp screamed in his frustration.

"Okay, boy. Good work." Lawrence Shaw reached out, opened the door and let the big cur slip inside the doctor's office. From the boardwalk, he turned back to the sheriff and townsmen, standing a foot above them. "Sheriff, get your posse together. Some of you men stay here and search the town. Get moving now. Lou Baines was your neighbor—and a good man! Find the ones who killed him!"

Sheriff Kemp collected himself quickly and turned toward the townsmen. "You heard him, get your horses. Let's go! Move it!"

As the townsmen dispersed, trotting away, talking hurriedly among themselves, Sheriff Kemp turned to Lawrence Shaw as he stepped back down beside him. "Thanks, Shaw." He sounded embarrassed. "I must have looked pretty ridiculous"

"No, you didn't," Shaw cut him short. "You're more involved here than I am. You've got more at stake." He offered a faint trace of a smile. "See why I don't do law work? It's not worth it for the few extra nickels and dimes you manage to squeeze out of it."

Kemp let it pass. "Shaw, I need your help. *Bad*. This time I'm not asking."

Shaw's jaw stiffened. "Telling never works with me."

"All right, then, I'm still asking." Kemp looked beaten. "But I've got to have you look after those two in there." He pointed at the doctor's office. "I've got to have somebody here who knows what they're doing while I'm gone with the posse."

Shaw considered it, letting out a relenting breath. "All right, go on. I can wait a day or two longer. You're covered here." He reached out and took the reins to the little dun horse. "I'll even take the horse to the livery barn. Now get going."

"I—I really appreciate it, Shaw."

"Yeah, yeah." Shaw waved him away and walked the horse off along the dirt street. "I'm just a civic-minded fool at heart."

It was near dawn before Sherman Ellsworth finally settled down and drifted off into a drunken sleep. At first, when he'd slipped into the room, he'd stuffed the new hat beneath his bed, hurried out of his dirty clothes, and washed in a basin of water on the oaken shaving stand. When he'd put his trousers and boots back on, feeling a sharp pain in his swollen ankle as he did, he'd gotten under the doubled sheets and laid there with the new pistol poised and ready on his bare chest. *Sit tight, boy . . .*

For a long time he listened and waited as boots and voices passed back and forth beneath his window. Nothing happened. At one point he'd nearly jumped from the bed and sailed out the window when the sound of boot heels came scraping up onto the porch, and a harsh knocking resounded throughout the quiet house. But the door opened, voices spoke back and forth, and in a moment the door closed again.

Amen, Ellsworth had smiled to himself. If only he'd brought along a bottle of whiskey.

Then, as the gray whisper of daylight seeped in through the window beside his bed, Ellsworth's eyes opened and fixed on the bottom edge of the door. He heard the soft turning of the knob, seeing the faint glow of lantern light beneath it. Under the sheet, he cocked the pistol slowly and quietly in his hand, and lay watching the door ease open, feigning sleep with his eyes closed to the slimmest point of vision.

"Mr. Potts?" The soft whisper of a woman's voice moved like velvet vapor within the faint glow of lantern light spreading into the room.

Ellsworth didn't stir. He watched through his eyelashes as the door silently shut and a white-cotton gown swept forward on silent bare feet, stopping beside his bed. A hand reached down to his naked shoulder above the edge of the sheet, moving back and forth, not quite a touch, but rather a suggestion of a touch. "Mr. Potts?"

"Huh? What?" He turned his face up now, hoping his expression looked like one that had been soundly sleeping. "Who is it?" He raised his free hand to his eyes as if rubbing sleep from them.

"Sssh. Be quiet, please. I'm Polly. Vera's sister." As she spoke, she trimmed down the lantern, moving to the nightstand and resting it there. "You told Vera yesterday that you wanted a woman. Remember?"

"Oh . . ." Ellsworth scratched his head. "Yeah, sort of." He looked her up and down, her hair loose and catching soft light from the low glow of the lantern. "I mean . . . yeah, sure I did."

"And she told you she didn't do that sort of thing for money?" She moved her free hand to her shoulder and lowered the strap of her gown. "But guess what . . . ? I do."

All right! Sherman Ellsworth raised up on his elbow, easing the hammer of his pistol down and slipping it beneath his side. He reached out and raised the wick of the lantern a bit, and laid back and smiled. "But maybe I changed my mind since then. Maybe I don't have any money."

"Oh." The strap on the cotton gown went back up over her shoulder. She reached a hand toward the lantern, but Ellsworth caught her wrist.

"Hold on, what's your hurry, Polly? Let's talk this over. I'm just waking up here."

She drew back her wrist, but not all the way. "It's two dollars, Mr. Potts. And I have to be out of here before everyone starts getting ready for breakfast."

"Two dollars! I didn't want to get married. I only wanted—"

"Then I'm sorry I woke you," she interrupted him in a soft voice.

"Come on, princess . . . give me a minute. I might have a little cash here somewhere." He stalled, turning her wrist loose and nodding toward the window. "Did I hear some carrying-on out there a while ago? What was it?"

"Then you weren't asleep?"

"Well . . . it woke me up for a minute." He ran his hand back across his hair. "Sounded like a herd of steers busting up and down the street."

"There was a robbery. Someone was killed, I think." She sat down on the side of his bed and laid a hand on his chest. "Will I be staying a while or not, Mr. Potts?" Her hand raised the cotton gown up to her knee and stopped there. "I have to know soon. I mustn't be seen leaving your room."

"Yeah," Ellsworth shrugged. "I've got your two dollars." His hand moved over onto her lap, pushing the gown up past her knee and squeezing the inside of her warm thigh. He sensed her breath catch in her throat as her thigh tensed a bit. "You're new at this, ain't you?"

"Why do you say that?"

"Because you would have already been gone by now if you were a seasoned sporting woman." He chuckled, kneading her warm inner thigh. "I believe you're only a make-believe whore."

She smiled. "Vera was lying. She *does* do this sort of thing for money. She just didn't want to do it with you." The strap came off of her other shoulder, and she let the gown fall down past her breasts.

"You're kidding. Why not?" Sherman Ellsworth flipped a corner of the sheet open and scooted over on the bed.

"She says you're rough Texas trash. Says she doubts if

you're a peddler at all—just some rambling gambler, is what she thinks."

"Well, she's got a good eye for judging men, then. I confess, I'm no peddler. Cards and dice *is* my stock in trade." He felt her skin, warm against him. "That doesn't bother you a bit, though, does it?"

"No. That's why I came here. I wasn't going to. But when I heard you slip in tonight, I changed my mind." Ellsworth tensed at her words as she continued. "I like tough men. The tougher the better." Beneath the sheet, she worked the gown the rest of the way off and laid it aside. *Oh, Lord . . .* He felt her hand move along him until it found the pistol, and she removed it from beneath the sheets and handed it back to him butt first.

"You didn't hear *me* slipping in earlier," Ellsworth said, his breath starting to race. "I don't know what you heard or *think* you heard, but it weren't me. Do you understand?"

"Don't worry, I didn't tell them anything."

"That's good, because there ain't a damn thing for you to tell them."

"I know, I know." She put her hands on his chest and clenched her nails into his skin. "Now put it out of your mind. Don't forget my two dollars before I leave."

"Shiiiit. You don't fool me. You didn't come here for money. I see what you're looking for." He grabbed her roughly and jerked her against him. "You like hard play, do you?"

"That's right. So don't be afraid I'll break, Mr. Potts. I can handle whatever you throw at me. I came here *wanting*. Don't make me leave the same way."

He nuzzled his rough cheek against her throat. He'd have to kill her . . . he knew that. He wasn't going to take a chance on her shooting her mouth off. But killing her could wait. Lord, yes it could wait! Ellsworth bit her neck, not too hard, but hard enough to make her clutch him tight. He laughed low, entwining his hand in her hair. "So you like it rough." He pulled her head back, and saw her pulse beating wildly in the side of her throat. She gasped, but only clutched him tighter. "Then hang on, princess. By God, you've struck yourself the mother lode."

At daylight, the blacksmith, Bob Starks, came to the doctor's office with a fresh pot of coffee and sat it on the cluttered desk. "Thurman said to tell you if you wanted something stronger, to just let him know."

"Thanks, Starks." Lawrence Shaw knotted his string tie around his throat and smoothed it down. "But I won't be drinking anything stronger as long as I'm keeping an eye on things here." He poured himself a cup of coffee and sipped at it. "Nobody's caught sight of the man on foot, I suppose?"

"Not a glimpse. He's lit out of here, don't you think?"

"Yeah, I think so." Shaw sat the cup down on the desk. "Keep a couple of men around the livery barn, though, just in case."

"Sure thing." The blacksmith started to turn and leave. But then he stopped. "Oh, I almost forgot. The stage clerk gave me this letter for you." He took the envelope from inside his coat and handed it to him. "All the way from Texas, it looks like. Kinfolk, I reckon?"

Shaw took the letter and cut him a sharp glance. "Yes, it is."

"Sorry, just being nosy."

"Yeah, I see you were." Shaw put the letter inside his coat and picked up his coffee cup.

"Aren't you going to read it?" The blacksmith leaned forward a bit.

Shaw ignored him. "On your way back to the shop, ask Thurman to tell you what happened to the last man who poked his nose into my business."

The blacksmith's eyes widened. "I best get out of here— meant no harm, of course."

Lawrence Shaw just stared at him until the blacksmith swallowed a nervous knot in his throat and left. When the door closed, Shaw smiled to himself, took the letter from his wife out of his coat, and read it. Then he sat still for a while with the coffee cup in his hand. He let out a long breath and read the letter again. He sat with the paper in his hand until the hollow loneliness passed. "Soon, darling," he said softly to himself. "Real soon, I promise."

From the other room, he heard a voice moan. He put the letter away, walked in between the two gurneys and looked down into the gaunt face of Andrew Daggett, the outlaw's eyes darting back and forth, unsure of where he was or how he'd gotten here. "Who . . . who are you?" Daggett asked in a strained voice.

"Never mind who I am." Shaw leaned down closer. "Who are you?"

"I'm . . . Andrew Turner," Daggett said.

"Sure, I bet you are." Lawrence Shaw studied his eyes. "Shame on you, whoever you are. I heard what you did to that poor boy out on the sand flats."

"All right, my name is Daggett . . . Andrew Daggett. But I never done . . . nothing to nobody, mister. For God's . . . sake. Can't you see . . . I'm dying?"

"Really?" Shaw smiled, a tight harsh smile. "You look fit enough to me, *Mister Daggett*—fit enough to hang, anyway. Had I known what you did, I would have left you out there in the sand. I hate a murdering coward." He raised the pistol from his holster, cocked it, and put the tip of the barrel against Daggett's nose. "*Bang!*" he said all of a sudden. Daggett's eyes flew open wide. "See?" Shaw lowered the hammer on the pistol and laid it on Daggett's chest. "You've got some life left in you yet. If I turned my back, you'd be strong enough to raise this pistol, kill this boy, and cut out of here, wouldn't you?"

Daggett raised his head, sounding stronger. "You serious? Is that an offer?" His hand went to the pistol as he spoke. But just as his hand closed down, instead of feeling the pistol butt, he felt Shaw's gloved hand slice beneath his like a streak of light off polished steel. Shaw snatched the pistol up and spun it on his finger. "No, you idiot. That's just my way of showing you I'm onto your game." With his black-gloved hand he jerked Daggett up close to his face. "Now get this straight. I'm in charge of your worthless hide until the sheriff gets back. You've caused me to change my plans, so I want to kill you real bad. Anything at all, any slightest problem, and *bang!* you're dead. If you complain that the coffee's too cold—*bang,* dead. Decide you need to spit, and miss the spittoon—*bang,* dead." He let Daggett fall from his hand. "Is there any question where you stand with me?"

On the other gurney, Samuel Burrack listened, barely conscious, but hearing the conversation. Who was this man? This man with the tight black gloves and the shiny pistol on his hip? A lawman? A man like Ranger Sazes? He had no idea. He only knew that he was still alive, and that this was the man who had saved him. Beside him on a metal tray lay the spur, its rowel stained with his blood. What kind of men were these, who would do such a thing, stab a man with a spur, cut a man's throat while he pleaded for his life?

A picture of Davey Riley came to his mind and he put it aside quickly. He didn't want to think about it. For now, he was still alive, and that was all that mattered.

Alive . . . Even hearing the word in his mind made him feel at peace. All right, he thought to himself, he was going to make it. He had to rest some more and get his strength back, but that was no problem. He'd done what he had set out to do. He brought in one of the men who'd killed his friend. And now he was here, and safe, and that was enough . . . for now. He drifted, the sight of the sharp spur rowel growing distant on the metal tray. There was nothing to fear here, he thought, as he felt himself float off somewhere in a soft billowy cloud. He had a feeling this man wouldn't let anything happen to him.

While Samuel Burrack slept, and Andrew Daggett lay on his gurney moaning—and at the same time looking all about the room for any chance of making an escape—Lawrence Shaw drank his coffee at the old doctor's desk. The doctor lay sleeping on a small divan in the corner. At the sound of horses coming to a halt, Shaw rose from the desk, walked to the window and saw Sheriff Kemp step down from his saddle and up onto the boardwalk.

Among the gathered horsemen, Shaw caught a glimpse of Cherokee Cousins and Clayton Mumpe mounted on Cousins's horse, a broad-chested grule with black stockings on its front legs. Shaw shook his head and chuckled under his breath. The door swung open, and Kemp stepped inside with a thumb hooked in his belt. Before the sheriff could speak a word, Shaw said, "I hate to disappoint you, Sheriff, but you've got the wrong men out there."

"Wha—?" Kemp looked stunned. "How do you know?"

"Saw them through the window, Sheriff," Shaw replied. "The tall Indian is Cherokee Cousins. The other is a gunslinger, or I should say he wishes he was. He's Clayton Mumpe. More than likely he's looking for me."

"Damn it to hell." Kemp slumped. His thumb unhooked from his belt. "That's the same thing they said." For a second he looked defeated. Then his eyes turned hopeful. "They could still be the ones, though—"

"Slim chance, Sheriff. Neither of them are thieves. Let's talk to them." As Shaw spoke, he put on his hat and walked toward the door. He stopped and nodded toward the other room where Daggett craned his neck sideways, watching them closely. "You might want to handcuff that outlaw to his gurney now that he's feeling better." Sheriff Kemp took a pair of handcuffs from his pocket and walked in to Daggett as Shaw stepped through the door, out onto the boardwalk. "Morning, Cherokee," Shaw called out, spreading a tight smile. "What brings you this way?"

"I've been searching for Junior Lake." From atop his horse, surrounded by shotgun and rifle barrels, Cherokee Cousins looked down with his wrists cuffed together and smiled and shook his head. "I never thought I'd be this glad to see you, Shaw." He gestured at the men around him, then added, "Would you mind telling these gentlemen that I'm no burglar?"

Behind Cherokee Cousins, Clayton Mumpe ventured a glance at Shaw. "Well, I don't know, Cherokee," Shaw said, eyeing Mumpe, "you weren't the last time I ran into you . . . but it appears you've fallen in with bad company since then." He looked at Clayton Mumpe, touching a finger to his hat brim. "Howdy, Mumpe."

Clayton Mumpe only grumbled. Cherokee looked back at him over his shoulder, then said to Shaw, "I just met this fellow last night. Didn't know he was looking for you—I wouldn't have brought him otherwise. Three drunks stole his horse. I was bringing him in from Mama Roby's when this bunch fell in around us."

Behind Shaw, Sheriff Kemp stepped out of the office door, saying, "We had no way of knowing any of that, mister. We were just doing our jobs."

"Yeah, is that a fact? Well, if I had of been on the dodge," Cherokee said, "half of these idiots would be laying back there right now staring up at buzzards. Think we'd be stupid enough to let you get the drop on us if we were ducking you?" He looked back and forth between Kemp and Shaw. "What about it, Fast Larry?"

"How'd you meet up, Sheriff?" Shaw asked Kemp without taking his eyes off Cherokee Cousins.

"Well, it's true." Kemp spoke in a grudging tone. "They didn't try to hide or make a run for it."

"Believe me, Sheriff," Shaw continued, "if Cousins wanted to make a fight of it, there'd still be fur flying out there. Let him go. Just don't shoot pool with him—not for money, anyway."

Kemp rubbed his jaw. "What about this cockeyed boy? Are you vouching for him, too?"

Clayton Mumpe bristled.

Lawrence Shaw shrugged. "So long as he promises not to shoot me in the back, yes I vouch for him, too. They're not the ones."

"I'm no back-shooter," Clayton Mumpe grumbled. "Anything I do, I do it eye-to-eye." He focused a twisted glare at Lawrence Shaw.

"All right, boys," Kemp called out to the posse in a disgusted voice, "turn them loose."

"Wait just a minute, Sheriff!" A hardware clerk named Bud Carlson swung down from his saddle and stepped over to the boardwalk. "Who's in charge here, you or him?" His finger pointed from Kemp to Shaw as he spoke. Another townsman named Rowe Beck stepped down from his saddle and stood beside Carlson. Beck carried a long rope coiled in one hand, a hangman's knot tied at the end of it. "Yeah, that's what I want to know, too."

But before Kemp could answer, Lawrence Shaw walked forward and stood a foot away from Carlson and Beck with his hand on his pistol butt. "The question is not who's in charge here, him or me. The question is: Who's gonna catch a jawful of pistol barrel?" His cold green eyes went from one to the other. "Is it going to be you, Carlson . . . or you, Beck . . . or *both* of you?"

"Stand down, Shaw!" Sheriff Kemp leapt down off the boardwalk, edging in between Lawrence Shaw and the two townsmen. "These men are all tired and disappointed—so am I, to tell the truth. We thought we had the killers. Can't you understand how we feel?"

Shaw took a step back, shaking his head slowly. "No. I'm no lawman, but I can't see why anybody would ever want to accuse somebody of murder unless they had some kind of proof."

Kemp looked ashamed. "I was going to check them out first, Shaw. I still am. Nobody was going to get out of hand here."

"Then check them out, Sheriff." Shaw's eyes passed across the coil of rope in Beck's hand. "Meanwhile, you've got my word they won't make a run for it. Right, Cherokee? Right, Mumpe?"

Both men nodded. Shaw turned to Beck. "Next time I see

you carrying that rope, you better have a cow on the other end of it, or I'll drag you out by an ankle and leave you hanging by your heels somewhere."

Rowe Beck let the rope fall straight down to the ground, then he backed away, a scared look in his eyes. "Sheriff, I don't deserve to be treated this way."

"Get on your horses, boys," Kemp said to Beck and Carlson in a calm tone. He turned to the others. "All right, men. We lost the whole night catching what *appears* to be the wrong men. Everybody go on home now, get some rest. Anybody feels like riding back out with me . . . I'll be leaving here again in four hours."

As the townsmen grumbled and dispersed, Kemp uncuffed Cherokee and Clayton Mumpe and stood back with Shaw as the two slid down from the saddle. "If you boys check out okay . . . all I can tell you is that I'm sorry. That's the best I can do."

"Aw, hell, don't worry about it, Sheriff. I know how it goes. I do some law work myself." Cherokee Cousins kicked the coiled rope across the ground. "We were headed here, anyway. Check out whatever you need to." He took the gloves from his hip pocket and put them on as he looked at Lawrence Shaw. "I suppose you expect I should buy you breakfast for this?"

Shaw grinned. "You better believe I do. What's the story on you and Junior Lake? I take it there's bad blood between you?"

"You're right, there is. I chased him down a while back, made him pay me some money he owed me—billiard money. Damned if he didn't steal my horse."

"The big paint horse?"

"Yeah . . . and now I hear he lamed it out and let it die. So, you know me; I'm on him hot and heavy."

"I always figured if you kept dealing with the likes of Junior Lake and his bunch, sooner or later it would cost you something. You're lucky it was only a horse."

Cherokee sighed and pushed up his hat brim. "You're not going to preach to me, are you?"

"Sure, a little bit," Lawrence Shaw chuckled. "I like saying I told you so. I always wondered how long you could step into that element and still keep your boots clean."

"Well, I learned a lesson from it. You know how I loved that paint horse. Junior's got to answer for it."

"Junior's got a lot to answer for, evidently," Shaw said. "Him and his boys killed a young buffalo hunter south of here the other day."

"That's nothing new for Junior and his bunch. They leave somebody dead everywhere they go." Cherokee Cousins gestured a hand toward a restaurant across the street. "Come on. Tell me about it over a plate of hash and biscuits."

PART 2

Chapter 8

Two days had passed before Samuel Burrack was back on his feet and able to leave the doctor's care. The rowel had slashed him deep between his ribs and it would take some time for him to heal properly. The doctor had shaved a patch of hair from the left front side of his head, where a jagged line of stitches now held together the deep gash in his scalp. He touched his fingers to the sore flesh beneath the stitching as he walked slowly across the dirt street to the Little Egypt Saloon. At his left heel the big cur moved along at a slow, steady clip.

"Look who's coming here, Fast Larry," Thurman the bartender said, gazing out over the doors of the saloon, seeing Samuel and the dog make their way closer, weaving through the thin wagon traffic in the early morning sunlight. "It's your new friend, I do believe." He chuckled under his breath and went back to wiping a shot glass with a clean white towel.

"You're kidding." Fast Larry was bent down over the billiard table to make a shot. But now he stood up and looked out through the dusty window. "What's wrong with that crazy kid? He's not supposed to be up and around for another week."

"Well, maybe he ain't supposed to be, but he is." Thurman sat the glass down and swung the towel over his shoulder. "He's paler than my grandmother's mustache . . . but here he comes, all the same."

On the other side of the billiard table, Cherokee Cousins

sipped his beer, a cue stick propped against his side. "Are you going to shoot the nineball or not?"

"In a minute." Fast Larry laid his pool stick down along the rail of the felt tabletop. He walked around the table and met Samuel as he came through the swinging doors. "Samuel Burrack," Lawrence said, "are we going to have to knock you in the head to get you to lay still and take care of yourself?"

Samuel offered a weak smile, touching his fingertips to the stitches in his head. "I hope not. I don't know how much more my head can take."

"Does the doctor know you're out here?" Lawrence Shaw gave him a skeptical glance.

"Yes, he does. I told him if Daggett could mend in a jail cell, surely I could do just as well in a hotel room. He finally agreed with me."

"Sounds right to me, then." Lawrence Shaw gestured him forward. "Come here, I've been telling these fellows about you." He turned to Cherokee Cousins and the bartender, saying, "Well, here he is. This is the young man who couldn't make up his mind whether or not to kill that outlaw . . . so he shot him full of holes with a peashooter, then dragged him all the way across the sand flats."

Samuel lowered his eyes, a bit embarrassed. Lawrence Shaw took note and added quickly, "Just joking with you, kid."

"Yes he is. But all joking aside, that was bold work, young man," Thurman said behind the bar. He hooked a thumb into the handle of a clean beer mug and slipped the mug beneath a long tap handle. "This one is on the house."

"Uh, thank you all the same," Samuel said, stopping him, "but it's a little early for me. And I've got some hides to sell." He turned back to Lawrence Shaw. "I just wanted to come by and thank you properly for all you've done for me."

Lawrence Shaw shrugged. "Don't mention it. Call it my

good deed for this decade." He smiled. "And forget about the hides, kid, they're already gone."

Samuel looked all around. "But where? How? Those were good hides."

"I sold them." As Shaw spoke, his fingers went into his black vest pocket and came out with a fold of dollar bills. "They were getting too ripe to stay in the livery barn, so I took them out to Jersey Dan's station and got them on a hide car out of here. Let them stink up St. Louis for a while." He held the money out for Samuel to take, but Samuel only looked at it, surprised.

"Go on, take it." Shaw nudged it forward. "It came to ninety-seven dollars and some change."

Samuel took the money, grateful. "I only figured eighty-four dollars for the whole load."

"Yeah, that's because Jersey Dan was clipping you and your friend by a dime per hide. I had to shake him by the collar a little. But he came around."

"Then I thank you again, Mr. Shaw." Samuel put the money in his shirt pocket and buttoned the pocket flap. "Now all I have to do is find me a hotel room for a while."

"You better forget about a hotel room in this town," Thurman called out from behind the bar. "There's only one hotel and it's full of lice and bed ticks."

"Bed ticks? Jesus!" Cherokee Cousins looked himself up and down and brushed a hand along his shirtsleeve.

"Go to Vera's Boarding House," Thurman continued, "three blocks down on the right. I hear the place is empty right now. She keeps clean beds, and she'll let your dog sleep on the back porch, provided he's not a howler."

"Then I'll go there. Blue's not a howler. Mostly he just hangs around." Samuel nodded. "I appreciate the advice."

Before Samuel could turn and leave, Cherokee Cousins asked as he came closer from around the corner of the billiard table, "When Junior Lake and his gang killed your friend, was he riding a big paint horse?"

"Yes, he was. Or I should say, he must have been. There

was a dead paint horse laying there when I came back and saw them kill my partner."

"Damn it." Cherokee Cousins sliced a breath. "Then that drunken bum at Mama Roby's was telling me the truth. Junior *did* leave my horse laying dead on the desert."

Samuel looked back and forth between Shaw and Cousins. "I don't understand."

Shaw looked at him. "This is Cherokee Cousins. He's been searching for Junior Lake. One of the men who robbed the mercantile store here the other night was one of Junior's men. He was passing himself off as a traveling peddler. He stole this man's horse, too, and almost got him and Cherokee hung for robbery and murder." Shaw nodded toward Clayton Mumpe who sat at a small table in the front corner of the saloon. Mumpe stared at the three of them over the top of a whiskey bottle, a sullen look on his face.

"So you see, kid?" Shaw went on. "You were tangling with some pretty low, vicious characters out there. You're lucky they didn't eat you up and spit you out."

"I suppose I *was* lucky." Samuel rubbed his chin thinking about it, catching a mental glimpse of Davey Riley's face as the blade drew back and laid a red streak across his throat. "Nobody has ever found the one who left here on foot?"

"No. He was staying at the boarding house Thurman told you about. But Vera's sister said he's long gone. There's no telling where he's at by now."

"I see." Samuel nodded. "Then maybe Ranger Sazes has at least caught up with Junior Lake by now."

"Sazes?" Shaw smiled. "Listen to me, kid. Put that crazy ranger out of your mind. If he hadn't busted up the gang and chased them out of the badlands and in close to town, none of this other stuff would have happened."

"That's right," Thurman joined in. "When Sheriff Kemp gets back from riding posse, ask him about Outrider Sazes. He'll tell you. Sazes carries all these badlands killers and lunatics around in his chest like a bad disease. Every now and then he coughs them out and they scatter on the wind. Wherever they land, they spread their infection."

Shaw and Cousins nodded in agreement. "That's a good way to put it, Thurman," Shaw said.

"But Ranger Sazes is only doing his job. " Samuel looked back and forth at them, confused by their attitudes. "Somebody has to hunt them down and stop them, don't they?"

"Well, sure, kid, that's true." Lawrence Shaw looked a little embarrassed. "Maybe all we're trying to tell you is to stay clear of Outrider Sazes. Sazes is not like other lawmen. He's lived so long in that lower element that he's consumed by it. Even other lawmen dread to see him coming. Take a man like Sheriff Kemp. He does his job, keeps peace in his town. But when he goes home at night he can put all that aside. Not Sazes. He's a part of that outlaw world—trouble looking for a place to happen."

Samuel looked at each of them. "Then what should he do? Let them get away with what they do to innocent people like Davey Riley?"

"All right, kid. I don't know what the answer is." Lawrence Shaw tried to dismiss the question. He walked back to the billiard table and picked up his stick. "I only know that Sazes is crazy as hell. He likes his work *too much*." Shaw stroked the stick back and forth between his fingers and made his shot, the nineball racing forward and dropping clean into the side pocket. "It's best to leave Sazes to his thieves and murderers. Who's got time for him? I sure don't."

Shaw raised up from the table and chuckled, smoothing down the front of his vest as Cherokee Cousins tossed a dollar onto the green felt and began to rack the balls. Shaw snatched up the bill, shoved it into his shirt pocket and nodded toward Clayton Mumpe at the small corner table. "You see, kid. I've got my hands full waiting for our Mr. Mumpe there to decide whether or not he's fast enough to lift his pistol and blow my head off. Most likely he's got money bet on it with somebody."

Samuel flashed a quick glance at Clayton Mumpe, then back to Shaw. "Oh, it's true," Shaw said, running the cue stick back and forth between his arched fingers as Cherokee lifted the wooden rack and waited for him to break the balls for a new game. "Somebody probably gave him hundred-to-one odds. The only thing that keeps him from trying me right now is that he's afraid it would look downright ungrateful of him—trying to kill me right after I kept him from stretching hemp."

"Bullshit," Clayton Mumpe hissed. "I'm ready right now if you are. You're the one putting it off, not me."

Ignoring Clayton Mumpe, Shaw looked up at Samuel Burrack as he stroked the stick with his fingers. "You see, what this poor fool doesn't understand is the unfairness of it. If he happens to get lucky and shoots me down, he gets big money and an instant reputation—something he's been craving for a long time. But when I kill him, which I will, of course"—Shaw grinned, staring at Clayton Mumpe through cold green eyes—"I don't make squat for my trouble. I've killed a nameless *nobody* . . . and in a few hours who will even remember it?" With that, Shaw slammed the stick forward, busting the billiard balls in every direction across the felt. Shaw chuckled, shaking his head. "It's just not fair anymore . . . I've got to get out of this business."

Samuel looked from one to the other, backing toward the saloon doors. "And you call Ranger Sazes crazy?" He heard Lawrence Shaw and Thurman laugh behind him as he stepped down into the street, the big cur rising up from his spot on the boardwalk and falling in behind his left heel.

After Samuel's third round of knocking on the boarding house door, he'd given up and started to leave, when the door opened a crack and a woman's pale face looked out at him. "Yes, can I help you?" Her voice sounded guarded; her eyes darted along the dirt street, then leveled back at him.

"Yes, ma'am, I need a room." Samuel still held his hat in his hand, rather than place it over the painful line of stitches.

She looked him up and down. "Sorry, but we have no vacant rooms." The door started to close.

"But, ma'am . . . the bartender at the Little Egypt said he heard you were empty here. I apologize for looking such a mess. The fact is I was injured on my way to Wakely and haven't gotten over it—"

"You're the man Fast Larry Shaw brought to town?" Her face seemed to change. The door reopened, this time a little further.

"Well, yes, I've heard some folks call him Fast Larry. He found me and my dog and oxen and brought us here." Samuel offered a meek smile. "I'm Samuel Burrack. The bartender said Vera's Boarding House has the cleanest beds in town. I have cash to pay." As he spoke to her, he noticed the dark circle under her right eye, the puffy swell of her cheek; and he saw the dark tracing of a hand print on her face. "Ma'am?" His voice lowered. "Is everything all right here?"

She hesitated, then caught herself and said quickly, "Oh, yes, of course. I'm Polly." Her fingers brushed meekly at her cheek, but then moved away. "My sister Vera didn't want to take on any more boarders at present. We had a terrible thing happen here the other night."

"Yes, ma'am, I heard one of your boarders was involved in the robbery."

Something flashed in her eyes, but only for an instant. "Yes, and Vera is very upset about it. But I'm sure she wouldn't say no in this case, after all you've been through." She opened the door wide and stepped back. "She isn't here now, but do come in." Her eyes went down to the big cur.

"Oh, this is my dog, Blue. I hoped maybe he could sleep on your back porch? If it's no trouble, that is. He's a real clean dog, Miss Polly. He doesn't howl or carry on."

"Then I'm sure that will be fine." Polly stepped further back and gestured Samuel past her into the hallway. "He can even stay on the *front* porch for now."

Samuel looked around inside the big, clean house, the

high-backed sofas and chairs in the parlor with white doilies on them. "I apologize again, Miss Polly, for my sore condition. I'll be getting myself a change of clothes and a hot bath as soon as I get settled in here."

"I understand, Mr. Burrack. We are used to working men from out on the plains. I should mention, though, that we won't be serving meals for the time being, until the weather cools some. I hope that won't inconvenience you too greatly. There is a good restaurant just down the street." As they spoke, she directed him to a long stairwell and gestured him upward with a sweep of her hand.

"That'll be just fine, ma'am. I wouldn't expect you to light a hot stove in this weather, not for just one boarder."

At the top of the stairs, he started down the hallway and stopped outside a closed oak door—the first door he came to. But as he reached for the knob, Polly stepped in front of him and said in a rushed voice, "No, not this room! Yours will be farther down—at the end of the hall."

Samuel noted the urgency in her voice. "Yes, down there," she added quickly, "where it's much cooler." She shot a glance up into his eyes. "It's on the rear of the house. It stays out of the sun longer than any other room."

"Oh . . . that's good, ma'am." He caught a faint familiar odor surrounding the door. For a second he sensed that someone was inside the room, but he dismissed it as he moved along, with Polly coaxing him farther down the hallway. He noticed that all the other doors along the hallway stood open a few inches with a key in each lock.

Once inside the room at the far end of the hall, Polly folded her hands in front of herself and stood by the open door while Samuel looked around. "Yes, this will do just fine." When he turned back to her, he noticed she seemed to be in a hurry. "I'll just rest here for a few minutes, then go to the store and get myself a change of clothes."

"All right." She stepped backward through the open door, took the key from the door and handed it to him. "I have to run out for a while. You'll find a front-door key for yourself on the key rack in the front hall. Feel free to take one, but be careful not to lose it."

"Yes, I will. Here, I'll pay you for a week in advance before you leave." He reached in his pocket for the money, but she held up a hand, stopping him.

"No, please. I really must hurry now, Mr. Burrack. You can pay me when I return."

"Whatever you say, ma'am." He watched her disappear from sight, and listened to the ring of her footsteps echo down the wooden stairs.

Outside, Blue stood up from his spot on the front porch and stepped aside as Polly opened the door and closed it firmly behind herself. "Get out of my way," she whispered to the dog in a harsh tone. The big cur stood watching her as she stepped down from the front porch and walked quickly around the side of the house toward the backyard.

In a moment, the crack of a buggy whip caused the dog to perk up his ears. He bounded down off the porch and ran back alongside the house. He stopped for a second and stood staring after her as the one-horse buggy pulled out of the yard and headed out across a rocky path leading north out of town. Then, as if stricken by a sudden impulse, the dog shot forward, following her buggy tracks as they snaked off in a flurry of dust.

Chapter 9

When he'd rested an hour or more, Samuel left the boarding house and walked to the mercantile store. A young man behind the counter explained how he was only filling in for Martha Baines, who was still deep in mourning over her husband's death. "It was the most awful tragedy you can imagine," the young man went on to say. "I hate charging her wages for my being here, but what else can I do?" He tossed a hand at the inequity of the world around him.

Samuel gathered himself a new bib-front shirt, a pair of summer undergarments and socks, and a pair of stiff denim trousers. Once he paid for his garments, the young man asked him if he was the one who brought in the wounded outlaw, Daggett. When Samuel nodded and said that he was, the young clerk let out a short sigh.

"Well, good for you, is all I can say. I only wished the sheriff could have done as much in catching the scoundrel who killed poor Mr. Baines." As the clerk wrapped Samuel's purchases in a length of brown paper and began tying string around the bundle, he looked up and added, "I fear this is only the beginning of an outbreak of crime here in Wakely." His eyes cut to the broken door of a gun cabinet that hadn't yet been repaired. "You may want to consider purchasing yourself a sidearm. I daresay, even some women in town are arming themselves—rifles, pistols." He shook his head. "It's terrible." Then as if struck by an idea, he tossed a hand toward the gun cabinet. "I can take as much as a dollar off the price of a new Colt for you."

But Samuel declined, thanking him for the offer. Once outside, he looked all around and didn't see the big cur. He walked to the barbershop with his bundle of clothes under his arm. After a shave, a haircut, and a hot bath, he dressed in his new clothes and left his old buffalo-hunting clothes with the barber to be washed and picked up later. Outside the barbershop he placed his new hat carefully on his head and walked to the restaurant a block farther along the dusty street.

When he'd eaten a full meal and drank two cups of strong coffee, he walked back to the boarding house, feeling better than he had in days. On his way up onto the porch, Samuel looked around once more for the big cur, but still saw no sign of him. It wasn't like Blue to stray off for this long at a time, and later inside his room, he caught himself going to the window every few minutes and looking down at the empty front yard. *Where are you, Blue?*

His eyes searched along the dusty street, and when he grew restless in his growing concern, he walked down onto the porch and called out the dog's name. Then he walked around to the back porch, looked out across the yard and called out again. Still no sign of the dog; but he walked to the back edge of the yard and saw Blue's pawprints leading off between the buggy tracks. Had the dog followed her? But why would he? Blue just didn't do that sort of thing.

Back inside the empty boarding house, Samuel walked up the stairs. Along the hallway, he caught the same faint odor he'd noticed earlier when he passed the closed door. The heat of the day had grown stronger now, and with it the odor had become more distinct. He lingered for a second and looked the door up and down, still sensing someone behind it. What was that smell? On the way back to his room, he thought about the pawprints following the buggy tracks, and about the bruise on the young woman's cheek. What was going on around here? he wondered.

*   *   *

At the Little Egypt Saloon, Lawrence Shaw took the
envelope from the little boy's hand. He thanked him and
handed him a nickel and fanned him toward the door. "Now,
out you go, young man. You shouldn't be in a place like this.
Tell the postal clerk that the next time I want *him* to bring
me my mail personally."

"Yes, sir, I'll tell him," the little boy said, padding barefoot through the swinging doors.

"And just what's *wrong* with a place like this?" Behind
the bar, Thurman spread his hands apart taking in all of the
place. Three men in dusty business suits stood drinking at
the bar, getting down as many shots of whiskey as they
could before going back to the livery barn and climbing
once more aboard the big Studebaker stagecoach.

Lawrence Shaw smiled. "Thurman, if you have to ask, I
doubt if you'd understand." He stepped over to the table in
the front corner where Cherokee Cousins sat sipping a beer.

"News from afar, huh?" Cherokee nodded at the letter
Shaw held in his black glove.

"Yeah . . ." Shaw drew out a chair with the toe of his boot
and sat down. "It's from my wife." He opened the envelope,
unfolded the letter, and held it down beneath the edge of the
table for privacy.

"Wife? I didn't know you had one of those." Cherokee
cocked his head a bit to one side. "Isn't marriage an occu-
pational hazard in your line of work?"

Lawrence Shaw glanced up at him, ignoring the second
part of the question. "Oh, I have a wife, all right. She's the
best thing that's ever happened to me. This is her second letter in the past week. I haven't written back to her, because I
plan on surprising her by just showing up on the front porch
some morning. I was ready to head home to her the other
day, but then all this business came up with the sheriff."

"Are you sure that's what kept you here?"

"What are you saying, Cherokee?"

Cherokee shrugged. "Maybe you're having a hard time

turning loose. It's hard sometimes, changing what you are, even when you know it's best for you."

"Naw." Shaw brushed the suggestion away. "I've got no problem turning this loose. I'm *already* gone, I just haven't caught up to myself yet." He smiled.

"Then cut out tomorrow," Cherokee said. "I'll watch things here for you." He watched Shaw's eyes, seeing if he'd take the offer.

"Thanks, but no. I gave the sheriff my word." Shaw lowered his gaze to the letter and said in a lower tone, "But I'm not fooling myself. I'm heading out as soon as he gets back—you can bet I am." His gloved hand brushed across the letter, smoothing it out as if caressing fine silk.

"You're not one of those people who keeps intending to go home but keeps finding reasons not to, are you?" Cherokee spread a crafty smile.

Shaw's face reddened a bit, embarrassed. Then he shook his head in denial. "Huh-uh. I admit I have let a couple of things keep me here. But not anymore. Life's too short, especially in my business."

"Just checking," Cherokee Cousins said. He raised a glass and sipped, letting his eyes drift out through the dusty window toward the street. "Well, there goes your buffalo hunter again. Looks like he has something on his mind."

"Oh?" Shaw raised his face from the letter and looked out, seeing Samuel Burrack move along the busy street. "That kid, I swear." Shaw raised from his chair for a better look. "He's the most *serious* person I've ran into in a long while. You know the first thing he said to me when I finally got him pinned down and into the oxcart?"

"What's that?" Cherokee didn't raise up, but he craned his neck a bit, watching Samuel trudge forward with a determined look on his face.

Shaw chuckled. "Get a load of this. He's got a spur sticking out of his ribs . . . blood running from four or five stab wounds, he's about bled to death—he says, 'Mister, have you got any water for my dog?' Can you believe that?" Shaw turned to Cousins with a bemused look on his face.

"I'd say he likes his dog real well." Cherokee tipped his glass in salute. When he sat the glass down, he added, "And I'd say you like that dumb buffalo hunter for some reason or another."

"You're right. The kid's okay." Shaw watched Samuel through the dusty window. "I don't know what it is about him. He's not the brightest man on two legs. But I get the feeling you can count on what he tells you. If he sets out to do something, I believe you can consider it done."

"Dumb but honest, eh?"

"Maybe so. " Shaw thought about it as Samuel Burrack moved out of sight along the street. "There's something about him that I miss in myself. It's something that got away from me somewhere along the line. Like I said, he's still serious about things, the kind of things people like you and I learned to laugh at or take for granted a long time ago."

"Well, give it time, this place will catch up to him."

"I don't think so," said Shaw. "Maybe that's part of what I see in him. Even if this place catches up to him, I don't think it will ever overtake him. I like seeing that in a person."

"Oh, then he's what I call a *righteous pilgrim*." Cherokee leaned back in his chair and hooked his thumbs in his belt, his right hand above the big Colt pistol at his hip. "One of those kind who can roll in the dung with the rest of the herd, but can stand back up, shake himself off, and manage not to carry the stench of it."

Lawrence Shaw stood silent for a moment with his wife's letter hanging from his fingertips. He watched Samuel come back into sight around the other side of a long freight wagon, then disappear once more around the side of the stagecoach. "A righteous pilgrim? I don't know about righteous. Maybe just *noble*."

"A *noble* pilgrim? Hmm . . ." Cherokee said the words as

if testing them out in his mind. "All right, I'll go with that. Just how noble do you suppose he is?"

Shaw cut a glance over to Clayton Mumpe who stared back at him from the far end of the bar with a grim expression on his face. For a second, a trace of the old hollow loneliness played across Shaw's mind. But he put it away and turned back to the window, catching a glimpse of his own eyes in a smoke-stained reflection. "We'll see," he said in a hushed tone, speaking more to himself than to Cherokee Cousins.

Sherman Ellsworth bounded down off the rickety cabin porch as the buggy wound down from the switchback trail. He paced back and forth restlessly and kicked at a stick in the rocky front yard where broken bottles and jagged-edged tin cans lay strewn in all directions. When the buggy sped forward and came to an abrupt halt, he stepped forward running a shaky hand across his parched lips and called out, "You better have some whiskey for me, girlie, or I'll smack your head so hard, hair'll grow on your elbows."

Polly looked frightened. She secured the buggy and said as she stepped down, "I, I didn't have time, Sherman! I hurried out here to tell you—"

"What?" He cut her short. "You didn't have time?" He stood shirtless, beads of sweat glistening on his chest, his galluses off his shoulders and hanging down from his waist. The stolen pistol hung from his neck on a strip of rawhide. "You better hope to God you're kidding me!" His fists clenched tight at his sides. He sprang forward and grabbed her by her wrist.

"Sherman, please!" Her voice quivered as she shied back from him. "Listen to me!"

As he held her pinned in place, Sherman looked past her and up the winding trail and caught sight of the big, blue spotted cur as the dog came into sight and stopped thirty yards back. "What the hell's this? I've seen that dog before. Are you being followed?"

Polly gasped as she spun around and saw the dog sit down in the dirt and watch them, its tongue lolling in the afternoon heat. "Oh, Lord it's his dog! The buffalo hunter's!" She spun back to Ellsworth. "It followed me here, Sherman!"

He shook her. "What are you saying, you stupid little whore? You led somebody here?" He drew a hand back to slap her, but she shielded her face.

"Please listen to me!" She spoke fast. "The buffalo hunter is staying at the house—he came by and asked for a room! I don't know if he suspects anything or not! I wanted to hurry here and tell you."

Sherman turned her loose and raised the pistol, his eyes scanning the high rise of rockland surrounding the cabin. "Is he back there?"

"I don't think so—I didn't see anybody's dust."

"But you didn't see the dog, either, did you, *idiot*?" He turned, searching the land, cocking the pistol. "See? You whores are all alike. Always more trouble than you're worth."

"Sherman, I'm sorry." She sounded hurt. "I wanted to warn you. Don't you think it's odd . . . that he just happened to come looking for a room?"

He gave her a strange curious look. "Odd? Well, let's see now. You run a boarding house . . . people rent rooms." He shook his head. "Am I not getting the picture here? Is there something I'm missing?"

"It's a sign, Sherman, don't you see?" She tugged at his bare shoulder. "They're closing in on us! We've got to get out of here, before it's too late!"

"Shut the hell up." He rounded his shoulder away from her and took aim at the dog. "You're just anxious to get underway to Texas. Watch this . . ." He steadied the pistol and began to squeeze the trigger. "One shot—no more dog." The big cur sat staring with the pistol sight honed in on his chest.

Sherman held his shot long enough to cast a sidelong

glance at Polly. "You *did* bring me some ammunition though, didn't you?"

"Sherman, there was no time!" Her voice pleaded. "I was afraid. I hurried straight out here."

He lowered the pistol with a long breath of exasperation. "I bet I kill *you* before this is all over." Then with the suddenness of a striking snake, his hand shot out across her face and sent her backward on the hard ground. "You rotten, stupid woman! No whiskey, no bullets!" He kicked at her, but she managed to roll away in time. A trickle of blood ran from her nose. "Now get out there and bring that damned dog in here. For all I know he could be scouting me out for the law."

Polly struggled to her feet, sobbing, her hand up to the new red welt on the side of her face. "But how can I get him?"

"I don't know. Get him the same way you got me for all I care. I wouldn't put it past you. Just get him in here!"

"Are you going to . . . to kill it?" She looked out at the big cur as the dog sat in the same spot, just staring back at them.

"Well, hell yes I'm going to kill it. I might skin him and make myself a blue spotted hatband." He walked away, kicking at an empty whiskey bottle, then ambled back up onto the porch and into the cabin with his pistol hanging from his hand. "Don't come through the door without that dog on a rope—I might just decide to make a hat band out of *your* sorry hide."

Chapter 10

Samuel Burrack had followed the buggy tracks out across the sand and mesquite brush for nearly an hour, on a big bay he'd rented from the livery barn. Always amid the tracks the pawprints of the dog did not wander in either direction, and Samuel could almost picture the big cur with his nose to the ground, serious in his pursuit. *But why?* Samuel had no idea as he heeled the rented horse forward up a bow in the trail between two tall upthrusts of rock.

He couldn't imagine what had prompted the big cur to follow the buggy, nor could he clearly say why he himself was now following it. But something urged him on—instinct, or a premonition? Whatever it was, he'd felt strongly enough about it that he'd shoved the small pistol Ranger Sazes had given him down in his waist and carried the big buffalo rifle across his lap. At a turn in the higher trail where the buggy tracks led down toward a leaning, weathered shack in a rocky valley, Samuel drew the horse back and sat still in a dark slice of afternoon shade, not quite sure what to do next.

The buggy sat empty in the littered front yard, and there was no sign of the dog. After a moment, Samuel shook off the doubt and wariness that held him in place and had just started to heel the horse forward when he heard the raised angry voice of a man inside the shack.

"Whoa, boy." Samuel stopped and drew the horse back once more, and sat listening now to the raging curses and threats echo up from the valley floor.

Inside the shack, Sherman Ellsworth snatched up a wooden stool and hurled it across the room. On a pallet in the corner, Polly hunkered down and shielded her face with her forearm as the stool crashed against the wall above her and fell tumbling across the dirty floor. "We leave when I *say* we leave!" He pounded a fist on his chest. "Not a damned minute before!"

"I'm sorry, Sherman!" Polly cringed, naked on the pallet, a red handprint rising anew on her cheek. She wiped a tangled strand of hair from across her face. "I'm just scared!"

"Sorry? Scared? I'll show you *scared!*" Ellsworth came forward, buttoning his trousers. He kicked his bare foot at the pallet. Polly scurried along the wall, getting out of range, snatching up a gray damp sheet and throwing it around herself. "You think I'm taking your worthless behind with me? You don't even have enough sense to bring bullets or whiskey!" He moved toward her, kicking again. "Get up! Open some of them airtights and fix me some beans!"

"I will, Sherman, I will!" She scurried farther away and stood up, wrapping the sheet tighter around herself. "Just . . . let me get my clothes on."

"Naw, you ain't putting no clothes on. I like you just the way you are. Now get busy before I take a stick to you!" Beyond a wooden door to a smaller room, the big cur growled and whined and scratched at the floor toward the sound of their voices. Sherman Ellsworth snatched up one of his boots and hurled it against the door. "Shut up in there! I'll drag you out and bash your head in!" Blue relented and paced the room in a circle, whining low, his eyes searching around the walls for an opening, but finding none.

Polly hurried to the battered table where a few cans of beans and corn lay in a pile. She stood one can up on its end, picked up the long butcher knife with a trembling hand, stabbed the point of it down into the can and began to open it. Sherman paced back and forth angrily, sweat glistening on his face and chest. He ran his fingers back through his damp hair. Seeing Polly fumble with the can, he bolted over, snatched the knife from her hand and shoved her aside. "Here, give me the damned thing! You can't even open a can of beans. And you're talking about going to Texas?"

Polly shied back a step from him, hiking the sheet up across her breasts. "I get—I get nervous when you act like this."

"Aw, now ain't that a shame." Sherman stabbed the blade down and rocked it back and forth in the can, opening it. "And you being such a tough girl and all. *'Don't worry about me.'* " He grinned and mimicked her in a harsh voice as he worked the knife back and forth. " *'I won't break. I like it rough.'* Well, here's *rough* looking at you, sweetheart. And it's going to get a lot rougher before this ride is over."

In the small room, Blue went into another round of loud whining and scratching at the wooden door. Sherman swung toward the sound with the big knife tight in his hand. "I've had it with that whining, crying, lousy cur!"

Polly cut in, seeing the insane rage in Ellsworth's eyes. "Why don't we let him go? He won't bring anybody here. He's just a big stupid pup."

"Oh, I'll let him go all right!" Sherman stomped over to the door, raised a bare foot, and kicked it open. The crash sent the big cur fleeing into a dark corner. He cringed there, his long tail wrapped beneath him. Sherman filled the open doorway, the big knife raised in his tight fist. "Okay, puppy, puppy, puppy! You want out? Come along with ole Sherman, boy. I'll make a *good* dog out of you!"

"Sherman, please!"

"You shut up!" Sherman raged at her over his shoulder. "See if you can pour those beans into a pot while I go walk the doggie! Surely to God you can do that much."

"Drop the knife," said a voice behind Sherman

Ellsworth. Ellsworth had started to let go a string of cursing over his shoulder before he realized that the voice did not belong to Polly. His back stiffened at the sound of the hammer going back on the big buffalo rifle. "I said drop it . . . drop it right now." Samuel stood beside the table with his feet shoulder width apart, the big rifle aimed and ready.

But Sherman Ellsworth didn't drop the knife. Instead, he turned slowly, the knife raised chest-high. His eyes darted to the pistol lying on the crumpled pallet in the corner. Then his eyes came back to Samuel. "Who the hell are you, boy? And what right have you got busting in here in the middle of a family discussion?"

"I mean it, mister. Drop the knife."

Even as he spoke, Ellsworth was sizing Samuel up, getting a feel for what he was dealing with here. He saw the big hammer cocked back; he saw the intent expression on the young man's face. But looks were one thing, pulling a trigger on a man was something else altogether. He took a slow step forward, a slight smile spreading across his lips.

"Heck, man." Ellsworth shrugged. "Me and her bicker like this all the time. We don't mean nothing by it. Do we, darling?"

"It's him!" Polly pointed a shaky finger at Ellsworth, speaking to Samuel Burrack. "He's the one who killed Mr. Baines and robbed the store—he told me so."

Jesus . . . Sherman Ellsworth stopped and gave her a stunned expression. His mouth gaped open. "Hon*eeeey* . . . ?" He slumped his shoulders.

"It's true! He has your dog—and he's holding my sister hostage! He said he would kill her if I didn't do what he wanted. He's one of the men who killed your friend!" Her words rushed out, tearful and frightened. She'd moved to one side of the table, clutching the sheet across her bosom.

"I figured as much, ma'am." Samuel Burrack kept his eyes on Ellsworth as he spoke to her. "Go ahead, get your clothes on. He's not going to hurt you."

"She's lying, mister." Ellsworth snapped out of it, and took a cautious step forward as Polly hurried over to her pile of clothes on the pallet.

Samuel nodded at the knife still in Ellsworth's hand. "I won't say it again. Drop the knife, or I'll shoot you in the knee."

In the knee? All right, that tells him something about this stranger, Ellsworth thought. He let his arm drop to his side and allowed the knife to fall to the floor. "Looks like you've got me." He lowered his head and added under his breath, "Damn the luck—and I was headed out of here for Texas."

Something clicked in Samuel's mind. He'd seen this man before. He noted the man's pale cheeks, the way he handled himself. Yet it was more than these things. There was something else. Samuel didn't know why, but as he looked the man up and down, something strong inside him told him that this was the man who'd killed Davey Riley. "Your name is Ellsworth. I've seen you before."

"Whoa now." Ellsworth saw the look come over Samuel's face, and he saw Samuel's hand tighten on the rifle. "Don't go jumping to any harsh conclusions." But now the expression on Ellsworth's face only confirmed it.

"You murdered my friend!"

"Easy. If you think that's true, let's wait for the law to settle it. Don't do something stupid here." Ellsworth had seen what the big rifle did to Daggett's shoulder.

Samuel stilled the rage in his chest. "Yep, we'll let the law settle it all right. I'm taking you in. I'll see to it you hang for what you did."

The big cur ventured his nose out from the doorway behind Ellsworth, probing the air toward the sound of Samuel's voice, then drew back inside the small room. "Come on out, Blue." Samuel called to him, but seeing the dog's reluctance, he moved forward a step, Ellsworth cautiously stepping to one side to let him pass.

"I didn't hurt him," Ellsworth said. "And that's the

truth." As he spoke, keeping Samuel's attention on the doorway to the smaller room, Ellsworth watched Polly reach down and pick up the pistol from the pallet. "I wouldn't hurt a dog for nothing in the world. My whole family is animal lovers—always was. I was just telling her, he ain't nothing but a big ole cuddly pup."

"I heard what you were saying," Samuel said. "You better *hope* he's not hurt." Samuel studied his eyes. Yes, this was Davey Riley's killer all right., He was sure of it. *Got him for you, Davey . . .*

Samuel moved past Sherman Ellsworth to the doorway, turning sideways to keep an eye on him. Ellsworth saw Polly struggle with the pistol, trying to cock the hammer back. When the sound of the hammer caused Samuel Burrack to turn toward her, Ellsworth knew it was his chance to make a grab for Samuel's rifle barrel. And he took it.

"Shoot him, Polly!" Jerking Samuel's rifle barrel forward, Ellsworth let a out a yell. But Samuel didn't let the rifle go, and the forward pull on the barrel caused his finger to pull the trigger, sending a blast of fire only an inch past Ellsworth's leg. "Damn it, shoot him!" From the small room, the big cur charged forward, teeth bared. The dog barked and bounced back and forth as Ellsworth and Samuel struggled for control of the rifle.

"It won't cock!" She screamed and gave up trying, and instead hurled the pistol forward. It bounced off the back of Samuel's shoulder, skidded across the rough floorboards and landed near the open front door.

Ellsworth jerked Samuel forward with the rifle, kneed him hard in the groin, and made a dive for the pistol while Samuel bowed at the waist and tried to right himself. The big cur snarled and shot forward at Ellsworth, but then cut away and pulled back when Ellsworth kicked at it. Ellsworth made another lunge for the pistol. Samuel forced himself to make a move, diving for Ellsworth and landing atop him right before Ellsworth managed to get a grip on the gun. "You son of a bitch!" Sherman Ellsworth raged beneath him.

The dog bellowed. Now Samuel reached out for the pistol as well, both their hands stretching forward on the dirty floor, Samuel with an arm around Ellsworth's neck, choking off his breath. With his free hand he finally managed to get the pistol, cock it with his thumb and swing the tip of the barrel to the side of Ellsworth's head. "It's over! Don't make me kill you!" Samuel's voice almost pleaded, yet at this point it was down to life or death. He would do whatever he had to do.

But Ellsworth still struggled with him, jerking sideways with Samuel on his back. Behind him, Samuel felt the weight of the woman straddle him; and he felt her fingers pull back on his hair. He tried to shake her free as Ellsworth struggled beneath him. A hot stinging chill shot through Samuel's face as the knife in Polly's hand came down hard across his cheek. The blow of the big blade stunned him for a second. He rolled off of Ellsworth and let out a moan. Behind Polly, Blue bounded back and forth, barking, but doing nothing more.

"Oh, Lord . . ." Samuel could hear Ellsworth scrambling away as he raised a cupped hand to his burning cheek. "You stabbed me . . ." The pistol drooped in his hand.

The room seemed to swirl, the barking of the dog resounding above all else. Samuel swayed to one side and caught himself. He looked up into Polly's wild hysterical eyes. He wanted to ask her why she did what she had. He wanted to stop time and go back to the point where he'd come into the shack with the rifle cocked and ready. There were things he should have done differently. Yet he knew even in his stunned condition that nothing could be changed now. He saw Polly draw the big blade back above her head for what would be a death blow to his chest. In stunned surprise he felt the big pistol buck in his hand as if the gun were a living thing and had seen that he was powerless and had taken it upon itself to act on his behalf.

"No!" Samuel yelled, seeing her fly backward in a belch of smoke and fire. She landed atop the table, pulling it over onto the floor with her. The big cur jumped back with a yelp and fell silent, poking its nose over to where Polly lay writhing with her hands clasped across her bleeding stomach. Outside the sound of horses' hooves pounded away from the cabin.

With his left hand cupped to the heavy flow of blood from the wide gash in his cheek, Samuel moved forward to Polly and raised her across his lap, holding her as she struggled in her pain. "I'm shot dead, aren't I?" Her words came out tight and pained beneath her failing breath.

"I don't know." His own voice sounded strained and slurred with his cheek open in a flow of heavy blood. "We're both . . . hurt bad. Lie still, I'll get something—"

"No." She held his arm, keeping him from leaving her, and it was just as well she did, because he had no idea what he might have gotten for her that would have warded away the glazed look coming into her eyes, or the gray pale color that rose upon her face like a thin shroud. "I need to tell you . . ." Her voice failed. "Poor Vera . . . I killed her, not him."

"You killed your sister?" Blood from his gashed cheek dripped onto her, and Samuel wiped it away as best he could with his bloody hand. "But why?"

"I—I don't know. I lost my mind. Now I'll burn in hell for it . . ." Her eyes filled and turned distant. "Pray . . . for me. I thought I could be an outla—"

Her words stopped. Against his chest, he felt her life spend out in a low, hushed sigh. At the end, her eyes looked no different than a second ago except that whatever spark had been there had now vanished. Her face turned to that of a pale porcelain doll. "Oh, God, I killed her." Beside him, the big cur whined low and leaned forward on its front paws, sniffing at the blood on the dead woman's face.

*   *   *

It was dark outside when Cherokee Cousins stepped on the boardwalk in front of the Little Egypt Saloon. He'd rolled a cigarette, lit it, blew out a stream of smoke, and leaned back against the front of the building. Inside, the sound of a snappy banjo strummed for the drinking crowd. He shook out the wooden match, flipped it out into the dirt street and watched Blue come out of the darkness into the soft glow of the saloon light. The dog sniffed at the burnt match, bounded up onto the boardwalk, and looked up at him wagging its long tail.

"What do you want? A smoke?" Cherokee Cousins reached a hand down and patted the big cur's neck. "Naw, you're too young . . . better stick to chewing for now." He laughed to himself. But then he fell quiet as he raised his hand and felt a dark sticky substance on his fingers. "What the—?" He rubbed his fingers together, then recognized what it was. "You're covered with blood! Get away from here." He nudged the dog away with the side of his boot. Then he looked up at the sound of the buggy moving in out of the darkness. In the soft glow of light spilling through the saloon doors, Cherokee saw the grim blank look on Samuel Burrack's blood-streaked face, and he let out a soft whistle. "Damn, young man, what have you done now?"

"I need a hand here," Samuel said just above a whisper.

"I can see you do." Cherokee stepped down from the boardwalk to the side of the buggy. Samuel slumped against him as he slid off the buggy seat. "Easy does it." He looked close at the rag pressed and dried against Samuel's cheek, then winced at the sight of the gaping end of the deep wound, which had cracked open again. A glimpse of white bone shown near Samuel's blood-crusted chin. "Your whole face is laid open!"

On the boardwalk, the swinging doors came open and Lawrence Shaw stepped out. "What's going on there, Cherokee?"

"It's our noble pilgrim," Cherokee said over his shoulder, helping Samuel lean back against the buggy. "Somebody's sliced him like a pound of pork." He reached up into the buggy, secured the reins, and stepped back as Lawrence Shaw moved from the boardwalk for a better look.

"Oh, no, not again," Shaw said. "You're going to wear that ole doctor out if you don't slow your pace. Who did this to you?" As he asked, Shaw looked at the corpse wrapped in a bloodstained sheet back in the buggy seat.

"She did. " Samuel tossed his head in that direction, then slumped back down. "It's Polly, from the boarding house. I killed her."

"You—?" Lawrence Shaw's words halted in his throat. He looked around at the curious faces gathering in the open doors of the Little Egypt Saloon. "Shhh, no you didn't, kid. Keep quiet." He held his face close to Samuel's, speaking in a guarded tone just between the two of them.

"Yes, I did. I didn't mean to—"

"I said you didn't." Shaw spoke in a harsh whisper. He shook him. "Listen to me. Keep your mouth shut out here. We'll get you to the doctor's office. Then you can tell me all about it."

"Her sister, Vera, is dead, too." Samuel shook his lowered head slowly. "I believe she's in the boarding house, in the first room at the head of the stairs."

Cherokee and Shaw looked at one another as the drinking crowd gathered along the boardwalk. Shaw leaned in close to Samuel's face. "You're not saying . . . ?"

"No. Not me. Polly killed her. I'm sure you'll find her body up there. Polly took up with the man who killed the store owner. His name is Ellsworth. I almost had him . . . but then she stabbed me. He got away."

On the boardwalk one of the drinkers chuckled and said to the others, "Damned if he don't look like he got in an argument with a hay sickle." He chuckled again, this time a thin man beside him joined in.

Shaw spun toward him, pointing a finger. "You, funny

man, take laughing boy beside you, and both of you go check out the boarding house."

"Do what?" one of them asked.

"You heard me, check out the first room at the top of the stairs. Get going."

Both men shrugged, looking uncertain. "Check it out how?"

"Just go there. Kick in the door if you have to. Come back and tell me what you see."

"Whoa," one of them said. "I don't want to go poking my nose somewhere it doesn't belong."

"It's not a question of whether or not you're going to do it." Shaw glared at them both. "The question is: Do you want to do it *with* or *without* my boot sticking out of your rump?"

As the two men shuffled off down the boardwalk, Shaw stepped around the buggy, unwrapped the top corner of the bloody sheet, and looked down at the cold dead face of the young woman. He shook his head, recovered the face, and said to the rest of the men on the boardwalk, "A couple of you get her over to the undertaker's, and don't even *think* about asking me what happened to her right now."

He stepped back around the buggy. "Come on, Cherokee. Let's get this mess over to the doctor's." He looked at Samuel's face again and shook his head. "If he keeps sewing you up, your head's going to look like a map of Oregon." Shaw glanced down at the big cur standing near their feet as he and Cherokee Cousins raised Samuel's arms up over their shoulders between them. "What about him? Is he all right? He's got blood all over him."

"He's all right." Samuel stood on unsteady legs and looked down at Blue. "That's my blood on him."

"Did he help any? Did he try to bite anybody?" Cherokee asked.

"No. Blue's not a biter," Samuel said as the three of them moved off toward the doctor's office.

"Then maybe you better start teaching him to," Cherokee

Cousins added. "The rate you're going, kid, you need all the help you can get." He cast a sidelong glance at Samuel's bloody face. "Give him to me for a few days . . . I'll teach him to bite." Behind them, Blue padded along with his tongue hanging out.

"He'll learn on his own," Samuel said, his jaw somewhat numb, his words slurring.

"That's right, kid," Shaw offered. "If it's in him to bite, he'll learn on his own. If it's not in him to bite, what good will it do to teach him?" Shaw looked over at Cherokee Cousins with a trace of a smile. "You're part Indian, you're supposed to know this stuff."

"I do know it." Cherokee Cousins gazed forward along the dark street. "One of them better learn to bite before this place eats them alive."

"Don't worry about that, Cherokee," Lawrence Shaw said. "He's going to make it. He's just a big pup yet. He's still got a lot to learn." No one was sure if he was taking about the dog, or Samuel.

Chapter 11

The three horsemen rode abreast slowly, making their way down the middle of the dark street. When they saw the small group of townsmen step down off the porch of the boarding house carrying the blanket-wrapped corpse and place it on a gurney, the horseman in the middle turned in his saddle and said, "What have we here, some late-night callers?" The other two horsemen turned slightly in their saddles in passing. At the head of the group of townsmen, they saw two lit torches leading the way. Firelight flickered across grim faces.

A stiff arm swung down from beneath the blanket and one of the townsmen stooped and raised it and put it back in place on the gurney. One of the riders grunted under his breath. "If they're calling on that one they sure won't get an answer." He cocked his head to one side in curiosity and added, "That's was a *woman's* arm—did you see it?"

"No." The rider in the middle gazed forward once more and heeled his horse a bit. "There's only one thing I want to see here, Ed. And I want to see it real soon and get it over with."

"Don't worry, Tommy. Fast Larry's here. He's been here over a month." Ed Gribbons gazed back and forth along the dark street from beneath his wide, low hat brim. "If I didn't know better, I'd swear I could already smell him." He allowed a tight smile and heeled forward. "Just think, this time tomorrow, you'll be *Faster* Tommy Deebs, the man who shot him. Hope you don't get a big head afterwards and forget me and Tomblin here." He cut his eyes to the third man. "What do you think, Tomblin? Is he going to still know us after tomorrow?"

Leo Tomblin caught his horse up to them a step. "I wouldn't be here if I thought otherwise."

"And neither would you, Ed." Tommy Deebs still stared straight ahead. "Good backup is hard to find. Keep me covered and keep this thing fair. That's all I ask." He watched the townsmen carry the corpse into the funeral parlor where a single lantern glowed in the window.

The riders stepped down at the hitch rail outside the Little Egypt Saloon, spun their horses' reins, and stepped up onto the boardwalk. Walking in through the swinging doors, Gribbons and Tomblin lagged back a step, letting Tommy Deebs make a slow deliberate entrance. Deebs stopped just inside the doors and began loosening his right glove one finger at a time. A big Colt with dark smooth walnut grips rested across his stomach in a Slim-Jim style holster. Behind the bar, Thurman froze for a second. But then he cleared his throat and said in a strained but cordial voice, "Evening, gentlemen. Welcome to the Little Egypt. What can I get you?"

"Fast Larry Shaw," Tommy Deebs said bluntly. He was down to loosening the last finger of his glove now, looking slowly around the nearly empty saloon. He noted the empty mugs, the half-empty bottles and shot glasses along the bar, and the cigar stubs and litter on the floor. "Where is he?"

"Well . . ." Thurman offered a nervous shrug. "As you can see, he's not here." He nodded at the far end of the bar where Clayton Mumpe and the old banjo player stood staring above their mugs of beer, the banjo player with his battered banjo slung up on his shoulder. "There's been a terrible killing in town," Thurman added. "Everybody's either turned out for it, or gone on home to tell their families about it."

"A terrible killing, huh?" Tommy Deebs leered at

Tomblin and Gribbons, who flanked him with their hands poised near their pistols. "Mister, you ain't seen nothing yet." He finished taking off his glove and walked straight to the bar, one slow step at a time, his big spurs ringing with each step like small church bells.

At the doctor's office, Lawrence Shaw and Cherokee Cousins stood over Samuel Burrack, watching as the old doctor finished up his work and patted a small wad of gauze against the blood seeping from the long line of stitches. "Boy, I hope this the last I see of you for a while." He examined the other stitches atop Samuel's head. "I'd like to get one wound finished up before I start on another. These will be ready to come out in another day or two. Think you can lay low that long? Give things a chance to grow back together a little?"

"I'll try," Samuel said in a wry tone.

When the old doctor stepped back and wiped his hands on a towel, Lawrence Shaw placed a hand on his shoulder. "Doc, you look like you could use a cup of coffee. Want to step out and get yourself one?"

"It's too late at night for me to be drinking coffee—" He stopped, seeing the look on Shaw's face. "Oh . . . well, come to think of it, *yes*, I believe I will just go fetch myself a cup." He flipped the stained towel over his shoulder, walked out of the room, and closed the door behind himself.

Shaw and Cherokee moved a step closer to Samuel, who sat on a short wooden stool. "Now, tell us the whole story, kid," Shaw said under his breath, "only forget the part about you shooting the woman."

"But I did shoot her." Samuel looked up, back and forth between them. "Not saying it doesn't change the fact that I did it. I'm sorry it happened, but she tried to kill me. I acted before I could stop myself."

"I understand, kid. Just tell us everything else."

As Samuel told them the story, they nodded, glancing at

one another. When Samuel finished, he let out a sigh and slumped on the stool. "It was stupid of me to go in there on my own. If I hadn't, maybe Polly would still be alive."

"Don't blame yourself," Cherokee Cousins replied. "She'd already killed once. She knew which side she was on. Nobody forced her to take up with that snake. It was her own doing."

"I'm sure his name is Ellsworth, and he's the one who killed my friend. Daggett told me his name. I heard the woman call him Sherman."

"Yep," Cousins said. "As soon as you said his name was Ellsworth, I realized it's that trash up from Texas. He threw in with Junior Lake right before Junior stole my horse. I never met him. But I've heard he's a straight-up lunatic. He would have killed her himself once he was through with her." Cherokee shook his head. "What makes a woman throw in with somebody like that? She must've been as crazy as he is. Don't blame yourself too harshly."

"That doesn't change the fact that I killed her." Samuel looked down at the floor. "I've got to live with it, I reckon."

Lawrence Shaw spoke in a quiet tone. "Kid, if she was trying to kill you, that's self-defense. Try to put it out of your mind. But don't go around telling people about it. It's not the kind of thing you want folks to know. You don't want to be branded as a woman-shooter."

"They're going to know," Samuel said. "As soon as the sheriff gets back he'll have to hear what happened. I won't lie to him."

Shaw and Cherokee Cousins cut one another a glance. "Listen to me, Samuel." Shaw put a gloved hand on his shoulder. "I'm not asking you to lie to the sheriff. He left me in charge, so until he gets back, I'm calling the shots here. Anybody wants to know what happened, you tell them to ask me, all right?"

"Yeah, but—"

"No 'buts', kid. This is the way I want you to do it. You won't be lying. I'll report it to the sheriff myself. You don't need to mention it again."

"If he asks, I'll have to tell him." Samuel gave him a determined look.

"That's fair enough—but he won't ask, I promise. As far as he's concerned, Sherman Ellsworth killed her."

"I can't abide with that." Samuel raised up from the stool. "I did it, and I'll own up to it. I know you're trying to help me, but I can't blame it on Ellsworth, even if he is a killer."

"Noble pilgrim," Cherokee Cousins whispered under his breath.

"What did he say?" Samuel asked.

"Nothing, kid, forget it." Lawrence Shaw grimaced and let out a breath. "Play it the way you've got to, then . . . only think it over until the sheriff gets back. As far as I'm concerned, you didn't mention it to me, all right?"

Samuel nodded. "All right." He looked back and forth between them again. "I know you're both only trying to help me, and I appreciate it. You both think I'm young and don't know anything. That's why you call me kid, although there's really not much difference in our ages." He shrugged. "But I know that what I do today, I've got to live with tomorrow. That's all I can go by, till I learn something better." He picked up his bloodstained hat from atop a peg on the wall, putting it down gently onto his head.

Lawrence Shaw looked at Cherokee Cousins, then back at Samuel with a slight smile. He seemed to consider something for a second, then he said, "You've managed to bring in one of your friend's killers, and you've put another one on the run. You've even uncovered a murder. You must've learned something. They haven't killed you yet."

Cherokee Cousins nodded. "I believe you're a lawman in the making, Sam. The question is, what kind?"

"If I am, I can't change it. None of this is anything I

asked for. Trouble came to me. How else could I have handled it?"

"Don't listen to us," Shaw said. "Stay like you are, kid— I mean, *Samuel*. Trouble with people like me and Cherokee is that we do things our own way so long, we start thinking it's the only way."

"Well. As soon as the sheriff gets back, I just want to square up with him, then get on my way."

"Yeah, me, too." Shaw adjusted his hat on his brow. "Home is sounding better to me all the time."

"I'm not talking about going home," Samuel said. "I'm talking about going after this Sherman Ellsworth. For what he did to Davey Riley . . . for what he did to that girl. The bartender was right about these kind of men being an infection. The longer they go unattended, the worse they spread."

Cherokee Cousins chuckled. "You're out of your mind. That was just bar talk. Ellsworth didn't do anything she didn't want done."

"Maybe so, but I'm going anyway. I need to get it settled myself." Samuel's voice softened. "Before she died, she asked me to pray for her."

"Then pray for her." Cherokee Cousins smiled, tossing the idea away. "Praying's cheap."

But Samuel saw nothing in it to smile about. "You don't see what she meant, do you? She was asking me to make it right somehow. Stopping Ellsworth is the only way I can think of to do it."

"Hold on, Samuel." Lawrence Shaw raised a hand toward him. "You don't want to start down *that* trail, especially over the likes of her. Leave Ellsworth and his kind to the law . . . or to fate. Those kind of men don't last long. Something will catch up to him. "

"Ranger Sazes warned me that it's easy to get caught up in that outlaw world—looks like he was right. I might have put it away had I not looked into Ellsworth's eyes. After seeing him face-to-face, coming that close to catching him, then seeing him get away." Samuel drew in a tight breath. "I've got to bring him down, not just for the woman, but for Davey . . . and for myself."

"For once I have to agree with Sazes," Shaw said in a cautioning tone. "If you get drawn into that world, you might never get out."

"I know. But I am in it, whether I meant to be or not. One thing just leads to another with these killers. I'm going to carry these scars from now on. I might just as well see it through."

Before Shaw could say anything more, a soft knocking sound came from the door causing the three of them to turn; the doctor's voice came low, unimposing, yet with a tone of urgency. "Mr. Shaw? Someone from the saloon's here to see you. It sounds pretty darned important. There's—"

Shaw opened the door, interrupting him. "Yes, what is it?"

The doctor stepped aside, gesturing a hand toward the banjo player who stood with a worried look on his face. "It's me, sir," the musician said, his hat hanging in his tense hand. "Thurman over at the saloon sent me to tell you there's three men asking for you." His eyes widened as he spoke. "They know I came here. I best warn ya, they've got their bark on."

"Do they now?" Shaw looked unconcerned. "Well, I better get over there and peel their bark, I suppose. Did they tell you their names?"

"Yes, sir. The one with the most bark on, he said tell you it's Tommy Deebs looking for ya. Said you'd get the idea why he's here."

"I've got it all right. Sounds like Deebs finally found something he can do with his pistol besides shoot the heads off of jack rabbits."

"I'll back you up on this." Cherokee Cousins made the offer and began taking his glove from his right hand.

"Why? There's only three of them." Shaw raised the big pistol from his holster and checked it, spinning the cylinder down his forearm, and letting it hang loose in his hand down his side. "Anyway, I don't plan on shooting Tommy Deebs. He's another nobody. I bet Gribbons and Tomblin got him all talked full of himself. If they're the other two with him, I've got no problem."

"I'm still backing you up." Cherokee loosened his pistol in his holster. "So don't argue with me. This will even us up for you vouching for me to the sheriff. Now I can start beating you at billiards without feeling bad about it."

"Oh? You've been *letting* me win?" Shaw gave him a skeptical look.

"No," Cherokee Cousins said, pushing a dark strand of hair back behind his ear and adjusting his holster belt, "I just haven't been letting you lose . . ."

The Little Egypt stood dim-lit and silent as a tomb. The squeak of the swinging doors sounded loud and long as Lawrence Shaw pushed through them slowly and stepped inside, his pistol already cocked, hanging down his thigh in his right hand. Behind the bar, Thurman stood rigid, a sheen of sweat glistening on his troubled brow. At the billiard table, Ed Gribbons and Leo Tomblin stood leaning back against the table's edge. Between them, with one hip propped up on the green felt table rail, Tommy Deebs sat rolling a billiard ball back and forth idly beneath the tip of his finger.

"Well, Tommy Deebs." Shaw's voice sounded calm, almost playful, as he stepped slowly and diagonally across the floor toward the bar. "A banjo player just brought me word that you'd like to see me—I couldn't imagine what for." A trace of a smile played across Shaw's lips, then vanished. Deebs's eyes went to Shaw's pistol and stopped there as Gribbons and Tomblin stepped away a foot or more, giving him room.

"Is that how you answer a challenge these days, Shaw?" Deebs stopped rolling the ball and nodded at the cocked pistol. "You come in with an edge?"

"Oh, this?" Shaw stopped at the bar and raised the pistol

slowly, jiggling it a bit in his hand then laying it down atop the bar. He rested his right hand a few inches from the butt. "Let's just put it right here for the time being. I wouldn't want to give your friends heart failure."

Leo Tomblin sneered. "Talk big now, Shaw. But when this is over you'll be—"

"Keep quiet, Leo." Ed Gribbons raised a hand toward him, keeping him from taking a step forward. "Let Tommy do the talking. We're just backup."

"Talk?" Tommy Deebs straightened up off the table, rolling the ball away to a corner pocket. "There's nothing to talk about." His eyes fixed on Shaw's. "I'm here to take you down, Fast Larry. That's all the talk needed."

Ed Gribbons whispered, "That's telling him, Tommy." Tomblin stood tense, ready.

"So, you want to be a duelist? Or is it *shootist* they call it now?" Lawrence Shaw raised his left hand slowly and pushed up his hat brim. "What's the oddsmakers paying on me these days?"

"You keep up on your own odds, Shaw. This ain't about money to me. Don't try putting me off." Deebs clenched his jaws tight. "I came here to see who's best."

"Then I'm sorry to disappoint you, Deebs. But the truth is, I've been thinking about retiring—hanging up my gun so to speak."

"What?" Deebs looked curious. "You don't retire. This is one game that plays on for keeps."

Shaw chuckled under his breath. "Apparently you didn't read the article in *Harper's* a while back." He smiled and went on before Deebs could respond. "According to them, this whole fast-draw, dueling thing was just a passing trend. They say it's about played itself out—said it's come and gone like French fashion wear." He shook his head. "Few years from now, it'll all be history and old-men tales. Yeah, I'm ready to hang it up."

"Hogwash!" Deebs had been staring, incredulous. Now he seemed to snap out of it. He worked the fingers of his right hand open and closed a few times, loosening them. "If you're retiring, what are you still doing hanging out in saloons? What's that big bone-handled gun still hanging there for? You're scared, that's all. To hell with *Harper's*. You heard what I did over in Principal to Rambling Joe Phipps. Now you don't want no part of me."

"Easy, boy." Shaw's voice took on a warning note, seeing Deebs work himself up to making a move. "I said I'm *thinking* about retiring—didn't say I've made up my mind yet." He gestured a nod over toward Clayton Mumpe at the corner table. "But I refused to fight him. How's he going to take it? Me shooting you three after turning him down?"

"Us *three . . . ?*" Tomblin cut a sidelong glance at Gribbons.

"I can fix that." Deebs spread a threatening grin toward Clayton Mumpe, then looked back at Shaw. "I'll shoot that cockeyed idiot first."

Clayton Mumpe stood up away from the table, not saying a word. He inched to the doors and slipped through them as Lawrence Shaw let out a breath and looked Gribbons and Tomblin up and down. "Well, Tommy, since you've gone to all this trouble, I suppose it would be rude of me not to oblige you. But before we start, I need to let your friends know my new policy regarding bystanders." His eyes fixed on Gribbons, then Tomblin as he spoke. "As soon as this commences, I'm going to shoot them first . . . then it'll just be you and me."

"If you're through running your mouth, Shaw, let's get on with it." Tommy Deebs nodded at Shaw's pistol on the bar. "Holster it. Step away from the bar."

But Lawrence Shaw ignored Deebs and said to the other two in a quiet tone, "Ready, boys?"

"Hold on a second, damn it." Gribbons raised his gun hand chest-high. "Me and Leo ain't shootists. We're just backup scorekeepers, you could say."

"I know." Shaw kept his gaze leveled on Ed Gribbons,

seeing the paleness spread across his face. "But that's my new policy. I always hated the ones who just like to watch. Ain't that all backup really means? You don't have the nuts and stomach for it yourselves—you put somebody else out front? If he wins, you make a couple of bucks, get to go around bragging that he's your buddy? If he loses, you haven't lost much. Hell, you might have him bet both ways." Shaw shook his head side to side, real slow, his fingertips tapping softly on the bartop. "This time we're doing things a whole different way—make you both *active participants*. Be proud, boys. Your names might even appear in the next copy of *Harper's*."

"Tommy, it ain't supposed to go this way." Gribbons whispered out the side of his mouth.

"Shut up, Gribbons. He can't take *me*. Even if he could, he can't take all three of us. He's just wants to rattle everybody a little. It's his style." Tommy Deebs spread a nasty grin. "Nice try, Shaw. Now let's get it done. Just you and me."

At the swinging doors, Cherokee Cousins stepped in and to one side, his hand poised near the pistol on his hip. "You were right, Shaw." He looked at the three gunmen. "They didn't believe you could handle all three of them."

"What's that half-breed doing here?" Tommy Deebs didn't look as eager as he had a moment earlier. "Cousins, you stay the hell out of this."

"He's *my* backup, Tommy." Shaw shrugged. "You've got two. Seems only fair I should have at least one."

"You've got two," said Samuel Burrack from within the shadows around the far corner of the bar, near the back door. Samuel stepped forward to the edge of the dim lantern light and leveled the rifle toward Leo Tomblin, the sound of the big rifle's hammer cocking in his hand.

The sound of Samuel's voice took Shaw by surprise, but he managed to keep it from showing. "So there, I have two." Shaw stood silent now. He wasn't going to be the next one to speak.

After a tense moment, Tommy Deebs let out a relenting breath. "A buffalo rifle? I never took Fast Larry Shaw for a coward. Looks like I was wrong." His gun hand came up away from his holster.

"But you're alive . . . for now, anyway." Shaw shrugged. "You really *should* read the article. There's better ways to make sport." He cast his glance at Gribbons and Tomblin, knowing that Tommy Deebs had just folded his hand. "What about you, backup boys? I don't want you leaving here with your feelings hurt. Want to go on with it?" His gaze turned instantly dark. "Or, have you had enough watching for one night?"

"Come on, Tommy, this is bad," Gribbons whispered under his breath. "You'll get another chance."

"Huh-uh." Deebs shook his head. "I brought it to him, he turned it down. Far as I'm concerned that's the same as him admitting I'm faster. The way I see it, I won this one. I've made my mark. Right, Shaw?"

Shaw smiled, his fingertips still close to the cocked pistol on the bar. "Sure. Why not? I've got nothing to prove. Now go tell the world how you backed me down."

"I will." Deebs moved slowly toward the door, the other two moving right along behind him. "If you ever get tired of hearing it, you come see me . . . we'll settle it then." When Shaw didn't respond, Deebs stopped for a second at the swinging doors and turned his gaze to Cherokee Cousins. "I meant no offense, calling you half-breed. And I ain't forgot the ten dollars I still owe you from back in Abilene. I'm just a little short on cash right now."

Cherokee Cousins nodded. "No offense taken, Deebs . . . pay me when you can."

When the three men had left the Little Egypt, Thurman ran his left hand across his brow. He lifted the sawed-off shotgun from beneath the bar, uncocked it, and put it back down. "Damn it, Shaw, maybe it's not a bad idea after all, you leaving here. I'm getting too old for this kind of carrying on." He chuckled and hooked three beer mugs onto his thumbs and stuck them under the tap. But then he stopped and looked at Shaw. "They won't be coming right back, will they, like that fool the other day?"

"Naw, they're finished for tonight." Shaw picked up his pistol, uncocked it, and spun it into his holster. "They'll go make camp somewhere and talk about it all night. Deebs is just doing what I did myself at one time." As he spoke, Clayton Mumpe slipped back through the doors, slid back into a chair at the front corner table, and resumed his twisted stare. "Better give him one, too, Thurman. All this moving around has probably got him thirsty."

Samuel Burrack came forward from his spot in the shadows, his hat brim down across the line of stitches on his head, the new stitches in his cheek still leaking a thin trickle of blood. "Samuel, Samuel." Shaw let out a breath. "You're full of surprises tonight. Would you have shot those fools?"

"I owe you a lot, Shaw." Samuel took a bandanna from his pocket and touched it to his wounded cheek. Shaw waited, but Samuel said no more. From the direction of the back door, the big cur slipped forward from the shadows and stood at Samuel's right boot heel. Shaw looked down at the dog, then back up at Samuel Burrack, and smiled as if already knowing the full answer. He turned to Cherokee Cousins as Cherokee walked over to the bar. "Ten dollars, huh? Tell me something, Cherokee. Is there anybody anywhere who doesn't owe you money for a pool game?"

"You don't . . . yet," Cherokee Cousins said. "Want me to rack them up?" He nodded toward the billiard table and the pool rack on the wall.

"Sure, go ahead. Why not?" Lawrence Shaw hooked his gloved hand into the mug handle and raised a foamy sip of beer. "There won't be any more games for me, once I get home to my woman." He turned to Samuel Burrack. "Take a good look around, Samuel. This is the world you're stepping into, and the one I'm stepping out of. It's a hateful, crazy place. Most honest working people don't realize it even exists. This is the dark underbelly of society . . . gunmen, murderers, thugs, and thieves." He winked. "Now if you'll excuse me"—he wagged his thumb toward Cherokee Cousins—"I better go put this pool hustler in his place." Outside, three horses galloped away into the night.

Chapter 12

Over the next three days, the wound on Samuel Burrack's face had lost its tender puffiness and began to heal properly. The stitches atop his head had been removed by the old doctor, and although there would be a lasting scar, Samuel could tell that once his hair grew back, it would be hardly noticeable. At Lawrence Shaw's invitation, rather than stay in the crowded hotel, Samuel had bunked in one of the three vacant cells in the sheriff's office. He stood examining his wounded cheek in the small shaving mirror hanging from the bars above a shaving mug and a pan of water. Two cells down, Andrew Daggett lay snoring in the early morning light.

"Look at it this way," Cherokee Cousins said, leaned back in the chair behind the sheriff's desk with a boot propped up on it. "A scar that bad . . . it's like carrying a circled date on a calendar. Every time you see it or touch it, you'll remind yourself who you were before, and what you've become since. You could get some good of it, if you pay attention to what it tells you."

"I suppose so." Samuel touched a careful fingertip to his cheek and turned away from the shaving mirror. "All I want right now is to get it healed and get on the trail." He stepped out of the cell over to the pot of hot coffee atop the potbellied stove, and poured himself a cupful. "Hadn't been for Shaw talking me out of it, I'd already be gone."

Cousins nodded. "A couple more days won't hurt anything. Never get in too big a hurry hunting down an outlaw.

I learned that riding for Judge Parker. If it's meant for you to get Sherman Ellsworth, you'll get him." Cousins shrugged. "Meanwhile, how's the shooting lessons going?"

"I've been a crack shot since I was a kid." Samuel adjusted the worn holster belt on his hip as he sipped his coffee. "But this gunslinging is new to me." Lawrence Shaw had found a used holster and a scuffed-up .45 Colt in a trunk marked CONFISCATED FIREARMS and had given them to him. Every day for a couple of hours, he and Lawrence Shaw rode out onto the sand flats where Shaw taught him to draw and fire. "Shaw still does most of the shooting, though. Says I'll learn more about gun fighting watching him shoot than I will doing it myself."

"He's right." Cousins tipped his hat brim up and looked him in the eyes. "You could practice drawing from now till the end of time and never get as good as Shaw—he was born gifted with a fast hand and a good aim, like some men are born with an ear for music. Watch what he does and pick up what you can from it."

"It's hard to see much, as fast as he is. He has me watch his eyes and guess when he's getting ready to draw."

Cousins spread a thin, knowing smile. "Yep, he's teaching you right. Like you said, you already knew how to fire a gun. He's just showing you the things that will keep you alive. If you can learn to tell when Fast Larry is getting ready to draw, I guarantee you, nobody else will ever get the drop on you. Just hope to God you never have to use what he shows you."

"I know. " Samuel stood silent for a second. "What about you, Cherokee? When are you heading out after Junior Lake?"

"Oh, I'm in no hurry now—the paint horse is dead, so there's no chance of getting back what he took from me. I'll wait and see how Outrider Sazes does. If Sazes misses Junior, I'll take a run at him. I know where he and his gang used to hole up down in Old Mexico. It's a place the Mexicans call *Cruz de la piedra de la sangre*."

"Blood Stone Crossing?" Samuel asked, checking his translation.

"Yep. The outlaws all call it 'Blood Rock.' Outrider Sazes won't go there because it's in Mexico. Sazes might do a lot of crazy things, but he won't cross the border. Neither will I when I'm wearing a badge, riding for Parker."

"But you have been there?" Samuel studied his dark eyes, but they revealed nothing.

Cherokee Cousins seemed to weigh his words. When he did speak, all he said was, "The difference between me and Sazes is that I don't always wear a badge . . ."

Lawrence Shaw had finished breakfast and left the restaurant. He was out on the street headed back for the sheriff's office when he noticed the three horses belonging to Tommy Deebs, Ed Gribbons, and Leo Tomblin hitched outside the Little Egypt Saloon. Thurman saw Lawrence Shaw looking at the horses from the boardwalk of the saloon, and he stepped down and hurried over to him, wiping his hands on a bar towel. "Listen to me, Shaw. They ain't acting like they did the other day. Deebs said they only came in to pick up some whiskey before heading back south. They'll be gone in less than an hour. I don't think they're looking for any trouble."

"Good enough." Lawrence Shaw looked up and down the street, then back at Thurman. "I'll stay away and keep an eye on their horses from the sheriff's office. This is my last day in town. I'd like it to pass quietly."

"Then you really are leaving this time?"

"Yes. I got a telegraph awhile ago from Sheriff Kemp. He's over in Humbly. He's called off the hunt and headed back. Should be here by tomorrow morning." Shaw smiled. "I'm headed out as soon as his boot touches the ground. Sell Deebs his whiskey and send him on his way. I'm out of business, for good."

"You got it, Fast Larry." Thurman slung the bar towel over his shoulder. "You'll be stopping by later, though, won't ya? You wouldn't leave without having a last drink with me?"

"You know better than that." Shaw touched a finger to his hat brim and moved off across the street. "I'll be by later—you can count on it."

On his way back to the Little Egypt Saloon, Thurman said good morning to the telegraph clerk in passing, and noted the pale blank expression on the young man's face as the clerk hurried past him with no reply. Thurman stopped and turned, and watched curiously as the clerk caught up to Lawrence Shaw halfway across the street toward the sheriff's office. He saw Lawrence Shaw slow to a halt when the clerk caught up to him. Thurman cocked his head slightly to one side, seeing the clerk take a step back when he handed Shaw the folded telegram.

Shaw stood with the telegram in his hand, glancing up at the clerk before unfolding it. "If this is about Sheriff Kemp coming back, the other clerk already told me."

The telegraph clerk stood rigid, his voice sounding grave but unsteady as he spoke. "No, sir, it's not about the sheriff. I—I think you better read it, sir . . . please."

Shaw, seeing the clerk's condition, chuckled under his breath as he opened the folded telegram. "Boy, settle down. No news can be all that bad, can it?" His gloved fingers smoothed the paper out on the palm of his hand.

Inside the sheriff's office, Cherokee Cousins had stood up from the desk and stretched, pressing a hand to the small of his back. Stepping over for a cup of coffee from atop the stove, he caught sight of Lawrence Shaw and the telegraph clerk through the dusty window. "Looks like Shaw is back. Feel like going over for some breakfast yourself? If you do, how about bringing back a plate of gravy and biscuits for the prisoner?"

"Sure thing," Samuel replied. "What about you? Can I bring you something?"

Cherokee stood with the coffeepot in one hand, a cup in the other. But he didn't answer. Nor did he pour. He stood looking out the window as if transfixed. "Jesus . . ." He whispered to himself, seeing Lawrence Shaw sink almost to his knees in the dirt street, his head shaking back and forth, the telegram clasped tight in his gloved hand. "What the—" Cherokee dropped the pot down onto the stove and pitched the cup to the side.

"Cherokee? What is it?" Samuel Burrack stepped forward, his eyes following the direction of Cherokee's gaze.

"I don't know." They both saw the clerk reach out with an arm and try to place it across Shaw's shoulder—Shaw straightened up and slung it away and walked in an aimless circle, then nearly went down to his knees once more before catching himself. Shaw wadded the telegram and tossed it away on a drift of breeze. Then he walked off as if in a trance along the dirt street. "Come on, kid." Cherokee hurried to the door and swung it open. "Shaw! Wait up!" He yelled as he ran down to the clerk who stood staring, frightened, bewildered. But Shaw didn't seem to hear him.

Cherokee spun facing the clerk as Samuel Burrack stooped down and picked up the crumpled telegram and righted it in his hands. "It's about his wife, mister!" The telegraph clerk spoke quick and nervous, stepping back from Cherokee Cousins with his hands raised chest-high. He swallowed a dry knot in his throat and leveled his shaky voice. "She's . . . well, I'm afraid she's *dead,* sir."

Samuel ran his eyes across the telegram and let out a sigh, passing it on to Cherokee Cousins. "Lord, Cherokee, it's true."

"Let me see that." Cousins snapped the telegram from his hand and read it. Then he let the paper hang down his side in his fingertips. He gazed off to the far end of the street where Lawrence Shaw had disappeared into the livery barn. "This will kill him," Cherokee said in a whisper.

"I better go see about him." Samuel started to turn toward the livery barn, but Cherokee grabbed his arm, stopping him.

"See about him how? What can you say? Nothing, that's

what. Leave him alone for a minute. With Shaw it's best to wait and see how he's going to handle it." He turned loose Samuel's arm, and added, "I know you mean well . . . but stay put for now." He looked around the street, folding the telegram and holding it tight in his hand. "Damn it, Shaw . . ." He whispered under his breath.

Thurman had seen how Lawrence Shaw acted, and now he came trotting over from the boardwalk. "What's wrong with Shaw?" Before Cousins could even answer, Thurman dealt the telegraph clerk a cold stare. "What the hell did you say to him?"

The clerk slunk back without a word. Cherokee Cousins stepped between Thurman and the frightened young man. "Go on back to your office." As the clerk turned and left in a hurry, Cherokee turned back to Thurman. "Shaw's wife is dead."

"Oh, no." Thurman pressed a hand to his forehead. "But how? Why?"

Cherokee handed him the telegram and looked over at the three horses at the hitch rail as Thurman read it. "Isn't that Tommy Deebs's horse?" Cherokee asked, already seeing dark possibilities taking shape in his mind.

"Yeah," Thurman answered as he gazed down reading. "I told Shaw, though, they're not looking for trouble. They're leaving any minute. Shaw said it's okay."

"That was then." Cherokee snatched the wrinkled telegram from his hand. "Maybe you better tell them to clear on out, right now. I don't know what this is going to do to Shaw. All he talked about was how much he loved that woman." Cherokee's voice wavered as he spoke. He looked down and shook his head, "Christ, Shaw," and when he raised his face again, he blinked his eyes and rubbed a finger across them as if clearing them of dust.

"You don't think he'd . . . ?" Thurman's worried eyes searched his.

Cherokee Cousins let out a long breath, looking away from Thurman and Samuel Burrack as he spoke. "I don't

know *what* I think." His eyes fixed on the livery barn at the
end of the street, where at the wide closed doors, a drift of
dust spun sidelong on a passing breeze. "But if they're leaving anyway, now is a good time to do it."

At the end of the bar inside the Little Egypt Saloon, Tommy
Deebs and his backup partners stood listening to Thurman
with their shot glasses in their hands. On the bar lay a pair
of saddlebags with a half-dozen whiskey bottles sticking out
of them. When Thurman finished telling them what had
happened, Deebs spread his hands along the edge of the bar
and looked down at his boots, tapping his fingers for a
second. "That poor sumbitch . . ."

After a second of silence while Tomblin and Gribbons
stood staring down into their whiskey in contemplation,
Deebs raised his face back up to Thurman and said, "Still, I
don't see what it's got to do with how soon we leave town."
His face took on a flat unyielding expression. "I finished it
with Shaw. I even left it open so's if he wants to settle
things, it's his choice." He shrugged and tossed back his
shot of whiskey. "But damned if I'll go running out of here
with my tail between my legs."

"That's not what this is, Mr. Deebs," Thurman said. "The
man has just lost his wife. Out of respect, wouldn't it be best
all around if the three of you simply took your whiskey and
left?"

"Respect, huh?" Gribbons grunted. "I'm sorry as hell
about his wife. But if I ever had any *respect* for Fast Larry,
I never knew about it. " He cut a glance to Leo Tomblin.
"Fact is, he talked to me and Leo here like a couple of dogs
the other day." Gribbons reached out to the saddlebags on
the bar, pulled out a bottle, pulled the cork from it with his
teeth. "So, nossir, I see no need to get in a hurry." He refilled
his glass and stood the bottle beside it. "We might stay till
these saddlebags are empty, then buy some more." He
grinned and winked at Leo Tomblin.

"Same here," Leo chuckled, raising his shot glass in a toast. "I say we drink to that poor dead woman—"

"Cut it out, Leo." Tommy Deebs had been thinking it over. Now he looked at the two of them. "Maybe the bartender's right. This is about who's fastest with a pistol, not about personal matters. I never disliked Shaw personally. He just happened to be standing where I wanted to be. I'm there now, so let's drink up and head south."

"Backing a man down ain't never as good as beating him straight up, Tommy. Let's be honest about it. It ain't like Shaw went crawling out of here on his knees and elbows. Looked more to me like he just didn't want to fool with ya— maybe thought you was a waste of time."

"Yeah?" Tommy Deebs upended his glass and let out a whiskey hiss. "That's not what you said the other night around the campfire."

"Well, that was different." Gribbons's voice was starting to sound thick with whiskey. "I figured that was the best we were going to get out of this thing." He refilled his glass. "But under these new circumstances, can't you see the opportunity that's being handed to you?"

Thurman backed away, drifted down the bar, reached under it, and without picking up the sawed-off shotgun, he cocked both hammers, and moved on, the three men not seeing a thing. He filled a mug of beer, walked to the other end of the bar and slid it before the old banjo player. Under his breath he said, "This one is on the house. Drink up and clear out. There'll be no music in here today."

Chapter 13

Once the news of Lawrence Shaw's wife had spread throughout the town, the streets of Wakely grew quiet and empty. As if upon hearing rumors of a coming storm, the townsfolk had drawn back, seeming to hold their breaths, and waited. Nearly an hour had passed. Nothing stirred but a drift of dust on a hot breeze, and the listless motion of the big blue cur as he trotted back from the livery barn and returned once more to Samuel's side.

"Good boy, Blue," Samuel whispered, reaching a hand down to scratch the dog's ears. "Now stay here with us." Across the street, a peal of drunken laughter rose and fell above the swinging doors of the Little Egypt Saloon. Hearing it, Samuel looked up at Cherokee Cousins.

"It's been long enough," Cousins said in a hushed tone, looking first at the saloon, then back over to the closed doors of the livery barn. "I better go try to talk to him. Trouble is, I know Shaw as far as shooting pool or talking road-talk." He hesitated for a second. "But, damn . . . how do you talk about something like this?"

"I'll go with you," Samuel offered.

"Naw . . ." Cousins kicked a boot toe at something unseen in the dirt. "I'll do it. Shaw and I speak the same language. You stay here."

Cousins leveled his hat brim and started forward. But then he stopped at the sight of Ed Gribbons moving away from the Little Egypt Saloon and cutting across toward the livery barn with a bottle of rye in his hand. "Oh, no. What's this idiot up to?" He raced forward.

Outside the livery barn doors, Ed Gribbons stopped, and pitched the bottle onto the softer ground near the doors. There was dark laughter in his drunken voice when he called cut, "Hey, Shaw! There's a drink for you! Heard what happened, figured you could use one. Bet you ain't standing so tall now, are you, gunslinger? Deebs says he'd like you to come by the saloon so's he can pay his condolences. Maybe sing a few hymns—"

"You rotten son of a bitch!" Cherokee Cousins dove the last ten feet, hitting Gribbons from behind and rolling with him in a spray of dust and straw. When he sprang back to his feet, Gribbons still lay on the ground, a trickle of blood running down the back of his hand. "Get up, you bastard! Get out of here before I kill you myself!" Cousins stood crouched with his right hand on his pistol butt.

"Easy, now, half-breed." Gribbons spread a sly grin, and from the look in his eyes Cherokee could tell he wasn't nearly as drunk as he'd pretended to be. Gribbons lifted his jacket open slowly with one hand. "I'm not armed." He raised his other hand to his lips and blotted the trickle of blood from it, still smiling, keeping his eyes on Cousins. "You going to shoot an unarmed man?"

"Well, hell yes!" Cherokee Cousins's pistol streaked up from his holster, cocked, and leveled down at Gribbons's forehead. "In your case, I prefer it!" The pistol bucked in his hand, the shot kicking up dirt an inch from Gribbons's boot.

Gribbons's face turned pale, his eyes widened as he scooted backward in the dirt, shot after shot from the pistol making him crawl faster. In his backward scramble, Gribbons managed to get to his feet and run. Cherokee aimed the pistol at the small of his back and cocked it. "No, Cherokee!" Samuel Burrack yelled, sliding to a stop, the blue cur beside him doing the same. "Not like this! He ain't worth it!" He reached out, shoving Cousins's gun hand away.

Cherokee Cousins slung his arm wide and turned the pistol toward Samuel, his dark eyes hollow and cold, the life gone from them now. Behind them lay death and nothing more. Samuel found himself looking into the eyes of a stranger, a harsh, brutal killer he'd offended, and who would now take his life as easily as he might swat a fly from his shirt sleeve. Cherokee Cousins's hand tightened on the pistol butt as a string of spittle swung from his lips. "Who the hell do you think you are—?"

"He's right, Cherokee." Lawrence Shaw's voice sounded calm and even above the sound of the livery door squeaking open. "Ease it down. He's on your side."

Shaw stepped out of the livery barn leading his buckskin, the big stallion curried and saddled and tacked for hard travel. It took Cousins a second to uncoil. When he did, the pistol lowered and uncocked. He blinked hard. Life seemed to come back into his dark eyes. "Whew . . ." He blew out a breath and looked at Samuel.

Samuel felt as if a tight steel cable loosened from around his chest. He caught his breath. The two of them turned, facing Lawrence Shaw as Shaw stopped and reached down to pick up the bottle of rye. "I'll drink his whiskey. Everybody stay calm. Move slow. Let me get through this."

"Yeah, Shaw, that's the way she'd want it, isn't it?" Cherokee's voice came low, careful, like a man touching a foot down on a thin layer of ice, testing its strength.

Shaw only looked at him and shook his head. "Let's not talk about her." He pulled out the cork, took a drink, and passed the bottle on to Cherokee Cousins. "Drink with me, Cherokee. This is a bad time to drink alone." Samuel watched Shaw's cold green eyes drift over past the Little Egypt, then back again.

Cherokee took the bottle of rye and studied it for a second. "Forget Gribbons, Shaw. He's just a big-mouth fool. I shouldn't have let him get to me that way—don't let him get to you."

"I've got a lot of miles between here and Texas. I best get going." Shaw didn't appear to see anything, or hear anything. His calmness seemed stilted and false to Samuel Burrack—a man playing the role of being in control while at any second something akin to a wounded panther might spring forth from inside his chest. "Cherokee, keep an eye on things here until tomorrow. Tell Sheriff Kemp I had to leave."

"Sure thing. You take it easy, Shaw."

When Lawrence Shaw had stepped up into the saddle and heeled the buckskin forward onto the street, Cherokee Cousins said to Samuel Burrack without facing him, "Sorry about a while ago. But never grab a man's arm in a gunfight, even if he's in the wrong."

"All right," Samuel replied. They watched Shaw move away slowly, a hot breeze nipping at his black hat brim. "I don't trust it, do you? He's not acting right at all."

"No, he's not," Cherokee said, "not at all . . ."

Inside the Little Egypt Saloon, Ed Gribbons had come in through the back door laughing, his narrow escape over, his adventure leaving him shaken but no worse for the wear. Tommy Deebs and Leo Tomblin had met him at the door and asked what all the shooting was about. Gribbons slammed the door and fell back against it and told them as he slung his head back, catching his breath.

"You said what? You dirty low-life poltroon!" Deebs snatched him by his shirt with both hands and jammed him upward onto the wooden door. "This ain't the way I want it! I'm not going to fight him, not while he's in this kind of shape!"

Gribbons's hands went up, trying to press Deebs back. "Tommy! Listen to me, you've got to! This is your chance! Get out there and do it!"

"I'll get out there all right. But not that way. I'll get out there and apologize to the man, for what *you* did! You rotten turd!" He slung Gribbons forward and shoved him out toward the bar.

"Take it easy, Tommy," Leo Tomblin pleaded behind him. "He's right. This is your chance. Maybe your only chance. Ed and I bet over two hundred dollars on you in Humbly! We should have told you sooner—"

"You did what?"

Behind the bar, Thurman hovered near the cocked shotgun, wiping a towel back and forth on the bar above it. He cut a glance at the three men as they came arguing and cursing from the stockroom. Tommy Deebs stopped at Leo Tomblin's words and spun around facing him. "Money? That's what this is about for you? To hell with your money! I came to make my mark! It ain't going to happen this way!" He shoved both men forward toward the swinging doors. Behind the bar, Thurman picked up the shotgun no sooner than they'd gotten out of sight. He held it at port arms, moving around the bar with it before the doors had even settled. He crouched and watch them move down from the boardwalk and into the street.

"Shaw! I want to talk to you!" Tommy Deebs shoved past the other two men and quickened his step, seeing Shaw atop his horse, moving away in the opposite direction. When Shaw's big buckskin stopped in the street, Cherokee Cousins and Samuel Burrack both spun toward the sound of Deebs's voice.

"Damn it. They just won't let this thing go!" Cherokee moved forward, Samuel and Blue right beside him. They all three slowed to a halt, Samuel reaching down and taking the blue cur by his ear as the big buckskin stallion turned in the street. Lawrence Shaw stared down at Deebs with a blank expression.

Tommy Deebs stopped cold in his tracks, seeing the look in Shaw's eyes. He raised his hands chest-high, away from his pistol. "It wasn't me, Shaw. I never sent Gribbons over with that bottle. I just want you to know that. That's not something I would ever do, no matter what."

Behind Deebs, Leo Tomblin whispered to Gribbons. "Hell, listen to Deebs crawfish—he's making me sick. Look at Shaw. The shape he's in, let's take him ourselves."

"Are you drunk enough?" Gribbons whispered in reply.

"Damned right I am."

"Make your move, then. I've got you covered."

As they whispered back and forth, Cherokee took note of them and readied himself. "Get back, kid, it's about to commence . . ."

Deebs continued speaking to Lawrence Shaw. "All I can say is I'm sorry . . . about your wife, and about the way things turned out here—"

"Are you ready?" Shaw's voice came as if from some distant place, cutting Deebs off. His cold green eyes leveled on Deebs as he raised the big pistol slowly from its holster and held it pointed straight up close to his shoulder. He turned the cylinder one click at a time and let three bullets spill down into his lap and fall to the ground.

"No, Shaw, listen." Deebs shook his head. "I came to set things right between us. Not to do this!" But even as Deebs spoke, Shaw lowered the pistol back into its holster and pressed both knees to the buckskin's sides, the move locking the stallion into place beneath him.

"Do it now," Gribbons said to Tomblin beside him; and as they both jerked their pistols free, Deebs yelled, "No!" But in the split second that followed, Shaw's big pistol came up too quick to be seen. Before Cherokee could draw his pistol to cover him, Shaw's three shots sounded like one explosion along the street, and all three men went down as if the hand of God had yanked the surface of the earth from beneath them.

The buckskin had not flinched. A ringing silence fell upon the street. Blue smoke curled around Lawrence Shaw's hand. His cold green eyes moved across the body of Tommy Deebs and stopped at Cherokee Cousins. "Shaw, it's me," Cousins called out, his pistol still in his hand, halfway up from his holster. "Let me know something!" Although Shaw had fired all three shots, his pistol now empty, Cousins wasn't turning loose of his own gun until he saw something settle down in Shaw's eyes. "Don't make me do something I don't want to do here."

Shaw sat for a second, Cherokee Cousins facing him, tense, ready. But then Shaw pressed his knees one short tap to the buckskin's sides and the big stallion slackened its stance and let out a breath. With that, Cherokee Cousins eased down as well and lowered his pistol . . . but still kept his hand on it. "All right, Shaw, it's over."

No sooner than Cherokee had spoken, the sound of a pistol shot resounded. A clump of dirt kicked up high near the buckskin's hoofs. Clayton Mumpe sped out from his cover in an alley and ran across the dirt street firing at Shaw on his way toward the swinging batwings of the Little Egypt Saloon. Two bullets whined past Lawrence Shaw, one of them grazing his shoulder; but Shaw only stared, and raised the empty pistol in his hand and clicked it over and over, a trace of a strange, weary smile on his face.

Cherokee Cousins and Samuel Burrack had acted quickly. They both came up with their pistols cocked; and as Clayton Mumpe hurled himself through the swinging doors, they'd fired. Clayton Mumpe let out a long hysterical laugh from inside the doors of the saloon. "Haaaaa! You missed, you sonsa—!"

The doors to the Little Egypt blew off their hinges in a wide explosion of splinters. Clayton Mumpe sailed backward out across the boardwalk and landed facedown in the dirt, smoke rising from his buckshot-riddled back. Thurman walked out among the debris and kicked one of Clayton Mumpe's crumpled boots off the boardwalk and into the street. He stood and looked over at Cousins, Samuel, and Shaw for a second with the shotgun over his arm. Then he turned around and walked back inside.

"And that's that," Shaw said, his voice sounding strange and somehow aloof in the empty street. Deftly, his fingertips went to his pistol belt, snapping out six cartridges. While he reloaded the pistol he looked down at the bodies on the street and said aloud to no one in particular, "Is that enough? Enough for now?"

"What'd he say?" Cherokee gave Samuel Burrack a concerned glance. Before Samuel could answer, he said to Shaw, "Why don't you climb down from there, Shaw? Get that shoulder looked at before you head out?"

"Haven't you seen enough—had enough?" Shaw backed the big buckskin up without taking his eyes off them. "You want more?"

Samuel took a step forward. "Please, Mr. Shaw, it's over. Let's get the doctor to take a look at you."

But Shaw yanked the big buckskin farther back. "Over? It's not over. I'll tell you when it's over! It's over when the devil says it's over!"

"Leave him be, kid," Cherokee said softly, stepping forward beside Samuel Burrack. "He's out of his head—doesn't know what he's saying."

"It's over when *I say* it's over," Shaw added. He turned the big buckskin in the street and looked down at them. "Don't ever get near me again, none of you. That's all the warning you get."

Samuel stood stunned, watching the big buckskin spin in the street and move away in a wake of dust. Beside him, Cousins nudged his arm. "Come on, Samuel. Let him go. There's nothing we can do or say. Shaw's got too much eating at him right now. He knows he waited too long to go home . . ."

To keep down the flies, a pail of soapy water had been pitched across each dark puddle of blood in the street, and a pair of makeshift wooden doors stood on new hinges in front of the Little Egypt Saloon. Later that day after the bodies had been carried off to the funeral parlor and the town had slowly returned to its normal pace, Cherokee walked into the sheriff's office with a plate of food for Andrew Daggett. The wounded outlaw stood at the bars to his cell, a crusty blood-stained bandage wrapped around his chest and shoulder. Another bandage lay bunched up beneath the bullet hole in his trouser leg. Yet another circled his waist.

"Now that Shaw's gone, I hope this ain't going to turn into one of those lynching deals like you hear about." He pressed his face to the bars and cast a sidelong glance past Samuel, who sat at the sheriff's desk, toward Cherokee Cousins as the tall Indian kicked the front door shut.

"Relax, Daggett." Cherokee shoved the tin plate through the break in the bars. "Wakely isn't that kind of town. I almost wish it was. It'd save a lot of time, not to mention your feed bill. "

"I heard all the shooting. Don't tell me it ain't that kind of town. I run into that sort of stuff everywhere I go. " Andrew Daggett took the plate in his hand and limped back to the cot and sat down. "People these days just as soon hang you as look at you. That's been my experience of late."

"Maybe you just bring the worst out of everybody, Daggett. Ever look at it that way?" Cousins moved back to the desk and looked down at Samuel Burrack. "How're you feeling now, Sam? You haven't said three words all afternoon."

"I'm all right. What is there to say? I can't help thinking about Shaw." Blue lay asleep at Samuel's feet, his body drawn into a ball, his long legs tucked beneath him. "What'll become of him now?"

"Forget him. I hate to say it, but that's all you can do. Shaw knows he dealt himself this hand somehow. He knows he should have gone home sooner. He's blaming himself for everything right about now, I imagine. He'll go after the man who killed her, that'll help a little. But it doesn't stop him from knowing the truth."

"The truth?" Samuel looked up at him.

"Yes. The truth is, her dying is a part of the kind of life Shaw made for himself. He'd be a fool not to know it. That's why he didn't want to talk about her. He was ready to walk the straight and narrow, but he couldn't quite get started— had to stay in it for one more day, for one more reason."

Cherokee leaned down on his hands on the battered sheriff's desk.

"You're judging him too harsh, Cherokee."

"No, I'm not judging him at all." Cherokee straightened up from the desk. "He's been a friend to me. I'm only turning over his cards in his absence—reminding myself how the game's played."

Samuel Burrack shook his head. "Shaw didn't ask for this."

"No. But he knew it was coming. He's expected it since the day he first drew blood."

"What about you, Cherokee? Are you any different? Do you expect any different?"

Cousins didn't answer. Instead, he walked to the dusty window and looked out. After a silent pause, he spoke without turning around. "Strange how when a man steps in a trap of his own making, he always acts within his nature. The preacher prays, and begs redemption. The statesman lies, denies, and points a finger of blame. A gunman . . . ?" He stopped and took a deep breath and let it out slowly. "Hell, we've seen what a gunman does."

"Why are you telling me all this?" Samuel stared at his back until Cousins turned and faced him.

"I don't know, Sam. Maybe it's because Shaw said he saw something in you that he admired. Maybe I'm just speaking on his behalf. I saw how you acted out there. How you drew and fired without hesitating. You've gotten past something, haven't you?"

Samuel answered in a quiet tone, "It's not the same as shooting buffalo . . . but, yes, I'm past it now."

"I thought so. I've watched you since you've been here, seen you thinking, studying, searching something out for yourself. So, what's it going to be for you? Lawman? Gunslinger? An outrider like crazy ole Ranger Sazes?"

"I don't know. I've seen all three. It's hard separating one from the other. Everybody calls Ranger Sazes crazy. But so far he's the only one with any clear direction. He's the closest I've seen so far to walking that straight and narrow you talked about."

"Ranger Sazes *is* the straight and narrow, Sam. Down deep, we all want to be like him." Cherokee smiled and lowered his eyes. "Down deep, maybe that's why we all call him crazy."

Chapter 14

A storm had come and gone overnight, and in its aftermath, morning set in, gray and heavy with rain. Samuel had awakened briefly during the night to the sound of thunder and the ghostly flash of lightning as it streaked through the window, licking blue-yellow stripes along the steel bars. Black shadows flickered and stretched across the rough plank floor, causing the blue cur to whine softly and move to where Samuel's boots stood beside the cot in the open cell. The dog curled down into a ball and lay against the boots as if they were some sort of talisman against the fury of the night.

"Go back to sleep, Blue," Samuel had whispered, although it may have been to himself that he was making such a request. He let a hand fall down from his cot to the dog's shoulder, and as he patted it, he thought once more about Lawrence Shaw, and about all that happened throughout the day.

Cherokee Cousins had been right. Samuel hadn't hesitated when Clayton Mumpe ran across the street firing in their direction. The pistol had came up into his hand just as smooth and as instinctively as Lawrence Shaw had said it would. He recalled Shaw's words those times when they'd fired their pistols out on the sand flats. Shaw would see the doubt in his eyes and tell him not to question himself. "Learn to trust your instincts without hesitation." Samuel could still picture Shaw spinning the pistol back into his holster as he spoke. "Staying alive is the only skill involved."

In the passing of the storm, Samuel wondered if he would ever see Shaw again, and if he did, would Shaw be the same as he had been before? He didn't think so. Samuel knew that from now on, he would be a part of Shaw's dark memory, the young buffalo hunter who'd stood there in the street the day Shaw's world had shattered and crumbled around him. Samuel touched his fingertips carefully to the healing scar on his cheek. "Fast Larry . . ." He whispered the name in reflection, wondering what would become of Shaw now.

"That's all I've got for you, Sam," Shaw had said, that last day on the sand flats. He'd watched Samuel draw and fire from atop his holster, and he'd nodded in satisfaction when Samuel spun the pistol back into his holster. "When you go after Ellsworth, just remember, kill him in your mind before you even start out looking for him. If you don't, he'll kill you. These kind of men never question anything they do. That's what makes them so dangerous. Don't give him time to talk, don't give him time to think. Once your gun sight falls on him, kill him quick." As he'd spoken, Shaw had drawn his pistol so fast that all Samuel saw was a blur. Then Shaw spun it backward and holstered it.

"I'll never be that fast," Samuel told him.

"No. But you're faster than most. It's the quickness that stuns them for a split second. And it's that split second that determines every outcome."

They'd stood in silence for a moment, then Samuel asked him quietly, "Do you regret anything you've done, now that you're getting out of it?"

"Regrets? No . . . regret is the stumbling block of a fool. I've done some wrong, and it'll catch up to me over time. But I knew the bill would come due someday. When it does, I'll pay it, swallow it, and find a way to keep it down. I've refused to stand in any man's line. Whatever that costs me, it's just the price of living."

Samuel gave him a piercing gaze. "What's it been like for you?"

Lawrence Shaw had hesitated, long enough to see that

Samuel wasn't asking to pry, but rather to consider something for his own future reference. Then Shaw had said in a personal tone, "The honest truth? I loved every minute of it. But now that it's over—it's been a carnival show, Sam. It's time to strike my tent and go home, leave room for the next performer."

It came to Samuel now in his slumbering state in the eye of the passing storm. Lawrence Shaw had not been teaching him *how* to use a pistol. Shaw had not even been teaching him *when* to use a pistol. Shaw needed to sound out his own life those days on the flats, and for some reason, Samuel had been the person he'd entrusted to listen. Samuel drifted back to sleep, and in doing so, saw the madness in Shaw's haunted red-rimmed eyes as Shaw turned his horse in the dirt street and rode away.

That was the part of Lawrence Shaw that had become instinctive to him over his time standing behind a gun. That was the base element of the man's nature that revealed itself when all thought stood in its barest form, and when all reasoning had abandoned him and left him alone and lost. As it turned out, the most important thing Samuel had learned about handling a gun, Shaw had taught him quite by accident. Through Lawrence Shaw's tragedy, Samuel had learned that the most important thing to know about a gun was when to lay it down.

A whole different thing than shooting buffalo. . . . Indeed it was, he thought, hearing the rain lash sidelong against the side of the building and rattle like buckshot across the tin roof. He pictured the dead, hollow eyes of the woman who had tried to kill him, and reminded himself that here in this lower world there were desperate, violent people, to whom his life meant nothing.

Three cells away lay Daggett, who was meek and silent now that he was jailed. Yet Samuel had to shoot him time and again to stop him. Daggett had kept coming at him like a crazed animal, relentless in his deadly intent. No. There was no room for hesitancy and indecision in this dark world

Sazes had warned him about. Samuel Burrack knew that, now that he lived there.

In the stillness of the gray dawn before the town began to stir, Samuel stood up from the cot, undressed himself down to his short underwear and walked out onto the boardwalk barefoot, watching the rain fall straight down now that the storm had passed. Blue sat in the open doorway watching him, as Samuel stepped down onto the mud street and raised his arms and his face into the downpour.

As if in some curious baptism ritual, Samuel closed his eyes and let the rain run down his wounded cheek until at length the stiffness in his face was gone, and all felt cool and clean and healing to him. Then he turned and went back inside, closing the door quietly behind himself. When he'd dried and dressed and readied his gear for the trail, he shoved the big rifle into its fringed-leather boot, laid it down on the cot, then sat down beside it.

Moments later, Cherokee Cousins stepped inside and slung rain from his hat. Stamping water off his boots onto the rough plank flooring, he looked over at Samuel through the open cell door and shook his head. "I brought Mumpe's dun horse over from the livery barn for you. But you might want to wait another day before heading out. You won't find any tracks after this belly-wash, anyway. "

Samuel thought about Lawrence Shaw. "No. I said today, so today it is." He stood up and swung the big rifle under his arm.

"At least stop by the restaurant first, get yourself a hot meal. Tell them it's on me."

"Thanks, but no. I've packed some elk jerk and biscuits. I'll eat as I travel."

"I swear, Samuel. I've never seen a noble pilgrim in such a hurry with so little to go on."

"I wish you wouldn't call me that." Samuel offered a faint smile. He walked quietly to Daggett's cell and stood for a moment looking in at the sleeping outlaw. "Pity I won't get to see him hang," he said under his breath.

"Do you really want to?" Cousins stood with his wet hat in his hand, watching him close.

"No. He'll pay for what he did. That's all I ever wanted." Then he raised his hat and placed it down on his head, and walked to the door, the blue cur at his left heel. With the door knob in his hand, he turned to Cherokee Cousins. "I appreciate you telling the sheriff what happened when he gets back today."

"Don't mention it, Samuel. Just watch your back out there."

"I will. You do the same if you run into Junior Lake."

Cherokee Cousins only nodded, following Samuel and the cur through the open door where he stood on the boardwalk and watched them move down into the rain. At the hitch rail, Samuel looked the little dun horse over. He checked the cinch, swung his spindle and rifle up behind the wet saddle and tied them down. Cherokee Cousins shook his head slowly, and watched him mount up, turning the dun onto the muddy street in the downpour.

When man, horse, and dog had faded deeper into the grainy morning pall, Cousins stepped back inside, walked to Daggett's cell and said in a harsh tone, "Wake up, you lousy bastard. Vacation's over for you. *I'm* in charge now. For two cents I'd blow your brains all over the wall and tell the sheriff it was a gun-cleaning accident."

Daggett rolled stiffly onto the side of his cot and wiped his hands up and down on his face. He blinked his bleary eyes at Cherokee Cousins. "Take it easy, half-breed. What did I ever do to you?"

Through the pouring rain, Samuel followed the tail of the storm along the mud-slick trail to the shack where he'd last seen Sherman Ellsworth. This was not the quickest trail for him to take to the badlands' border, nor was this a place he ever wanted to see again. Yet, for reasons unclear in his mind, the hunt for Sherman Ellsworth had to begin there, at the weathered shack in the remote canyon of sand and rock where Samuel had watched life slip away from the young woman in his arms. Something of himself had been left there, suspended, awaiting his return.

Once he arrived, Samuel stood on the porch as rain pelted the roof like steel darts. He hesitated for a second before pushing the door open and walking inside. Once crossed the dusty threshold, he found himself walking softly, as if not to disturb whatever dark memories still lingered there. Blue moved about the shack in the same manner, cautiously touching his nose to a stain on the floor.

"Get away from there, Blue." Samuel nudged the dog away with the side of his wet boot. He took his time walking from one spot to the next, stopping for a moment at the dust-covered pallet on the floor. He touched his boot toe to the handle of the bloodstained knife where it had fallen, and for a moment he stood still in one spot and listened to the rain until something inside him was at last resolved.

Then he turned, walked out onto the porch and closed the door firmly behind himself, and stood searching the gray, endless land and the rain-shrouded sky, toward the dark images of what lay ahead. The storm had turned, a vestige of it now boiling black and low at the far end of his vision. Somewhere ahead of the storm lay the world Samuel was now a part of, as if that world itself moved from place to place in its entirety, illusive, terrible, and taunting, ever drawing toward it those who would give it chase.

"Ranger Sazes . . ." He whispered the name in contemplation, his eyes looking forward; he touched his fingers to the tender wound on his cheek. "Come on, Blue. Let's get started." He turned his collar up against the rain and leveled his wet hat across his brow. "We've got a long ride ahead."

PART 3

Chapter 15

Behind a large boulder atop a switchback trail overlooking an old mine shaft, Ranger Clyde Sazes looked back across the sky. He judged the storm to be no more than three days behind him. At dusk there was little sign of a weather shift moving down from the northwest, other than a faint haze on the far horizon and a tight feeling deep down in his bones. But these were signs enough for him.

Sazes puffed on his briar pipe as he cleaned each of his pistols in turn. He inspected each of them and put them away, letting the Mad Russian ride a bit high in the holster across his stomach. "Don't worry," he said to the pistol, running his hand across the handle. "There's plenty for you to do down there."

He'd managed to get closer to Junior Lake and Morris Braydon over the past week, "dogging their heels," he called it, making sure they saw his line of dust in the sky between them and the border. Junior Lake was no fool, Sazes calculated, letting go of a stream of pipe smoke. Junior understood that the only way to get to Mexico and on to Blood Rock was to ride through Sazes's gun sights. So far, Sazes had managed to keep this game in check.

Yet Sazes knew that once the storm caught up to him, especially once it moved past him, everything could change out here in a hurry. He would lose their tracks in the deluge, and with that his knowledge of where they were at all times. That would give them an advantage. Sazes wasn't about to let that happen if he could help it.

Up until now, both his and the outlaws' hoofprints remained joined, each running to the end of a long winding ribbon of upturned sand across the badlands. There was nothing Junior Lake and Braydon could do to shake him off their trail, and Sazes knew it was driving Junior crazy thinking about it. Sazes chuckled to himself, drawing on the pipe and watching the smoke lift and swirl away on the evening breeze.

He stood up, picked up his rifle, walked to the edge of the large boulder, and looked down on the opening to the old mine shaft. A patchwork of dried boards, wire, and mesquite brush formed a ragged makeshift corral against a jagged wall of rock. On the outside edge of the corral, four horses stood with their heads bowed, their reins wrapped around a leaning cross-timber brought up from the bowels of the old copper mine. Inside the corral, a half-dozen lank cattle milled in place and swished their tails amid a looming cloud of flies.

When Sazes had finished his pipe, he tapped the bowl against the edge of his boot sole and walked back to the blanket on the ground where he'd cleaned his weapons. He picked up a worn folded sheet of paper from beneath a cartridge box, opened it in his hand and studied for a moment, then put it away inside his riding duster. He took up the reins to the Appaloosa and led it to the edge of the boulder, looking down once more at the mine shaft below.

Thirty yards back inside the mine shaft, gathered around an oil lantern, a cattle rustler named Lumpy Rigglen slapped his cards down onto the dusty saddle blanket and laughed as he looked at the three pairs of eyes staring back at him. "Boys, read them and weep is all I can tell you." He reached out and pulled in the small pile of change and let it jingle from his grimy palm. "All donations gratefully accepted here at Lumpy's Hole-in-the-Wall Saloon and Cattle Emporium." He grinned across green, broken teeth.

A young slick-headed outlaw named Duck Burnston

turned his face to one side and spat, running a hand across his thin goatee. "Shitfire! I'm sick of you cheating us, Lumpy."

The other two outlaws, Billy Raggs and Joe Pearl, shied back a few inches, looking back and forth between them.

Lumpy kept his broken grin. "That's a terrible thing to say to me, Duck. I have to admit, I am struck *conster-nate* by such an accusation."

"Well, it's the damn truth." Duck shot the other two a glance, but saw no sign of them taking his side.

"Hell, of course it's true!" Lumpy tossed a grimy hand. "I ain't denying it. But unless you can prove something, you just as well keep your mouth shut."

"And if I could prove it? Then what?"

Lumpy shrugged, raking in the cards, stacking them and shuffling them. "It wouldn't matter much. I ain't giving no money back."

"Yeah, Duck," said Joe Pearl, "so shut up and ante. You know any other games nearby?" They all laughed. All except Duck Burnston, who stood up and dusted his seat, moving away grumbling under his breath.

"Where you going, Duck?" Lumpy called out as he licked his thumb and started to deal a new hand.

"To relieve myself, damn it. Why? You want to watch?"

"Not this time," Lumpy chuckled. "Last time you wouldn't let me leave till I sang you a song!" The three outlaws hooted and roared.

"Peckerwoods . . ." Duck sliced the word under his breath and headed toward the glow of daylight at the front of the shaft.

"Watch yourself out there, Duck," Billy Raggs called out as he picked up his cards. "You heard what Junior said before he left. That old Outrider ain't far behind."

"Screw Junior. I ain't afraid of Outrider Sazes, or damn well nobody else."

The two outlaws bowed over their cards as Lumpy took

two discards from his hand and dropped them onto the saddle blanket. "Did either one of yas bring the horses in a while ago?"

Without looking up, Billy Raggs said, "Yeah, Joe brought them inside."

"Me? No I didn't. I thought you did." Joe Pearl worked a short cigar stub to one corner of his mouth as he spoke.

Lumpy leaned back and looked at each of them. "Nobody around here does anything." He laid his cards down and had started to get up when the crack of a rifle echoed down the stone walls of the shaft. The three outlaws stared at one another, frozen in place, their expressions puzzled, until Joe Pearl said, "Duck *shot* hisself?"

"No, you damned idiot!" Lumpy caught his arm and kept him from running to the front of the shaft. "Somebody's out there!"

Billy Raggs quickly reached out with a shaky hand and trimmed out the lantern. "The Outrider, you think?"

"That would be my *first* guess," Lumpy said in a sarcastic hiss, "since Junior said he was right behind him. I can't believe neither one of yas had enough sense to bring in the horses!" He raised his pistol in the darkness, and moved off along the wall toward the glow of daylight.

"Us?" said Billy Raggs. "Why didn't you, if you wanted it done so bad?"

"Because I'm in charge, fool! I ought to shoot you both myself. I will, too, if that Outrider don't kill us all."

"Damn Junior and Braydon for ever stopping here," Joe Pearl said, running a hand along the wall where he'd stood his rifle earlier. "Where the hell's my Winchester?" His hand groped along the hard stone, finding nothing.

"I don't know," Billy Raggs said, moving past him in the darkness, following Lumpy Rigglen. "I saw Braydon checking it out before they left."

At the entrance to the shaft the three outlaws hugged the walls and ventured a peep out into the evening light. Ten feet from the corral, Duck Burnston's body lay sprawled facedown in the sand, a dark pool of blood spreading beneath his chest.

From behind Billy Raggs, Joe Pearl whispered, "Do you think that might be some Comanches come to rustle the steers?"

"Yeah," Billy Raggs whispered back over his shoulders, jacking a round up into his Spencer rifle, "you're wishing it's Comanches."

From within the towering stones forty yards away, the sound of Ranger Clyde Sazes's voice echoed down to them. "I've got six names on my list. Junior Lake . . . Morris Braydon . . . Lumpy Rigglen . . . Billy Raggs . . . Duck Burnston . . . Joe Pearl. You all know why I'm here. Come on out, give yourselves up."

Lumpy Rigglen called out from the mine shaft. "You missed Junior and Braydon. They're already gone. That's Duck laying there with his heart blown out, Sazes. You didn't give him much of a chance, did you?"

"No."

A silence passed, and when Sazes said nothing more, Lumpy called out, "And you expect us to give up and get the same thing? Do you think we're damned fools?"

"Yep."

Another silence passed. "Well, by God!" Lumpy called out. "We ain't giving up, then, not without a fight!"

"I was hoping you'd see it that way," Sazes called out. A shot exploded, spraying dust and rock chips from the inside wall of the shaft. Lumpy rocked backward a step, then came forward and fired. But he had no target in the high reaching rocks along the switchback trail. His shot grazed the top of a large boulder and whistled away.

Before Lumpy could press himself back against the wall of the shaft, three pistol shots rang out, each one ricocheting back and forth across the shaft like angry hornets. The three outlaws hit the ground with their arms thrown over their heads. "Jesus, ranger! Hold your fire a second!" All three men crouched, moved back a few feet, and took aim out through the evening light. "What are you doing with our names on your list? You know all I do is rustle cattle. When did you get so interested in steers?"

"I'm not interested in steers. I'm after Junior Lake. You pieces of punk just happen to be on my way. How long since he left here? What's his plans?"

When no one answered from inside the mine shaft, three more shots fired in rapid succession. "Lord God, man!" Lumpy cried out. "Give a body time to think! I don't want to tell you something wrong, now do I?" As Lumpy spoke, he turned to the other two and motioned for them to tuck a pistol behind their backs. He whispered, "We've got to get out there where we have a chance to take him down, else he'll wait us out and shoot us dead."

"That's right, Lumpy. The mood I'm in, wrong information would get you killed quicker than anything," Sazes replied from the cover of rock.

"Are you crazy?" Billy Raggs whispered to Lumpy Rigglen. "We can't take that old devil by surprise!"

"We can damn sure try," Lumpy hissed. "It's better than sitting here like rats in a trap." He turned back to the front of the shaft and called out, "Hey, what if we've changed our minds? Can we still give ourselves up?"

"I don't know, Lumpy," Sazes called down. "I kind of like it this way. I won't have to feed you all the way to Humbly."

"For crying out loud, Sazes! What kind of lawman are you? We're talking about going along peaceable here! You can't just kill us like we're dogs!"

"Sure I can, Lumpy. I found those three bodies yesterday out on the flats. Ain't that how you killed those people? Like they were dogs? You burned their wagon—"

"Whoa, hold on now, Sazes. Is that what's got you all stoked up? Because if it is, we didn't have nothing to do with it. That was Junior and Braydon's handiwork. They did that on their way here. If you'd been following them closer, you'd know that. There was two kids in that wagon, too. Junior traded them both to the *comadrejas* for fresh horses after he got here. That's the gospel truth."

A brief silence passed while Sazes thought about it. Then he called out, "*Comadrejas,* huh? Since when did Junior start trading with the desert weasels?"

"I'm just telling you what he told us, Sazes. And I ain't saying no more unless we talk face-to-face." As soon as he'd spoken to Sazes, he turned to Billy Raggs and Joe Pearl. "Get ready, boys, we'll be stopping his clock any minute now."

Sazes stepped out from behind the tall boulder into full view, with his rifle butt propped on his hip, the Mad Russian hanging in his right hand. "Pitch your weapons out, then step out here slow and easy, all three of you at once."

"There he is," Billy Raggs whispered, "shoot him!" He raised his pistol in the cover of darkness inside the shaft. But Lumpy shoved Raggs's pistol down.

"Hell no, fool! Not yet. If we miss from here, he'll never let us out. Just follow me—and be ready." With his Colt stuck down his back, Lumpy pitched out a small-caliber pistol he carried in his trouser pocket. "There's mine, Sazes. See it?"

Sazes only stood staring. When the other two pitched out a weapon each, Sazes moved down along the trail toward them, leading the Appaloosa by its reins. He watched the three of them file out and stand abreast, facing him with their hands chest-high. "Lord, Sazes." Lumpy grinned and shook his head. "I wished you'd asked us about that wagon to begin with." He nodded at Duck Burnston's body on the ground. "Bet ole Duck wished it, too. He wouldn't be blown all to hell. We could have cleared it up and you gone on your way. I'm a straight-up rustler. We all are. If it ain't on four hooves with a pair of horns, we don't want nothing to do with it."

Sazes stopped fifteen feet back from them and looked down at the small-caliber pistols in the dirt, not fooled at all. Then he shoved the Appaloosa to one side out of firing range and said to Lumpy, "What about the two children? I saw no sign of there being any children at the wagon."

"Well, there was, sure enough. I hated seeing it. Junior made the swap right up yonder plain as day." He pointed a finger toward the top of the trail, but Sazes did not cast a glance in that direction. The other two outlaws inched a step away from Lumpy Rigglen. Sazes watched them, but didn't say a word.

"Which direction did the *comadrejas* take them?"

"That's anybody's guess." Lumpy shrugged, letting his hands fall a little bit lower. "You know how those desert weasels are. They fade into the ground. One minute they're there, the next minute they're gone."

"Which way did Lake head out across these rocks?" Sazes asked, not seeming to pay any attention when the two outlaws on either side of Lumpy Rigglen took another step away from him, fanning out. Sazes kept his eyes on Lumpy.

"He's gone toward Humbly. But the truth is he's wanting to cut over the border real bad. Says you've dogged him in a way he can't risk getting past you."

"How long ago?" Sazes asked, still not appearing interested in the others' hands lowering down, not seeming concerned about the way they'd planted their feet shoulder-width apart, getting set.

"Oh . . . I'd say an hour, more or less." Lumpy raised a hand and scratched his head up under his hat brim. "If you tried real hard you could probably—" His hand came down quick, swinging around behind his back. "Get him, boys!"

The Mad Russian came up cocked in Sazes's hand, and bucked with each shot as he walked it left to right across where the three of them stood. Billy Raggs fell dead with the first shot before he got the pistol drawn from behind his back. Lumpy slammed back against a bracing timber, spinning sideways and dropping down with one arm slung over a long scrap of barbed wire in the corral fence. His pistol hung from his hand but was stuck on the fencing, useless. Joe Pearl had managed to get a shot off, and the bullet grazed Sazes's forearm. But then Joe Pearl flew backward, a boot coming off his foot before he fell dead to the ground.

Sazes walked over to Lumpy Rigglen, breaking the Mad Russian open and letting the three spent shells fall to the ground. He stared down at the dying outlaw as he reloaded and recocked the pistol. "You . . . You saw it coming, didn't ya?" Lumpy's breath was halting and weak, a gout of blood pumping forth from his chest with each beat of his heart.

"I'm not blind, Lumpy." Sazes stooped down on his haunches at face level and swung the rifle over his lap. "Was you lying about there being children on that wagon?"

"What's the difference? You . . . wouldn't stop long enough to go after them. You're . . . a heartless piece of work . . . you are."

"You're dying, Lumpy. Now's the time to tell the truth." As Sazes spoke he untied the bandanna from around his throat and wrapped it tight around the graze on his forearm.

Lumpy struggled, managing to nod his head. "Yeah . . . it's the truth. Junior swapped them off for horses. Can I have . . . a drink of water before I die here?"

Sazes looked at him, cutting a passing glance at the cocked pistol still in his hand, hanging over the strand of barbed wire. "Sure, why not?" He raised up, stepped over to the Appaloosa, lifted a canteen by its strap and started to turn when he heard the sound of the twanging barbed wire as Lumpy swung his arm free of it.

Almost without looking Sazes swung the Mad Russian and fired a shot. The bullet slammed Lumpy's head back at an odd angle and left it there, bobbing on the barbed wire until it settled and stopped. Sazes stepped back over, uncapped the canteen, took a swallow and let it hang from the same hand holding his rifle. "I saw that coming too, Lumpy," he said to the dead face hanging in the fencing.

Clyde Sazes broke the gate open to the corral and fanned the cattle out onto the bare rocky terrain. In the wake of their dust he turned three of the four outlaws' horses loose, slapping their rumps and sending them off in bewildered procession to fend for themselves. He kept one horse for a spare, a big scrappy roan that he led on the end of a short rope. He climbed atop the big Appaloosa stallion and heeled it upward on the high switchback trail.

From a higher ridgeline, Junior Lake had watched the whole bloody show from three hundred yards away. He sucked air through his teeth and said under his breath, "Damn. I figured Lumpy and his boys would put up some kind of show for themselves. Sazes killed them quicker than it takes to swat a fly. It looked like Lumpy even had the drop on him from behind. Sazes blew his fool head off!"

"What's he doing now?" Beside Junior Lake, Morris Braydon lay against the side of a rock rubbing a bandanna back and forth along the barrel of the Winchester rifle he'd taken earlier from the mine shaft while Joe Pearl wasn't watching. "Is he gonna ride into our ambush, or what?"

"I don't think so." Junior sounded disappointed. "Whatever Lumpy told him has him changing directions."

"Think it's to look for the kids?"

"Not a chance. Sazes doesn't give a damn about a couple of snot-nosed kids any more than we do. It ain't his style." Junior raised onto his knees, watched for a moment longer, then stood up and dusted his trousers. "This just rips it! He's heading out toward the *comadrejas'* trail, not ours."

"Then you must be wrong. He *is* going after them kids."

Junior chuckled at the irony. "Jesus, just when I would've had him cold, he decides to become a do-gooder on us."

"Well, that's better than having him dogging us all the time, ain't it?" Braydon continued to wipe the rifle's barrel.

"I suppose so, but I had my heart set on blindsiding him,

killing him right here." He noticed the Winchester for the first time and chuckled. "You thieving little wretch! That's Joe Pearl's rifle."

"Not now it ain't," Braydon grinned. "Joe knew I was a thief. He shouldn't have left it laying around. Besides, he's dead now. What good's it to him?"

"Come on, Braydon," Junior said, looking down at Sazes in the distance, "he just drew himself a lucky hand today. Let's cut for Humbly, then hit the border."

"Sounds good to me." Braydon shoved the bandanna into his hip pocket and swung the Winchester up under his arm. "I'd like to see Cherokee Cousins step into my sights with this baby pointed at him."

Junior let out a long breath. "Are you still fretting that half-breed? He's old news. If I run into him, I'll drop him like a bucket of lard."

"Well . . . just in case you don't." Braydon patted the rifle stock and grinned. "I'll keep ole *Pearl* here close at hand."

Junior shook his head and walked to his horse. "You've got some gall, naming a rifle after the man you stole it from—a dead man, at that."

Sazes rode to the top of the switchback trail, scouting the tangles of brush until he came upon the many hoofprints of the *comadrejas*. He stepped down from his saddle and pressed his fingertips gently to the earth. The prints were fresh, less than a couple of hours old, and at first he asked himself why he had not seen their dust earlier in the day. Then he reminded himself that here in their home terrain, the *comadrejas* had the ability to move like ghosts.

With no one on their trail, the band of desert vermin had separated somewhere ahead, picking their footing across boulder facings and rock ledges until they hit the flatlands. Down there they would regroup in some remote dry wash or canyon and travel in strength across the border, where they seemed to be able to vanish into thin desert air.

Sazes stood for a second in the closing grayness of evening, knowing his odds on finding the children were slim—and freeing them from the *comadrejas* even slimmer. To the northwest he saw a first glimpse of the storm lying in a thin dark line on the far horizon. *Damn the luck* . . . He turned and looked almost longingly toward the trail leading the other direction, the trail Junior Lake would have taken only an hour ago.

"This one's on me, Junior." Sazes whispered toward the empty towering rockland, not knowing that at that very second Junior Lake and Morris Braydon had slipped atop their horses and stepped them carefully away from where they'd lain watching him. "You're smarter than I thought," Sazes continued as his eyes scanned the high barren earth. "You knew I'd have no choice but to go for the children, didn't you, you dirty sonofabitch?"

Chapter 16

Samuel had flanked right of the storm as it loomed low and rolled forward in the sky before him. At a point atop a high ridge, he watched a line of deer cut across a sandy canyon floor, their backs wet from the heavy rain. Seeing the deer appear briefly in sight, only to vanish away into a deep crevice, reminded him once again that with the harsh weather at hand, washing away all signs of the man that preceded it, finding Sherman Ellsworth here in this vast expanse was next to impossible.

He slumped in his saddle for a second with his wrists crossed. In the face of endless rock and sand and high stretching ridgelines that lay sprawled before him, a flicker of doubt set in. He questioned how in the name of heaven he had ever expected to find something as small and insignificant as man in this wide wilderness. He straightened himself with resolve and pushed up his hat brim, running a gloved hand down the healing scar on his cheek. The man was out there, he just had to find him.

They had come upon him before, Junior Lake and his men, like violent specters from some cruel netherworld. They had caught him unprepared and unseasoned and forced their game upon him. And they'd beaten him, their victory so attested to by the shallow grave of Davey Riley, which by now had been laid open by scavengers and strewn to the desert winds.

Samuel's hands tightened on the reins. He forced the lingering doubt from his mind and heeled the dun horse for-

ward. At his horse's heels, Blue rose up from his seat in the
dust and fell in behind him. He would come upon them
again—this time he'd be prepared, he thought. Somewhere
out there, Outrider Sazes hunted this species of man, day in
day out. Sazes knew their ways and their thinking, a master
hunter whose prey did not elude him. Samuel Burrack
would learn these things as well. He had to.

"Take up, Blue," he said down to the big cur, determined.
Reining back, he let the dog trot past him fifty yards, and he
saw the dog move back and forth before him, lowering its
nose to the ground. "Don't worry, Blue, it'll come to us," he
added under his breath.

The following morning, the darkness in the sky had
swung farther southwest toward the border. With his buffalo
rifle, at a distance of two hundred yards, he took down a single buck deer as it topped a draw, hesitating in his sights.
When he rode forward to gather his prey, he caught sight of
the cur sniffing at a jut of rock, and when he'd ridden closer
he saw the washed indentations in the sand. "All right," he
said, rubbing the dog's head. "Maybe it's Ellsworth, maybe
it's not. Either way, we're not without resource, are we?"

When they'd eaten, they moved on.

With the land drying quickly in the heat of the sun, glassy
pools of water were rapidly being swallowed by the thirsty,
parched earth. The next day Samuel moved over into the
black shade of a long stretch of rock shelves beneath jagged
rocky hills. At dusk, when the rocky hills had leveled back
down into the flat belly of the land, he came to a worn cross-
trail that snaked east to west across his path.

While he'd never been on the cross trail, he knew that the
only place it could lead was to the small town of Humbly to
his distant left, or on to a scattering of abandoned relay sta-
tions and border shack towns to his right. From here, Sherman Ellsworth would have cut for the border, Samuel
reasoned, stepping down from his saddle and pressing a
hand to the small of his back. Come morning, Samuel would
do the same.

He found a wide, damp dry wash nearby, where rainwater from the storm had already diminished down to a thin trickle. By dark he had grained the dun from a small bag of feed he'd brought along, and had picketed the animal twenty yards downstream where wisps of pale grass stood amid the stone bed. He made no fire, taking a short meal of dried meat, biscuits and fresh water.

Once he'd fed the blue cur, checked his pistol, and took stock of his meager supplies, he laid down on his blanket, and with the saddle for his pillow, slept soundly with his big rifle drawn to his chest. Against his back, the blue cur coiled into a ball and let out a long breath and rested, its eyes gazing into the shadowy darkness.

At some point deep in the night, Samuel was awakened by the dog. Not by the sound of the low growl in its throat, but rather by the feel of the dog's body rumbling against him. Without a word, Samuel rolled over with his rifle and stilled the dog, placing a hand on its tensed, wary head. *What was it?* He had heard something himself through his veil of sleep, but it had taken the warning of the dog to call his senses to it.

He lay as still as stone, listening to the ringing silence of night above the faint trickling of water. He heard nothing for a time, and yet the dog remained rigid beneath his hand, its senses alert toward something unseen. When the sound came again he recognized it as men's laughter, low and distant. The unexpectedness of it caused him to blink his eyes and listen closer to make sure he wasn't mistaken. But in a moment he heard voices again, still faint, but not laughing this time.

The voices spoke back and forth, drawing near on the flatland above him. Listening, he recognized the words as the broken, mutated Spanish-English language of the *co-madrejas*. His hand tightened instinctively on the big rifle's stock. *Desert weasels!* Samuel's breath drew shallow. Then he collected himself quickly, picking up the saddle and the blanket. He rose up into a crouched stance and with the tip of his rifle barrel nudged the dog back downstream where he'd left the horse. He moved slowly and silently toward the horse, and unhobbled it. But before he could move the horse back he realized the voices were closer than he'd thought. He sank to the ground with his rifle and listened, with one hand resting on the big cur's neck to keep him quiet.

"If jou askz me, I saz we slitz the boy'z throat and keepz the girl por ourselves." The voice spoke in the darkness above the edge of the dry wash. Samuel heard the sound of their horses' hooves slow to a halt.

"Jou shutz up," a voice replied. "Jou knowz nothing. The girl iz too young. It iz best we takez them to *Mejico*. We sellz them, eh?" In the darkness, the owner of the voice rubbed his thumb and finger together in the universal language of greed.

Samuel listened, hoping the horse beside him wouldn't make a sound. Blue stood silent, as if listening to their words himself.

Among the broken English voices, an American named Jasper Witt added his opinion. "We were nuts, trading good horses for these Mexican brats in the first place. What the hell was Imdigo thinking, doing such a fool thing?"

"Imdigo iz the boss. Juo can askz him when he joinz us."

"Shit." Jasper Witt grunted under his breath. "Even Imdigo can be wrong, I reckon." He reached a hand out in the pale moonlight and playfully slapped the frightened little boy on his head. "Scared, ain't you, kid?" The child only shied back from him and put a trembling arm around the little girl beside him. Jasper laughed and added, "I don't blame you a damn bit. If you knew what I was thinking, it'd scare you both to death." The other four *comadrejas* laughed with him. Samuel heard the whimper of the frightened children and felt a sickness stir deep in his stomach.

"We spendz the night here, where there iz water," said the first voice. "Others will joinz us tomorrow . . . perhapz Imdigo himself. Then jou tell him how foolish he iz, eh?"

"Makes me no difference," Jasper Witt replied. "He

never shoulda dealt with Junior Lake. Anybody with one eye and half sense would've known better."

Samuel heard Junior Lake's name and tried to picture in his mind what had happened out there in the badlands. Whatever these children's situation had been, it was now up to him to deal with it. He looked all around in the pale moon-lit darkness. He'd counted five of them as their silhouettes had moved down toward the dry wash. Then he'd seen the two small figures lifted roughly from a horse and tossed to the rocky ground. The little girl let out a short muffled scream, and then fell silent as the boy whispered something to her in Spanish.

Samuel reasoned that if these men had been in contact with Junior Lake, they must have done so with Ranger Sazes still on Junior's trail. Did Sazes know about the children? If he did, would he have abandoned his search for Junior Lake and struck out after these men? Was he somewhere nearby, the way he'd been the day Davey Riley met his fate at the hands of his murderers? If so, Samuel could certainly use his help; if not, Samuel still knew what he had to do. There were five gunmen here, but Samuel wasn't about to leave the boy and girl behind.

Crouching, silently, he moved the horse back an inch at a time, holding his breath as he did. When he'd gotten around a bend in the dry wash, he and Blue moved up onto the flatland, Samuel pulling the horse behind him until he was a good thirty yards out into a stand of mesquite brush. When the horse's shoe clicked on a rock, Samuel froze, hearing the voices stop for a second. Jasper then said, "Hold it! Did ya'll just hear something out there?"

A tense second passed, Samuel standing frozen with his rifle in one hand and the horse's reins in his other. Finally a voice chuckled. "Jou are too nervous, I thinkz. Es nada out there. Getz some sleep now, all of us. Jazper, you standz guard, eh? Since jou hearz so good."

Samuel let out a tense breath and stilled his racing heart. He inched another few feet into the cover of mesquite and high rocks, sank down with his rifle across his lap, and waited. Nearly a full hour had passed by the time the voices ceased and the sound of snoring loomed above the circle of men. Samuel waited yet, as a glow of tobacco flared and fell in the darkness. He rehobbled the horse where it stood and made sure the dog stayed still in place.

Then he lowered onto his belly and crawled forward, following the glow of tobacco until he judged himself to be within fifteen feet of the man sitting watch. Again he waited, and when the glow snuffed out and the sound of a man coughing and settling onto the ground stopped, Samuel eased back up in a crouch and moved forward, quickly now, the butt of the big rifle drawn back and ready.

At the last second before Samuel swung the rifle stock around, the man might have opened his eyes and seen the dark image coming at him. Samuel wasn't sure. But he did not hesitate. The butt of the rifle made a sharp crack as it struck the sitting man and sent him sidelong and limp on the rocky ground. Samuel crouched in silence for a second, listening, making sure the sound hadn't disturbed the sleeping *comadrejas*. Then he moved forward into their midst.

In the darkness, the boy tried to let out a scream, but Samuel's hand clamped over his mouth. Samuel drew both startled children to his chest and whispered in their ears, cautioning them. *"Facil, facil, esta quieto . . ."* While the men slept, Samuel withdrew with the children until they were a few yards away. Then, Samuel whispered to the boy, *"Habla Ingles?"*

The little boy nodded and whispered in reply, *"Si, algunos."* Yes, he knew some English. His eyes were large and fearful in the pale moonlight.

Samuel saw the doubt in his eyes and whispered, "Don't worry, we'll get by." He patted both of their shoulders to reassure the two of them. The girl whimpered softly and buried her face against the boy's arm. "Wait here," Samuel whispered, "and don't make a sound, *comprende?"*

"Si," the boy whispered, his voice trembling, *"Esta*

usted uno de ellos?" he asked, thinking that Samuel might be one of the *comadrejas.* Beside him, the girl only shuddered and kept her face hidden.

"No, le tomo ambos exterior de aqui," Samuel whispered, struggling with his Spanish. Then he added in English, "I am taking you out of here. *Ahora guarde quieto*—now keep quiet." As Samuel knelt beside them, he felt something cold and wet brush the side of his face and almost swung his rifle around before realizing it was the big cur's nose.

"Blue!" he whispered harshly. But the dog only poked its nose past him and sniffed at the two children. Samuel caught his breath and calmed himself. "All right, then stay." He pressed the dog firmly against the boy and placed the boy's free arm across the dog's shoulders. "Keep him here with you," Samuel whispered, *"Comprende?"*

The boy nodded. Then Samuel moved away to the *comadrejas'* horses. When he returned, he led the horses, hearing them grumble under their breaths, their hooves sounding far too loud to him.

Samuel lifted the children up onto one of the horses and whispered to the boy, "Can you hold her? Can you ride?" When the boy looked confused, Samuel asked in his broken Spanish, *"Puedo montar?"*

"Si," the boy nodded in reply, *"monto bien, asi hace a mi hermana."* He could ride well, so could his sister, he'd said.

"Good, then." Samuel steadied the girl against her brother's chest, and placed the reins in the boy's hands. "Follow me and stay close." The children both looked confused now as the girl stared down at him and wiped her eyes. Samuel repeated himself in Spanish, hoping he was saying it right. *"Sigame, queda cierra, si?"*

"Si!" The children nodded in unison.

Samuel allowed himself a tight trace of a smile as their eyes moved warily across the long wound on his cheek. "Don't worry, it's not as bad as it looks. I'll get us through this." He led them off to where he'd hobbled the dun, and in a moment they'd slipped away into the darkness.

When the first *comadreja,* a man named Todjo, stood up in the gray wisps of dawn and walked to the edge of the dry wash to relieve himself, he rubbed his eyes with his free hand and looked over toward the spot where he and the others had tied their horses the night before. For a moment he only stared blankly. Then he pawed at his eyes as if to make sure they were working properly. "Damn itz to hell! The horsez are gone!" He spun, hiking up his trousers, and kicked one of the sleeping men on the ground in passing. "Get up, *estupido!* The horsez are gone! So are thez chidrenz!"

The others threw aside their ragged blankets and sprang to their feet, pistols jerking upward as they looked all around in confusion. Todjo stopped and reached down to where Jasper Witt lay sprawled on the ground. He snatched Jasper up by his collar and shook him. "Jou bastardo! Where are the—?" He stopped short, seeing Jasper's bleary eyes trying to focus, a bloody knot standing blue and wide on the side of his head. "Damn itz to hell!" He slung Jasper back to the ground and turned to the others.

"Whatz haz happened here, Todjo?" one of them cried out, running over to him. "This pig of a gringo had letz someone steel our horsez, that's what!"

The four *comadrejas* looked all around bewildered, still waking, turning in place. One of them called out from a foot away, "Over here . . . there arez the trackz! One man, and he haz dog with him!"

"One man, and a dog! *Jesus Christo!*" Todjo looked up from the hoofprints leading out across the flatlands. He stood with his hand on his pistol, studying the outline of distant hills in the faint morning light. He let out a resolved breath as the others joined him, two of them having dragged Jasper Witt to his unsteady feet and bracing him between them. "Nobody steals ourz horsez," he added, slicing out his words through clenched teeth while gazing off to the distance.

When the two *comadrejas* turned Jasper Witt loose, he fell to the ground murmuring, "What—? What happened?"

Witt started to struggle to his feet but Todjo planted a boot down on his shoulder. "It iz best jou stay out of myz sight, Jazper, jou idiot!"

"What doz we do, Todjo?" one of the others asked.

"We goz on, jou fool. What doz jou think we do?" Todjo nodded out across the flats toward the jagged hills. "This manz and hiz dog? They do notz go far. Imdigo and the others will seez him." He turned and grinned, a dark nasty grin. "I would notz want to be in hiz bootz today, no?"

"Why he didn't killz us in our sleepz, Todjo?" one of them asked, looking puzzled, scratching his head.

Todjo shrugged. "Because hez a fool, iz why. Nobody in theirz right mind would have left us alive." He stared in silence, then turned, went to his blanket on the ground, picked it up, shook it out, and slung it over his shoulder. "Come on, *vamanos!* I wantz to be there when Imdigo cutsz off his eyelids and skins himz alive."

Chapter 17

Samuel pushed the horses hard throughout the remainder of the night, and yet at daylight the barren flatlands still stretched far before them as if they'd hardly gained a mile. At midmorning, when they stopped to change horses, Samuel handed the children a canteen; and as they drank from it, he scanned the short jagged hill line to their left and saw a drift of dust moving in their direction. "Up you go," he said, scooping both children into his arms and raising them up onto the sweaty back of one of the *comadrejas'* horses. "Drink as we ride."

The children looked confused at his words, but then the girl's eyes caught sight of the distant dust. She tugged at her brother's sleeve. The boy looked away with her, and after a quick glance turned back to Samuel with dread in his eyes. "I know. There's plenty more of them." Samuel patted his knee. "But they're at least an hour away. We'll be all right." Samuel hurried, swapping his saddle and supplies from the shaggy dun to a big deep-chested bay. He slapped the three spent horses on their rump, sending them off across the sand, and had started to tie the reins to the last fresh *comadreja* horse to the tail of the bay. But looking at the horse, a small, shallow-flanked roan, he realized it was not in much better shape than the ones he'd turned loose. His eyes went once more to the rise of dust, judging their distance.

"Go on, get out of here." Samuel slapped the roan's rump and watched it falter slightly as it turned and trotted off behind the other three horses. On the ground, Blue sat panting, his tongue lolling in the heat, his breath rasping, near exhaustion. "Come on, Blue," he called out, already raising his boot to a stirrup. But as the dog rose to its tired feet, it only swayed a bit to one side, and sank back down, whining lamely through the pounding in its chest.

"I've got you, boy." Samuel swung away from the stirrup, gathered the limp dog in his arms and raised him up across the saddle. "Nobody gets left behind." Then he stepped up behind the overheated dog, cradled him in his lap, and heeled the horse, slapping the rump of the other horse and sending the children on ahead.

At the front of the line of dust, the *comadreja* leader Imdigo drew his horse to one side, letting the others ride past him as he wiped a grimy hand across the field lens and raised it to his eye. He focused in on Samuel and the children and whispered a curse under his breath, catching a glimpse of Samuel's big rifle butt. *A buffalo rifle?* He wasn't sure. From out of the line of a dozen riders, a young *comadreja,* an American known only as The Rat, slid his horse in beside Imdigo and checked it down. "What do you say, Imdigo? Is it the Mexican kids, for sure?"

"Si." Imdigo grunted, sounding disgusted. "What other childrenz do jou suppose it would be?" He lowered the lens and closed it between his dirty palms. "Todjo has letz some gringo get the best of him. I should keel him!"

"Who is the gringo?" The Rat squinted out across the flatlands, not seeing a thing except the rise of dust from Samuel's, and the children's horses.

"Howz should I know whoz is the gringo?" He gave The Rat a cold glance. "Youz all look alike, eh?"

"All except me." The Rat tilted his chin to one side, and spit, running a hand across his parched lips. "Whoever it is, he'll never make it to cover. It's a three-horse stretch from here to the badlands hills."

"Si, but he iz over halfway there alreadyz." Imdigo heeled his horse forward. "There are more of ourz men coming this wayz from the storm. We willz cut him off between us. I want thosez children. Theyz cost me three good horsez." He lowered his voice and added, "Damn Junior Lake to hellz."

"You ain't the first one Junior Lake ever skint in a swap. Let's go get them little boogers." The Rat gigged his horse and sped past Imdigo toward the rest of the riders. He called back over his shoulder, grinning, "It's all just good sport to me."

Imdigo grumbled to himself, waving The Rat on ahead. "Goodz sportz to jou, eh? I hate allz jou damnz gringos."

For the next hour, Samuel and the children pounded across the flatlands, only slowing for a moment now and then to let the horses catch their breaths. He did not like killing good horses, yet that's what he be would doing if he didn't stop and allow the animals a good long rest out of the scorching sun. But looking back at the closing rise of dust, he knew that stopping was out of the question. Ahead lay an upright string of rocky buttes. He judged it to be at least an hour's ride away.

To make matters worse, even as he studied the distance and weighed their chances, he caught a flash of sunlight streaking off of a rifle barrel from a thin trail leading down between two buttes. Looking closer, he saw another group of *comadrejas,* four of them riding down onto the flatlands. Reining his horse down quickly, Samuel reached out, catching the bridle of the children's horse and checking it down with him. "We've got to stop!"

"No habla!" the boy said, looking into Samuel's eyes. The girl looked back and forth in bewilderment.

"We have to stay *here,"* Samuel said, pointing down at the ground. At first he wondered whether or not to tell them what was about to happen out here on this desolate plane. He looked back once more, seeing the encroaching rise of dust as if it were some large living thing come to devour all that stood in its path.

"Climb down," he said to the children, sliding down himself, bringing the dog with him. The big cur took to the ground moving, circling and shaking himself out. He was rested, but still put upon by the staggering heat. When the dog pressed close to Samuel's leg, Samuel nudged it back with the side of his boot. Then he said to the boy, "Hold him back. Take him and your sister to the other side of your horse."

The boy only shrugged in confusion. *"No habla."* The little girl stood huddled silently behind him.

Samuel shook his head, not able to find the right words to relay his intentions. "Here, see this?" He bent and raised the big buffalo knife from his boot well. The boy shied back a step on his bare feet. Sam pointed with the knife toward the buttes, where the first of the four riders had come down onto the flatlands in a rise of dust. "Out there? See them?"

The boy turned back to Samuel, a sick frightened look in his eyes. "You *habla?*" Samuel showed him the knife in his hand, then turned to the tired horse beside him.

"Si," the boy whispered. He led his sister away a few steps with the dog at their side. The three of them lowered down to the ground, the boy shielding his sister's eyes and whispering near her ear.

Samuel looked back once more at the riders gaining behind them. Then he turned to the buttes and caught a glimpse of the other three riders joining the first one down on the flatlands. He thought of how strange this must all look from some higher level, this collection of spent, frightened creatures on a flat hot griddle of sand. What was this struggle for? Simply to remain here in this harsh furnace? And what of these two forces advancing on them like packs of wolves? What was their gain? Didn't they realize that this was only one passing day? Only one thin slice of time out of the broad, tough breast of the universe?

Enough of that . . . He shook his head back and forth, clearing it. The heat had dazed him for a second. But now he collected himself, stepped in front of the tired horse and raised its sweat-streaked head with his left hand, turning its face upward to the stark empty sky. "Easy, boy," he whispered. With all suddenness and all of his strength, to keep it quick and get it over with, he plunged the knife blade in and up, and felt the horse's damp chest tense and shudder, and then go slack against his bloody hand.

Imdigo stopped at the head of the column of riders and looked westward where the sun had begun its slow fiery descent. Shadows stretched long off the jagged hills and buttes. Beneath the buttes, dust from the other four *comadrejas* had settled as they'd stepped down from their saddles and squatted on the open flatlands. Imdigo lifted the field lens to his eye, scanned back and forth across the four *comadrejas,* then across the dead horse farther out on the flats where Samuel and the children had taken cover.

"Whatz are those four cowards waiting forz?" Imdigo said, referring to the four *comadrejas* huddled beneath the buttes. They each had a rifle across their laps, yet they seemed not at all interested in advancing farther onto the flatlands. "They sitz there doingz nothing!"

The Rat rubbed his raw sweaty neck. "Well, it's too damn hot to prolong this thing. Let's ride on out and do what we got to do."

Imdigo waited, thinking, wondering why the other four had dropped down and stalled in the midst of the afternoon heat. He recalled the fleeting glimpse of the rifle he'd seen earlier. After a moment's more consideration, he turned to The Rat, and spread a crafty smile. "I think maybe jou move in closer and seez what goes onz, eh?"

"Shit, why not?" The Rat looked all around. "Maybe take a couple of boys with me?"

Imdigo shrugged. "Take a couple."

When The Rat returned with two others riding beside him, Imdigo looked one of the men's horse up and down. "Change horses withz me, Adlea."

The man, Adlea, looked at him. "Butz why, Imdigo?"

Imdigo had already stepped down to make the swap. "Do notz argue to me! Change horses!"

Adlea looked around, worried, then climbed up on Imdigo's horse. The Rat chuckled and said to Imdigo as he and the other two filed past him, "You don't think we're coming back, do you?"

Imdigo only jerked his head toward the dot on the horizon where the dead horse lay. "Go on, Rat. We willz seez." In the sky above the horse, a buzzard drifted, suspended on an updraft of air.

With the field lens to his eye, Imdigo watched The Rat and the other two ride out in a loping steady pace across the sand, a tail of dust wiping back and forth with the beat of their horses' hooves. He judged the yardage. At what he speculated to be a thousand yards out, The Rat rose slightly in his saddle, a rifle raised above his head. He spurred his horse hard, let out a war whoop, and swung his arm forward. The other two followed, each of them letting out a cry of their own.

Imdigo watched them in the small circle of lens. The Rat rode hard at the lead until he'd left the other two a hundred yards behind him. But then, as if having ran under a low lying branch, The Rat lifted up and back out of his saddle and seemed to hang in the air for a second with a red ribbon spiraling out of the middle of his back.

"Si, I was rightz," Imdigo said to himself, watching The Rat roll away in a spray of blood and sand as the blast of the big rifle cracked across the flatlands. "Soz itz really *was* a buffalo rifle I sawz." As the sound of another blast pealed across the desert, Imdigo turned to the rest of the *comadrejas*. "All rightz, nowz we know what to do. You menz circle him. We charge allz at oncez and killz him."

"Imdigo, whatz about the childrenz?"

"Whatz about themz?"

"You saidz you wanted themz."

"I did. But so whatz? Now we killz everything!" He raised an arm, circled it the air and put it forward. The men spurred their horses out and rode abreast across the burning sand.

Behind the dead horse, Samuel reloaded as the last of the first three *comadrejas* pitched backward dead on the sand, his horse slowly coming to a halt. Samuel leveled the buffalo rifle back across the dead horse's side. "Here they come," he said back to the boy and girl. "Keep that horse down."

"Si!" The other horse was down on its side, the boy holding it in place with an arm and a leg thrown over its neck. His sister patted the horse's side, trying to soothe it against the crushing noise of the buffalo rifle.

The butt stock of the big rifle slammed against Samuel's shoulder. Another rider, horse and all, rolled sidelong in a high sheet of sand. He turned to reload, and in doing so caught sight of the four *comadrejas* from beneath the buttes who had now mounted their horses and were charging forward. Smoke blossomed from their pistol barrels. Being closer than the main force of *comadrejas* charging their front, Samuel swung the big rifle toward the four riders, steadied it on his knee, and fired. As one of the four *comadrejas* flew backward from his saddle, Samuel had already turned, reloaded, and aimed the rifle out once more across the dead horse's side.

At four hundred yards, Imdigo spun his horse to the left as the next rifle shot sliced through the chest of the man beside him, hurling him away. "This is notz working! Getz him, jou fools!" he shouted to the other riders, who upon seeing the deadly accuracy of the big rifle, and knowing that nothing lay between them and its line of fire, had already begun to veer and draw their horses away.

Two of Imdigo's riders managed to get in closer, dropping from their horses and taking position behind the lip of a flat rock. They fired, and Samuel felt the bullets thump into the dead horse's rump.

He turned to the children, saw that they were protected by the other horse, the big cur standing above them with his tail tucked between his legs. Samuel glanced at the ammunition laid out on the ground beside him—he had only seven rounds left. From the buttes, the three remaining riders charged straight in and were now flanking to the left, still firing, but their pistol rounds fell short and kicked up sand thirty yards out.

"Stay down, Blue!" Samuel yelled, seeing the big cur start back and forth at the sound of pistol fire. Samuel turned toward the three riders, leveled the buffalo rifle, and had only started to pull the trigger when he heard the blast of rifle fire from somewhere among the buttes and saw one of the riders fly sidelong from his saddle.

"Sazes?" he said hopefully. Then with no time to dwell on it, he turned and fired on the two *comadrejas* behind the flat rock a hundred yards away.

Not afforded any cover in the flat desolate land, Imdigo had taken to the sand, holding onto the horse's outstretched reins as the animal thrashed, whinnied, and tried to pull free. One of his men came crawling quickly through the sand on his belly. "He is shootingz us to pieces, Imdigo! Now some-one is firing fromz the buttes!"

"I seez that!" Imdigo raged at the man. "Callz the men back! We go now!"

"What about those twoz?" The man pointed a shaky fin-ger toward the flat rock where two *comadrejas'* rifles still exploded toward Samuel's position.

"Leave themz!" Imdigo looked off at the distant sky and shook his head. "The stormz caused all this!" He shook his fist at the clear blue heavens.

Behind Samuel, a shot from one of the rifles behind the rock nipped at the other horse's hoof, and the startled horse slung the children away and bolted. Samuel caught the little girl in the crook of his arm and pressed her down against the dead horse's belly. The boy slid in beside him. Blue flew into a fit of barking, circling out a few feet in the sand.

The boy started to make a leap for the dog, but Samuel grabbed him and held him back. "No! Lay still!" Turning to the big cur, Samuel yelled, "Blue, get in here!" Two rifles barked from behind the flat rock. Sand kicked up near the big cur and he dodged back from it. Samuel turned and fired, his shot taking off a chunk of rock, but he was unable to hit the men. From the buttes, rifle fire barraged on the other two riders steadily, until they gave up the fight and raced away across the sand. Samuel reloaded—he was down to three cartridges now—and leveled the rifle across the dead horse's side, taking aim on the *comadreja* who yanked his horse's reins, trying to settle it enough to climb into the saddle. The other *comadrejas* were moving back now. He squeezed the trigger, felt the rifle slam against his shoulder, and saw both man and horse go down as the bullet tore through the man's back and embedded itself in the horse's chest. Samuel reloaded, but this time he held his fire, alternating his rifle sights back and forth on the fleeing riders.

For a moment there was dead silence. Nothing stirred but a hot gust of wind across Samuel's back. No more shots resounded from behind the flat rock where the *comadrejas* were. Beyond it, he saw the two figures crawling swiftly away. Samuel let out a breath, patted a hand on the little girl's back, who cringed with her face hidden against the dead horse's belly. "Move around here," he said to the boy. "Take care of your sister."

A few feet out, Blue thrashed in the sand, blood spilling from his right front shoulder. Samuel crawled out and dragged the dog back to the cover of the dead horse. "Easy, Blue . . ." He jerked the bandanna from around his neck and pressed it to the gaping wound. The dog whined and tossed its head; pulling him across his lap, Samuel leaned back against the belly of the dead horse. "I've got you, Blue." He pressed the bandanna to stay the flow of blood, and looked out toward the buttes where a single rider came into sight, waving an arm back and forth slowly above his head.

"Look, I was right! It's Sazes, Blue," Samuel whispered to the big cur as if the dog understood his words. He let out a relieved breath, and taking a second to clear the heat of battle from his chest, he said to the wounded dog, "You're going to be all right now."

Samuel held Blue and sat quietly while the boy and girl huddled against him, watching Ranger Clyde Sazes slow his big Appaloosa down to a walk the last few yards. The big stallion sidestepped at the sight of the dead horse. Sazes steadied the animal, looking back and forth along the horizon. He stopped the Appaloosa and sat looking down at Samuel, without a word of acknowledgment. He lifted his hat brim, propped his rifle up on his thigh, and got right down to business. "That was Imdigo's men," he said. "And that's Imdigo laying dead over there. I saw you shoot him through my field lens. Good shot, young man."

Samuel only nodded. The children made room for him to stand, and he did so with the big cur lying across his forearms. "Can you help me with Blue? He took a bullet in the shoulder."

Ranger Sazes looked him up and down, seeing the long healing scar on his face. "It appears you've had another confrontation since last I saw you."

"It's a long story." Samuel lowered the injured dog to the ground as Sazes stepped down from his saddle, lifting a canteen of water from around his saddle horn.

Sazes handed Samuel the canteen, then nodded toward the children who stood quietly beside the dead horse. "I came this way looking for them. It's a good thing you found them before the *comadrejas* took them across the border. You took quite a chance." Now that he saw the children were safe, Sazes turned from them, and stooped down to the wounded dog, scratching its ears.

"I had a hunch you'd be on their trail," Samuel said. "Couldn't see you leaving them to the *comadrejas* if you knew about it."

"A hunch?" Sazes looked at him. "There's not many folks who would have figured me that way."

"I'm not many folks." Samuel attended to the dog.

"No, I reckon you're not." Ranger Sazes watched him, studying the deep wound on his cheek. Samuel wet the bandanna with water and dabbed at the dog's shoulder wound.

But when he drew the knife from his boot well, Sazes stopped him and said, "We'll get the bullet out of him, once we get into the shade of the buttes."

"What about the rest of the *comadrejas*?" Samuel cut a glance out across the flatlands.

"They've had it for now." Ranger Sazes examined the dog's seeping gash as he spoke. "With Imdigo dead, they'll hightail it across the border and lick their wounds for a few days. They won't be bothering us." He stopped examining the dog long enough to fix his gaze on Samuel for a second. "If your hunch about me had been wrong, all three of you'd be dead."

"But I wasn't wrong about you," Samuel said. "Even if I had been wrong, what other choice did I have?"

Sazes's eyes went to the children. "Good point." He spread a smile and returned his attention to Blue. "Let's get going." Then he spoke down to the big cur as if the dog understood him. "Are you going to live long enough to learn anything?"

"He's doing a little bit better every day," Samuel said on the dog's behalf.

Chapter 18

Junior Lake stepped out on the boardwalk in front of the Blue Eagle Saloon in Humbly, puffing on one of the cigars he'd taken by the handful from behind the bar. He and Braydon were not alone now. Three days earlier, they'd teamed up with three border outlaws while on their way to town. These men had heard Ranger Clyde Sazes was in the area and they had been headed for Mexico to avoid him. It didn't take Junior Lake long to convince them to join him.

Of course, Junior hadn't mentioned that Ranger Sazes was hot on his own trail and had been for some time. All he'd mentioned was that it would be better to travel in strong numbers, a notion that was hard for the three men to dispute, knowing Junior's reputation. As he puffed the cigar, Junior Lake grinned and tipped his hat to two women who had hoped to get past the saloon without being seen. They hurried past him. "Good afternoon, ladies . . ."

Junior chuckled under his breath as they gave him a frightened look and quickly disappeared into a doorway. On the street, Braydon stood among a hitch rail full of horses he'd gathered throughout the town. On the side of the telegraph office, lines sagged to the ground where one of the outlaws had cut them the day they rode in.

It was a stroke of luck running into these three hard-cases, Junior thought, puffing his cigar. His intentions had been for him and Braydon to slip into town, gather fresh horses, some supplies, then cut straight for the border. But now, with three more guns backing him, he could afford to make a little bolder stance here. He could take what he wanted. Who could stop him? In the single jail cell across the street in the sheriff's office, Sheriff Lovelet lay on the floor of the locked cell with a bloody knot on his forehead. The few townsmen in Humbly had armed themselves, but they stayed back now, fearing what would happen to the sheriff if they made a move on Junior Lake and his outlaws.

"Garrett, Clancey, Stubs," Junior called out to the three outlaws who came walking through the broken doorframe of the mercantile store, their arms full of supplies, weapons, and ammunition. "You boys get on over here and pick yourselves a good horse, compliments of the local gentry."

"By God! Don't mind if I do," said the one named Lester Stubs, who dropped an armload of supplies to the ground and stepped over them toward the line of horses. "This is the most generous bunch of folks I've run into in a long time." Stubs was a short outlaw with three fingers missing from his left hand. He wore a tall silk top hat shoved down over his battered Stetson brim and had put on a long swallow-tailed dress coat over his dusty sweat-streaked range clothes. "I'll just take that big chestnut bay, then."

"Any one but that one," Braydon said. "That one's mine." He stepped in between Stubs and the big chestnut as Stubs bounded forward.

"The hell he is. You heard Junior. He said take my pick. So get out of my way." Stubs started to shove Braydon to one side, but Junior Lake's voice stopped him cold.

"Don't put your hands on my little buddy, Stubs. Pick yourself another horse, before I wear a pistol barrel out over your head."

"Huh?" Stubs turned to him, Junior looking down on him from the boardwalk. "Your little buddy? Thought we was all in this together—"

"You heard me, Stubs." Junior glared at him. "Braydon's my good-luck charm . . . he's like a rabbit's foot to me. Any problem with that?" Junior's hand rested on the Hoard pistol hanging down his chest on a strip of rawhide.

Stubs shrugged. "Not at all. One horse is as good as another, when it's free anyway." He grinned and snatched the reins to a big line back dun. But as he'd unwound the horse's reins and pulled it away from the rail, he shot Braydon a hard glance and whispered something under his breath. Braydon only smiled. This was the first time Junior had ever referred to him as a good-luck charm. He liked that.

The other two outlaws, Garrett and Clancey, stepped in and picked a horse. Garrett stood barefoot in the dirt, a rifle with a scorpion carved in its stock in his right hand. He looked up at Junior Lake and said, "He might be your good-luck charm, but that's my leather tobacco pouch hanging out of his pocket—I want it back!" He turned his stare from Junior Lake to Braydon. Braydon squirmed in place.

"Jesus, Braydon." Junior Lake shook his head in disgust. "Did you take his damn pouch? Can't you leave anything alone?"

"Wasn't my fault this time," Braydon said, looking sheepishly down at the ground. "He left it laying on the bar, I swear he did." Braydon lifted the pouch from his rear pocket and handed it over.

"That's right I did, right next to my hand, you little turd!" Garrett snarled, snatching the pouch from Braydon. "It's bad enough I can't find boots to fit me, let alone being robbed of my personals."

"That's enough, Garrett. You got your pouch back." Junior laughed low, and added, "Braydon can't help stealing. Says it's born in him. Right, Braydon?"

"It's not something to joke about," Braydon said, looking embarrassed.

Garrett took a horse, and pulling it past Braydon, whispered between the two of them, "Touch something else of mine, I'll walk around your little chicken neck with a paring knife. I'm an assassin . . . I tolerate no fool's play."

Braydon swallowed hard and moved back a step.

"If everybody's through with their bullshit," Junior called down to them, "let's get this show on the road. It's a long ride from here to where we're going."

Clancey, a tall thin man wearing dusty eyeglasses, had also pulled a horse from the rail, checking its cinch and saddle. Now he looked up at Junior through his thick glasses and said, "We're going to ride out of here, just like that?"

"Well, yes, Mr. Clancey." There was a sarcastic snap to Junior's words. "I feel like it's the right thing to do. Why, did we forget something?"

"It's just that . . ." Clancey paused, looking all around the empty street. Ten yards up the street, a dead mule lay in its wagon traces where one of the men had shot it down earlier. Along the boardwalk, broken glass lay glistening in the sunlight. "I'd kind of like to burn something down first." He looked back up at Junior Lake. "It would make up for the bank not having any money in it, don't you think?"

Junior just stared at him blankly for a second, then said in an exasperated tone, "Hell yes, by all means . . . set something on fire." He turned to Braydon, Garrett and Stubs. "You three get the supplies together while Mr. Clancey here amuses himself."

Junior stood watching the empty street while Clancey ran giggling like an excited schoolboy to the saloon. In a moment, he ran back into the street with a lantern burning in his hand. He bounded back and forth, whooping like a wild man. Then he stopped in front of the telegraph office and hurled the burning lantern through the large glass window. Junior Lake shook his head and murmured under his breath, "Yeah, laugh, you crazy bastard, it's going to be a pleasure getting rid of you . . ."

*   *   *

With the two children and the wounded dog, the ride to Humbly took a day longer than it should have. Ranger Sazes led the way on his big Appaloosa. Behind Sazes, the children rode on one of the two *comadrejas'* horses they'd found wandering the flatlands. Samuel rode a few feet behind them with the bleeding cur draped over his lap. Before starting their trek toward Humbly, Samuel had held the big cur down on the ground, in the shade of the buttes, with a blanket pressed over his head, while Sazes dug in and unlodged the bullet from the dog's shoulder. The dog had lost a lot of blood and was too sore to walk, but otherwise was doing as well as could be expected. The wound was clean, with no signs of infection. Sazes had covered the gash with a bandanna held in place by a length of rope tied around the dog's chest, to keep out the sand and dust.

The night before while they made a camp alongside a sparse stand of pinyon trees, Sazes had cleaned and rechecked the dog's wound. When he finished, he poured himself a cup of tea, and waited until the children were asleep on a blanket near the fire. Then he turned to Samuel and asked about the scars on his face and his head and about what had happened on his way to Wakely. As Samuel told him everything, about taking in Daggett, about Ellsworth, the girl, and what had happened to Lawrence Shaw's wife, Sazes just listened and sipped his tea and seemed to consider all of it as part of some grand design.

"So capturing Daggett bought you a hand in the game," Sazes reflected, taking out his briar pipe, packing and lighting it with a twig from the campfire. "Then when you got to town, instead of sticking with the sheriff, you threw in with Shaw and Cousins." He let out a breath and a long stream of smoke.

"I didn't throw in with anybody," Samuel said. "Things just seemed to have been led that way."

"Either way, that's where you were headed and that's where you ended up." Sazes said it as if it didn't matter whether a man's course was steered by his intention or blind happenstance. The end result was still the same.

"All I know is, if it hadn't been for Shaw, I would never had made it to Wakely."

Ranger Sazes looked Samuel up and down in the flicker of firelight, taking note of the Colt pistol in the low-slung holster on his hip. "I suppose Shaw had something to do with that pistol tied on your hip, too."

"Yes, as a matter of fact. It's one that he found in the sheriff's office."

"And he taught you to use it?"

"I've been a good shot since I was a kid," Samuel said. "Nobody had to show me how to use it." He saw the look in Outrider Sazes's eyes. Then he added, "Shaw knows a lot about gunfighting. We talked some about it."

"I see." Sazes drew on his pipe and sipped tea from his tin cup.

"Shaw and Cousins both treated me like a friend. I can't say nothing against either of them."

Ranger Sazes let out a puff of smoke and with it a sigh. "No, I suppose you can't. But don't consider them friends, not in any sense that gives allegiance to what they are or how they conduct themselves. I warned you about stepping into that world. Now that you're in it, don't go making friends with those who live there."

"Shaw and Cousins aren't outlaws," Samuel said in the two men's defense.

"No, but they walk a fine line on the edge of being one. Shaw, for the sake of recognition, has gotten stuck with what he is. Cherokee Cousins, by his own avaricious nature, puts himself in a place where the wind can sweep him in either direction."

"Cousins is a lawman. Him and Shaw both told me so."

"A lawman? Well, *sometimes*, when it's convenient to him . . . but he can never commit to it fully. He's a gambler and a roundabout *all* the time, because that's what comes to a man when he can't make a choice." Sazes drew on his pipe and watched Samuel's face to see how he took it. "I know you don't like what you're hearing. But if Cousins were a real lawman he'd be after Junior Lake and that bunch for what they've done to others, not for what they've done to him. He's on a man's trail for stealing his horse?" Sazes chuckled. "That's pretty puny in the overall scheme of things, wouldn't you say?"

Samuel shrugged. "It's not my place to judge him."

"But of course it is." Sazes let out a long stream of smoke and examined the glowing bowl of his pipe. "The less a man judges others the more he loses sight of himself. Judging is what we all do—we just ain't suppose to *admit* to doing it." He spread a crooked smile and wagged the pipe back and forth in his hand. "Don't confuse judgment with acceptance. You might accept what Cousins is. But you better do so only after judging him and you best judge him wisely. If you can't, you better spur your horse down a different trail. Else this one will kill you graveyard-dead."

Sazes's eyes darkened even in the glow of the firelight. He then added, "I've learned to judge and accept all comers within the boundary of man's law . . . because that's the clearest and most simple principle to live by."

A silence passed as Samuel considered Sazes's words. Then he asked, "What about me, Ranger Sazes? How have you judged me?"

Sazes took his time, inspecting the bowl of the pipe and tapping out the ashes against the heel of his boot. "You're set upon to right the wrongs done to others—to what was done to Davey Riley, not what was done to you. I believe you would have felt the same had you not even known Davey Riley, and had only seen what was done to him from afar."

"A noble pilgrim," Samuel offered in a quiet tone. "That's what Cherokee Cousins called me."

"Then he might've been right on that account. I judge you as just and honest. If you weren't, you wouldn't have come looking for me."

"I never said I came looking for you." Samuel tilted his head a bit and eyed him in the flicker of firelight.

"No, but you did, whether you knew it or not."

"Oh?" Samuel offered a weary smile. "Either by intent or blind happenstance? Is that what you think?"

"What do *you* think?" Sazes finished off the last sip of tea and laid his tin cup beside the fire. Before Samuel could respond, Sazes leaned over the sleeping dog, saying to Samuel as he inspected the wound, "Now that you bear the scars of this world, will you carry them as a memory, or as a guide? If they're only going to be a memory, then happenstance is the whole of it. But if they become your guide . . ." His words trailed off.

"I want to see men like Sherman Ellsworth and Junior Lake brought to justice," Samuel said, his words surprising himself as he said them. "I can't abide the trouble they cause, or the evil they spread about themselves. I want to be a lawman . . . not a gunman like Shaw, not a rounder like Cousins. I want to be a lawman like you, Sazes . . . out here, where they live."

Ranger Sazes only looked at him. Samuel nodded and looked him in the eye. "There, I've said it. I reckon I've known that for a while and just couldn't admit it to myself."

"It's good that you took your time, didn't jump to the decision. Law work's not for most folks, especially out here." Sazes had been holding the empty pipe in his hand. Now he put it inside his shirt pocket and leaned back against his saddle on the ground.

"Well . . . what do you say?" Samuel studied his eyes in the flickering fire. "Will you take me with you, help me become a lawman? I'll carry my own weight."

"We'll see." Sazes tilted the brim of his hat down over his brow. "Let's get these children to town, then go get Junior and his boys. When it's all over, you let me know if you still feel the same."

Chapter 19

Although it had been a full day and a night since Clancey set fire to the telegraph office in Humbly, a thin spiral of smoke still drifted from the blackened bed of ashes and twisted metal debris. Had it not been for the old sheriff, Horace Lovelet, catching sight of the two children as Ranger Sazes and his party rode in off the last stretch of sand and creosote bushes, the armed townsmen might have fired upon them. But seeing the children gave Lovelet pause, at least long enough to recognize Sazes's big Appaloosa stallion. When the Appaloosa drew closer, Sheriff Lovelet recognized the Outrider himself. By then, the townsmen had gathered behind the old sheriff, and awaited his decision.

"Easy now. Everybody stand down," Lovelet cautioned over his shoulder, both of his hands supporting the old Dance Brothers pistol, a weathered thumb lying tense across its worn hammer. "It's Outrider Sazes . . . and a group of youngins with him. Most likely the Mexican children from the missing land wagon."

"Outrider Sazes, huh?" A voice spoke from amid the armed townsmen. "That explains the likes of Junior Lake cutting through here in the first place. That blasted old ranger keeps those badlands stirred up like a hornets' nest."

"Quieten down now." Lovelet turned slightly toward the sound of the voice behind him. "Let's try to show some manners here." Yet when Sazes stepped his horse past the smoldering debris, eyeing it closely his last few yards up the middle of the street, the old sheriff called out to him, "There, Sazes! That's what happens every time you dog those hard-cases in our direction!"

Sazes reined his Appaloosa to a halt a few feet back, and nodded at the pistol in Sheriff Lovelet's hands. "Good morning to you, too, Sheriff. I'd appreciate you giving that pistol a little breathing room. Wouldn't want these children to get a bad impression of their northern neighbors, would we?" Sazes turned in his saddle and looked the town over, shaking his head. "The fact is, I wasn't dogging him at the time. If I had been, he wouldn't have stayed long enough to do all this. I broke from his trail to hunt for these children."

"You did?" Sheriff Lovelet looked surprised for a second, as if having trouble picturing Outrider Clyde Sazes doing such a thing. But then he relented a bit, rubbed his drooping mustache and let go of a tense breath. "Well, I'll be . . . are they the ones from the wagon we heard about?" Lovelet raised his thumb from across the pistol's hammer and took one hand off the pistol butt, letting the big Dance Brothers hang down his thigh. His brittle right shoulder slumped from the weight of it.

"Where'd you hear about it?" Sazes eyed him, the Appaloosa stepping sideways to the townsmen in the dirt street.

"From that lousy pack rat Morris Braydon, who rides with Junior Lake, that's who. He got drunk and couldn't keep from bragging to the bartender how him and Junior traded them kids for horses. It'd make your skin crawl . . ."

"That figures. Braydon's always been an idiot." Sazes gazed off toward the flat trail on the far end of town. "How long ago did they leave, Sheriff?"

"Yesterday, about this same time, Sazes," Sheriff Lovelet answered. "Of course they had to burn something down first." He thumbed toward the charred telegraph office. "All five of them rode out of here like tom cats slathered up from a prowl." Lovelet spat and ran a hand across his mouth in disgust.

Samuel had slipped down from his saddle and laid the wounded cur on the ground. The dog swayed and righted himself, then stared forward at the group of men and their rifles and shotguns. His hackles rose in suspicion.

"Five, huh?" Sazes raised the brim of his hat. "So they've taken on three others. I suspect there'll be more joining him along the way to the border. Junior does have his ways when it comes to attracting followers."

"Yep, he does," Lovelet agreed. "They all took plenty of arms and fresh horses, too. I expect you'll have your hands full when you catch up to them."

"Feels like I've been on Junior and his boys half the summer . . . trying to keep them from cutting over to Junior's hideout at Blood Rock," Sazes said. "Was anybody killed here?"

"No. Not this time." Lovelet seethed just thinking about it. "But only because we knuckled down to him. I'm no match for Junior Lake . . . might as well admit it. The men here wouldn't make a move, feared they'd get me killed. They were right in thinking it, too." Lovelet raised his hat an inch. "Look what they did to me."

Sazes looked at the swollen knot on the side of Lovelet's head, and nodded. "Your men did the right thing, Sheriff. Don't worry, I'll bring Junior Lake down."

"When you do, don't bring him by here, unless you want him hung quick without a trial." The old sheriff glanced at the men around him for support. They nodded and murmured among themselves.

"Gonna blow his damned head off, Outrider?" a voice called out from among the townsmen.

Sazes only glanced across the faces of the townsmen and, ignoring the remark, turned back to the sheriff. "I'd like you to witness me swearing this boy in as my deputy, Lovelet." Sazes gestured toward Samuel. "His name is Sam Burrack.

He's going to be riding them down with me. He'll need some proper legal authority."

"A deputy? Since when did you ever have a deputy, Sazes?"

"Since I asked you to be a witness to it, Sheriff." Sazes's eyes took on a hard edge. "Will you do it or not?"

"Hell yes, indeed I will. If it'll help close Junior Lake's eye forever . . . I'll witness anything it takes." He looked past Ranger Sazes at Samuel and added, "You send them straight to hell, young man . . . you hear me? There ain't one in that whole lousy bunch fit to live."

Samuel only nodded.

From one of the shops along the boardwalk, a woman came forward to the children and bent down to them, speaking to them in Spanish, in a low soothing tone. While the men talked of who should live and who should die, she led the children off with her, raising the little girl up onto her hip while the boy tagged along barefoot a short ways back. The boy lingered at first and looked back at Samuel and raised his small hand to him.

"Gracias, amigo. Dios esta con usted siempre." He'd told Samuel goodbye, and asked that God be with him always.

"De nada. Dios esta con tambien." May God be with you also, Samuel answered in his broken Spanish. He gave the boy a reassuring nod and watched him turn away, this time walking a little closer to the woman beside him. On the ground, Blue, finding himself alone in the dirt street, limped over stiffly and stood a few inches behind Samuel's boot heel.

"We need supplies, and some fresh horses under us," Ranger Sazes said to Sheriff Lovelet. "How bad did they clean you out?"

"Pretty bad." The sheriff gestured a hand about the broken glass and bare shop windows along the boardwalks. "But we'll get together whatever we can for yas." Sheriff Lovelet stopped and scratched his swollen head, looking

Sazes up and down. "You really broke off of Junior's trail to hunt for those children?"

"That's right, Sheriff." Sazes just looked at him. "Why do you ask?"

"Because . . . *damn,* that just doesn't sound like you, Sazes. From what I always heard of you—"

"All right, then, Sheriff." Sazes cut him off. "Let's put it this way. This young man here found the children. I just happened along at the right time. Does that suit you better?"

"No offense, but yes, it does." Lovelet spread a thin smile and leveled his hat down on his head. "Come on, let's go see what we can find for you." Sheriff Lovelet motioned Sazes off toward the livery barn.

"But Outrider Sazes was already on the children's trail," Samuel put in. "He kept the *comadrejas* from killing all of us."

"I understand." The sheriff cut Samuel a disbelieving glance, and said to Ranger Sazes as they walked together through the parting group of townsmen, "Luckily we managed to get the money out the back door of the bank without them seeing us. Left a few dollars in there to keep them from being suspicious. They beat the hell out of the teller, but he stuck to his story, told them there hadn't been any money in the bank since last Christmas."

Samuel shook his head, listening as they walked away. He picked the big cur up in his arms, gathered the reins to the horses, and followed a few feet behind the two lawmen. "I don't really care who saved who from what out there, Sazes," Sheriff Lovelet said. "I just want to see an end to that son of a bitch, Junior Lake."

With two fresh horses in tow and ten days' worth of supplies divided between them, Ranger Sazes and Deputy Ranger Samuel Burrack left Humbly and followed the day old tracks across the flatlands and upward into the badlands hills. They pushed hard, for two days and nights, swapping the horses back and forth every four hours, keeping the animals as rested and ready as possible. The big cur spent most of the first day riding across Samuel's lap. But by evening when the dog began to squirm and grow restless, Samuel lowered him from the saddle and watched him as he stretched his stiff legs, shook himself out, and tried trotting ahead of them a few yards. He limped badly, yet pushed himself on, his wounded shoulder drawing him into a crooked gait. "He's coming along fast enough," Sazes said, sitting atop his Appaloosa, watching Blue from the sparse shade of a lone cottonwood tree. "Before you know it he'll be back strong as ever. He might be a different dog by then. A bad wound has a way of bringing about change in man and beast alike."

"We'll see." Samuel whistled for the big cur, and when the dog came limping up to them, Sazes backed his horse a step and turned it and put it forward on the trail.

"Getting wounded changed you some, didn't it?" Sazes asked over his shoulder as Samuel stepped down and raised the dog across his saddle.

"All it did was make me more careful." Samuel stepped up into the saddle and adjusted the panting dog across his lap.

"And you don't call that a change?" Sazes heeled the Appaloosa forward, leading his spare horse behind him. They rode on. At a narrow cross-trail, Sazes and Samuel looked down at the ground where four new sets of hoofprints had moved in from the east, joining the others. "And now there's nine." Ranger Sazes spoke in a lowered tone, and gazed upward along the high ridgelines in the distance. At a clearing in a shallow rock basin, they saw where the five men had stopped and rested. Sazes stepped down and kicked an empty whiskey bottle out across the sand. "Junior will get more brazen as his numbers improve." He allowed a crooked smile and turned and stepped back up onto his saddle.

In the long encroaching shadows of evening, Blue took the lead while Samuel and Outrider Sazes moved their horses along at a walk. When they stopped that night to make camp, the big cur lay on the sand and managed to stretch his stiff neck around, poking his nose beneath the bandage and licking the wound. "Yep, he's on the mend," Samuel said, raking together a short bank of sand for their cook fire while Ranger Sazes attended the horses.

"No fire tonight," Sazes said in a matter-of-fact tone, gazing ahead toward the next higher level of terraced rockland. "They're up there somewhere, pretty close. They can't see us with the naked eye in broad daylight . . . but they'll see our fire at night. Let's keep Junior Lake looking over his shoulder, wondering where we are."

"All right." Samuel smoothed away the sand. He went to his saddlebags on the ground and returned with canteens of water, a handful of jerked meat, and the remaining dried biscuits they'd brought from town. They sat down to eat. After considering something that had been on his mind since they'd first arrived in Humbly, Samuel took a short sip of water and asked Sazes why he'd let the sheriff think that he'd only happened upon the children, when Sazes had been trailing them all along.

"Aw, what's the difference? The main thing is the children are safe. Like most folks, Sheriff Lovelet thinks what he wants to think, sees what he wants to see." Sazes tried to dismiss it with a toss of his gloved hand.

"But he's wrong about you, Sazes. So are a lot of people." Samuel chewed his biscuit and jerked meat as he spoke. "Don't you mind?"

"No, I suppose not." Sazes looked down at the canteen in his hand and swished it around. "I use to, a long time ago. But this is what I am, and what people make of it neither makes the sun rise nor set, now, does it?" He smiled, but Samuel thought he saw a trace of sadness, regret perhaps.

"No, maybe not." Samuel sipped water from the canteen and studied Sazes's shadowed face in the coming darkness.

Sazes saw the look in Samuel's eyes and turned his face from him and shrugged, playing it off. "Besides, having

people think they know you when they really don't might be
a good thing out here. It's not wise for me to let the kind of
people I deal with know what I'm up to, what I'm thinking,
what my next move might be."

"Keep them off balance and guessing?"

"As much as possible. It's not important that people
know who I am. Only what I stand for." He tapped the
badge on his chest. "The man who has to justify himself
and explain his actions is a man who's missed his calling. I
know why I'm here. I deal a hard game, but I play it
through. The day I lose, I'll ask no mercy . . . no more than
I've given."

"Sounds fair enough to me." A silence passed. Samuel
finished his biscuit and jerky and sipped from the canteen.
"Why didn't Junior Lake cut straight for the border when he
had a chance? Why'd he wait around for you to get back on
his trail?"

Sazes capped his canteen and lay it on his lap. "Because
he's like every other hardheaded outlaw. He wants to get
across the border, but he's always looking for one more
thing to gain first. It's my notion that deep down inside,
every outlaw wants to get caught. They just don't realize it."

Samuel only stared at him.

Sazes shrugged. "A boy like Junior Lake don't want to
just get away nice and easy. What's the excitement in that?
He likes to feel the world hounding him, feel the air tight
around his throat. He wants to keep life pressed to its breaking point, then at the last second, slip out by the skin of his
back, with bullets flying. That way he feels he's accom-
plished something. In the end, they all want to go down in a
blaze. If not, what's been the point to their whole miserable
life?"

Samuel slumped a bit and shook his head, having a hard
time agreeing with it. "And you say this is something they
don't realize?"

Sazes chuckled and relaxed against his saddle. "Hell no.
If they realized it, they wouldn't be an outlaw."

Samuel capped his canteen, and picking up Sazes's canteen, carried them both a few feet away and laid them on a rock near the horses. "I'll take first watch," he said.

"No need for you to tonight," Sazes said from beneath his lowered hat brim. "Get yourself some rest."

"They could slip in on us," Samuel said, glancing around at their wide open campsite, and up at the black line of hills above them.

"Trust your dog." Sazes pointed a hand out to the big cur where it lay on the sand, licking at its wounded shoulder. "From now on, this ole boy won't let anybody within a hundred yards."

Chapter 20

On a rock overhang high up in the badlands hills, Junior Lake took only a short sip from the bottle of rye and handed it back to Max Reed, one of the four outlaws who'd fallen in with him on his way up from the flatlands. "Max, ole buddy. You can't imagine how glad I was to see you and Bud Dannard coming." Junior nodded toward Clancey and Stubs, who sat passing a bottle back and forth with Braydon and Bud Dannard. A few yards away, Coy Garrett lay passed out drunk with his horse's reins wrapped around his hand. "Those three peckerwoods have just about drove me to killing them all."

Max Reed looked at the dusty bottle of rye, rounded his palm around the tip of it, and threw back a long drink. "What'd they do?"

Junior shrugged. "It's not so much what they've done. They just don't know nothing. Those two are a couple of bungling jailhouse rats, is what I've concluded. Stubs barely has enough fingers to pick his nose. Clancey, the one with the eyeglasses, likes to watch fires. I believe he'd thrown open his fly and grabbed a handful of himself had we not been watching him."

"One of those kind, eh?" Max Reed said.

"Yeah, and that one, with his reins around his wrist." He nodded at Coy Garrett sprawled on the ground. "He can't even find boots that'll fit him. Look at those feet! I feel like goosing his horse and letting it drag him to death. He keeps chastising poor ole Braydon for stealing. Hell, you know how Braydon is. He can't help it."

"Yeah, I know." Max Reed ran a hand behind his back, making sure his Bowie knife was still there. "You just have to keep an eye on your stuff around him." He checked the watch fob in his leather vest pocket and idly touched the bullets in his pistol belt.

"Anyway," Junior went on, "that one, Garrett, claims he's some kind of assassin, or wants to be if he could ever stay sober. He showed some promise till he started drinking—carries a rifle with a scorpion carved in the stock. Claims he came down from Wind River just to kill Outrider Sazes. Never said why. Said he used to be a hired assassin for the railroad." Junior sucked air between his teeth. "I swear, it's getting hard to find anybody worth a damn anymore." He nodded toward the two men who'd ridden in with Reed and Dannard. "What about those two? Think they're worth anything? If they are, their looks sure keep it hidden."

"The Moore brothers?" Max laughed. "Man! Talk about some straight-up inbreeds! The one on the right, Kirby, smells like he's had recent congress with a sow grizzly—the other one, Dillard, said he has a mortal fear of the number nine."

"The number *nine?*" Junior gave him a bemused look. "What the hell is that about?"

"Don't ask me. He said just being around the number causes him trouble breathing. Asked me and Dannard if we'd *please* not say it around him." Max Reed shrugged. "I told him sure . . . but you can tell Dannard's busting to let it rip any time."

"Jesus . . . !" Junior looked down for a second, considering it.

"I know," Max Reed chuckled, "he's one flat-out idiot! Me and Dannard ran into them cutting across the sand, scared to death. Like the devil was after them. Had to run them down to tell them we weren't the law. Turns out them and your boy, Ellsworth, screwed up a robbery back in

Wakely and had to get their knees in the wind. Ellsworth's saddle fell off his horse during their getaway. Said ole Ellsworth screamed like a woman. Said he was laying down a long stride of boot leather, last they saw of him."

"Sherman Ellsworth . . . lost his horse." Junior grinned. "Good ole Sherm. I never thought I'd miss that dirty, rotten, Texas bastard. He was supposed to head for Blood Rock and wait for us. I figured he'd take his time, though, stick his nose into something—get a hanging party on his trail first. Braydon stole his watch and half his money before he left. He'll be wanting to kill Braydon, is my guess. So there's one more thing for me to deal with. It's tough leading a bunch like this."

"I bet." Max chuckled and took another drink. "Speaking of losing a horse, what ever come of the trouble between you and Cherokee Cousins?"

"Don't know. Haven't seen him. When I do, I'll figure how to settle with him and be done with it. He's just one more sore loser, far as I'm concerned." Junior put the subject of Cherokee Cousins aside and nodded once more toward the Moore brothers and Clancey and Stubs. "Do you suppose all four of them together could even slow down Outrider Sazes, if I got them drunk, left them behind, and gave them a good talking-to first?"

"It's worth a try. Me and Dannard already decided, the Moore brothers ain't long for this earth. We're just biding our time. Far as Sazes goes, I figured as long as he's been dogging you, you'd have become friends by now." Max Reed grinned.

"I'll *friend* the son of a bitch. You watch."

"Not to turn this on a sour note . . . but why haven't you killed him already?" Max Reed tilted his head slightly and stared at him.

"Don't worry." Junior looked at him and winked. "I've got plans laid. I want to get the Outrider well fed first." He nodded once more toward the Moores and Clancey and

Stubs. "While he's picking them from his teeth, I'll shoot him hard, from a long ways off."

"We could break it off right here, get on over the border and come back next spring. The way Sazes has everybody stirred up, there's no telling how many men we'll have with us by then."

"Huh-uh." Junior shook his head and took the bottle from Max Reed's hand as Max offered it to him. "There's a lot of little pig-shit towns along the border. I'd like to work my way through them first—call me a tourist at heart." He grinned, took another short sip from the bottle, and handed it back. Max Reed turned the bottle up, emptied it, and pitched it to the ground.

Junior continued. "We'll get higher up, make Sazes think we're headed straight for *Mejico*. Once he finishes with these fools, he'll get in a hurry to stop us. Then we nail him, and go on about our business."

"I like your thinking, Junior." Max Reed laughed under his breath, and cut a glance toward the unsuspecting outlaws. "If you ever done me that way, I'd have to kill you."

Junior's eyes flashed hot, but Junior managed to check himself down and feign a smile. "Hell, Max, you think I'd be telling you all this if I ever planned on doing you the same way? We're two good buddies, you and me. Eh? Right, *mi amigo*?" He nudged Max Reed in the side with his elbow.

"Si, mi amigo." Max Reed chuckled. "We're both too smart for that . . ."

At the start of the day, while the first light shimmered in a silver thread on the horizon, Samuel cleaned and rebandaged the dog's wound, and fed him scraps of dried meat and biscuits. A gusting wind had set in with the rising sun, whipping the horses' tails and manes. Sazes led the animals forward, one hand holding his duster collar up against the sting of wind-driven sand. "It'll be a hot blow all day," he said in passing, as Samuel finished with the dog and stood up and tightened his hat down onto his forehead. "Going to be hard following tracks unless we get up closer," Sazes added.

Samuel watched Sazes ready the Appaloosa for the trail, and heard him murmur under his breath and pat the big Russian pistol with his gloved hand. "Maybe we'll catch them all in a short draw and shoot the hell out of them." When Sazes led the horses back to where Samuel stood looking at him with a curious expression, Sazes looked him up and down, handed him a set of reins and said, "Well, what are we waiting for, Deputy? Let's get to it."

By noon they'd stopped and rested their horse on the downwind side of an upreaching boulder. Sazes reached out with his boot toe and kicked another empty whiskey bottle off the trail. It landed spinning near Samuel's boots. Sazes looked at him with his crooked smile. "Getting bolder by the mile, I'll wager."

"Doesn't he realize that the more they drink, the slower they'll go?" Samuel kicked the bottle farther away and watched Blue limp over to it, sniff at it, and turn away.

"Oh, yes, Junior knows that. I'd say he's getting them drunk on purpose. But you can bet he's sober as a judge. He's good at cutting out and leaving somebody else to take the heat. I'd say these are not his regular boys. Probably some drifters and saddle bums who've taken up with him. He'll jackpot them, sure enough."

"I understand," Samuel said. "He wants us to see these empty bottles?"

"If he didn't they wouldn't be lying here. Junior's smart, but not as smart as he thinks. He figures he knows what I'm thinking right now." Sazes tapped a finger to his temple. "He thinks we'll charge right ahead and jump into a gunfight with these men, just to hurry through them and get to him and Braydon. Junior knows I won't cross the border, so he figures I'm anxious to catch him before he makes it there."

"Well, aren't you?" Samuel looked at him.

"Of course I am. But I won't get in such a hurry that it'll endanger us. Before it comes to that, I'll sit on the border and wait all winter if I have to. He can't stay away for long. Hiding out eats Junior up."

"Cherokee Cousins told me you wouldn't cross the border, no matter what."

"He told you right." Sazes stepped back up on his Appaloosa and crossed his hands on the saddle horn.

"Why is that? Jurisdiction? Cherokee told me there's a lot of lawmen who slip over and bring back—"

"Naw, it's more than just a matter of jurisdiction," Sazes replied, cutting him off. "It's a boundary I set for myself a long time ago. There has to be something that separates a lawman from the kind of men he hunts. For me, it's the border. The law says I can't cross it. So I won't, no matter how well I might justify doing it. If I crossed it once, it'd be easier to justify it the next time." He stared ahead along the upward winding trail into the rocklands. A haunted expression came over his face. "Soon there'd be no border at all."

Samuel stepped up onto his horse and sat in silence while Sazes sorted something out in his mind. In a moment the big cur came trotting back toward them. He looked back at Samuel and Ranger Sazes and whined, limping in a circle. "Sazes?" Samuel said his name quietly as if not to disturb him. "Are we ready to go?"

"Huh?" Sazes snapped a glance at him, as if suddenly remembering he was there. "Oh . . . yes, of course, let's get going." He fidgeted with his reins and collected himself. "I sense we'll soon have a reckoning somewhere up ahead." Sazes heeled his Appaloosa forward. Samuel held back, giving him the lead. Then, with the spare horses on a short length of rope behind him, Samuel nudged his horse's sides and followed Sazes up onto the winding trail.

They rode on upward, deeper into the high badlands hills where stone passes opened onto narrow rock ledges, and where the tops of pinyon and cedar swayed in canyon beds more than two hundred feet deep. In the late afternoon the gusting wind had ceased to roar low in the canyons, and now whistled across sharp edges of cliffs and terraced ledges.

Ahead of Samuel and the two spare horses he led, Outrider Sazes stepped down from his saddle and pulled his Appaloosa into the shallow rock basin where Junior Lake and his band of outlaws had rested earlier. "Here we go, got more signs of them here . . ." Sazes looked down at the three empty whiskey bottles lying in the basin and beckoned Samuel forward. As Samuel led the horse to the edge of the basin's edge, Sazes bent down and picked up the battered silk top hat and the dusty swallow-tailed dress coat the outlaw, Stubs, had pillaged from the store in Humbly. "One of them drunk himself out of his coat, it appears."

"There's a canteen," Samuel nodded.

Sazes picked the canteen up and shook it, the sound of water within it causing him to raise his brow. "Now that's careless, leaving a half-full canteen behind in this country. I'd say Junior has gotten these boys pretty well primed for action."

Sazes looked down at a stain of horse urine on the stone basin. It hadn't fully dried yet. He stooped down, picked up one of the empty whiskey bottles and ran a gloved finger down into the neck. Then he rubbed his thumb against his wet finger as he pitched the bottle away and gazed ahead, toward a towering ridgeline. "Perfect ambush, right up there . . ." On his way back up to the edge of the stone basin, Sazes drew the Mad Russian from its holster and checked it.

"You think so?" Samuel followed behind him, looking back over his shoulder, scanning the same jagged rocky edge, his hand on the big pistol at his hip.

"Count on it." Ranger Sazes led the Appaloosa back around the side of a tall standing rock. Samuel joined him. A few feet out on the trail, Blue lifted his nose into the air and stood with his front feet spread apart and braced, his hackles beginning to rise. "Get him in here," Sazes said in a lowered tone. "If we play this thing right, we'll have Junior in the bag by nightfall."

Samuel stepped out, took the dog by the scruff of its neck and eased it in beside him, the dog still leaning toward the trail ahead. "I'm ready when you are." Cutting a quick glance around the rock, Samuel yanked the pistol up from his hip.

"Take it easy now," Sazes cautioned him. He put a hand around Samuel's wrist and guided the big pistol back down into the holster. "They can't see us until we ride in between those rocks and round that next turn. This is the kind of setup that Junior's good at. He left some men here to ambush us. But he's long gone. What we've got to do is get around this as quick as possible, then run Junior down and hit him before he figures out we're still alive."

"All right, tell me what you want me to do." Samuel felt himself rushing, and he took a deep breath to calm himself. "I'm ready now."

Chapter 21

Junior sat atop his horse between Max Reed and Bud Dannard. On the ground, Stubs, Clancey, and the Moore brothers checked their rifles and pistols and glanced at one another with uncertainty. "Hurry up, all of yas," Braydon said, scurrying back and forth, holding the reins to their horses. "We haven't got all day here!" He looked over at Coy Garrett who slumped against a tree, passed out, a bottle against his leg and his horse's reins tied around his ankle. Then he turned to Junior. "What about our big *assassin* there?"

"Assassin my arse." Junior spit. "Forget him, Braydon. Once the shooting starts, he'll go for the wildest ride of his life."

"I don't see why you're keeping all our horses way back here." Stubs gave Braydon a suspicious stare, then turned to Junior Lake. "And why is it you three ain't staying with us? We're all supposed to be in this thing together."

"Because, you stupid drunken rag!" Braydon shouted at him from two feet away, leaning toward him with his hand tight on his pistol. "This is the smart way to do it. I hold your horses so they don't get hit." He swung an arm toward Junior Lake, Max Reed, and Bud Dannard. "They're going farther along the trail, so you'll have cover to run to in case the ranger flushes you out! We've been through all this. Now shut your damn mouth and get moving. Do you want to look like a craven poltroon coward? After drinking all the man's whiskey? For God sakes, man! Where's your self-respect?"

As the four men turned grudgingly and stalked off the trail up the thin path leading to the ridgeline, Junior nodded at Braydon and said to Reed and Dannard, "See why I keep that little rooster around? He can always get things done."

Braydon heard himself being talked about, and looked up at Junior with a sly beaming grin. "Thinks he can question me? That drunken tramp? Lucky I didn't kick his flea-bit ass for him." Braydon took off his hat, dusted it against his leg, and put it back on, puffing his skinny chest out a little.

Junior Lake waited and watched until the four men had disappeared up over the edge of the ridgeline and dropped down, taking position above the trail. "All right, Braydon," he said, turning his horse along with Reed and Dannard. "Give us about ten minutes, wait till they're settled in good, then get on out of here. We'll meet you on the other side, down on the flatlands. Don't forget the horses."

"Will do." Braydon grinned and tipped his hat brim, watching them ride off at a trot.

"How does he know you won't jackpot him," Max Reed asked above the sound of their horses' hooves as they moved along the trail.

"He doesn't." Junior smiled, staring ahead. "That's what I admire about the little son of a bitch."

Along the high ridgeline, the four riflemen separated into twos. Clancey and Stubs took cover behind the same upturn of flat rock. The Moore brothers moved thirty feet farther along, taking position behind the sun-bleached remains of a gnarled pinyon whose bare roots clung onto the jagged cracks of the rocky surface beneath it. Settling in, Kirby turned to his brother and asked in a whisper, "How the hell did we end up here?"

"Damned if I know. Just drunk I reckon." He looked back at Clancey and Stubs and waved his hand back and forth at them. "Bet they're wondering the same thing."

"That's right, wave at us, you stupid drunken bastard," Clancey hissed from his spot behind the rock. He turned to Stubs. "He'll be lucky if he doesn't shoot his foot off." He craned his long neck and looked back toward the trail, but was unable to see past a jagged line of rock. "Another thing. I don't trust that thieving little fish-eyed turd Braydon no farther than I can spit a walnut."

"Then why didn't you back me up a while ago?" Stubs stared at him. "Maybe we could've done something different."

"Yeah, like what? You saw the look in those boys' eyes. They were set to do some killing. It wasn't about us drinking their whiskey, either. One cross word and they'd left us stone-cold dead. You can bet your daddy's shaving mug on it."

"Still, you should've said something. It pays to let your protest be heard, I always say."

"Shit." Clancey spat, grunting under his breath, and looked away. But in a moment he perked up at the sound of horses' hooves pounding forward from around the sharp bend in the trail below. "Uh-oh! Get ready, Stubs! Here he comes."

"All right, then, let's get this thing over with and get out of here." Stubs raised his rifle and braced his forearm across the rock.

Ahead of them, Kirby Moore looked back and waved an arm back and forth again. "We hear it, you son of a bitch," Clancey cursed in a harsh whisper. "Why does this fool keep waving at us?"

A hundred yards down the other side of the bend in the trail, Morris Braydon heeled his horse forward, leading the other four horses behind him. He cut down off the trail onto a narrow elk path and followed it toward the flatlands where Junior, Max Reed, and Bud Dannard had already kicked their horses forward in a rise of dust.

"Damn it, Junior, wait up," Braydon said to himself. The sound of rifle fire exploded in a volley behind him, and the horses spooked and sawed and tugged at the lead rope. "Aw, Lord, no!" Braydon felt his horse begin to slide down the path, its hooves skidding in loose rock, the four horses pressing him, jamming his horse forward. "Whoa, damn it! Whoa!"

Behind Braydon, the four horses seemed to all lose their footing at once and became one tangled, tumbling ball of hooves, manes, and saddle leather. In an instant the lead rope jerked free from his hand as the snarled horses rolled screaming and kicking off the edge of the path and plummeted out of sight. "Lord God Almighty!"

Braydon's horse went down on its rear haunches. He slid back off of the saddle, off of the horse's rump, and grabbed its tail. Holding firm, with his boot heels dug in, he slid forward as the horse thrashed and struggled, finally stopping itself. Braydon sank to his knees, the horse's tail still clutched tight in his hand. The horse stood straddled on the path, blowing, shaking out its mane.

"Easy, boy, easy now." Braydon rose up, steadied himself against the horse's rump and climbed shakily back into the saddle. "That's the way, boy, nice and slow now," he purred, soothing the animal, feeling the horse collect itself and move on, step after careful step. The sound of rifle fire still exploded from atop the ridgeline as Braydon urged his horse forward, not about to look down at the deep canyon floor below.

From behind the rock atop the ridgeline, Clancey stood up and screamed at the top of his lungs amid the rifle fire, "Stop shooting, you sonsabitches! Stop shooting! There's nobody there!"

Levering a new round into his rifle chamber, Kirby Moore looked back, hearing Clancey yell. But unable to make out Clancey's words with Dillard Moore firing round after round down at the riderless horses on the trail below, Kirby only waved an arm back and forth, turned, and resumed firing. "That's it! I'm killing that arm-waving bastard!" Clancey leveled his rifle on Kirby Moore's back. But Stubs shoved his rifle away and the bullet went screaming off a flat rock near the Moore brothers' feet. They ducked, and stopped firing long enough to look around.

"Hold your fire," Stubs called out to them. "There's nobody down there—just horses! It's a trick!"

"Did they shoot at us?" Dillard asked Kirby, jacking a round into his chamber. "I'll blow their damned heads off!"

"No, wait! He's saying it's a trick. There's nobody down on the trail."

"I see that . . . they ran a couple of horses through. So what? Sazes will be coming next!" He swung back toward the trail as the two frightened horses sped past them, out of their line of fire, and raced along the main trail down toward the flatlands.

As soon as Samuel had slapped the spare horses' rumps, sending them pounding along the trail, he ran and slipped over the edge, hurrying down the narrow elk path to catch up with Sazes. The big cur had lagged back waiting for him; and as Samuel hurried past him, the dog turned and limped along behind. A hundred yards farther down the steep path, Sazes led the horses by their reins. "Be careful not to spook the horses," Sazes called back, raising a hand toward him.

Samuel slowed to a quiet walk, so did Blue behind him. Samuel glanced over the edge of the path, but Sazes said, "Don't look down there. You don't want to see it."

"What happened?"

"Braydon lost some horses over the side. The little sucker got in too big a hurry, and tried to ride this path instead of walk it. He's running scared. Must think Junior's lit out on him." Sazes pulled the two horses forward. "Come on, we've got him nearly within spitting distance. Get your rifle ready. Take him down as soon as we get some ground beneath us."

Atop the ridgeline, the Moore brothers had slipped back across the rocks to join Clancey and Stubs. The four of them crouched tense and silent, watching the trail below. "What do you think, Kirb?" Dillard asked his brother in a whisper. "Think we turned that ranger back toward Humbly with his tail tucked?"

Kirby Moore looked frightened. "We didn't turn that ranger back. He's down there somewhere." He turned his gaze back down to the trail.

Clancey spoke in a hushed tone. "What's the chances he snuck around us? Maybe wants to get to Junior so bad, he bypassed us?"

They considered it. "Well, the rest of you do what suits you best," Kirby Moore put in, standing all the way up. "Myself, I'm going to withdraw back to the horses and skin out of here."

"Horses, ha!" Clancey raised up, also. "If there's any horses waiting back there, I'll kiss your ass in front of witnesses. We're jackpotted, boys. Let's admit it."

The realization came to Kirby Moore and he slumped and shook his head. "I swear, every time I put trust in somebody, it ends up this way." He shook his head slowly. "It sure makes you wonder, don't it?"

"Shit," Clancey said in disgust. "We better wonder how we're going to get out of here on foot."

At the base of the jagged hills, Sazes pulled the horses to one side and raised the field lens to his eye. Samuel kneeled on the sand and made a quick adjustment to his buffalo rifle. "Braydon's kicking it hard," Sazes stated, keeping his voice calm and even, not wanting to rush Samuel and cause him to force his shot.

"I've got him." Samuel stretched out on the sand, dug his elbow down into it and leveled the rifle out toward the rising stream of dust in Morris Braydon's wake. Blue shied away from the rifle and circled back behind Sazes and the horses.

Nearly a full mile away across the long stretch of flatlands, Junior Lake slowed his horse, turning it in a short circle and looking back at the same rise of sand. "Come on, Braydon," he said to himself in a tight voice.

"Here, catch." Max Reed circled beside him and pitched him a battered pair of binoculars. Junior wiped the lenses quickly on his shirt. He reined his horse to a stop and raised the lenses to his eyes. "That's not near enough dust for five horses," he said to Reed and Dannard, the two of them checking their horses down beside him.

"Uh-oh, Sazes is dead on him!" Junior scanned from Sazes to the figure on the sand, a glint of sunlight dancing on the tip of the big rifle. "Hell, he's got a long-range shooter with him. Can't see the man's face, but he's putting the hurts on Braydon. Damn it, Braydon! Where's the horses?" He scanned back to Braydon, seeing the look of terror in his ferretlike eyes.

In the sand a thousand yards back, Samuel took in a breath, let it out smoothly, then held it, his finger starting to press back on the trigger. Yet in the split second of the hammer's fall, Samuel heard Ranger Sazes let out a short, powerful grunt, and the sound of it distracted his attention. The blast of the big rifle muffled the sound of another rifle shot, this one coming from high up in the hills behind them. Samuel saw his own shot go left. "Missed," he said. As he quickly reloaded, he glanced around and saw Sazes slumped to the ground, the big cur jumping around him, whining, scared, not knowing what to do. The big Appaloosa had bolted away, and with a long whinny raced west across the sand flats.

"Sazes?" Samuel saw the blood spill from Ranger Sazes's chest and he spun to his feet and ran to him. "Sazes! No!" Even as he dropped the buffalo rifle in the sand and threw himself down beside the ranger, his eyes cut upward along the high distant ridge and caught a glimpse of a lone rider back his horse out of sight.

"Lord, Samuel—" Sazes gasped and gripped his shattered chest. "Never saw . . . that one coming." Blood flowed.

"Oh, God, no! Hold on, Sazes, *hold on!*" Samuel threw his gloved hand over the gaping wound, frantic, trying to stave off the heavy rush of blood. Desperate, he looked back and forth, for something—anything! Blue eased forward, his nose probing toward the downed ranger. Samuel snatched the dusty bandanna from the dog's shoulder wound and shook it out quickly, thrusting it against Sazes's hard-pulsing wound.

From the dark end of the flatlands, Junior Lake turned to the other two with a stunned expression. "Jesus Christ. Somebody just killed that sucker." He sounded as if he doubted his own words.

Reed and Dannard looked at one another, equally stunned. "Killed who? Sazes? Braydon?" Max Reed stood in his stirrups and craned his neck up, trying to see better.

"Sazes, by God." Junior stared at them, letting it all sink in. "Somebody just blew him the hell away."

"He's really dead?" Max Reed stepped his horse closer to Junior Lake and took the binoculars from his hand. He raised them to his eyes.

"That long-range shooter is working on him, trying to do something for him. But I got news for him." Junior shook his head slowly. "Sazes is meat-grease on the desert floor." He stifled a short laugh. "Can you make out the shooter?" he asked Max Reed, seeing Reed stare through the lens.

"Naw, Braydon's dust has got me. You're right about Sazes, though. They can nail that sucker's list to his head stone. He's quits for sure."

"Who shot him?" Bud Dannard asked, cocking his head a bit to one side, curious.

Reed and Junior looked at one another for a second. A faint disbelieving smile came to Reed's face. "You don't suppose . . . ?"

"One of them fools?" Junior glanced at the distant hills, then back to Reed. "Nawwww. Not unless they hit him aiming for something else."

"Maybe that drunk assassin?" Dannard grinned.

Junior Lake laughed at the notion and slapped his leg. "Damn it all to hell, I don't care *who* shot him." His laughter rose, Reed and Dannard joined in. "He's dead! He's dead!" Junior drew his pistol and spun his horse, and let out a long cackling yell, firing the pistol toward Morris Braydon.

At three hundred yards now, Braydon closed fast toward them, his hat sailing off his head and spinning away on the hot desert air. At the sound of Junior's pistol and the sight of sand kicking up ahead of him, Braydon ducked low in his saddle and slid the horse down and sideways in a high spray of sand. "Now look what you've done, Junior," Max Reed laughed. "You've scared the blue living hell out of him."

Junior fired another shot, straight up into the air. Then he waved the pistol back and forth and yelled out, "Get on in, Braydon. Hurry up."

But Braydon shied back, cautious. "What'd I do, Junior? Lose the horses? Because I couldn't help—"

"Shut up, Braydon," Junior chuckled. "Nobody's mad at you. Sazes is dead!"

"What?" Braydon didn't trust it. "What do you mean dead? Dead how?" He shot a glance back through the dust, but he couldn't see a thing. He turned back toward Junior and yelled, "Junior, if it's about the horses, I swear I couldn't help it! A wasp must've stung them or something!"

"Get on in here, before I shoot you for real!" Junior laughed aloud, bellowing and turning to Reed and Dannard with tears in his eyes. He held a hand to his aching side, caught his breath, and settled himself. "See? See what I mean? 'A wasp must've stung them or something.' That little rooster just tickles the hell out of me."

Chapter 22

Like cautious wolves, the four men moved down under the cover of darkness, drawn toward the glow of light seeping from within the narrow jagged crevice in a high wall of stone. Outside the crevice, a horse perked its ears toward them, catching not their sound but rather their scent. The horse nickered long and low and shied against its tied reins. Over the edge of the trail, the men crouched in the thin light of a quarter moon. In front of the other three, Kirby Moore looked back and whispered, "I don't like this one bit . . . Sazes will kill us if he catches us out here."

"Without horses we're dead, anyway," Clancey replied, his voice little more than a thin rippling wisp above the brush of a night wind.

"There's only *one* horse." Kirby stalled, scared, wanting no part of this. "It ain't worth it."

"One horse beats a blank." Clancey hissed now. "If you're not going, get the hell out of the way. *I* will."

"All right, all right. I'm going. Just wanted it understood is all. Don't blame me if he kills us."

Inside the slim crevice, where a small fire burned in the tight stone clearing, Samuel kneeled beside Sazes and touched the wet bandanna against his pale damp forehead. "Sam?" Ranger Sazes's voice came from deep in his throat, struggling against his failing lungs.

"I'm here, Sazes," Samuel whispered. "Don't talk. Rest."

But Sazes shook his head slowly back and forth. "No—got

to talk. I'm going for sure . . ." His weak eyes looked up
from the fire toward Samuel.

"I know, a fire's risky." Samuel touched the wet bandanna to Sazes's cheek, then down to the fresh trace of
blood on his lips. Behind Samuel, Blue turned to the darkness beyond the crevice opening and whined softly under
his breath. "Quiet, Blue," Samuel said without turning.

"Fire's risky . . . but I'm glad." Sazes tried to smile his
crooked grin. "Rather die in the light than the dark."

"Don't talk about dying. You can beat this."

Sazes tried to chuckle, but it turned into a weak, racking
cough. "Shape I'm in . . . dying *is* beating it."

"I'll get them for this, Ranger Sazes. I promise—"
Samuel words stopped short. Sazes's hand gripped his wrist,
clutching it with his failing strength.

"Listen to me, Sam—I lost this one." He coughed and
struggled to catch his breath. "There wasn't time to teach
you . . . what I wanted to. Let this go . . . get back to your
own life."

"This *is* my life, Sazes. There's no going back. We
haven't known one another long . . . but it feels like it." He
raised the canteen and poured a trickle into his hand, patting
it against Sazes's parched lips.

Sazes studied the resolve in Samuel's eyes. "Yeah . . . it
feels like a lifetime." Sazes's frail hand gestured toward the
blood-soaked riding duster lying beside Samuel. "My
list . . ."

Samuel pulled the duster closer. He reached inside it and
pulled out the wrinkled, folded paper, the paper still wet and
heavy with Sazes's blood. He tried to unfold it in his hands,
but then he stopped and shook his head. "It's no use, Ranger
Sazes. I can't make out a thing."

Sazes coughed and caught his breath and clutched
Samuel's arm once more. "Doesn't matter . . . I just raised it
at the right time . . . and called out a name."

"I see," Samuel nodded.

"And . . . the Appaloosa. He's yours now."

Samuel winced. "He's gone, Ranger Sazes. He took off when you went down."

Sazes managed a weak chuckle, and coughed. "Ornery ole stallion. I had a feeling . . . he wanted out of this. Just couldn't see no way till now." His eyes searched deeper into Samuel's. "You take care with Junior . . . you hear me?"

"I will." Behind them the big cur took a step closer to the front opening in the crevice and let out a low growl. "Easy, Blue," Samuel said over his shoulder.

"Pay attention to your dog . . ." Sazes gestured toward the big cur with his narrowing eyes. "Go on . . . get out of here."

"I—I want to wait, a while longer." Samuel lowered his eyes from Sazes's.

"Why? To bury me?" Sazes shook his head back and forth slowly. "No hole in the ground . . . no rocks on my chest. I like it here. Go on now . . . this work won't stop for you. It never did for me."

Blue growled more persistently, taking another step forward, his hackles raised high and stiff. "Hold on, Sazes. I'll be right back. Please, hold on for me."

Samuel moved toward the darkness with his pistol drawn and cocked, his back pressed to the wall of the slim crevice for cover. At the front edge, he looked past the horse and across the narrow clearing. He caught a vague glimpse of the shadowy figures spreading out among the rocks and brush. Beside him the big cur fell silent, but stood tensed, ready to spring forward.

"You want the horse?" Samuel called out. "Come and get him!" He fired four rapid shots, the blaze of powder streaking like lightning out into the shattered silence. The horse whinnied, rearing against its reins. Boot heels stumbled on rocks and sand, as the men moved away. Samuel stood for a second, then looked down at the dog. "Watch them, boy."

He hurried back inside, but even as he called out Sazes's name, he saw his slack face turned toward the low flames, his lifeless, hollow eyes staring into the glowing embers. He let out a breath and holstered the big pistol, a sliver of warm smoke still coiling upward around the steel barrel and the knuckles of his hand, entwining the two in the flickering glow of firelight. He stood staring down at Sazes's body until something leveled inside his chest and loosened, allowing him to breathe. "You're right," he whispered at length. "It seemed like a lifetime. *More* than a lifetime."

The first place Junior Lake led them to was not a town at all. It was only a short scattering of crude, crumbling adobe hovels that at a glance might have swollen up from the arid earth after a long rain, like blisters that had callused over time and would not go away. Dusty blankets hung and flapped in the hot winds off the desert floor, in place of doors where sun-bleached boards had long dried brittle and come apart.

A swollen dead goat lay at the end of a long swipe in the dirt where someone had dragged it from the dark circle of blood in the street where it was slaughtered. The goat's hindquarters were cleaved away as if in afterthought, and blowflies circled and nursed on the stark white tips of its udders. "Looks like our boy Sherm might have passed through here," Junior chuckled. "I believe he'd eat the arse out of a still-running goat."

"Jesus, Junior." Max Reed slapped at a fly as it circled close to his ear. "If this is your idea of touring I'd hate to see where you grew up."

"Take heart, Max. This is just a piss-stop. We'll cool out here a day or two out of the sun. Give me a chance to straighten out this stallion's attitude. The Outrider had him ruint. Right, boy?" Junior reached down and patted the Appaloosa's withers. "I liked to never got a loop around his neck." The stallion tensed at Junior's touch.

"Should've let him go. He's bad luck, in my book."

"Bad luck? Come on now, Max, you're more sophisti-

cated than that. Don't make me sorry I've confided in you."
He nudged the Appaloosa stallion on, the big animal moving grudgingly, blowing out a muttering breath. "I didn't get
to spit in Sazes's face before he died. I ought to at least get
to enjoy his leavings."

Beneath him, the stallion swayed in reluctance and
quartered and bowed as if ready to buck. "Whoa, boy." Junior lifted the reins high and tight and steadied the stallion. "Don't make me geld you and tie a ribbon in your
tail."

"Max is right," Bud Dannard said.

"There's better places ahead, Bud, if this one doesn't
suit you." Junior smiled to himself. "I always say a man
ought to see as much as he can of his country. Never know
when you might be called upon to impress some foreign
dignitary."

"Well . . . looking at it that way, you've got a point," Max
Reed said, allowing himself to smile, slapping once more at
the buzzing insect circling his ear. "Let me ask you this. Are
we at all concerned with that long-range shooter you saw
with Outrider Sazes?"

"I see no need to be." Junior gazed straight ahead, where
in an open doorway littered with empty whiskey bottles, a
young woman with tangled red hair stood smoking a thin
cigar. "I've got a hunch who that long-shooter was—that
blue cur looked awful familiar to me."

"What blue cur?" Braydon asked, sidling his horse closer
to Junior. "I didn't see no dog."

"That's because you were too busy trying to maintain
your stool and ride at the same time." Junior shot him a look,
muffled a laugh, and gazed forward. "Remember that buffalo hunter that leaned too close to Sherm's big knife blade
a while back?"

"No." Braydon stared blankly ahead, seeing the young
woman in the doorway lift the edge of her dirty long skirt
and pucker her lips forward in a long stream of cigar
smoke.

"Well, shit . . ." Junior rolled his eyes upward, patient but perplexed, and stopped the Appaloosa in the middle of the narrow dirt street and looked at Braydon. "You mean to tell me you have no recollection *whatsoever* of the man you helped kill less than a month ago? Damn it, Braydon. What's the matter with you?"

"Oh, yeah . . ." Braydon still looked a bit uncertain, but nodded and ran a dirty finger across his throat. "You mean, that one?"

"Yes, Braydon, *mi amigo,* I mean *that* one." Junior winced.

"But what's all that got to do with a blue dog?" As Junior Lake, Braydon, and Max Reed sat on their horses in the street, Bud Dannard heeled his tired horse forward toward the young woman in the doorway, his hand going to his hat and tipping it.

"Listen to me, Braydon, *please!*" Junior reached a hand over onto Braydon's saddle horn and shook it back and forth, Braydon wobbling in the saddle like a limp snake. "They had a *dog* with them. A big *blue* dog. I saw it when I looked back, about the time Daggett got shot by a long-range rifle." Junior gave him a close questioning gaze. "Getting any of this?"

"Aw, to hell with it."

Beside them, Max Reed grew disgusted and shook his head. "Wait up, Bud," he called out, heeling his horse forward.

"Yeah, I get it." Braydon shrugged his thin shoulders. "What about it?"

"Never mind, Braydon." Junior Lake let out a breath of exasperation. "It's not that important to you." He glanced at Reed and Dannard as the two stepped down from their stirrups and spun their reins on a remnant of a weathered hitch rail, headed for the open doorway. Junior heeled the Appaloosa forward.

Behind the bar, a big man wearing a pair of extrawide galluses raised a thick hand out toward them as Junior and the other three stepped inside. "Everybody hold it right there and hear me out." He spoke in a tone of determination, so much so that even Junior Lake slowed to a halt.

"Start talking, then," Junior said with a bemused smile. "It's a free country." The young woman slunk to one wall and leaned there, caressing her bare left shoulder with her right hand. Bud Dannard managed a guarded wink at her. Junior saw it and said, "Pay attention, Bud—the man needs to get something off his chest." Junior turned back to the big serious-looking bartender. "Go ahead, then, shoot." He caught himself, raised a hand toward the bartender, and grinning, added, "That's just a figure of speech."

The bartender nodded stiffly. "All right, here it is. I had lots of trouble with a fellow who rode through here the other day." He nodded toward a mounted deer's head that had bullet holes where its eyes should have been and half its antler rack missing. In a rear corner lay an accordion beat to pieces, beside it a bloodstained straw sombrero, and a broken table leg with a clump of hair stuck to it. "I just want to tell every one of you, if you're here to cause trouble, shoot and kill, and rip and tear . . . let me know right now and I'll walk out and let you have this damn place, lock, stock, and by-God barrel."

Junior glanced at the others, smiled, then turned back to the bartender. "You sound like a man who's lost that keen interest so necessary in running a profitable business."

"Ha! Mister, you said it. This place ain't worth its weight in heartache to me anymore. My wife ran off with a stagecoach driver six months back. Since then I've said to hell with everything." He tossed a thick hand. "So there's where things stand—you want it, you've got it. Just let me get my hat—I don't *have* another shirt." He turned and reached for a threadbare bowler hat on a peg behind the bar.

"Wait a minute." Junior stifled a laugh, giving Max Reed a look, then turning back to the bartender. "I'm as sorry as I can be about your wife—I'm sure we all are. But we don't want this place. What the hell would we do with it? Just stay and pour, it'll make you feel better. If we get too rowdy, you'll know when it's time to run."

The bartender drew his hand back from the hat. "You won't none of yas get blind-drunk? Go nuts? Shoot me or Little Lacy there?" He nodded toward the young woman. She hooked the tip of a finger on her lower teeth and smiled, rubbing her back to the wall like a cat marking its scent.

"I can pretty much guaran-*tee* you nobody in this bunch is going to shoot Little Lacy. As far as shooting you goes, we'll just have to wait and—"

"No thanks." The bartender's hand went back to the hat peg.

"Lord, man! Can't you tell when somebody's only joking with you?" Junior spread his hands, stepping closer to the bar. "I'm not going to beg you to stay, but *damn!* Give this thing a chance."

The bartender lifted the bowler hat, tugged the hat down on his head, and came around the corner of the rickety bar. "See? It always starts off that way, joking and cutting up. But then somebody says the wrong thing, and somebody gets shot over it. I've seen it too many times. Come on, Little Lacy, I'll ride with you as far as—"

"Whoa, whoa, *whoooa!*" Junior Lake cut him off sharply, stepped in front of him, and held him in place, his gloved hand on the bartender's broad chest. "Talk about saying the wrong damn thing! You go on and leave, if the spirit so moves you . . . but let's be *realists* here. Do we look like the kind of men who are going to let you breeze out of here with the only warm living woman 'twixt here and hell—her already rubbing the wall and us ole boys just hot off the trail? We might should discuss this a little more seriously."

"Mister." The bartender's square jaw tightened. "I've told you how it is with me." He pressed forward against Junior's gloved hand. "Now I'm not going to stand here and argue abou—"

The sound of Max Reed's pistol cut him short as Max circled past him in a casual gait and shot him straight down through the foot.

"Oh, *God . . . !*" The bartender staggered back and sank to the dirty floor, clutching his foot with both hands against the spew of blood. "I knew it! Damn it to hell! *I knew it!*"

Junior stepped over and patted the bartender's hefty shoulder and straightened his crooked galluses strap for him. "Well, you asked for it. Now drag ass back there, wrap that foot up, and pour us some whiskey like you've got some sense. Gonna leave here with that woman, ha!" Junior mimicked him, shaking his head. "How the *hell* did you ever come up with that?" He laughed and turned to Little Lacy as the bartender crawled off behind the bar. "Sweetheart, do you do your best work against that wall, or do you have a place somewhere?"

She smiled, coy and suggestive. "I have a place across the street. It's clean."

"I'm satisfied it is." Junior looked her up and down. "Can you whistle?"

"You better believe it . . ."

"Well, good. Hurry on over there, wash whatever needs washing, pick off whatever needs flipping. Then when you're ready, say, in about three minutes? You whistle real loud for us."

"You got it all," she said in a breathless lilt, moving slow and fluid across the dirty floor, giving each of them a promising look in turn.

"Damn it, *go,* sweetheart!" Junior clapped his hands toward her. "We're already so impressed we can't stand against the bar." She quickened her pace a step. "And do something with that hair!" he called out as she disappeared through the doorway. "Don't want none us having bad dreams!"

Behind the bar, down out of sight, the bartender moaned. Junior stepped around the bar and stood over him. "Excuse me," he said as he picked up four dusty bottles of mescal and stood them on the bartop. "How's that foot coming?" Junior stepped back around the bar and looked at Max Reed, spreading a broad grin. "See, Max? This place ain't so bad, now, is it? Sometimes you find a party waiting, sometimes you just have to make one as you go."

While the men drank and the sound of their coarse talk and rough laughter resounded, at the weathered hitch rail, the Appaloosa stallion drew back hard against its reins, testing the strength of both leather and rail. He let out a hot bellowing breath and came forward, chesting the rail. The sun-grayed wood creaked forward, but held. Dust flurried and spilled. The other horses shied back from him as he shook out his mane and lowered his head. He stood like a horse made of stone. But only for a moment.

He twisted his muzzle sideways, raised his frothed lips and bit at the wrapped reins, then dug his teeth at the wood. Beside him, a dusty roan leaned slightly and touched its wet muzzle to the Appaloosa's neck. But the big stallion, having none of it, stiffened, laying his ears back. He swung a vicious tooth-filled glare at the roan and snapped at it like a wild dog. The roan ducked away and stamped a hoof. The Appaloosa continued to pull at the reins and butt the rail. Then he snorted, and resumed chewing at the wood.

Inside the small cantina, Junior Lake pulled the corks from the second round of mescal bottles and slid one to each man along the bar. "What I was trying to say back there, before our Mr. Morris L. Braydon got *amnesia* on me," Junior said, reaching around Max Reed at the bar and jerking Braydon's hat brim down tight over his eyes, "is that the long-shooter with Sazes was the other buffalo hunter we ran into a while back." Junior paused and flashed a wicked smile, the first quick bottle of mescal dancing inside him. "He came up over the edge of a draw, and pro-

ceeded to put a slug the size of a buckeye through Andrew
Daggett's shoulder, from about fifty yards or less." Junior
looked into the new bottle of mescal with one eye closed.
"Which is why we didn't meet you boys like we said we
would in the first place."

"I see." Max Reed chewed at the inside of his lip in contemplation. "But now we have no reason to worry about
him?"

"Did you hear me, Max?" Junior lifted the bottle of
mescal to his lips and drank deep, letting out a hissing
breath. "From *fifty* yards away? With a buffalo rifle? And
hits Daggett in the *shoulder?*"

"Just spell it out, Junior," Max said, feeling a little agitated by Junior Lake's sarcasm. "I never had the benefit of
proper schooling." He shot Bud Dannard a testy glance, then
looked back at Junior. Bud Dannard closed his eyes and
raised his brow, liking the warm ripple of mescal in his
belly.

"What I'm saying, Max, is, the boy is either blind as a
mole or wrestling with some unnatural convictions against
killing a son of a bitch. If he shoots that poorly, he would
have already starved to death hunting buffalo. See?"

"Yeah, I see, when you start just saying it straight out."
Max nodded in understanding. "You figure with Sazes
dead, whoever the long-shooter is, he's going to go away,
right?"

"There you are." Junior Lake shrugged one shoulder
and took a drink. "Who knows, he might be the one who
shot Sazes. Nobody could stand that ole Outrider. How
could they? Max, you have to learn to look at all possibilities."

Max Reed felt the effects of the mescal settling inside his
head. "Oh? Well, I believe I've learned about as much as the
next fellow when it comes to—"

"Hey, Max." Junior stopped him, looking at him
through mescal-lit eyes. "I seem to have said something
that's stung you high up on the shanks. You're getting

drunk and testy. Let's not show one another our bad side, what do you say?"

Max turned facing him. "You're not going to show me a damn thing that I ain't seen many times, many places."

"Well, by God." Junior turned facing him, a strange gleam coming into his eyes, mescal boiling on his brain pan.

Bud Dannard took a cautious step away from the bar. Braydon followed. "Now, boys," Braydon said, "did I ever tell you about the family traveling up to—"

"Shut up, Braydon," Junior hissed.

"Yeah, keep your nose out of this," Max Reed growled.

In the midst of the mescal-ladden tension, a shrill whistle sounded from across the street. "Hear that?" Braydon looked worried, trying to smile. "We all need to settle down here. There's a woman over there been searching her whole life for something like me. Let's not break her heart."

Junior and Max Reed stood tense, eyes locked, their faces drawn tight, their tempers fueled by alcohol. But then something flickered in Junior Lake's eyes. His chest rose and fell, his eyes cut to Braydon, then back to Max Reed's. "Max," he said in a low whisper, "did you hear that fool?"

Something in Max Reed uncoiled. He nodded his head slowly, a tight, wary smile forming. "Yeah. If we had any sense, we'd both turn and shoot him. What do you say? On three?"

"Hey! Come on now!" Braydon jumped back another step. "Don't joke around like this! This ain't funny."

"Get out of here, Braydon," Junior said, letting it all go and turning back to the bar. He lifted his bottle. "You go first. That's our treat for you not letting us get out of hand."

"Hey, what about me?" Bud Dannard thumbed himself on the chest as Braydon turned and raced out the door. "I don't want to follow that little snake!"

"Hell, Bud, why not? You'll hardly know he was there."

Junior laughed and threw back a drink. He threw an arm up around Max Reed's shoulder. "Hey, sorry, ole buddy. It was just the mescal talking. This is the first time in a long time that I've been able to let down and enjoy myself and do some serious drinking. Me and you, hell, they don't get no closer than us, you know?"

"Yeah," Reed looked embarrassed. "I know. We're both so used to dodging Sazes. Now that he's dead, we won't know what to do with ourselves for a while." He stepped from under Junior's arm, picked up his bottle, and took a long drink, considering it. "You know, Junior, it's a lot like when my daddy died. Through it all, I was real happy, down deep, right here." He pressed his fist to his chest. "I felt good and free and knew I'd never have to look at that bastard's face again. But still . . ." He shook his head slowly, reflecting on it. "It took some getting used to. It really did."

Behind the bar, on the floor, the bartender finished cleaning and bandaging his wounded foot, and when Junior Lake called out to him, he painfully raised himself up and leaned on the bar. "I hope you're not going to turn out to be a slacker," Junior said. "I shouldn't have to keep coming around there, doing your job."

"What can I do for you?" The bartender sliced out his words through clenched teeth, and stood crestfallen before them.

Junior looked him over and laughed a little. "The man you were talking about having trouble with? Was he a big ole bearded boy? Stood about this tall? Liked to talk about Texas a lot?"

"Except for the beard, that could be him. This one's name was Sherman Ellsworth, if that means anything to you."

"Right on target." Junior chuckled. "Ole Sherm . . . telling the whole world who he is now. What'd he do here, if you don't mind my asking."

"Killed a goat, for staring at him, he said." The bartender lifted his eyes to the shot-up deer's head. "Then he did that, broke a table all to pieces, beat an old musician half to death with a table leg. Then he went door to door and robbed what few folks are left here. And he hacked the hindquarters off the goat with a big Bowie knife and rode out with it."

"Yep, that's his style, up and down." Junior threw back another drink.

Chapter 23

There were few people left in that time-locked swelter of sand and rock grit, where abandoned adobes stood, their collapsed tin roofs swaying down into their bellies. Weathered *chozas* with door- and windowframes missing stood leaning amid encroaching mesquite and coarse bracken, like the flat hollow skulls of some ancient race of giants.

Behind one of the rickety shacks, an old man with skin that matched both the texture and hue of the land around him, pressed forward against the weight of the afternoon heat on a dried-vine cane. Leading his last goat behind him, he stopped at a small dust-covered cart and backed the goat onto it.

At a window scalloped with dust and soot, two old women who had long been his wives, muttered in French, watching him. They'd gone to him earlier, having seen Junior Lake and his men arrive. Now one placed a brittle hand on the other's shoulder, and they turned to their gathered belongings on the dirt floor. From the hovel next to theirs, they heard the muted laughter of the young woman, and above it the sound of what could have been a rutting pig.

The Appaloosa stallion settled each time one of the men came out of the cantina, crossing the dirt street to take his turn with Little Lacy behind the swaying blanket of her hovel. The other horses would blow, seemingly relieved for a time. But once that man was out of sight, the big stallion started in again, chewing at the rail, butting hard against it, at times ramming it with his head. When he stopped for a moment to catch his breath, the dusty roan next to him, long tired and agitated by the Appaloosa's behavior, reached in while the stallion wasn't watching and sank its teeth in his withers.

"Jesus, Braydon," Junior said from his side of the table, "go check the horses, see what's the ruckus."

"I can already tell ya," Braydon said, rising to his feet. "It's that damn Outrider's stallion. He reminds me so much of Sazes, every time I look at him, I feel like boxing his jaws." Braydon moved toward the doorway as he spoke.

"Leave him alone. Just check on him." When Braydon stepped outside, Max Reed said to Junior in a slurred voice, "Should've turned him loose, that stallion. He's bad luck."

"We're going to fuss again, are we?" Junior lifted his heavy head and looked with bleary eyes at Max Reed.

"Nope . . . just stating my opinion."

"Good." Junior Lake nodded, took a drink, and sat his bottle down. A worn deck of cards lay spilled on the floor. The bartender watched and listened from behind his bar, nervous, sensing doom. Junior's voice slurred. "Because I can't help feeling there's something important at work between me and that stallion."

"He ever gets a chance he'll kick your brains out," Max Reed said.

Junior considered it. "Well, there's that, too. Maybe that's the whole of it. But I won't cut him loose. He's like having a little bit of the Sazes at arm's length. I like that, for some reason."

Outside, Braydon ventured close to the Appaloosa, and looked at him across the hitch rail. "You big trouble-making sonofabitch ya." He drew back an open hand. "I oughta smack the hell out of you."

But instead of the stallion cowering, he leaned forward, his eyes big and fiery. Braydon jerked back a step as if having seen the face of the Outrider himself, in the eyes of the animal. "Damn it, now! Settle down! Don't make me come

back out here or I will do it! I swear I will." He lowered his
cocked hand and walked back inside, glancing back over his
shoulder. "Creepy sonofabitch . . ."

"Who?" Junior Lake asked. "What is it?"

"Nothing. What's taking Dannard so long over there?"
Braydon asked, still looking back.

"He's a lover, Bud is." Max Reed grinned and took a
drink. "I've seen him fall in love quicker than some men can
spit. He falls out of love just as quick. Says he's been that
way since he was a little bitty thing. Don't be surprised if he
takes her and a blanket and gets up on the roof." Max looked
all around the dirty cantina. "Are you all as hungry as I am?"

"On the roof? Why?" Junior asked, leering at him
through heavy eyelids.

"That's just Bud," Max said. "He's a poet of the heart, I
reckon." He turned to the bartender. "Anything fit to eat
around here?"

"A poet of the heart . . ." Junior repeated it and nodded
his drunken head.

At the hitch rail, the Appaloosa perked his ears toward
the footsteps across the street and the sound of the woman's
muffled voice. The stallion nickered deep in his chest, standing still while the man and woman moved as one, the man's
arm around her naked waist, a blanket draped over his bare
shoulder. "What do you think?" The man spoke quietly, and
with their arms around one another, the two strolled around
the hovel, looking up at the roofline.

Her words were soft, playful and loose. "It's your
money . . ." The sound of her voice jingled melodiously, like
the spill of coins on a soft velvet tray.

When they had moved out of sight, the stallion went back
to the rail with his teeth. The roan kept its distance. Cribbing
his teeth on the same spot over and over until the wood was
worn thin, the stallion jerked back as if suddenly perplexed
by a pointless task, and butted it hard, much harder this time
than the times before. The wood creaked, yet held; and the

stallion sank down, appearing to bow before that which had bested him.

The other horses milled in place and settled, glad to see an end to it as the Appaloosa rolled partially onto his side, his reins taut, the bit pulling his jaws upward and askew. His eyes lifted and searched the empty sky. Then, in a final, blind, desperate effort, he rolled back and hurled himself forward, lunging upward, the hitch rail across the center of his thick neck.

The horses whinnied and thrashed together at the sound of wrenching wood and snapping leather; and when the rail broke in half across the stallion's neck, they backed hurriedly around in the dirt street as one. The roan snorted and blew and whinnied loudly, stomping a hoof. "What the hell's going on? Braydon, get out there!" Junior said.

"Damn Sazes!" Braydon stomped off toward the doorway.

The horses grumbled and milled. They watched the big stallion spin a full circle and race away with half of the hitch rail still wrapped in his reins.

Beans and red sauce the color of blood dripped from the wall of the dirty cantina. The tin plate spun like a coin on the floor, then wobbled down, rattling to a stop. On the floor by the bar lay the deer's head, its other antler gone, and straw hanging from its broken mouth and its neck where the mounting board had been ripped away. Junior Lake raged, drunk and furious at the loss of the stallion. He'd emptied the big Hoard pistol into the ceiling, dust and splinters from it covering his shoulder. In a corner where Braydon and Reed had dragged the table, they sat looking down into their bottles, not saying a word. Outside, the creaking sound of a goatcart's wheels stacked high with earthly belongings moved past the cantina. Beside it the two old women and their ancient husband with his dried-vine cane pressed forward toward the desert.

When the bartender had left moments ago to relieve himself, Junior had screamed at him and told him he'd better hurry up. So he had. But when he came back and caught a glimpse of Braydon slipping out from behind the bar, he limped around to the battered cigar box beneath the bar where he kept a picture, an old letter, and a lock of silky yellow hair tied in a faded ribbon. They weren't here now. He'd slapped the box shut and walked back around to where Braydon had slipped into a chair behind the table.

"Give it back," the bartender demanded; Braydon, looking embarrassed, asked the bartender what the problem was, since he was going to leave earlier without it, anyway.

"Never mind earlier. Give it back, now."

"Braydon, have you got something belongs to this gimp-legged peckerwood?" Junior stood with a smear of beans on his chin and the warm pistol still in his hand.

"He says I do."

"Then give it back, you hear me?" Junior cocked the pistol.

"Shit . . . All right. But it ain't stealing if something's left laying."

"Just let him have it!" Junior bellowed, then turned to the bartender, his voice thick with mescal. "It's something he can't help. I find myself constantly at odds with it."

"Well, all right . . ." The bartender felt better and bolder and had broadened his chest. He told the three of them that there was no reason to steal something like this—after all, he'd given the place over to them, hadn't he? What more could he have to give them?

"You're right." Braydon had smiled crookedly and stood halfway up from the chair. But when the bartender put out his hand, Braydon flew into him with a knife from his boot like some small devil swooping down from the night sky. He stabbed him repeatedly across the floor, and at the end of it, the bartender lay dead. Junior and Max Reed had watched with detached interest, Junior lifting a bottle and tossing his eyes upward, not surprised.

"So there, you foot-shot sonofabitch—accuse me of stealing, will ya!"

Now Braydon sat moist with blood to his elbow, drinking his mescal.

"How long will Junior carry on like this?" Max Reed asked Braydon in a lowered voice, shooting a guarded glance at Junior Lake.

"Your guess is as good as mine. He's not the kind of man you can knock in the head and let sleep it off. That's been tried. He never forgets a thing like that. He'd kill you over it."

"What do we do, then?" Max raised a drink from his bottle.

"Let him blow it out, is all." Braydon nodded. "It's more about the Outrider than it is about the stallion. And that's the damned truth."

"I hear you," Max said. His eyes went across the bartender's body on the dirt floor, then rolled upward to the bullet holes in the ceiling and back down to his bottle. "Maybe it's time we moved on . . ."

They drank, to the sound of Junior Lake stomping about the small room swinging the leg from the broken table. Glass shattered and sprayed. An iron stove pitched over on its side and slung ashes out of its open door as it rolled through. Then, Junior Lake calmed himself and dropped into a chair and tossed the table leg away and said in a spent and rasping voice, "I hate losing that stallion."

"I can see you do," Max Reed offered, scooting a bottle of mescal over to him. "Maybe we could all go hunt for him?"

"Naw, if I found him now, I'd just kill him. Nothing or nobody does me that way and lives to tell about it." He swept the bottle up and drank.

"Jesus, Junior! It's a dumb animal. Who will it tell? Another animal?" Max Reed chuckled.

Junior glared at him and wiped a hand over his mouth. He started to say something, but stopped himself when Bud

Dannard and Little Lacy came through the door. "Is it safe in here?" Bud Dannard grinned and kicked a length of tin stove pipe out of his way. Little Lacy stared, her mouth agape, naked from the waist up with the blanket doubled low around her hips. Her breasts, shoulders, and face had burned before the sun went down and her skin glowed red and grainy, the color of raw cedar shavings.

"Oh, my God!" She moved forward with a hand to her mouth, at the sight of the bartender lying dead in a circle of drying blood. "He's dead? Stanley's dead? Oh, my God!"

"Don't make a big thing of it." Junior shrugged. "He's been dead over an hour."

"But—he's—I mean, who? Why?" With her arms cradling her breasts like small pups in a basket, she reached out a toe and poked it against the dead bartender's wet belly. Then she drew back and wiped her toe on the dirty floor. "I want to know who did this. And why?"

"Here we go, hon." Bud grabbed her arm and pulled her away to the bar as the others lifted their eyes to her. "Don't mind us, boys," Bud spoke back to them over his shoulder. "We just stepped down for some refreshment." He pulled her with him behind the bar, and busied himself with the bottles on the wall as he spoke in a hushed whisper. "Don't ask nothing. Don't look at anything. See what I was telling you earlier? See what they'll do?" He picked up a bottle and shoved it under his arm.

"Why did they do it?"

"Hush! It wasn't their fault. He should've left when he started to."

"They wouldn't let him. He tried to—they shot him."

"He didn't try hard enough, then. Let's go. Don't look at nothing."

On their way to the door, Junior called out, "Get caught up, Bud, we're leaving here come morning."

"All right, Junior." Bud pulled the woman along until they were all the way across the street. "If they come to you tonight, I've got to give you up to them . . . just for tonight, though, do you understand?"

"I understand. It's only money to me."

He looked at her, a bit hurt. "But remember what we talked about? I meant every word I said. Didn't you?"

"Sure, I did." She slipped her arm around his waist, took the blanket from around her and tossed it back over her shoulder.

Dannard whispered, trembling, looking her up and down in the soft glow of moonlight. He stroked her tangled hair. "Oh, Lord. Let's get on up there, what do you say?"

Chapter 24

At the end of the first long day, Samuel's hat was missing and he had no idea of how or where he'd lost it. It had been there, then it was gone. Resting his horse in a slice of saguaro shade, he'd searched through his saddlebags and found his last folded bandanna and shook it out, forming it to his head like a seaman's skully and tying it back. Then he'd ridden on against a cross wind full of sand lifted burning-hot from the desert's rolling loin.

At dark, he sat down beside a thin bed of loose rock where water trickled from behind two boulders then snaked around a deadfall of cottonwood and was gone. "We'll camp here," he'd said to the dog and the horse, and to himself.

Blue lapped water from the ground while the horse stamped a deep hoofprint in it, and drew from that small pool of its own design. Samuel stripped the bandanna off his head, pressed it to the shimmering water, fell back on the ground and spread the wet bandanna over his burning face. When his clothes and body had cooled to some extent, he raised Outrider Clyde Sazes's Mad Russian pistol from his waist and held it up to the white half shell of moonlight, flat across his palm. He turned it back and forth, admiring it.

"He spoke to you like you were alive," Samuel said. As the weight of pistol grew on him, he spread a tired, thin smile and lowered it to his chest. "But I won't . . ."

He slept for an hour or so, and only awakened when the dog prodded his side, whining, scratching at his ribs as if digging him out of the ground. "All right, all right." Samuel

struggled up onto his stiff legs and shoved the Mad Russian
back down in his waistband. He rubbed the damp bandanna
across his face, feeling the dull bite of the healed stitches in
his cheek. The horse had wandered up to the two boulders
and stood in the grainy darkness, grazing on a coarse lump
of spindly wild grass.

At the horse's side, Samuel took down jerked meat from
the saddlebags and threw some to the big cur. He took out a
small feed sack and lifted a handful of grain and chaff from
it, stooping down and holding it to the horse's muzzle. When
the horse finished, Samuel wiped his hand on his trousers,
took down the two canteens that hung from the saddle horn,
and lay them open against the thin trickle of water. As they
slowly filled, he slumped down against one of the boulders
and lay his head on his crossed forearms.

In the quiet, on the cusp of sleep, his senses stirred at the
sound of the horse letting out a low nickering in its chest. He
raised his face and looked at it. He became more alert at the
sound of Blue's low growl toward something unseen in the
distant night. "Easy, boy," he whispered, rising up in a
crouch, lifting the horse's reins as he moved to the dog. He
lay his free hand to the big cur's back, feeling the rise of
short hair across the dog's shoulders. "Shhhh, what is it?"
He whispered, asking the dog as if Blue would tell him.

The faint sound of a horse nickering drifted in, the noise
seeming to skim the sand. The big cur tried to move a step
forward, but Samuel held him back. "Be still."

The sound came again. It was faint and carried in it the
essence of pain. Samuel held the dog in place, and listened
closer until the sound came again. He tried to judge the distance of it. "Stay here, Blue. *Stay,*" he whispered, and turned
and moved the horse quietly back to the two boulders and
tied its reins to a short sprig of brush. He turned back around
and saw that the big cur had not stayed at all, but had just
slipped out of sight across the sand.

Samuel sliced his words in a harsh whisper, "Blue! Blue,
come back here!" He waited for a second, then sighed in ex-

asperation when the dog didn't return. He shook his head. *Doesn't listen to a word I say . . .* Then he raised the Mad Russian from his waist, leaving his own Colt in its holster at his hip, and willed himself forward into the darkness.

Samuel crept from a low rise of sand to a jagged rock spur until he heard the low nickering of the same horse, and at length the low sound of a woman's voice. He crept closer, his senses charged, and froze in place as a torch flared, lighting up a small dome on the sand. As soon as the torchlight rose, Samuel heard the loud growl of the dog, the bleat of a frightened goat, a man's voice crying out, and the sharpness of a woman's scream. He raced forward, the Mad Russian out at arm's length, cocked and pointed.

"Por favor! Por favor!" The old man's dried-vine cane fell to the ground as his thin arms shot upward, his broad sleeves dropping down around his bony shoulders. Beside him, one woman cried in French at the sight of the pistol boring right at them. At the goatcart, the big cur backed a step and braced, ready to lunge again as the goat bleated aloud. It nearly fell, trying to back away itself, the weight of the cart the only thing stopping it from fleeing its harness.

Samuel cut his eyes toward where another woman looked around. This one was down on her knees at the muzzle of the Appaloosa stallion, a water gourd in one wrinkled hand, a short flickering torch in the other. She neither started nor shrunk at the sight of the big pistol. She spoke in French, and her words may as well have been the calling of a crow for all Samuel understood.

"Por favor," the old man said, his breath bated. "She tells you we help! We only try to help *el caballo*—the horse!" He ventured a step forward to Samuel. *"Por favor,* do not kill our goat, he is the only goat we have left!"

Samuel moved to the horse, lowering the pistol, calling out to the big cur, "Get back, Blue! Get over here!" He sank down beside the woman and looked at the big stallion lying limp and spent on the ground. "Oh, no . . ." He spread his hand out and placed it gently on the horse's neck, feeling the slightest ripple of the Appaloosa's skin at his touch.

The old man and the other woman moved in to Samuel's side. "Is your *caballo,* this one?" The old man had picked up his cane and pointed it down at the stallion, speaking softly. "We only want to help him, *si?*"

"Si, gracias," Samuel answered without looking up at him.

"But I think he dies, this one . . . if we cannot get him up."

"Then I've got to get him up," Samuel said. He looked down into the Appaloosa's eyes as the horse raised its head slightly and let the woman pour water across its parched lips. "You have to stand up, boy," Samuel said. "Don't die on me, Sazes . . . you better not."

"It is the horse's name, si?" The old man bent down and placed a hand on Samuel's shoulder.

"What?" Samuel looked at him, then realized what he'd called the stallion. "He belonged to a friend of mine . . . but someone killed my friend."

"Oh." The old man nodded. "And the one who killed your friend took from him this *caballo?*"

"I . . . don't know. The stallion took off, day before yesterday." Samuel stroked the Appaloosa's neck as he spoke, looking at the loose reins with the three feet of broken hitch rail still wrapped in them.

"I think he did. I see a man riding him, back there." He pointed off into the distant darkness. "Four men came . . . bad hombres, these men—"

"When was this?" Samuel cut him off.

"Only yesterday. We left because of them. *Mi esposas* and I are old, and I think there is always much trouble where these men are. Another such man came, and when he left, he killed my other *cabro* and butchered it before this one's very eyes." He swung a finger toward the goatcart where the goat stood rigidly still, keeping its eyes on the big cur. "And this one could only stand and watch and do nothing, even though the slain *cabro* was his mate." He shook his bowed head. "This is what has come to where we live. So we go."

Samuel stood up and wiped off the Appaloosa's sweat on his trouser legs. "Can you help me get him up?"

"We will try . . . but maybe he don't get up. Maybe he dies here."

"Then let's get started." Samuel called the dog to his side, then added to the old man. "I have a horse and a rope back there. We'll be right back."

The old man turned into a talker when Samuel returned. He'd made the connection between the big Appaloosa and the name Samuel had called the stallion as he kneeled beside it on the ground. He asked Samuel, and Samuel told him that yes, his friend had been Outrider Clyde Sazes, the ranger. Samuel told him this as he threw the rope over the top of the goatcart, and tied the other end to his saddle horn. Both of the old women moved together, staying close enough for Samuel to benefit from the torchlight.

The old man followed him around the goatcart where the other end of the rope lay near the stallion's muzzle. As Samuel fashioned a hackamore type of sling around the Appaloosa's head, the old man said he had long heard of Sazes, but never knew him.

He asked if Samuel was also a ranger, and Samuel told him no, but that he had been sworn as a deputy back in Humbly to help Sazes hunt down the very men he'd spoken of. The old man sighed and said that at first he'd feared Samuel might be such a man as the ones who'd killed his other goat, but then, "I did not see the look of them in your eyes."

Samuel finished with the sling and patted the stallion and stood up. "What look is that?"

"These men all look wild in their eyes," he said, "like the wolf who has drank bad water. I did not see this look in your eyes. If I had I would've fought you, make no mistake of this." He held his gaunt chest out and gestured a weathered hand toward his wives, the goat, and the goatcart. "Because what manner of man would not fight and die to protect what is his?" He told Samuel the reason he had not fought the man who killed his other goat was only because his wives had stopped him.

"I understand," Samuel said, and he stood tugging at the stallion's head to test the head sling. "Are you ready to help me get him up?"

"Si, of course," the old man said, shuffling behind Samuel. He spoke over Samuel's shoulder and told him he had never known Sazes because to tell the truth he had avoided him over the years. He himself had been a wild young *pistolero* in Mexico, and left there years back to settle down here with his wives and let time overtake him.

Samuel turned and looked at him in surprise. "Yes, it is so," the old man said, and he lowered his eyes for a second. He went on to say how for years he'd lived in fear that Sazes might someday place his name on his list and come to his home and drag him off for past transgressions. By then he'd grown so fond of his two French wives that he would not have been able to bear such a thing and would have had to shoot the Outrider.

Samuel put the horse's reins in the old man's hand. "He wouldn't have come for you unless you'd given him reason, I don't think."

"I know . . . but when a man hides from his past, he sees only the worst ending to what peace he enjoys."

"Well, I'm glad you found peace. Are you ready to help me get him up?"

"Gracias . . . si, I am ready." Yet before Samuel walked away, the old man tugged at his sleeve. "I have not always been so old, I tell you. When I was your age I was strong and brave and nothing could stop me. At one time I had seven wives." He held up five gnarled fingers. "And all of them had been what you call *'lookers.'* It is true. Many of them even French, from the north country, as you can see." He squared his frail chin toward the two old women. "And when they left there with me, that country mourned."

Samuel stood looking at him with patience even though he needed to hurry with the stallion. "Then you've done well for yourself—raised many children, I suppose," Samuel said, hoping to move on to the task at hand.

But the old man's eyes lowered to the ground. *"Nada."* He shook his head, then raised it in defiance of fate and continued, "It has been my misfortune that all my wives have been barren. I say this has been my punishment for all the wrongs I did in the past." Then he turned away with the reins in his hands. "Tell me when to start leading the horse. He will do as I say, don't worry about my end."

"I'm not," Samuel nodded as he walked to the stallion and into the narrow torchlight where the two women had stood back and waited. The stallion lifted his head slightly as Samuel crouched and took the big knife from his boot well and leaned down over his belly. One of the women whispered in French, and the other gasped; and Samuel shoved the blade under the downed stallion's cinch, sliced it loose, and shoved the saddle with his boot until it flapped over on the ground.

The stallion snorted, rumbled, and rasped, and tried to toss his head, but was too weak to ward away his perceived tormentor. Samuel stepped around him and lowered down on his haunches, his back to the stallion, and braced himself. The stallion raised his head again and nickered and grumbled. "Don't back talk me," Samuel said over his flexed shoulder, "you're coming up, like it or not."

The old man led the horse forward in short steps, drawing the rope taut across the top of the goatcart. On the other side, the stallion's head rose at an odd angle, limp at first, then jerking a bit as if to protest the whole thing. But the pull against it left it no choice but to roll a few grudging inches onto one spent knee, and in doing so gave Samuel leverage against its back. Samuel strained and shoved with all his weight.

One of the old women moved in, hiked up her long cloak and squatted beside him, pushing as well. "Careful he don't

roll back on you, ma'am." Samuel felt the mass of horse
muscle quiver and give a little; and he dug his boot heels in
and strained harder. The stallion cried out, Samuel's hips
pressing hard on the spot where the flailing hitch rail had
bruised it. But Samuel only pushed harder. The stallion
struggled now to escape, finding the pain of living more in-
tense than the resolve that death had promised. "That's it,
come on, Sazes!" Samuel called out to the stallion and grit-
ted his teeth in effort. He raised his voice to the old man.
"Keep it taut! Don't let the rope go slack!"

The stallion wallowed and for an instant tried to roll back
against them. Samuel felt himself lose an inch of ground.
Beside him, he heard the woman cry out and knew the stallion's side was rolling down on her. "Get out!" Samuel
strained and braced. But the old woman either could not or
would not move from beneath the weight. Rather, the other
woman moved in with them, the torch in her hand too near
Samuel's face. He felt its searing heat, but could not escape
it.

The three of them pushed now, and once again Samuel's
back and the bony hips of the women pressed sorely on the
stallion's wounds. The big animal cried out long and loud
and, yet in his pain rolled up onto his knees. Froth swung
from his lips. The old man urged the other horse forward a
step, the weight on the goatcart pressing the cart down. The
goat stood bleating at the strange scene. Blue sat just outside
the glow of torchlight, cocking his head curiously.

Samuel realized the pain he was causing the stallion, but
still he pressed harder, the women pushing with all their
strength, the torch coming so close to Samuel's face that he
felt the dry stitches in his cheek tighten like hot steel wire.
He winced. They pushed. The stallion screamed and raised
up on one faltering leg and dug in with his other hoof until
both its front hooves stood spread before him. "Slack off!"
Samuel yelled.

Samuel sprang to his feet. He ran to the front of the stallion, his breath heaving in his chest, and grabbed both sides

of the head sling and threw his weight back against it. "Hold on, boy! That's the way . . . hold on." The big stallion sat wobbling on his rear haunches, froth slinging side to side as he tried shaking out his mane. Samuel eased his weight a bit, seeing the stallion grow more steady on its hooves.

Beside him the old man appeared with the rope coiled in his hands. The two women stepped back and dusted themselves off. The one with the torch moved around behind them and raised the light for them to see by. "What now?" the old man asked. Samuel sank to his knees, his hands still on the stallion's head sling, his breath broken and rasping. He pressed the wounded side of his face to his shirtsleeve and held it there for a moment, catching his breath.

"Now . . . I get behind him . . . and we get to do it . . . all over again."

Chapter 25

"Me and Lacy's been talking some," Bud Dannard said. He stood back from the broken hitch rail, wary, studying the men's faces as he spoke.

"I bet," Junior Lake said, not looking at him, shoving bottle after bottle of mescal down into Morris Braydon's saddlebags.

Bud Dannard swallowed, passed his gaze from Braydon, across to Max Reed, then back to Junior. "Well, yeah . . . and the thing is, I'm staying. I mean if it's all the same." He looked at Max Reed and saw Reed shake his head slightly, as if warning him against some deadly consequence. Dannard went on, speaking to Junior, "That is, if you have no objections . . . wouldn't stay if I thought it was—"

"If you thought it would get you killed." Junior grinned, finishing his words for him.

"Well, that, too." Bud Dannard looked nervous.

Junior pushed up his hat brim. "Ordinarily, it *would* get you killed, calling it quits midtrail this way. But in keeping to my character as a giving, caring man," he said, as his grin widened, "I wish you and the lovely young woman all the best."

Reed and Dannard looked at one another, a little surprised. "You mean it?" Dannard asked. "No hard feelings?"

"You're still alive, aren't you?" Junior turned back to Braydon's horse and adjusted the cinch. Bud Dannard kept a close eye on Junior's gun hand. "The fact is," Junior chuckled, "I was wondering how to break it to our boy,

Braydon, that he was going to be afoot the rest of the way."
He dropped the stirrup and patted the horse's dusty shoulder.
"See how things always work out for the best?"

Bud Dannard eased down. "Thanks, Junior—"

But Junior cut him off. "Of course, you realize you're
forfeiting your part of the bank money stashed over at Blood
Rock."

"Jesus, Junior," Max Reed cut in. "That's not fair. I can
bring it to him next time through."

Something white-hot flared in Junior's eyes, but he
caught it, concealed it, and smiled at Bud Dannard, his hand
resting now on his chest near the big Hoard pistol hanging
around his neck. "It's your decision, Bud. Love or money?"
Morris Braydon found cause to look down at something in
the dirt, and stepped back out of the way.

"No problem, Junior." Dannard spoke calm and even,
making sure his words were clearly understood. "I'd like
you to keep my share, and think kindly of me as you
enjoy it."

Junior looked at Max Reed. "See? See how love can
soothe the savage beast right out of a man? Are you going
with us, Max?" Junior looked around the empty dusty street.
"Or you gonna stay here and look for love yourself?"

"That's a sucker's deal," Reed said. "I'm sticking close to
you. That's money I earned."

"Well, all right." Junior turned back to Dannard. "What
about that shooter with Sazes?"

"What about him? You said yourself he wouldn't come
around here. If he does, he wouldn't know me from Adam."
Dannard swept a hand back toward the cantina behind him.
"Me and Lacy are going to make a go here—just good ole
cantina keepers. We've got plans to expand this business."

"Expand it to *what?*" Junior chuckled. "This ain't exactly New York City here." He gestured toward the swollen
goat carcass. "Ole Sherm already moved through and cor-
nered the livestock market."

Dannard's face reddened. "You'd be surprised what goes

on here. Lacy said there's miners that come through once or twice a month. Says on a good weekend, we can take in twenty, thirty dollars or more."

"Awww, Bud!" Junior lowered his brow, playful, skeptical, and winked at him. "You're just saying that, hoping I'll stay, ain't you?"

Bud looked stuck for a reply. "Well . . . you're always welcome here, you know that. I'm hoping you'll come back and maybe even tell all your friends about us. It'd help us get on our feet."

Junior seemed reluctant. "I don't know, Bud. I've learned to be careful what places I endorse. I suppose the first thing you'll do is raise the prices."

"Not for you boys, no sir."

"Well, then . . ." Junior seemed to reconsider. "In that case, I'm satisfied you can count on our support. Don't take this the wrong way, Bud," Junior added stepping up across the saddle, "but from one businessman to another, you oughta tell her to do something about her hair."

Morris Braydon grinned, took the reins to Bud Dannard's horse, swung up on it, and heeled it behind Junior, following him up the dirt street. "Damn it, Bud," Max Reed said in a guarded tone. "I thought you were a goner there."

"Had to take the chance, Max. I meant what I said about you all coming back . . . but I'd want all of you to respect my place, you can understand that, can't you?"

Max Reed just looked at him for a second, then shook his head, and turned and stepped up into his saddle. He passed a searching glance toward the open doorway, then leaned down a little and said under his breath, "Junior's right about her hair, Bud." He straightened, backed the horse into the street, then turned it and left.

Bud Dannard stood watching until they were well out of sight and their dust had started to settle. *Whew* . . . He ran a hand across his forehead and walked inside, past the bar and to a small cubbyhole in the rear corner. He opened it and Little Lacy stood up out of it and stretched and wiped sweat from her face. "How'd it go? What did they say?"

Bud took a deep breath. "Oh . . . nothing really. Junior came close to causing a ruckus, but I straightened him out."

She looked out through the doorway at the empty broken hitch rail. "Where's your horse?"

"Oh, him?" Bud milled and rubbed his chin. "Well, I had to give them something, we're friends you know?"

"Sure." She shrugged it away, looked around at the wreckage, and at the body of the bartender still lying on the floor in a pool of dried blood. "Well, let's get started cleaning up. I'll go find some rags and a bucket—"

Bud took her by the arm and turned her to him. "Let's take a break first. We'll get started in a day or so. Ain't you burning up in all those clothes?"

She gave a playful little giggle that caused her to squirm and rub against him before pushing him away. He looked at her with the eyes of a starved suckling calf.

"Not right now, Bud . . . we've got too much to do." He stared at her, his face pleading. She added, ruffling her hair with her hand, "We do want to make some money here? Right?"

"You know what I want to make." He stepped toward her again.

"Bud, please . . . !" She sidestepped him, spinning away with the accustomed grace of her profession. "It's hard to get in the mood with flies sucking on Stanley's back. Look at this mess."

"Hell . . ." He relented. "I'll drag him out of here, and be right back." He swayed toward her, a soft look of reflection. "We can get on the roof."

"The roof . . ." A hand went to her hip. "It could kill a person this time of day."

"I thought you liked it up there." He looked hurt.

"It's all right, I suppose, for a night . . . now and then. It's not something I'd want to make a habit of." She looked around at the mess and sighed. "I suppose this could wait. What about the old bandit?"

"The what?"

"You know. The old Mexican bandit I told you about. Weren't you listening?"

"Sure." Bud shrugged.

She tossed a hand and shook her head. "You weren't listening. The old Mexican bandit? His two wives? I told you he had money stashed all over the place."

"Oh, yeah. I was listening." Bud scratched his head.

"We could go check it out." She smiled. "I've always wanted to. But I couldn't by myself. I was always afraid to."

"Does he have a firearm?"

"I've never seen one."

"How old is he? How big?"

"Oh, Bud, he's an old man. I mean *old* old."

"Well, what the hell? I'm not afraid. Want to shake him down, after we hit the roof for a while?"

"No. Let's go get his money—then the roof, maybe. If my head quits hurting."

"Your head's hurting?"

"Bud, it hurts all the time. Like there's a drum back here. It pounds and pounds. I hardly see a minute's piece."

Junior Lake, Max Reed, and Morris Braydon rode abreast across the flatlands, then closed into a single file with Junior at the lead where the trail narrowed and snaked upward. They'd ridden on, ascending gradually at first, then more steeply, climbing three miles or more until the trail veered left and down around a sheer cliff ledge. At the top of the trail, they rested their horses.

"We could have saved two miles staying in the rocks," Max Reed offered, standing beside his horse with a canteen in his hand, a wet bandanna pressed to his face.

"I always liked this view." Junior pulled up a bottle of mescal from the saddlebags behind him, and stepped down from his saddle. He moved up beside Reed while Braydon stepped down and bent and checked his horse's hooves. "Does Braydon get on your nerves sometime?" Junior asked Reed in a hushed voice.

Reed cocked his head sideways to him. Junior whispered, "Now tell the truth."

"I've never cared much for the thieving little turd," Max whispered in reply. "Never saw what you seen in him. Why?"

"Nothing. I just think it's time we did some culling."

Max looked out over the deep canyon and sucked a tooth. "He's your friend, not mine. I've no say in it." Max looked back over his shoulder and saw Braydon drop his horse's hoof. He then drew his rifle from its boot and ran a hand along the barrel. Braydon stood watching them from twelve feet away, the rifle cradled in his arm, his hand on the stock, his thumb across the hammer. "Is that why we came this way?" Max asked Junior, seeing the strange flat grin on Braydon's face.

"Yep, that's why." Junior reached over and slipped Max's pistol up from his holster and stepped back. "Let me see this a second."

Max Reed looked at him and at the big Hoard pistol hanging at his chest. "What's wrong with yours?"

"Nothing." Junior grinned. Max saw the dark gleam in his eyes.

"Well, shit . . ." Max looked back out across the deep canyon, defeated. "Why all this, Junior? Why not just straight-up, face-to-face? That's how I've always done things."

"Yeah, and that's why you're there, and I'm here." Junior stepped around behind him now. "You started in making remarks as soon as we met up with you, Max. I swear, you wore me out."

"I didn't complain about nothing. I just said what was on my mind at the time."

"I know. And I understand." Junior cocked the pistol and raised it.

"Nothing we can change, then, I don't suppose?" Max Reed stiffened at the harsh sound of the hammer going back, metal clicking against metal in the high stillness.

"Naw . . . I've just gotten sick of ya."

Max rushed his words. "I hope to God Cousins catches up to you and—"

The Colt bucked in Junior's hand. The sound of it brought up a flapping of wings off the side of the canyon wall, and caused a loose trickle of sand and small stone. Max's body went limp, pitching forward off the edge. Junior stepped forward and peered down, lowering the pistol. "Whooee! A bounce . . . another bounce. A roll . . . another *bounce!* Lord have mercy what a drop." As pistol smoke wafted in the thin air at Junior's shoulders, he turned to Braydon and grinned in satisfaction.

"I saw it coming." Braydon lifted his head back, grinned upward with his eyes closed and shook his head. "Saw it coming plain as day."

"He saw it, too, sooner than you think," Junior said. He checked the Colt pistol in his hand, turning it back and forth, judging the feel of it.

"You reckon? He was smart enough. But I don't know. I saw it coming, though, make no mistake about it." Braydon laughed, started to step forward. But the Colt in Junior's hand lifted its barrel to Braydon's chest the way a snake might lift its fangs before striking.

"Did you see this coming, too?" Junior's eyes turned dark and devoid of feeling. A streak of high, thin cloud drifted on their surface.

"Junior . . . ?" Braydon's thumb was still ready across the rifle hammer, but he jerked it away. His hand raised chest-high, like a lesser dog showing its belly. "Lord, Junior, don't kid around. I hate this! I never know what you're thinking!"

Junior held back until his face gave him away. He let out a short laugh, spun Reed's pistol on his finger, and shoved it down in his waist. "You didn't hear what he said back at the cantina about when his pa died, did you?"

"Naw, what?" Braydon ran a trembling hand across his brow beneath his hat brim and swung the rifle up over his shoulder. He stepped forward and looked down into the canyon.

"You would not have appreciated it in the least," Junior Lake said. "Told me all about how happy he was the day his poor ole daddy died."

"You're right, I wouldn't have liked hearing that kind of talk at all."

"I knew you wouldn't." Junior stared at him with a flat expression until Braydon moved back from between him and the edge of the cliff.

"What, Junior? What's that look?" Braydon fidgeted and stepped even further back from the edge. "I never done nothing! Hell, I wasn't there most time! I was in jail! Your mama slapped the fire out of ya, they say. I should have! But I never did!"

Junior reached out and pulled Braydon's hat brim down over his eyes. "Let's get moving. I wouldn't want you soiling yourself this high up."

PART 4

Chapter 26

At the end of the night, with morning spreading silver to the east and the pale half-moon still seated in the sky, the Appaloosa stallion had finally stood up. In the chill of the desert air, Samuel's shirt clung wet and clammy against him. The stitches in his cheek felt drawn and numb and when he'd raised his tired fingers and carefully touched the scar, one of the women turned to the old man and spoke low in French to him.

The old man nodded, but then waited a moment before coming closer to Samuel and saying to him, "I think it is best we make a camp. You can rest. We will look after *el caballo* for a while, eh?" Then he added before Samuel could answer, "I will ask my *esposas* to remove the thread from your face. I don't think they will mind." Behind him the two women stood in silence with the torchlight flame burning low.

"Gracias." Samuel let out a weary breath. "I need to get him to the water, keep him out of the sun a day or two . . . "

By daylight, back at the thin trickle of water, the women and the old man had spread a tarpaulin atop two boulders and using the poles from the goatcart, staked the other ends of it high enough for the stallion to stand beneath. Once up, the stallion stayed up.

Samuel, after rubbing the animal down gently with a wet shirt while the old man told him of his life as a bold *pistolero,* collapsed near the stallion against one of the boulders and slept the sleep of the dead, until the sun stood high and the winds came and flapped the tarpaulin, awakening him. As soon as his eyes opened, Samuel stood up and looked hurriedly toward the stallion as if fearful that while he'd slept the stallion might have faltered once more.

"He is doing well," the old man said. Samuel slumped back against the boulder face and rubbed his eyes. He noticed a stiffness had left his face, and realized that in his sleep, the women had managed to remove his stitches without him knowing it. "Feels better, no?"

"Yes . . ." Samuel looked over at the women who sat huddled in the sun with their serapes shielding their heads. "Gracias." The women scratched in the trickle of water, pulling back handfuls of wet sand and forming a pool of five or six inches.

"They never sit still, *mi esposas*. Always they are together, at times it feels I have but one wife with four arms and four eyes. And always they make things better." He gestured at Samuel's face, then at the horse, then at a small cook fire beneath a blackened tin pot where the thin flames lay licking the ground in the wind. Mesquite sparks raced the sand like fleeing fire ants. The big cur sat back a few feet from the women in a stately pose with his nose lifted to the sidelong coil of scented steam. "They do for *el caballo,* they do for you, they do for all they come upon."

"You've been well blessed, sir," Samuel said, and turned to the stallion and touched a careful hand to the long welts on its sides.

While Samuel looked the stallion over, the old man leaned on his cane and commented on how the pain from the very wounds that had staggered the big stallion and felled him to begin with, was the very thing that had brought him up from the ground. "And when his strength is back, he will be stronger and bolder than ever before. You will see. Because he will not only have his strength, he will then have knowledge of it—he will trust it more, and death will know he will not die easily, and for that reason death will shun him."

Samuel turned and looked at him, and the old man looked a bit embarrassed having spoken for the stallion. He shrugged and told Samuel it was true . . . and was not the same true of man? Of all things born of quickened blood? Did man not live as much on the beat of his pulse as he did the thoughts of his mind? And what man could say that he lived any less on his knowledge unrevealed, as he did on that which was known common to all?

"Well . . . " Samuel rubbed his healed cheek at the end of it when the old man paused for a breath, and rather than let the old man start up again, he said, quickly, "Yep, I reckon so, excuse me, I need to step behind a rock."

"Si." The old man gestured him away with a weathered hand, then stood with both hands on his cane—a brittle tripod in the dust.

At the close of that day, Samuel had led the stallion out a few yards and turned him and brought him back. "He is better, si?" the old man asked, watching Samuel bring the stallion beneath the tarpaulin, giving two handfuls of grain each to the horses, and one handful to the goat.

Samuel only nodded. When he finished, he walked back to the Appaloosa stallion and watched it eat. The big cur sidled closer to the two women and sat down with them, begging softly for the remains in the tin pot. "He is better, si?" The old man asked again about the stallion, as if Samuel's nod was not enough. "Better? Stronger? Eh?"

"Yes, he's going to be all right," Samuel said, rubbing the stallion's side, careful of the places where the skin quivered at his slightest touch. One of the women patted the big cur's head. She reached out, took the pot by its handle and poured warm chunks of meat and beans from it into a shallow tin plate. The big cur went into the plate and emptied it straight away. Then he licked and followed the plate as if it were alive as the plate moved across the ground, until without warning the dog's paw stabbed it to the ground in place and finished with it.

"And you? You are rested now, si?"

"Yes, I'm rested."

"Good." The old man patted the ground beside him. "Come sit down then. We can talk . . ."

Throughout the following day, Samuel took the stallion out now and again and walked it back and forth in the wind. After the sun had passed its hottest point, he took the stallion out farther on the desert floor past the deadfall of cottonwood. Beyond a proud saguaro, with its lifted spiny arms, and on past a stretch of cholla and rough bracken fern, Samuel stood back and dropped the reins, letting the stallion graze. The old man watched from beneath the tarpaulin.

The women huddled like schoolgirls in secret. They spoke low between themselves in French. Dipping water from the small pool of their own fashion, they poured cup after cup through a straining cloth into a water gourd. They chattered and laughed quietly. One of them reached out and patted the other's wrinkled cheek. They went back to dipping water; and the old man smiled to himself and shook his head and gazed back out at Samuel and the horse . . . and for a moment wished he was young again.

"So tomorrow you go?" he asked when Samuel led the stallion back in from land the color of copper and fire in waning sunlight.

"Yes, tomorrow. Early." Samuel stooped down before him with the stallion's reins in his hands. "So I'll say goodbye and thank each of you tonight."

The old man waved a hand. "I will be up when you leave. Come sit here." He patted the ground beside him. Samuel spread a patient smile and dropped onto the ground beside him.

Instead of starting right in talking as he had the past two days, the old man sat quiet for a while, gazing out into that blazing swirl of shadow and light. When he did speak it was not as it had been, nor was his voice the voice of some ancient *pistolero* who'd stood on a cane, who could only coax the horse step-by-step while Samuel and the women struggled with the stallion in the sand. His voice now sounded lofty, with wisdom and strength. "These men that you hunt? What would you have me tell you about them?"

Samuel considered his words, then answered as best he could, asking him what *could* he tell him about these men. "You don't know them, do you?"

The old man replied, "I know all men such as these. Ask me anything—anything that will help you."

Samuel struggled with it, wanting to ask him something, rather than shaming him. But finally he had to give up. "Forgive me," Samuel said, "I don't know what to ask . . . I have so little knowledge of these kind of men. Only what I've learned the past few days."

The old man seemed satisfied with Samuel's response, and he nodded, looking out across the sand. "Oh . . . and yet you go to kill them? Does this not sound foolish to you? Did you not ask the ranger, Sazes, *anything*?"

Samuel replied, "We—that is, he talked some, but not exactly about what I should do. We weren't together long enough for me to learn much from him. He did say something about these men—said, men like these wanted to get caught, deep down, they just don't realize it."

The old man snapped his eyes to Samuel. "Nonsense! He must have been crazy . . . as crazy as everyone said. No wonder he taught you nothing. He had nothing to teach you."

"I can't say that's true," Samuel said quietly. "He taught me something. I'm just not sure *what*. But it doesn't matter now. I'm going after them. Whatever I don't know I'll have to figure out when the time comes."

"For years I was one of those kind of men!" The old man rapped his fist on his sunken chest. "*I* never wanted to get caught."

"Begging your pardon. I believe you were a *pistolero*. I believe you were a bold man. But you were never one of those kind of men. If you were . . . you would have died as one of those kind of men."

"Oh . . . ?" The old man cocked an ancient eye to him,

sensing wisdom at work. "Then what kind of man was I? Tell me this."

"The man you are now, is the man you've always been." Samuel gestured a hand toward the two women and past the goat and the goatcart. "Because this is where you've brought yourself. You lived in that world for a while, but it wasn't the world you wanted. Not truly . . . or it still would be."

The old man spread a thin smile. "I was wrong. Maybe Sazes taught you something after all."

"Maybe. Or maybe I knew this much to begin with. But will knowing this keep me alive? Or will knowing it mean nothing when I stand before their guns? What good will this do for me in matters of life or death?"

"Si, this is true . . ."

They sat in silence for a long while as a ball of red fire melted in the west and flowed like lava across the far breast of the planet. When one of them finally spoke, it was Samuel, in a quiet and hollow tone. "I saw a good friend die for no reason, except that he was there. Saw a young woman die because she resented herself and her sister—nothing more. Saw another man lose the woman he loved because even though he wanted her, he couldn't give up something he hated in order to go to her." Samuel shook his head, then lifted his face to the cooling evening breeze.

"All this you have seen lately? Since hunting these men?"

"Well, sort of. It's been a long summer." He took a deep breath. "I found Sazes on the desert floor, or he found me, I don't know which. At first he told me to go back home— consider it all just a bad dream. Said this badlands would rip my heart out. Said if I stepped into these outlaws' world I could get stuck there . . ." His words trailed. "Sazes was right, only it was him who drew me in, not them. He didn't mean to, but I'm out here now, ready to hunt men I never should have met, let alone want to kill."

The old man shook his head slowly. "Life . . . she is such a strange lady. She lies, she cheats, she takes what you have, and leaves you to die. Ask for her help, she laughs or doesn't hear you. Offer her your heart, she breaks it. Be mean to her, she gets even." He raised a thin finger for emphasis. *"Always* she gets even. She gives you a God to pray to, and if this God answers your prayer it is God's will . . . if God does not, it is *still* God's will." He shrugged. "So why bother?" His expression turned to concern, and he studied Samuel's eyes as he asked, "You do know how to shoot a gun, eh? Surely to God you do?"

Samuel chuckled dark and low, but didn't answer.

The old man palmed himself on the head. "What am I saying, of course you know how to shoot a gun."

"Oh, yes, I know how. And I will. Tomorrow I'll ride on, I'll find them . . . and I'll use my gun, the only way I know how. And I'll kill them, or they'll kill me."

"You sound as if you do not want to shoot anybody."

A silence passed and at the end of it, Samuel said, "God help me if I ever *want* to shoot anybody. So far it's the only difference I've seen between them and the lawman."

"You will do all right." The old man nodded and patted Samuel's knee. "The sadness you feel? The uncertainty you question? The loss that haunts you? I have felt these things before. It is your destiny calling your name, pulling you to its heart. Sazes did not have to teach you what your destiny demands you must know. Like all men of serious intent and nature; when the time comes . . . you will know. You will learn from yourself and be all the stronger for it."

Samuel jiggled the reins in his hand. "Like the stallion?"

"Si . . . like the stallion."

Chapter 27

Although they'd said their goodbyes the night before, the old man was up on the silver cusp between morning and night and had come forward alone out of the gray sheen, holding a tall sombrero to his chest. Samuel had made ready his saddle and tack and dressed out his riding horse, leading the big stallion out beside him on a lead rope. When he saw the old man, he stopped what he was doing.

"Buenos Dias." The old man spoke low, as to not disturb the women, or the goat, or perhaps the hour itself. Samuel nodded in reply. On the ground, the big cur lifted his nose to the old man's knee and sniffed it lightly. "I bring you this." The old man held the sombrero out to Samuel. "For the sun, the wind, and the rain when it comes. It is old, but I think there is life left in it yet."

"Gracias . . ." Samuel turned it in his hands and saw that it had been well kept, but unworn in a long time. "But what about you? You may need it."

"No. It is a young man's sombrero. A serious piece that belongs on a *pistolero,* or a lawman. I wore it very little, because always for me, my hat was black . . . black as the heart of death, and trimmed in silver of the finest grade."

Samuel placed the sombrero down on his head without removing his bandanna skully. He squared it and looked at the old man as the old man went on to say that even though his hats had always started out as black as the heart of death, in this desert sun all things, be they black or white, turned gray in time. "So this one is already gray and ready for you to wear."

"Gracias," Samuel said again. "I'll take better care of it than I did my last one."

"Si, I know you will." The old man reached a hand down to Blue's nose and rubbed it. Samuel swung up onto his saddle with the lead rope in his hand, and touched the wide brim of the sombrero and said to the dog, "Come on, Blue, take up."

The big cur whined softly and hesitated, but then rose forward off his rear haunches and trotted on ahead. "He will miss *mi esposas*—the way they feed him and rub his head. The touch of a woman is a touch of peace to all things, eh?"

Samuel nodded. "I'm sure it's so." But even as he said it he thought of the scar on his cheek. He tapped his heels to the horse's side.

And he rode on.

No more than a mile had fallen behind him, when Samuel saw the big cur turn around and sit down in the sand in front of him. He nudged his horse forward, and coming to the dog, he stopped and looked down at him. "What is it, Blue?" Samuel looked all around the flatlands. The dog only sat and whined and looked back to the distance.

Samuel studied the dog for a moment, then nodded, turning his horse. "All right, let's go back." He heeled the horse back toward the camp as the big cur shot from the ground and raced ahead of him. Samuel halted his horse after a few yards and sat still until he saw the dog stop and turn, facing him in the distance. "Go on, Blue." The dog perked his ears, and bounded in place, barking, coaxing Samuel to follow.

But Samuel only backed his horse once more and turned around on the trail, heeling it forward. He looked back once and saw the big cur step back and forth, barking. Then the dog quieted, turned and loped away along the trail with his head down. Dust rose from his heels. "I can't blame you," Samuel said to himself. "You belong in a peaceful place . . ."

* * *

In the height of day with its heat, its fire, and its hard glare boring into his eyes as he scanned the flatlands, Samuel might have lost track of the time, or of the place itself—this terrible world now engulfing him. He spent the night at the base of a rising hillside, clearing his mind with water from the canteen and a wet bandanna draped down his face. The following morning he rode upward to the crest of a hill and looked down on the crumbling adobes in the sandy basin below.

He took out Sazes's field lens and pulled it open. Lying on his belly, he scanned the place from a distance of over a thousand yards. The small town looked deserted, no horses stood at the broken hitch rail, no movement in the narrow dirt street. One adobe had been taken down to the ground, its mud-block walls lying in broken clumps, a wide fresh parting of earth in its open floor where a shovel stood in the ground, a boot toe sticking up from it. He watched in empty silence.

By noon, two old men leading a pack mule walked bandy-legged out of the swirl of distant heat and onto the street. Samuel saw them tie the mule to a broken hitch rail outside the cantina. They walked inside, then ran back out. A man ran out shirtless, buttoning his trousers. He waved his arms and appeared to be yelling after them as the two miners took up the mule's rope and hurried away. In one hand the shirtless man held a long pair of shears. He raged in silence in the circle of Samuel's lens, at one point flailing his arms so wildly he fell to the dirt. Scrambling to right himself, the man fell again. Now a young woman ran out naked, to help him. But the man swung the shears at her and she disappeared back out of sight.

Samuel collapsed the telescope between his palms and stood up, dusting off his trousers and his shirt.

In the cantina, Little Lacy stood naked in a crouched fighter's stance, the neck of a broken bottle held out in her hand. On the floor, half of the hair from one side of her head lay strewn in clumps and strands, much of it sticking to her sweaty bare feet. "You son of a bitch! Nobody tries to stab me!" She taunted Dannard forward with her other hand. "Come on, I'll show you a *stab!* I'll slice your worthless nubs off!"

Bud Dannard stood heaving, wet with sweat and covered with dust from the street. The shears fell from his hand. "I . . . wasn't trying . . . to stab you. Jesus! I just lost . . . my temper."

"Temper your arse. You bastard! Wasn't no temper up on the roof, when you said, *'Honey, I think I luuuuv you'!"* She mocked him in her rage. "You want to see some temper? Come on!" She waved the broken bottle neck back and forth. "I even let you cut my hair, damn you!" She tugged at a ragged strand of hair cropped short above her left ear.

"Sweetheart . . . listen to me." He raised a hand toward her. His breath still rasped, but he calmed himself, moving in a wide cautious circle around the room, toward the table where his pistol lay. "This is what you'd call our first little spat. I'm sorry I swung the shears at you. It's hot, I lost my head. We spent all day yesterday and half the night looking for that old bandit's money. I went nuts when I saw those two customers turn and leave."

"What the hell would you do if you were them? Nobody likes seeing something like *that*, going on, just coming through the door!"

"Nothing like that ever bothered me." He shrugged his shoulders high, moving closer to the pistol.

"I know my business! I know what men don't want staring them right in their face! Those are miners, Bud! Good, honest, hard-working miners." She settled, but not much, and wiped a hand across her sweaty face. "You? You're a . . . a . . . !" Her words trailed, unable to define him. "I just want you to go! Get out! I'll run this place myself."

At the table, Bud reached down, picked up the pistol lying there and cocked it at her. "I just want things like they was. Honey, look at us. We shouldn't be acting this way—

you, all upset, wanting to slice me up. Me, ready to shoot you. I swear, we're better people than this."

She looked at the cocked gun in his hand. Her eyes welled, her hand lowered the bottle neck. "I know," she whispered, settling. "You're right . . . we're both upset, crazy from the heat, all the digging. Then this." She passed a hand over her short cropped hair, her head nearly bald in spots as if he'd practiced scalping her. "You said you knew what you were doing." A tear fell from her eye.

"Aw, honey, I'm sorry. I sheared a few ole boy's heads in prison. I don't know what got into me. I loved your hair, I swear I did."

"It didn't even *need* cutting," she sobbed, moving around the edge of the bar.

"I know, I know. Don't cry. Jesus, lamb!" He lowered the pistol, stepping toward her. But she raised a hand stopping him.

"Just, just stay back, Bud. Let's breathe . . ." Behind the bar, her right hand dropped down, feeling for the butt of the old shotgun, but not finding it. "I need a drink." Instead she found the handle of a short kindling ax and ran her thumb along its edge, testing its sharpness. "How about you? Want a drink? To cool us off?" She tightened a grip on the handle.

"Sure, let's just relax, take a break, and try to work things out." Bud moved across the bar from her.

She sniffed and ran a knuckle beneath her eye. "Does it— does it look awfully bad?"

"No, no . . . not at all. It's short, that's all."

"I need to see it in a mirror."

Bud looked worried. "Let's have that drink first."

With the ax hidden in her right hand, she stood the fresh bottle of mescal on the bar with her left. "Pull the cork for me, Bud, please?"

Bud Dannard laid the pistol down on the bar, feeling better. He reached out with both hands and pulled the cork as her hand beneath the bar gripped and tightened around the

ax ready to sink it into his forehead. "Here you are, sugar."
He grinned.

"There's a man."

"All yours, too," Bud said, reaching a hand over to her
breast.

"No, Bud, behind you," she whispered, "a man, in the
doorway."

His hand slacked and dropped to the bar. He turned,
looked Samuel Burrack up and down, and said, "We're
closed for repairs. There's another place about two days
down the road," As he spoke, he saw the folded paper in
Samuel's hand—this young man, standing there in a tall
sombrero, a big Russian-model Smith & Wesson pistol
hanging cocked at hip level, the weight of it seeming to
draw his right shoulder down a bit. Bud Dannard stared at
him. *The long-shooter . . . ?*

Samuel raised the list in his hand, feeling wooden, slow,
and awkward. Without looking at the list, he said, "I'm looking for the following men—" Then he stopped short as if
he'd lost his place on some important page. A tense silence
passed.

"Well, they ain't here, so get out." Bud's hand lay near
the pistol on the bar. Behind the bar, Little Lacy moved a
step to one side, keeping the ax in her hand. "I told you
we're closed, boy. Are you simpleminded?" Bud saw who it
was now, the shooter, carrying Sazes's list like some aveng-
ing angel. Wanting to be like Sazes? Thinking he *was* Sazes,
maybe?

Samuel didn't know what to say next, or what to do. He
knew this was one of Junior Lake's men. He wasn't about to
back away. He'd gone this far. "Where's Junior Lake? And
the rest of them?"

"Beats me."

"Who's the dead man in the hole across street?"

"Oh, him? Just some poor soul who tried to ride a wild
Bowie knife." Bud Dannard grinned. "We dug the hole looking for some money. Then we figured, he was dead . . . the

hole was already dug anyway. So . . ." He rolled his left hand as he spoke, but Samuel noted his right hand inch toward the pistol on the bar.

"Stop your hand! Get it back from that pistol!" Samuel raised the Mad Russian halfway up.

Bud's grin widened. "You mean this pistol?" He nodded his head slightly toward it without taking his eyes from Samuel's. Both Shaw and Sazes had told Samuel to always watch their eyes—said their eyes were the giveaway. But Samuel couldn't read this man's eyes any more than he could read the eyes of a blind bat. Samuel swung the pistol the rest of the way up, leveled it, and shot him.

The blast of the Mad Russian brought dust from the ceiling and floor alike. The bottle of mescal rattled on the bar. The woman screamed and jumped back, clutching the ax to her quivering naked breasts. Bud Dannard slammed back against the bar and fell, his hand slapping the pistol off the bar and halfway across the floor. "God . . . man! I wasn't reaching . . . for it . . ." Bud Dannard's voice sounded broken. Blood ran down his back where the bullet had bored its way out.

"I couldn't tell." Samuel stepped forward, the Mad Russian cocked again and aimed down at him arm's length. Behind the bar the woman screamed again, then stopped short and hugged the ax, her cropped hair trembling.

Bud Dannard laughed, a crazed sobbing laugh full of blood in his chest. "You couldn't *tell?* So you just shot me?" He dragged himself toward the pistol. "Damn you!"

"Stop right there, mister," Samuel warned. "I can tell now."

"Oh!" Bud struggled forward. "*Now,* you can tell. Lacy, honey! You're a . . . witness to what he's done. " His hand closed around the butt of the pistol. Samuel shot him again. "Oh, my . . ." Bud Dannard rolled over and tossed a dying look at the woman, seeing the ax in her hand. She shrugged with a sad look, tears in her eyes, shaking her head slowly.

"Well, hell . . . why not?" He lowered his face to the dirty floor, let out half a breath and expired.

Samuel swung the Mad Russian toward the woman. "Lay the hatchet down and step out from there, ma'am."

"He's my man," she sobbed, looking over at Bud Dannard's body.

"Lay the hatchet down, ma'am! Step out of there!"

"I can't, I'm naked. Look at me!" She hugged the kindling ax between her trembling breasts.

"Ma'am, I won't ask again. Step out, and lay it down!"

"Or what? You'll shoot me? I don't care. We were in love!"

"Then I'm sorry for you, ma'am. But I've been down this road before."

"I'm not moving till you hand me some clothes."

"Then I will shoot you stone-cold dead. Do you understand me, ma'am?"

She saw the look in his eyes. "Okay, okay. I'm coming! Mister Big Shot Gunman! Here!" She flung the ax to the floor, and backed around the corner of the bar, her eyes making one more pass beneath it, looking for the shotgun—but not seeing it.

"Easy now." Samuel glanced around and saw the thin cotton dress on the floor, strands of hair lying about it. He stepped over and picked it up, then pitched it to her. He wanted to ask what had happened to her hair. But he wouldn't, not yet.

Chapter 28

When she'd dressed, Samuel helped her drag Bud Dannard's body to the site of the dismantled adobe. Beside the shallow hole where she and Dannard had placed the bartender's body, Samuel took up the shovel and dug another hole. As he filled in the dirt over both bodies, the young woman sat on the ground and told him that perhaps she hadn't really loved Bud Dannard, but had only thought she loved him. Samuel asked her the difference between loving someone and *thinking* she loved someone. She had no answer. Instead she went on to ask if she was in any trouble with the law for what had happened here. Samuel told her no, not that he could see.

"But I'm not the one to ask." Samuel dusted his hands together and leaned on the shovel handle.

Little Lacy looked around the empty street. She sighed and cocked her head to one side. "How long have you been a ranger?"

"I'm not a ranger, only a sworn deputy."

"I didn't know rangers had deputies."

"I was riding with Ranger Sazes, searching for Junior Lake and his gang."

"So, you're not really a lawman at all?"

"Well . . ." He looked down at the two fresh graves. "It feels like I am." He looked all around at the broken walls lying on the ground. "What made you think the old bandit would have money hidden here?"

"It wasn't my idea. Bud had some crazy notion. I was just with him. I tried to talk him out of it," she lied.

Samuel just looked at her. She shrugged and added, "Until somebody tells me otherwise, I'm going to run the cantina. There's no point in it sitting there empty."

Samuel didn't comment. He stepped over to his horse and took down a canteen and drank from it. "Do you see any problem? Me doing that?" she asked.

"I can't say, one way or the other." He capped the canteen and put it away.

"Have you ever thought of running a business?"

"No, ma'am. When I'm finished here, I'm riding on."

"Oh?" She seemed a bit offended. "From what I've seen of Junior Lake and the others, you'll be lucky if they don't kill you."

"I know it."

"You know it?"

"Yep, but I'm still going."

"Why? It makes no sense at all." She ran a hand down the side of her hair that hadn't been cut and tried to offer a pleasant smile. Samuel glanced up the empty street where now a man, a woman, and a small child ventured out from behind the blanketed doorway of a small adobe, looking around cautiously. "Look," the woman sighed. "They must know everything's over now. They're crawling out of their holes."

Samuel only nodded and checked the cinch on his saddle horse, then took up the lead rope to the big stallion. He stepped up onto his saddle and heeled the horse out of the ruins and onto the dirt street. She stood up and said to his back, "They'll all be talking about you, you know—the big lawman who rode in and made things right. They'll forget that the real trouble was already gone when you got here. You'll be a hero here, for a while, anyway." She laughed, mocking him. "My, my, won't that make you happy? I'll sell some drinks because of it. You hear me?

Once they're drinking, I'll tell them anything I want
to . . ."

Samuel didn't look back, or acknowledge her in any way.
On the dirt street, the man, the woman, and the child stepped
to one side and looked up at him as if he were some dark
silent parade passing through . . .

By evening he'd followed the tracks of three riders up
along the high trail and rounded the turn to where Junior
Lake had killed Max Reed. There was an aura of death that
he would have felt even if the buzzards were not circling
low. He would have felt death even if he didn't see where
the bootprints of three men had stepped close to the edge,
but only the bootprints of two men led back from it. He
stepped down and picked up a spent cartridge shell and
turned it in his hand.

Swinging back up into the saddle, he looked all around.
He saw no empty bottles, no place in the dusty trail where
these men had rested for long. They were on the move now,
just the two of them. Did they have any idea he was on their
trail? He doubted it. But for some reason he felt that Junior
Lake had gotten something out of his system right here on
this spot. Why did he feel it? He wished he knew. But he felt
it just the same, and he felt it strong. "You're learning,"
Samuel said to himself. He bounced the empty brass shell on
the palm of his gloved hand, then he closed his hand around
it and rode on.

The next afternoon he came across another small settle-
ment, this one no different than the one he'd left. In a clearing on the desert floor between two rises of rocky hillsides,
he cantered his horse forward on the empty dirt street,
knowing for some reason that Junior Lake had already been
here and gone. On the lead rope, the big Appaloosa stallion
moved more easily now, his bruises less stiff and less
painful.

Faces came forward from the black shade of their adobes.
They watched him warily as he stepped down from his horse
at a common watering trough. While the horses took water,

he looked all around. Tied to a weathered board and propped against the front wall of an ancient Spanish cathedral, he saw the corpse of a man on public display.

"Did you come checking on us?" An old man with a faceful of bristling beard the color of burnished sand, stood a cautious step back from the trough. "If you did, you can see we ain't moved him—we won't, either, until you say we can."

Samuel looked back and forth at the six or seven faces drawing closer. Yet they did so with fear in their eyes. "What are you talking about, mister? I've never been here before."

"But you're one of them, ain't ya? Mr. Lake said somebody would come by to check in a day or two."

Samuel tried to weave it all together. He nodded at the body on the weathered board. "Who is that man?"

"He was our sheriff, sort of. Otto Clapeake was his name."

"I see. And Lake killed him?"

"You know he did," the old man said. "He told us to leave him there. Said one of his men would be back through to make sure we did." The old man gestured a hand toward the bloated body with its black-ringed eyes still open and dust in its blood-matted hair. "You can see we made good our word. We don't want no more trouble here."

Samuel turned to the trough, dipped his bandanna, and pressed it to his face. "Take him down," he said. "Get him buried."

"What?" The old man looked worried. Behind him the others looked at one another with the same expression.

"You heard me. Take him down . . . he's your sheriff, man! Don't treat him this way."

"Then you're really not one of—"

"No," Samuel answered with a snap in his voice. "I'm on Junior Lake's trail. How long since he left here? How many were with him?"

"Just one. A thieving little rat named Braydon. They left sometime night before last. There ain't a pocket watch or a bag of tobacco left in town. Are you out to kill them? I sure hope so. They killed ole Otto knowing he was no real lawman—just an ole boy trying to keep things on the straight and narrow here. Mr. Lake told us to hang him on a board for any other make-believe lawman to see—" He caught himself and added, "You are a lawman, I take it?"

Samuel didn't feel like explaining. "Yeah, I'm a lawman. Is there any grain I can purchase for my horses?"

"Hell, mister . . . if you need feed to go kill that bastard, there ain't a man here who'd charge you for it. I'll fetch you some myself."

"Thanks. How much farther to Blood Rock across the border?"

"You mean Blood Stone Crossing," the old man said. "It's hard to find. But follow this trail on down to Pitchly, the old trading post. It's a day, more or less. Cut west out of there across the border. Blood Stone is about a half day's ride somewhere from there, they say. But if you're a sworn lawman you can't go crossing the—"

"Good enough." Samuel cut him off. He tied the wet bandanna back around his neck, took off his tall sombrero, and stuck his head, skully and all, down into the water. Then he slung the water from his head and put his sombrero back on. "If I can get that grain and fill my canteens, I'd like to get on my way."

"Right now? Today?"

"Right now," Samuel said. He looked around the small town again, at the three men who were lowering the body from the wall and carrying it away on the board, out of the sun. Was it a message for him from Junior Lake? He thought about it. The man had said the body was there for the next make-believe lawman passing through. He still doubted if Junior knew he was on his trail . . . so what was this? What would Sazes have made of it? Was this just Junior playing the odds, figuring if someone *was* on his trail, this message would give that person pause? If nobody was

on his trail, this was no more than a sick twisted joke—
Junior's way of torturing these people even in his absence.

The old man looked him up and down as Samuel stood
considering it. "You'd do well to rest the night here, get
started early on the morning."

That was it, Samuel thought—Junior was simply playing
the odds for whatever might come. Well, he wasn't going to
think about it. He wasn't going to try to figure out Junior
Lake. Whatever the message or the meaning, it made no difference to Samuel. Nothing would change the reckoning between them. He'd had it with Junior Lake. All Samuel
wanted was to face him, one way or the other. "Young fellow," the old man added, looking Samuel up and down, "if
you don't mind me asking, just how long have you been a
lawman?"

Samuel turned to him with eyes the texture of polished
stone, the sharpness of tempered steel. "All my life, mister.
Now how's that grain coming along?"

Samuel took the grain and fresh water and pushed on
through the night. He even swapped saddles to the big stallion for a while, seeing how it felt, checking its strength. At
the end of the night he stood looking down from a dark ridge
into the small town of Pitchly and saw one dim light at a distance of a few hundred yards. In the misty dawn light, he
drew the horses back, dropped his saddle to the ground and
slept until midmorning. When he awoke, he took Sazes's
field lens out and looked down onto the crumbling adobes
and tilted weathered shacks, no different than the two towns
past.

He might have thought he'd ridden in a circle if not for
the thin stream running past the far end of the street, where
an old stone bridge stood heavy with moss and besieged on
either side by spiky beds of prickly-pear cacti. A thin woman
coaxed a burro across the bridge with a load of mesquite
kindling tied to its bony back. On the stone edge of a long
dry fountain of Spanish design, a man and a boy sat whit-

tling. A town at peace, he thought. Had Junior Lake even been here?

Before lowering the lens, his eyes swept past the horse on the street; then he jerked the lens back to it in surprise. Tied to the ring of a stone hitch post, he saw the big grule horse with two black front stockings. *Cherokee Cousins's horse?* Indeed it was. There was no mistaking it. Letting out a breath, Samuel collapsed the lens with a slap of his palm. It was about time he got a break, he thought, rising quickly from the ground. Samuel dusted himself off, feeling better than he had in days. "Come on," he said to the horses, stepping to them with his saddle slung over his shoulder, "it's time we saw a familiar face."

Cherokee Cousins had been on the way to his horse across the street when he saw the lone rider leading the Appaloosa down the trail. He stepped back out of sight behind the single standing wall of adobe block and watched until Samuel reined down to a halt near the hitch post. Seeing it was Samuel Burrack, Cousins smiled to himself. He relaxed, drew his pistol, and took a step forward into the sunlight. "Hey, noble pilgrim!"

Samuel turned in his saddle and saw the pistol pointed at him from twenty yards away. "Bang!" Cousins said. He saw the startled look on Samuel's face, and smiled, spinning the pistol back into his holster. "That'll teach you not to ride in without checking first."

Samuel didn't mention that he had indeed checked the town over first. He slipped down from his saddle, tied both horses to the post and turned to Cousins. "I am glad to see you, Cherokee."

"Same here." Cousins ran a gloved hand across the Appaloosa's rump. "Sazes's stallion?"

"Yep. Ranger Sazes is dead." Samuel faced him, the Mad Russian at his waist.

Cousins nodded at the pistol, recognizing it. "I can see he

is. Otherwise you wouldn't be carrying his big Smith and Wesson. Junior and his boys killed him, I take it?"

"I didn't see the one who shot him. But I've been dogging Junior's trail ever since." Samuel glanced around the street. "Junior and another man were headed this way. They should have been through here in the past couple days. I'm surprised you haven't run into them."

"I just got here late last night myself," Cousins said. "Rode down hard from the high passes."

As Cherokee Cousins spoke, Samuel took note of his horse at the hitch post. The big grule looked neither tired nor sweat-streaked, nor gaunt in its flanks. But Samuel didn't comment on it. "To tell you the truth," Cousins added, "I figured you'd be headed to the same spot. I hoped I'd find you." He smiled. "If you weren't dead, that is. Figured if you'd lived this long, you'd be good backup when I get to Blood Rock and take ole Junior down."

"Sounds fair to me." Samuel looked into Cherokee Cousins's eyes. They were different somehow, he thought, and for reasons he could not understand, he felt leery of the man. "From what I heard, Blood Stone Crossing can be hard to find."

Cherokee Cousins said, "Yeah, it can be."

Samuel thought he'd just caught a glimpse of regret in Cousins's eyes. "Everything all right, Cherokee?"

"Oh, sure, I'm a little spent from the ride." His smile looked tired, but he tried to manage a short laugh, nodding at Samuel's tall sombrero with the edge of the bandanna skully showing beneath its brim, the tails of the bandanna hanging down to his shoulder. "You look like you haven't had an easy go of it yourself."

"I haven't, but I'm all right. I'm ready to get on the trail anytime you are."

"Suits me. We can leave as soon as you've watered your horses."

Samuel nodded. "I'll pick up something to eat along the way. What about you? Are you hungry?"

Cherokee Cousins seemed to have trouble facing him, Samuel thought. Cousins shook his head, looking down. "No. But you go ahead. Grab what you need. I'll wait here for you."

Chapter 29

Samuel felt almost guilty when he asked the store clerk to put a pound of pemmican powder into a deep canvas bag for him. But he reminded himself that if the suspicion he felt toward Cherokee Cousins was wrong, nobody would ever know it but himself. There was no betrayal here, he thought, only caution. Watch a man's eyes, both Lawrence Shaw and Ranger Sazes had told him. They'd both said that a man's eyes change when he's about to kill you. But neither of them had said at what point that change took place. They'd been talking about a gunfight.

He'd seen nothing in the eyes of Bud Dannard, yet he knew Dannard was going to make a move toward the gun on the bar. Maybe Samuel had moved too quick. He'd never know for sure. Yet given the choice, he'd prefer to live with the doubt than to die with the certainty. So it was now with Cherokee Cousins. There was a marked difference in Cousins. If Samuel was wrong, so be it. Cousins himself had been the one to tell him back in Wakely that the man most likely to kill you is the man you most trusted—you never see it coming. "Are you sure you wouldn't prefer a good cut of jerked meat?" the clerk said, sitting the canvas bag on the counter. "This pemmican powder has been here all summer." He grinned. "It's like eating a mouthful of sawdust if you don't boil it down."

"I chew it like tobacco," Samuel replied absently, his mind on other things. He hefted the canvas bag and looked it over.

The clerk nodded. "Buffalo hunters do that, I hear. You must be one, eh?"

"Used to be," Samuel replied, sliding a coin across the smooth countertop.

Cherokee Cousins was also the one who always talked about playing the odds. Good advice, Samuel thought, putting the bag of pemmican under his arm. Cousins himself would have to agree that what Samuel was doing now was merely the act of a prudent man. Who could call it otherwise?

"Your horses are watered and ready to go," Cherokee Cousins said, when Samuel walked past him to the saddlebags on his riding horse. Samuel let Cousins see him raise the Mad Russian from his waist and shove it down in the saddlebags and drop the flap. "So am I." Samuel took the bag of pemmican from under his arm and held it toward him. "Beef powder, for the trail," Samuel said, offering it to him.

Cherokee Cousins turned it down. "No thank you. I ate so much of that stuff as a kid . . . I went around smelling like a calf every winter."

Samuel smiled, swung up on his saddle, and took the lead rope from his hand. "Lead the way, Cherokee. I'm right behind you."

They rode on for the next hour, dropping off the main trail and onto a lower, older trail grown over in places by sage and stretches of short cactus. They moved on for a time through tangles of thorn and wild grass as high as the horses' flanks. As they rode—Cherokee Cousins in the lead—they spoke back and forth about Lawrence Shaw and what might have become of him by now; and they talked about Sazes and how he'd died. Samuel rode with the canvas bag of pemmican resting on his lap, and from time to time cradled a fresh wad of it in his jaw, sucked juice from it, and spit it away.

At a slight widening in the overgrown path, Cherokee Cousins suddenly gigged his big grule forward, and spun i and stopped. Samuel braced himself in his saddle. He'd just then lowered his hand into the canvas bag for a wad of pemmican. But he stopped now, and looked into Cousins's eyes. Cherokee Cousins smiled, taking note of Samuel's hand in the canvas bag, the pistol on his hip. "Hold it, Sam. Feel anything here?"

"What?" Samuel only stared at him.

Cherokee's smile widened. "Do you feel any different all of a sudden?"

Samuel watched his dark eyes. "No . . . should I?"

Cherokee seemed to ease down some. "The border, Samuel. You know? That sacred line ole Sazes would never cross? We've been across it for the past three miles."

Samuel eased a bit himself. "Oh." He raised a fresh wad of pemmican from the bag and put it in his mouth. Then he faced Cherokee Cousins again. "Sazes said he crossed the border only once, but that was years back." He studied Cherokee Cousins's eyes even closer. "Said he wouldn't cross because a lawman had to draw himself a boundary."

"Yeah," Cousins shrugged, "I've heard all that. Sazes wasn't the only lawman to ever think that way. Fact is I once believed it myself."

"But not anymore?"

"That's right, Sam. Not anymore." Cousins turned the big grule back to the path and heeled it forward.

They rode on the better part of the day, Cousins speaking very little now, Samuel noticed. They crossed northwest through a tangle of dried thorn, through cholla and mesquite. Reaching the crest of a long sloping hill of sand and rock cliff overhangs, Cherokee stopped and pointed across a winding stream in the valley below. "There's Blood Rock, Sam. We'll be there within the hour." Cousins stepped his horse to one side, and backed it beside Samuel, less than ten feet away. "If you want to change your mind, now's a good time to do it. Nobody will ever know but me . . . and you."

Samuel felt Cousins's eyes on him as he looked out

across the valley. On the far slope a large boulder stood blood-red in the evening light, its shadow stretched long across the crest of the hill, like the black entrance to some lower world.

Samuel didn't answer right away, because in the knowledge and the dread of what was about to come, he wished for a moment that he could call it off, right here—simply back his horses and turn them away. He let out a breath, and reached his right hand into the bag for a fresh wad of pemmican. "No. It's too late to stop now."

Beside him, he heard the quick slip of gunmetal across leather, and his hand froze in the canvas bag. "I was afraid you'd say that, Sam." Cherokee's voice had gone low, a trace of sadness in it, Samuel thought. He heard the click of the pistol hammer cocking and turned his face slowly to Cherokee Cousins.

"You don't even look surprised, Sam." Cousins held the pistol cocked at him, ten feet away on his left side.

"I had some doubts," Samuel said. "I'd hoped I was wrong. Sazes told me you walked a fine line . . . said sooner or later you'd run afoul." He sat rigid, facing Cousins now, his right hand still in the bag. "How'd Junior get to you, Cherokee?"

Cherokee shook his head slowly. "Money, what else? But that was long before I met you and Shaw in Wakely. Junior owed me money from shooting pool. I saw the only way I'd ever get it was to throw in with him on a bank job. So I did, figuring I'd make a big roll and that would be the end of it." He shrugged. "But the bastard stole my paint horse and left me stranded—kept my share of the money. I've been after him ever since."

"But now you're right back in with him . . ." Samuel stared at him. "And you'll kill me for him? Even after he stole your horse and killed it?"

"Seven thousand dollars cuts an awful lot of ties, to man or horses. Junior and I settled things between us the other night when I got here. Sorry, Sam. But you're part of the deal. He didn't know if you were on his trail or not. So he sent me over here to be sure. If I thought you'd go away, I wouldn't do it. But you can't let it go—noble pilgrim that you are."

"We've all been playing the odds, Cherokee." Samuel sat rigid, facing him. "I played them myself, on you, before we ever started out today. You're right, I won't stop. Not until Junior Lake and I get straight. If I thought you'd leave, right here and now . . . I'd let you. If not, I'll have to kill you. Don't make me do it."

Cherokee Cousins's eyes went to the canvas bag pointed at him. He considered it for a second, then shook his head slowly. "Come on now, Sam. Nice try, but I know better. I saw you put Sazes's pistol in your saddlebags before we started."

"That's true, you did. You saw it go in . . . problem was, you didn't see it come out. If you want to ride away, Cherokee, now's the time to do it."

Cousins studied his eyes, then said in almost a whisper, "Anybody ever advise you not to gamble, Sam? You really don't have the face for it." His hand might have tightened on the pistol butt. Samuel wasn't sure. He couldn't be sure of anything, it seemed, when it came to these faces that wanted to see him dead in the sand.

"I've been advised of that," Samuel said. "I never could bluff worth nothing." The canvas bag puffed wide, the explosion of the Mad Russian blowing the bottom from it, in a blast of fire, smoke, and pemmican dust.

Cherokee Cousins rolled on the ground, his hands flinging his gun away and quickly pressing to the flow of blood from his chest. His horse stepped wide of him, then pounded away down the slope behind them, in a billow of dust. "Damn!" Cousins struggled to rise to his knees. But Samuel was down from his saddle now, and he sank down beside him and lowered him back to the ground.

"Easy, Cherokee." Samuel started to jerk the bandanna from his neck and press it to Cherokee Cousins's chest. But

seeing the location of the bullet hole and the size of it, he
knew it was useless effort, and drew Cousins across his lap.
"Just lay real still," he whispered.

Cousins looked up into his eyes. "Damn it, Sam . . . don't
you cry on me." He struggled for a rasping breath. "Sazes . . .
was right. I walked it . . . too fine. It tangled . . . my boots."

"Lie still, Cherokee." Samuel had trouble breathing himself.

"You . . . learned it . . . didn't you?" Cherokee Cousins's
eyes were fading fast. "Damn . . . we all looked away and
blinked. You turned into . . . a lawman." Cousins gave in to
the ebbing feeling inside himself and ceased struggling
against it.

Samuel held him. "Lord, Cherokee," he whispered, his
voice trembling. "What becomes of us now?" He looked off
across the winding stream and up to the tall standing rock
that loomed the color of blood. "Sazes was right. This life
will rip the heart right out of you."

Chapter 30

Junior Lake leaned back in his chair with a boot propped up on the tabletop. "Get away from that window, Daggett. You're starting to get on my nerves." Across the table, Braydon sat counting his pocket watches, his locks of hair, and his pipe stems. On a wooden bench along the wall, Sherman Ellsworth cleaned his rifle and cast sharp glances at the pocket watches on the table, cursing under his breath.

"I can't help it," Andrew Daggett said, looking back over his shoulder at Junior Lake and Morris Braydon. "I don't trust that half-breed. You wouldn't, either, if you'd seen how chummy he was with the sheriff and Shaw and that buffalo hunter."

"Here we go. More of that Cherokee Cousins crap." Junior Lake rolled a glance across the ceiling. "If I was as afraid of that half-arse Injun as you boys are, I'd put one between his ears and be done with it. Boys, Cherokee's a gambler at heart. A gambler keeps a tally on his life by how much money is in his pocket. As long as I'm holding Cousins's cash, he's my lap dog. He'll do as I say. If anybody's on our trail, he's killed them dead in the street, the way I told him to. He ain't about to lead nobody here."

"It pays to be careful of Cherokee Cousins, is all I'm saying." Daggett said. "I've never seen him without one last trick up his sleeve. Everything he does, he plays all the angles, just in case something changes."

"Shut up, Daggett," Sherman Ellsworth said, looking up

from his rifle. "He could've left you in Wakely—let you hang."

"Don't open your damn mouth, Ellsworth," Daggett hissed. "I ain't forgot what you done to me. I ought to kill ya." Then he said to Junior, turning from the window, pacing the floor, "I still don't like riding with Cousins."

Junior shot Morris Braydon a sly smile, saying to Andrew Daggett, "I doubt if Cousins will be around for long anyway, Daggett. So quit worrying about it."

"How long we going to hole up here, Junior?" Sherman Ellsworth spat a stream of tobacco juice on the floor and pushed up his hat brim.

Junior looked at Ellsworth. "You keep spitting indoors, I guarantee you won't be here long, Sherm. This ain't *Tejas,* you pig. Either spit out the window or in your boot. If I slip and fall in tobacco juice, it's going to make me awfully cross."

Morris Braydon laughed under his breath and when Ellsworth glared at him, Braydon picked up a watch by its chain and swung it back and forth, slowly, taunting Ellsworth with it. Sherman Ellsworth hissed, "I want it back. I'll get it back, too, you thieving little degenerate sonofabitch you."

"Hey, hey, *hey!*" Junior Lake's chair bumped forward and he snapped up halfway to his feet. "Don't you ever talk to him like that!" Junior's pistol cocked coming up from his holster. "Nobody talks to him that way as long as I'm around—"

"Hold it, Junior! Listen!" Andrew Daggett stopped midstep and swung toward the window. "Hear that? Somebody's out there!"

Junior listened, lowering his pistol away from Sherman Ellsworth. Braydon stood up and back from the table. Ellsworth rose, cocking his rifle. "So?" Junior glanced out the window. "If there is, it's only Cherokee. You boys are awfully tense. Somebody must've poured some *scaredshitless* in your drinking water."

"Wait!" Daggett's voice dropped low. His eyes moved along the wall to the rear of the shack. "Somebody's out there, and he's circling us."

"Shhh, I hear it, too," Junior said, his voice dropping to a whisper, the smile fading from his lips. He heard the sound of hurrying footsteps at the rear of the shack. "What the hell is this?"

The four of them stood in silence, their eyes cutting across the back wall. "Daggett!" Junior whispered. "Get out there. Check it out."

"By myself?"

"Right now, damn it!" Junior's pistol lifted toward him.

"Wait, what's that smell?" Sherman Ellsworth sniffed the air. "Jesus! It's smoke! We're on fire!"

"It's a posse! They're burning us out!" Daggett started to panic.

"It's not a posse, idiot!" Junior snatched him by the shirt and shoved him back against the wall. "This is *Mejico*! There's no posse out there!"

"That may be, but we're on fire," Sherman Ellsworth said, moving to the rear wall where smoke began curling through the boards.

"It *is* that damned Cherokee," Daggett cried out. "I told you not to trust him!"

"Shut up, Daggett, or I'm going to shoot you!" Junior turned to Morris Braydon. "Get the money up out of the floor! Hurry up!" He snapped back to Daggett. "Think Cousins is stupid enough to burn up the money? You damn fool!" Junior shoved Daggett away to the side. "Give me some rifle cover from the window!" He stepped over and swung the door open wide, his pistol cocked and ready. "Cherokee Cousins? Is that you? What are you doing? Don't tell me you're mad at me again?"

"It ain't Cherokee Cousins," Ellsworth whispered to Braydon. He pushed Braydon away from the table, snatched up his pocket watch from the tangled heap and moved to the window with Daggett.

"Hear me, boy?" Junior Lake called out. He searched the small clearing, then upward along the rocky slope toward the tall standing boulder in the shadowy evening light. "Whatever's bothering you, we can straighten it out. Don't be a fool—and burn all this money up? I know you're smarter than that!"

Only silence from the rocky slope. Junior Lake stepped back and kicked the door shut. "It ain't Cousins."

Their eyes went to the thickening smoke on the back wall. Braydon had lifted up two saddlebags from beneath a loose board in the floor.

"Who is it, then?" Ellsworth's eyes looked lost and wild.

Before anybody could answer, a voice called out from halfway up the rocky slope. "Junior Lake . . . Morris Braydon . . . Sherman Ellsworth. I have your names on my list. Come on out."

"What the hell? Outrider Sazes?" Sherman Ellsworth stood stunned.

"Sazes is dead! Get out of the way!" Junior shoved him away from the window and looked out with Daggett.

"I'll be damned," Daggett whispered, seeing the figure step out from behind a rock, a tall sombrero atop his head, a pistol hanging from one hand, the big buffalo rifle hanging from the other. "It's that buff hunter. Let me handle this, Junior. I owe that bastard!" At the back wall, the sound of burning wood crackled. Smoke billowed.

"Then get it done, before we roast in here!" Junior fanned a hand back and forth. "Does he think he's Sazes, back from the dead?"

"Don't worry, I've got him," Daggett said, moving to the closed door. "Just cover me. He ain't going to kill nobody! He's just a scared young pup."

Daggett grabbed the door and jerked it open. "All right now, buffalo-boy, I'm coming ou—" The blast from the buffalo rifle lifted him clear off his feet, hurling him backward across the table and slamming him face down on the plank floor.

"So much for Daggett!" Junior Lake fired through the open door, backing a step. Ellsworth poked his rifle barrel through the window in a spray of broken glass. They both laid down a barrage of lead. Behind them Braydon hurried, snatching up pocket watches and locks of hair from the table, shoving them down into his pockets. The two saddle-bags slung over his shoulders slowed him down.

Junior Lake stopped firing long enough to scan the slop-ing hillside. "Hold it, he's gone!" Junior turned from the window and looked back at the rear wall, seeing flames lick-ing through it. Smoke rolled up, filling the ceiling, spilling out through the open door and the broken window. They coughed, their eyes watering.

"We've got to make a move!" Sherman Ellsworth dropped his empty rifle and snatched up a pistol from his waist.

"I know it!" Junior had emptied his Colt and snatched the big Hoard pistol from around his neck. "Come on, get Daggett up here! Give him a toss!"

They dragged Daggett to the open doorway, the smoke choking them. "Ready? Go!" They heaved his limp body out the door. A rifle shot lifted off the top of Daggett's head, as Junior, Braydon and Ellsworth broke in the other direction, toward the small corral where they'd pinned their horses.

"The horses are gone! Damn it to hell!" Junior spun in place, the big Hoard pistol up and cocked. Braydon crouched down behind a broken rain barrel lying in the dirt. Ellsworth slipped away a few feet and sank down on the dirt. Smoke rolled black and low from the burning shack. "All right! We're out here! That's what you wanted!" Junior Lake raged at the empty hillside. "Come on now, show yourself!"

But Samuel didn't show himself. Instead, he lay behind the rock halfway up the slope and took his time slipping an-other cartridge into the buffalo rifle. He let Junior Lake rage until his voice went hoarse in his throat. Then Samuel eased upward above the rock, aimed into the drifting gray smoke and shot Junior Lake's right leg out from under him. As

Samuel lay back down and reloaded, he heard Junior's long scream end in a curse.

Samuel raised up, and took aim again, this time at Sherman Ellsworth as he ran for the cover of brush. The shot hit Ellsworth in the left hip and nailed him down into the dirt. Braydon ran wildly from behind the broken rain barrel toward Junior Lake where Junior rolled back and forth in the dirt with his hands clasped to his bleeding leg. The big Hoard pistol was still in his hand. "Junior! Junior!" Braydon dropped down beside him, the saddlebags over his shoulders. "What do I do, son? Tell me what to do!"

"Get out of here, Pa, damn it to hell!" Junior turned loose of his bloody leg and shoved him away. Braydon struggled to his feet and turned to run. But the rifle shot hit him in the center of his neck. His head jerked sideways in a broken angle, and he lay dead in the dirt. "Oh, no! Jesus! No!" Junior dropped the Hoard pistol and hurried forward, bumping along on his good knee. He jerked the saddlebags away from Braydon's shoulders and stared down. "Damn it, Morris L. Braydon! Just look at you!" His bloody hand patted Braydon's lifeless back.

Sherman Ellsworth came crawling back, his hip shattered, his leg dragging useless behind him. His pistol lay in the dirt, and as he reached for it, a shot rang out from Samuel Burrack's Mad Russian as he stepped down the hillside. Smoke curled from the barrel. Ellsworth screamed, his arm flopping up and down, then he fell back to the dirt, his elbow spurting blood.

Junior Lake looked around wildly in the drifting smoke. He saw Samuel Burrack walking closer, taking his time, the pistol in one hand, the rifle in the other. Junior swung his eyes to the big Hoard pistol lying where he'd dropped it. He lunged for it. Samuel's next pistol shot hit Junior's hand and shattered it. Ellsworth crawled closer, his voice sobbing. "Junior, help me."

"Get away, Sherman!" Junior shoved him away with his good hand. "The son of a bitch is crazy! Look at me! Look at my knee! My hand!" The wind lifted the smoke in a wide drifting streak, and Samuel Burrack stood twelve feet away, staring at them, his eyes icy and blank. He looked from one face to the next on the ground. All four of them, the same faces he'd seen that day on the sand flats. For all the trouble, the killing, and the misery they'd caused, it seemed strange somehow that they should be gathered here, as if the bad virus the bartender in Wakely had referred to had all blown back together on the same ill wind.

It seemed even more strange to Samuel that he should be standing over them now, two of them dead, two of them groveling bloody in the dirt. "What the hell is the meaning of this, mister?" Junior Lake demanded in a strained voice, looking up at him, outraged by the whole thing. "You damned lop-eared buffalo hunter. Look at us! Look what you've done here!" He gestured his bloody hand toward Morris Braydon's body. "That fine ole man you've killed like a dog is my father! My *father,* you son of a bitch!" Junior Lake demanded an answer. "Now just who the hell do you think you are?"

Samuel stared down at him. "I'm Sam Burrack, the next make-believe lawman." His eyes moved across them. "Who killed Outrider Clyde Sazes? Tell me his name, and where can I find him?"

"In a pig's eye!" Junior glanced over at the big Hoard pistol lying in the dirt. "What right do you have crossing the border, killing us this way? It ain't *legal!* It ain't *fair!* What right do you have asking us any damn thing!"

"All right, then . . . get armed. Let's finish it." Samuel stepped over and kicked the big Hoard pistol closer to Junior Lakes's left hand.

"You low, lousy--!" Junior cut his words short. He raised his shattered right hand. "Look at this! You want to fight me now? Now that I'm shot all to pieces? Is that the kind of coward you are? What chance have I got now?"

"The same chance the Mexican kids' parents had when you killed them. The same chance Outrider Sazes had when one of you shot him from behind." He looked at Sherman Ellsworth. "The same chance Davey Riley had." Samuel shook his head slowly, staring at Ellsworth, but noted Junior's left hand slip toward the big Hoard pistol.

"Who the hell is Davey Riley?" Junior asked Sherman Ellsworth. But before Ellsworth could say a word, Junior made a grab for the pistol with his left hand. Samuel's shot punched through his heart and laid him flat on the ground. Junior Lake let out a long breath and went limp.

Samuel stared at him for a second, then reached out with his boot toe and kicked the Hoard pistol over near Sherman Ellsworth and repeated the question he'd asked Junior Lake. "Who killed Outrider Sazes? Where will I find him?"

Ellsworth swallowed a dry knot in his throat. "I wasn't there and you know it." His eyes went to the big Hoard pistol. "There was some ole boys with Junior—maybe one of them did it."

"Give me names." Samuel stared down at him.

"What if I do? Will it do me some good?"

"It might . . . give them to me."

Ellsworth spoke fast. "Junior said there was the Moore brothers, Dillard and Kirby—the same saddle tramps that left me in Wakely. You oughta kill them for their own good. And there was a couple of ole boys named Clancey and Stubs . . . and a drunk named Garrett. Junior said Garrett claimed to be some kind of assassin—carries a rifle with a scorpion carved on it. Maybe he killed Sazes, you think?"

"Maybe." Samuel leaned the rifle against his side, shoved the Mad Russian down in his belt, and took the folded paper and the short pencil from his shirt. He touched the point of the pencil to the tip of his tongue and wrote the names down, one by one, taking his time.

Sherman Ellsworth stole a glance toward the big Hoard pistol. Then he looked back up at Samuel. "That whore sure ruint your face, didn't she?" He scooted his hand another inch toward the pistol. "I wished she hadn't done that. I didn't tell her to, you know." He nodded toward the saddlebags full of money lying near Braydon's body. "Do you realize how much money is there? Let me put it this way—we're both rich! Neither one of us have to worry about money ever again. How's that sound to you? A good ole two-way split? I saw how you set Junior up to go for that pistol—hell, you're just an outlaw yourself. Look at all that money. Go on, look at it!"

"You look at it," Samuel said, folding the paper, putting it away. "Take a long look at it. It's money you'll never spend."

"But you said if I gave you the names . . ." Ellsworth's eyes pleaded.

"I said *maybe* it would do you some good." Samuel stared down at him. "Turns out it didn't help you at all. If I were you, I'd make a grab for that pistol."

"Uh-uh. If you kill me, you'll have to do it in cold blood. I'm not making a move for that gun."

"Suit yourself." Samuel raised his pistol, and stepped toward Sherman Ellsworth.

Atop the sloping hillside in the black shadow of the tall standing rock, the Appaloosa and the saddle horse stood with their heads down. Only when the last shot echoed out across the canyon did the Appaloosa swing its muzzle up and down slightly, scraping a hoof in the dirt, seeming to know somehow that the killing was over. In a moment when the wind had shifted and thin wisps of smoke drifted upward, curling about the rock in the failing twilight, the animals turned their muzzles to the sound of Samuel's boots crunching upward on loose rock and red sand.

Both the stallion and the saddle horse scooted sideways a few inches as if to include Samuel into their small haven of shadow. Samuel ran a hand across the stallion's rump and then along its side. Then he stood the rifle against the face of the rock and dropped the saddlebags full of money beside it. Leaning back against the rock, he let out a long breath, feeling the barrels of the Mad Russian and big Hoard pistol, still warm, pressed beneath his belt. "Let's go home," he said; and the way he said it, he might have been talking to the pistols in his belt, or the horses at his side, or to any number of faces or voices that now seemed at peace in his mind.

Epilogue

There were no signposts beside the trail, nor was there so much as a line in the dirt. Yet somehow inside himself, he knew at what point the border slipped beneath the horses' hooves. And as surely as he knew this, he knew as well that he would never cross that border again—not this way, not for these reasons. The Appaloosa stallion rode whole and strong now, quick to his touch, and Samuel felt as if he'd ridden this stallion throughout his life. But these were not memories, of course, only gray vague shadows— a kindredness of spirit perhaps, that he could neither explain, nor understand.

He crossed the stone bridge into the first small border town, and rounded the old dry fountain in the street without stopping. He rode on, not wanting to look at the eyes of the few people who stood back and watched him pass, because he knew what those eyes saw in his face, and he did not want those eyes to haunt him.

At the next small town, he looked toward the old Spanish mission as he drifted past it, preferring the silent ancient facade of stone to the face of the old man with the burnished sand beard when he came trotting out to him. "Well? Did you find them?" The old man walked along beside the stallion. "Did you, huh? Did you kill them dirty bastards? Let me know something here, Ranger."

Ranger? Samuel turned his face to the man, but only for an instant. "I found them. They're dead." Then as the old man came to a halt and just stared at him, Samuel nudged the stallion forward without looking back. He rode on, another day and another night, up and down the rise and fall of badlands hills. When he neared the town where he'd killed Bud Dannard, rather than look at the face of the woman with her short-cropped hair, he swung wide of that town and only saw it from a distance, across shimmering sand flats in the early morning light.

By noon of the sixth day, he was on the trail back toward Humbly, and he found himself standing inside the small crevice where he'd left Sazes's body. The body was gone as if it had never been there. Only a scrap of shirt and the battered ranger's badge lay in the dirt among countless pawprints that filed in and out across the clearing, then disappeared downward into the endless swirl of sand. Amid the prints, Samuel saw where someone had ventured in barefoot. But where these big footprints had stopped, they did not return. Instead, he saw big boot prints lead out of the crevice.

Sazes's boots . . . Samuel shook his head. "Anyway . . . I got them, Sazes." He spoke softly to the scrapings in the dust. Then he picked up the badge, rubbed it on his sleeve and put it inside his shirt pocket. *Amen.*

The next morning, he circled down to the flatlands and rode on. He didn't stop until he saw the flapping tarpaulin in the near distance and heard Blue's eager bark as the dog ran out to him.

"He is here! He has come back!" The old man ran out yelling and waving his arms. When he stopped within a few feet of Samuel he added, "He is all in one piece!" Samuel couldn't help but think the old *pistolero* looked surprised to even see him at all, let alone in one piece. "What happened? Did you catch those hombres? Did you kill them?" The old man's words trailed and stopped as Samuel stepped down from the Appaloosa without answering and patted the big cur's head. The dog leaped up and down beside him. "Oh, I see . . ." the old man added in a hushed tone, seeing the closed dark look on Samuel's face.

"Come with me, then. Tell me about it when you feel better. We get you some food. I have something I must tell you—something I must show you." The dog bounded forward leading the way.

Beneath the tarpaulin, the two women came to Samuel, welcoming him. One of them touched her fingers to the healed scar on his cheek, examining it. Then she spoke to the other woman in French, and they stepped back nodding and whispering to one another. "They say that the scar is not noticeable." The old man shrugged. "They can hardly see where it was."

"Gracias." Samuel knew better about his appearance, yet he thanked the women all the same. Then he said to the old man, "I don't think I can eat right now. I want to sit and think, and maybe talk later. What did you have to show me?"

The old man shot the women a glance, pulling Samuel away by his forearm. *"Por favor."* His voice lowered "We must not talk of it here in front of them. They are still very upset."

As they moved away with Blue at Samuel's heels, Samuel looked back across the campsite and noted how much had changed in the brief time he'd been gone. The small hole the women had dug out to catch the water had been widened and lined with rocks. It looked deeper now and a small spade stood in the ground at one edge. Near the tarpaulin a small stack of fresh adobe blocks stood drying in the sun. Next to them, long branches from deadfall cottonwood lay in a stack for roof poles and support members.

Samuel followed the old man and the dog up into the rocks to a spot where small rocks had been formed into a mound. The old man turned to Samuel and said in a guarded tone, "You must not blame the dog for what you see here."

Samuel just looked at him. The old man held up a finger

and added, "I tell you this . . . if not for the dog, *mi esposas* and I would all three be dead. This is the truth!"

Samuel watched him kneel beside the mound of rocks and begin to pitch them aside one at a time. "Who's in there?" Samuel asked already catching the faint scent of rotting flesh as the mound grew shorter. As he asked, he bent down and began helping the old man move the rocks away.

"A killer, that is who! A madman who at first would murder me for my socks. Then when he saw that I had no socks, he would kill me for not *having any!* This was the kind of man he was. He would have shot us! But then the dog—" The old man glanced around as if making sure no one heard him on that desolate stretch of land. "The dog killed him."

"Blue? *Killed* him?" Samuel looked at the big cur, then back at the old man.

"Si! When the man began to curse and threaten us and raise his rifle toward us, the dog flew into him and clamped his jaws on the man's throat. I took the rifle from his hands and tried to call the dog back. But he would not turn loose until the man was dead. It was terrible to watch!"

Samuel shook his head slightly, trying to get it straight in his mind and accept it. "*Blue* killed him?" He repeated himself, watching the old man roll away the last stone and reel back from the wavering stench. Samuel took off the sombrero and fanned it back and forth. Then he held the sombrero brim against his nose and leaned down. "Whew . . . Lord have mercy." He stepped back, his eyes watering. "His face is gone. Blue couldn't have done that."

"No, I did that." The old man picked up a stone and threw it back on what was left of the death-blackened face. "I shot him many times with his own rifle, so if someone came along before I buried him, they would not blame the dog." He reached a hand out and patted the big cur's head. "Because you know how people are. They say once a dog has tasted the killing of a man, he will kill and kill again. I did it to protect the dog."

"I see . . ." Samuel only stared at him, not knowing what else to say. He watched the old man pile rocks back onto the body. Beside him the big cur looked up with its tongue lolling in the heat. When the old man had finished, they walked back to the camp where the two women were busy preparing a meal. "I'm not really hungry," Samuel said just to the old man as the old man flipped open a blanket and took up the dead man's rifle and handed it to him.

"Si, I understand. But perhaps you will be by the time the meal is ready." He watched Samuel turn the rifle over in his hands. He saw the strange stunned look come into Samuel's eyes when his gloved hand moved over the carving in the rifle stock—a scorpion with its tail held high and ready to strike. "What is it? What is wrong?"

Samuel stood in silence. He looked down at the dog, then back at the old man, and handed the rifle back to him. "Nothing's wrong. It's a fine-looking rifle."

Later that evening, when they'd eaten, and the women had cleared away the utensils and poured food for the dog while the big cur sat watching them expectantly, Samuel asked the old *pistolero* how it had been for him back when he'd done his share of hard killing. "How long was it before you felt like you were part of the world again?"

"Absolution is what you are asking me about." The old *pistolero* looked at him closely and said, "There are three questions you must answer yes to before you will find the absolution you seek. First of all, do you *feel* in your heart of hearts that you were *just* in what you have done?"

"Yes," Samuel answered.

"Do you think these men would have caused more suffering for others if you had not stopped them?"

"Yes, I do. I'm sure of it."

"Do you know there is nothing you did that you should have done differently?"

Samuel hesitated, catching a glimpse of Sherman Ellsworth's eyes as he'd closed in with his pistol. "Well, I—"

"Forget that question." The old man shook his head, seeing the dark vision stir behind Samuel's eyes. He shrugged. "I never thought that question was so important, anyway. The important thing is that you come to peace with what you feel and think." He smiled and sat in silence.

After a pause, Samuel looked at him and said, "I have felt cold inside . . . deep down in my bones, even in the desert heat, ever since I left there."

"I know that feeling," the old man said. "That is one that only passes in time. And it passes without you knowing it is gone. One day you will simply realize it is gone and that it has been gone for a while." They gazed quietly into the flickering flames of the small fire.

Before dawn, Samuel was up early and moving carefully so as not to disturb the sleeping camp. Yet when his horses were ready and he stepped up into his saddle, the old man came forward out of the darkness of the dawn and stood back, looking up at him. Samuel crossed his wrists on the saddle horn. "Tell me something, *mi amigo*. How long will you and your wives stay here?"

The old man smiled. "Forever, or until the water no longer flows." He gestured a hand toward the trickle of water and the widening pool. "Who knows what the earth has in store for us, eh?"

"Yes, who knows."

"Does the dog go with you?" On the ground Blue paced back and forth, a sliver of steam wafting on his breath.

"No. He's better off here," Samuel said.

"Si, you are right." The old man dropped a hand to the dog's head and rubbed it as he spoke. "Here, my women will pamper him and make him fat—and I will fill him with tales of when I was one bold *pistolero*." He smiled at Samuel and winked. "These are things he has grown to enjoy. But it was good that he saw the world through your eyes for a time . . . and you through his, perhaps."

"I understand," Samuel nodded.

The old man stood back, raised a hand, and bid Samuel adios.

Samuel heeled the stallion forward, leading the other horse behind him. At noon when he stopped in the shade of a tall saguaro, he took out the list and marked the name GARRETT off it. That evening he slept in the shelter of a cliff overhang, and the next morning he turned the stallion away from the trail back to Humbly and struck out for the distant ranger station he knew lay northeast of the bad-lands hills.

He would introduce himself as Sam Burrack—not Samuel anymore for some reason. He would give a report on all that had happened. Then, if they would have him, he would take up where Sazes left off. Ranger Sam Burrack, he said to himself, and he nodded, liking the sound of it. There was no end to this work. This was what Sazes had meant about getting caught up in the outlaw's world. He knew that now.

The following morning his tracks led away from the overhang and out across swirling sand. He thought about what he would say when he handed over the money and told the rangers what had happened. He would tell them the truth as best he could, noble pilgrim that he was. Although, he thought, it might be best not to mention that he'd crossed the border.

He considered it some more and decided it would serve no real purpose to tell them everything. He certainly didn't want to tell them that Blue had killed a man—that wouldn't be prudent, for the dog's sake. But otherwise, he'd tell them the truth, because that's what a lawman had to do to walk the straight and narrow. Yes, he thought, the straight and narrow . . . those boundaries of the mind and heart that all men had to set and keep, even an old ranger like Out-rider Clyde Sazes . . . even a young ranger such as himself.

When man, and horse, were out of sight, a large lizard came up out of the lower earth and stood where they had just stood. It swished its coarse tail back and forth and settled there. In a moment nothing remained of the ending parade save for the swirl of the heat and the winding tracks in the sand. On the wind, a drift of dust spiraled upward and bobbed and played . . . like some devil, at dance, on the lone desert floor.